THE IMMORTAL COWBOY

This is respectfully dedicated to the "American Cowboy." His was the saga sparked by the turmoil that followed the Civil War, and the passing of more than a century has by no means diminished the flame.

—◆—

True, the old days and the old ways are but treasured memories, and the old trails have grown dim with the ravages of time, but the spirit of the cowboy lives on.

—◆—

In my travels—to Texas, Oklahoma, Kansas, Nebraska, Colorado, Wyoming, New Mexico, and Arizona—I always find something that reminds me of the Old West. While I am walking these plains and mountains for the first time, there is this feeling that a part of me is eternal, that I have known these old trails before. I believe it is the undying spirit of the frontier calling me, through the mind's eye, to step back into time. What is the appeal of the Old West of the American frontier?

—◆—

It has been epitomized by some as the dark and bloody period in American history. Its heroes—Crockett, Bowie, Hickok, Earp—have been reviled and criticized. Yet the Old West lives on, larger than life.

—◆—

It has become a symbol of freedom, when there was always another mountain to climb and another river to cross; when a dispute between two men was settled not with expensive lawyers, but with fists, knives, or guns. Barbaric? Maybe. But some things never change. When the cowboy rode into the pages of American history, he left behind a legacy that lives within the hearts of us all.

—Ralph Compton

W9-BUQ-513

RALPH COMPTON DOUBLE

ROUGH JUSTICE #2

TWO WESTERNS BY
RALPH COTTON

BERKLEY
NEW YORK

BERKLEY
An imprint of Penguin Random House LLC
penguinrandomhouse.com

ISBN: 9780593441183

First Edition: January 2023

Printed in the United States of America
1st Printing

Book design by George Towne

CONTENTS

RIDERS OF JUDGMENT

DEATH ALONG THE CIMARRON

RIDERS OF JUDGMENT

PROLOGUE

NEWTON, KANSAS. SEPTEMBER 7, 1871

For the past two weeks, Danielle Strange had been recovering in bed in the upstairs back room of Dr. Lannahan's office. Her gunshot wounds had been healing quickly, but not quickly enough to suit her. Now that she was up and able to dress herself, she was restless and wanted to get on her way. She had spent over two years of her life hunting down her father's murderers, a gang of desperadoes who had left his body hanging from a tree. There had been ten outlaws in the gang that had killed Daniel Strange. Posing as a young gunman named Danny Duggin, she had used the gun-handling skills her father, the gunsmith, had taught her early in life. Danielle had tracked the killers down, one and two at a time, and had taken her vengeance upon them. Only one of those outlaws remained alive. His name was Saul Delmano, and she eagerly wanted to get back on his trail before it grew too cold to follow.

"The longer we stay here, the more time Delmano will have to prepare himself for a fight against us," Danielle said. On a chair beside her bed lay the cloth binder that Danielle was accustomed to wearing. The binder kept her breasts flattened enough that when worn beneath her loose-fitting shirt, no one could tell she was a woman. The only reason she wasn't wearing it now was because the binder constricted her painful wounds.

Her twin brothers, Tim and Jed Strange, looked at each other, then turned back to Danielle. Tim said, "Danielle, you're still too weak to ride and fight. You've done more than most any man could have done. But you're only human. We can't traipse out of here and take a chance on that hole in your side breaking open again or that fever settling back upon you."

"Tim's right," Jed joined in. "The way the doctor explained it to us while you were unconscious that first week here is that you'll be walking on new legs for a while. He said it could take half the coming winter getting all your strength back."

"I can't spend half the winter here if that's what you're getting at," said Danielle. She nodded toward the supper her brothers had brought her on a wooden tray. The plate and bowl on the tray sat empty on the nightstand beside the small feather bed. "I've got an appetite again, and I'm starting to get around pretty good, all things considered." She patted the mended bullet hole in the side of her clean boiled shirt. "By morning I ought to be able to ride."

"By morning?" Tim Strange shook his head. "That's pushing things too hard, Danielle."

Danielle turned a firm gaze toward him. "Quit calling me Danielle. I'm Danny Duggin until this thing is over."

"Sorry," said Tim. "I just wasn't thinking there for a second."

"All right, but be more careful," she replied. She offered him a slight smile to show she wasn't angry, and said, still patting a hand on her side, "I'm still pretty sore in my ribs, but it'll go away soon."

"Yes, it will," Tim Strange said, "and when it does, we'll talk about leaving here and getting on Saul Delmano's trail. But not a minute before. Besides, the doctor still needs to give me and Jed a clean bill of health."

Danielle took a breath and tried to regain her patience. In her attempt to convince her brothers that she was ready and able to ride, she'd almost forgotten that they, too, had suffered wounds at the hands of the outlaw gang they had fought and left dead on the ground before coming here to Newton. "I'm sorry, Tim," Danielle said, looking from one of her brothers to the next. "How are you two doing?"

The twins nodded in unison. "We're doing all right, Danielle," said Tim. "We're mostly healed up pretty good." He nodded at Jed. "Just so you won't think we're not keeping busy, listen to what Jed found out at the saloon."

Danielle looked at Jed expectantly. "Well, what is it?"

A grin spread across Jed's face. "You remember Bob Dennard, the bounty hunter you had trouble with back in Fort Smith?"

"I remember him," said Danielle. "He wanted us to ride with him and find Saul Delmano."

"That's right," Jed said. "Well, I've talked to him some, and he knows a lot about Saul Delmano. He said Delmano's family operates a large cattle business that stretches all the way across the border into Mexico. He said Saul Delmano's father, Lewis Delmano, is not much more than an outlaw himself, except that he's made lots of powerful political connections over the years. Dennard says if Saul Delmano is holed up with his crew along the border, he's going to be awfully hard to get to."

"Sounds like Bob Dennard is still trying awfully hard to throw in with us," Danielle said. "I appreciate him giving you the information, but we've still got no room for him riding with us. Does he still think I'm Danny Duggin?"

"Yep, he does," said Jed, "and so does everybody else except the doctor. We've done good keeping your secret. I told Dennard that Tim and I are your younger brothers, that we're here as family helping you out. He seems to believe it. He wants to ride with us awfully bad. Said if he's not riding with us, he'll be going after Saul Delmano alone. If he does, let's hope he doesn't cause us trouble getting to Delmano."

Danielle Strange thought things over for a moment, pacing slowly back and forth across the small room, one hand held to her tender side. Tim and Jed Strange stood quietly watching her.

Across the street, other eyes were watching her, too. Atop the mercantile store, an outlaw named Clyde Branson stood with his rifle lying across the edge of the roof. He watched Danielle each

time she stalked past the dusty window. Thinking Danielle was
the deadly young gunman Danny Duggin, Branson whispered to
himself, "Come on, Duggin, let's get this over with."

Danielle was pacing slowly, and that was to Branson's advantage. He knew he would get only one shot, so he'd better make it
count. He wet his thumb against the tip of his tongue, then ran it
across his rifle sight. There was two thousand dollars riding on this
shot. He couldn't afford to miss.

Clyde Branson counted off the seconds it took Danielle to walk
past the window in the light of the lantern, then turn and come
back. For a moment there, she must have stopped out of sight,
probably talking to someone. Branson had eased down and waited.
When nearly a full minute had expired, he saw her move past the
window again, and he tightened his hand on the rifle stock. He
would let her make a couple of more passes; then he would take her
down. It would take a few days for word of Danny Duggin's death
to make its way to the Delmanos. But that was all right with Branson. He would already be waiting at the Delmano spread by then.
All he'd have to do was pick up his money and head over into
Mexico.

Inside the room, Danielle stopped pacing again and said to her
brothers, "How are the horses doing? I haven't seen Sundown since
the day we got here."

Sundown was the chestnut mare her father had ridden the day
his killers had come upon him. The big mare had managed to find
her way back to the Stranges' small ranch, and Danielle had been
riding the animal ever since.

"Sundown's fine," said Jed Strange. "All three of our horses are
fine. To tell the truth, they needed the rest. We've pushed them
pretty hard all summer."

"Well," Danielle said, turning and starting to pace again,
"they've had all the rest they'll be getting for a while—"

Her words stopped short when she stepped in front of the dusty
window and the sound of the rifle exploded across the street. The

shot sprayed shattered glass across the room, the bullet barely missing Danielle's head.

"Look out!" Jed shouted as he and Tim sprang forward to grab Danielle. But she had already dived past the window and onto the floor.

"I'm not hit!" she said, crawling back hurriedly across the floor toward her brothers. A trickle of blood ran down her cheek from where a small piece of flying glass had nicked her. "Give me my guns!"

"Stay down!" Jed shouted as Tim reached over, grabbed one of Danielle's pistols from its holster slung over a chair back, and pitched it over to her.

Danielle caught the pistol and, rising into a crouch beside the window, peeped around the edge of the frame into the darkness outside. Another shot exploded, this one ripping a long sliver of wood from the windowsill. Danielle ducked back, but not before seeing the rifle's muzzle flash.

"Quick! It's coming from the mercantile roof!" Danielle shouted to her brothers.

The twins wasted no time. They were out the door and running down the wooden stairs as Danielle poked the barrel of her Colt through the broken window and fired three shots toward where she'd seen the rifle flash.

In seconds Tim and Jed had raced across the dark empty street. Cutting through an alley as they saw Danielle's pistol firing from the broken window, they turned and ran through mud and broken whiskey bottles to the rear of the mercantile store. A few feet back from the rear wall, Tim stopped and brought his brother to a halt beside him. He nodded at the ladder reaching up to the roof and said, "We've got him. There's only one way down unless he makes a jump for it." Twenty feet back in the darkness, partially hidden by stacks of firewood, a horse stood waiting, its reins hitched to a cedar post.

"I'll get his horse just to make sure," said Jed in a lowered voice.

"Yeah, good idea," Tim agreed. "Do it while Danielle keeps him pinned down up there."

Pistol shots barked from the window where Danielle stood, taking aim at the roofline. Tim ventured forward, Colt in hand, and kicked the ladder away from the wall. Meanwhile, Jed slipped across the muddy path to the waiting horse, calming it with a raised hand. He unhitched its reins and led it farther back into the darkness, noting the animal's fancy silver-trimmed bridle and reins.

"Whoever he is, he rides in style," Jed whispered to himself, running a hand along the hand-tooled California saddle with its Mexican silver inlay.

At the rear of the mercantile, the shooting had stopped as Danielle reloaded her Colt.

"You up there!" Tim called up to the roof. "You'd best come down with your hands raised. We've got you surrounded."

There was no answer from the roof, but behind Tim came the sound of running boots, and he almost turned and fired before he recognized the red-bearded face of the bounty hunter Bob Dennard coming closer.

"Don't shoot. It's me!" Dennard called out.

"You'd better hug this wall, Dennard," Tim called out, gesturing toward the roof with his pistol barrel. "If he's alive up there, he might start shooting down here any second."

Bob Dennard flattened back against the wall beside Tim Strange, glancing up along the roofline, drawing his pistol from his tied-down holster. "I heard the shooting and came running. What happened?"

"Whoever's up there took a shot at Dan—" He caught himself, about to say "Danielle." "Somebody shot at Danny through the window!"

"I should have figured as much," said Bob Dennard, peering upward, scanning the roofline as he spoke. "I tried telling you, these are big people you're wanting to lock horns with."

"I believe you, Dennard," said Tim Strange, "but Danny says he wants nobody else riding with us—no offense." As he spoke,

Tim's eyes searched along the edge of the roof, sweeping darkness in case the rifleman tried to jump down and make a run for it.

"No offense taken," said Dennard.

"Hey up there!" Tim called out again. "Either give it up and come down with your hands raised, or I'm coming up after you. Make up your mind!"

This time a weak voice called out from atop the roof. "I can't come down. . . . I'm hit bad."

"Then throw down some hardware, pronto!" Tim responded. He looked over through the pitch of the night and saw that Jed had taken the horse to a spot where if anybody jumped down from the roof on the far end of the building, he would spot it immediately.

"Here . . . comes my rifle," the halting voice said. After a second, a rifle fell to the soft ground a few feet out from the building.

"Now your pistol," Tim Strange demanded.

"I . . . can't get it drawn. I'm hit . . . bad and lying on it."

Tim gave Bob Dennard a questioning look.

Bob Dennard shrugged.

"I wouldn't take his word for it," Jed warned.

"I'm not going to," said Tim. He called up to the roof, "We're coming up. If I don't see both your hands empty when I step onto the roof, you're worm bait. Is that clear enough?"

Danielle came limping from the alley, a Colt in one hand, her free hand pressed to her side. She'd thrown on a riding duster and closed the front to conceal her woman's figure. "He's not lying about one thing," she said, stepping up to her brother and Bob Dennard. "He is hit. I don't know how bad, but I shot him when he rose up with his rifle."

As Danielle spoke, her eyes met Bob Dennard's. "I reckon you remember me," Dennard said, looking a bit sheepish.

"Yes," Danielle replied, none too friendly. "You're the one who mistook me for an outlaw and tried to ambush me outside of Fort Smith."

"I sure don't want any hard feelings between us, Danny Duggin," Bob Dennard said, taking a quick glance at the cocked Colt in Danielle's hand. "I made a mistake and I admit it. Lucky you didn't shoot me for my ignorance. I've been telling your brothers that I want to—"

"Not now," said Danielle, cutting him off. She turned her gaze to Tim. "Help me raise the ladder. I'm going up there."

"No," said Tim, taking her forearm and preventing her from walking over to the ladder on the ground. "You've got no business climbing a ladder, the shape you're in." He raised a hand and waved Jed in from the darkness. "Jed and I will go up there."

Danielle started to protest, but thinking about it, she knew Tim was right. She let out a breath. "All right, I'll stay here," she said. "You and Jed be careful."

"I'm going, too," said Bob Dennard, "in case you two need some help."

Tim gave him a firm look. "You can go up there, Dennard, but don't think you need to watch over me and my brother, Jed."

Bob Dennard looked embarrassed. "I should have said that a different way. I'm only interested in seeing who that is. Call it my nosy nature."

Danielle stood back and watched with her Colt ready in her hand as Jed joined Tim and Bob Dennard. Tim and Jed raised the ladder and set it in place while Bob Dennard kept an eye on the roofline.

Tim was the first to carefully climb the ladder, his Colt poised and ready. Jed climbed close behind him; then Bob Dennard followed, seeing Tim step over onto the tin roof.

Tim stepped across the roof as quietly as possible. Seeing the man lying in a heap against the front facade of the building, his hands empty and slightly raised, Tim called out, "Don't try any tricks, ambusher, or I'll kill where you lie."

"It's no . . . trick," the man said, lying over on his right side, his holster beneath him. "I'm . . . done for, sure enough."

"Serves you right, mister," Tim said, stepping closer, hearing Jed move in and beside him. "You tried to kill, but ended up getting killed yourself."

"I don't . . . need no sermons," said Branson.

"And you're getting none either," Jed Strange cut in. "Who are you anyway? Why'd you bushwhack our brother?"

"Name's Pete . . . Bristol. I was going to—"

"He's a damn liar," Bob Dennard interrupted. "He's a hired assassin named Clyde Branson. I've seen him a dozen times over the years. Most likely he's working for the Delmanos. Ain't that right, Branson?"

Clyde Branson raised his face weakly and said, "Is . . . that you, Dennard?"

"Yes, it's me. Tell these men who you're working for, Branson, before you make your trip to hell, you back-shooting snake."

Branson coughed, struggling to catch his breath. "Don't . . . act . . . so innocent, Dennard. You've done the . . . same thing before."

"Who is it, Branson?" Dennard insisted, ignoring Branson's remark. "It's the Delmanos, isn't it? They're paying you to kill Danny Duggin."

"What's . . . the difference?" gasped Branson. "It never got done."

"How much?" Dennard asked, stepping in closer, looking down at the wounded man.

"Two . . . thousand dollars," Branson said, his voice faltering more and more. "But not . . . just for me. It's open to all takers. Saul Delmano wants . . . Duggin dead . . . real bad. You might even be tempted—"

"How many men know about this two-thousand-dollar reward?" Dennard hissed, cutting him off.

Even as his breath weakened, Branson murmured, "Hell . . . every gunman from here . . . to El Paso. Now tell . . . these boys how you make . . . your living."

"That's enough of your mouth!" Bob Dennard cocked his pistol and aimed it at Branson's head.

"No! Don't shoot him!" Tim started to reach over and stop him, but even before he could grab Bob Dennard's gun hand, Dennard let the pistol down with a sigh and nodded at Clyde Branson.

"Never mind. This mangy cur is dead," said Dennard, straightening up and lowering his Colt into his holster.

Tim and Jed Strange both looked at the dead, hollow eyes of Clyde Branson, then back at Bob Dennard.

"We don't hold with what you were about to do, Dennard," said Tim.

Dennard shrugged. "Well, as you can see, it never got that far."

The three of them turned at the sound of Danielle's footsteps on the tin roof behind them. "Is he . . . ?"

"Yes, he's dead," said Jed Strange. "Bob here knew him. His name is Clyde Branson—a killer for hire. He said Saul Delmano has a two-thousand-dollar reward on your head."

"Yeah," said Danielle, "heard most of it while I was back there on the ladder."

"What are you doing up here, Danny?" Tim asked. "You were supposed to stay down there and take it easy."

"Don't worry. I took it as easy as I could," Danielle said. As she spoke to Tim, she turned a cold gaze to Bob Dennard. "You were pretty quick to want to kill a dying man, Dennard. What's wrong? Was he saying things you didn't want known?"

"Now look, Duggin," said Dennard, "I don't deny what I am. I make my living hunting down men for money. If it's wrong, why do you think the law allows it? Because the law knows it can't keep up with all the riffraff out here, that's why."

"I don't care how you go about making your living, Dennard," said Danielle, "but I saw what you were about to do." She looked away from Dennard to Tim and Jed, getting their approval from the look in their eyes. "My brothers and I won't be having you ride with us. Will we, Tim, Jed?"

The twins only shook their heads, lowering their pistols into their holsters. Danielle stepped past Clyde Branson's body, over to the front edge of the roof, where she looked down at the gathering crowd on the dirt street below.

"Somebody go get the town sheriff," she called down to the uplifted faces. "Tell him there's a man shot."

The people on the street looked back and forth at one another; then a young man turned and raced away toward the sheriff's office, where a light now glowed through the window.

"You're making a mistake not riding with me, Duggin," said Dennard as Danielle turned back around. "Ask your brothers here. Branson said the price on your head is open to all takers. Do you realize how many cold-blooded killers there are between here and the border? You'll never make it past Dodge City."

"I already know there's a lot of cold-blooded killers out here," replied Danielle. "But at least none of them will be riding beside me." She turned to her brothers. "Come on, Tim, Jed—we've got to make some plans and get out of here."

As the three turned to walk away across the tin roof, Bob Dennard called out, "All right, then, play it your way, Duggin. But I'm going after the reward on Saul Delmano and anybody with him with or without you!"

"It's a free country," Danielle called back over her shoulder.

"Damn right it is!" Bob Dennard called out. "We get out there in the thick of things, I'm warning all three of you . . . stay out of my way!"

At the threat in Dennard's words, Tim Strange started to turn from the ladder and issue some warnings of his own. But Danielle grabbed his arm, stopping him.

"Let it go, Tim," she said. "Dennard just showed you what kind of man he is. Let him rave and threaten and curse all he wants to. We've got work to do."

CHAPTER 1

Danielle recounted the events of the past months in her mind, most of the memories bringing a bitter taste to her mouth. Before Daniel Strange's death at the hands of his killers, he had been known as the best gunsmith in or around St. Joseph, Missouri. He and his wife, Margaret, had raised all three of their children to be decent, God-fearing, law-abiding, and equally as important, to be respectful of others regardless of that person's station in life. Along with these indisputable values, the Stranges had taught their children to be independent to a fault, for life along the Western frontier was not a kind place for the meek, the helpless, or the reluctant of spirit. While the Strange children were honest and soft-spoken, they had a presence beyond their years and knew how to handle themselves in most any situation.

Along with all the other things a frontier child must learn, Daniel Strange had taught his daughter and sons at an early age the skill, safety, and responsibility of handling and carrying a firearm. By the time his children were able to read and write, they could handle a Colt as well as any grown man and, of the three, while Daniel didn't make it a habit of saying so to Tim and Jed, young Danielle was by far the best. And the fastest. At thirteen, Danielle Strange could strike sulfur matches at a distance of thirty feet with the customized Colt her father had designed to fit her hand.

Tim and Jed Strange had taken up their father's trade of

gunsmithing and had mastered it at an early age—so had Danielle. When it came to repairing or even designing and building a firearm, the Strange children were equal in every regard. Yet, when it came to pulling the trigger, while the Strange twins were both excellent marksmen in their own right, it was daughter Danielle who had what her father always referred to as the *gift*. Whether she was firing from the hip or from horseback, Danielle Strange's talent was undeniably the best in the family.

Had it not been for the tragic death of Daniel Strange nearly two years earlier, Danielle might well have spent the rest of her life in St. Joseph, Missouri. She might have married and raised a family, or have taken courses at the women's college in St. Louis and spent her life teaching school. But these things were not to be, not for now anyway. Fate had dealt her a different hand, and all she could do was play the few cards left to her. She thought of this now in the dark hours of night as she sat cleaning and checking her brace of Colt pistols.

Her father, Daniel Strange, had left home on Sundown, the big chestnut mare, and had gone off on a cattle-buying trip, his trail snaking across Indian Territory. Days later, the chestnut mare had returned by herself, lathered and weary from the road. The following day, a note from U.S. Federal Marshal Buck Jordan had arrived along with Daniel Strange's wallet at the sheriff's office in St. Joseph. From that day to this, Danielle Strange had ridden the vengeance trail, seeking out her father's killers one at a time. What had begun as a list of ten names—the names she'd extracted from one of the killers before he died—was now down to one. Saul Delmano.

Danielle whispered the name to herself in the darkened room. The only light was the halo of the lantern by which she'd cleaned and checked her Colts. She looked around at Tim and Jed, the two of them having fallen asleep in her room, Tim leaning back in a wooden chair against the wall, Jed curled down on the floor, wrapped in a blanket he'd taken from the closet. Danielle smiled to herself, feeling closer to her brothers than she ever had.

It had been Tim and Jed who had come and found her in Indian

Territory, where she'd taken up with some of her father's killers in order to draw all of them into a trap. Tim and Jed had broken the news to her about their mother's death, and she had suffered her loss alone, with no time for proper grief.

"Sorry, Mom," Danielle whispered now in the darkness, thinking about it.

Feeling herself give in to deep sadness, Danielle shook the melancholy off before it got the better of her. She stood up from the side of the bed and dressed herself quietly, winding the cloth binder methodically around her torso as she had done so many mornings before on this trail of blood. Then she clenched her teeth against the pain in her side, pitched the pistol belt around her waist, buckled it, and tied the rawhide strip around her leg, securing the oiled holster in place.

Finishing, she walked over to her sleeping brothers, looked at each of them in turn, and said, "Rise and shine. We've got a long day ahead."

In a moment the twins were up on their feet, picking up their hats and adjusting them down on their foreheads. Having slept no more than a hour or two, and in their clothes and gun belts at that, Tim and Jed rubbed their hands on their faces, forcing themselves awake, and soon the three of them left the room and descended the wooden stairs. On the front porch of the doctor's office, Danielle took an envelope from inside her shirt and slipped it under the door. She looked back at Tim and Jed, who stood watching her questioningly.

"I wouldn't think of leaving without paying the doctor his due," she said.

They turned and walked abreast to the livery barn at the far end of the street. Before dawn, Danielle, Tim, and Jed Strange were in the saddle and riding single file along the dirt street out of town. There was no more to say about whether or not Danielle was fit to ride. They had talked it out last night until both Tim and Jed saw there was no use in arguing any further on the subject. Danielle had made up her mind to go, and nothing was going to change it.

As the three of them rode past a darkened alley, they did not see the five men standing back in the far shadows, watching them ride by. One of the men, a gunman named Loot Harkens, started to raise his pistol from his holster, but beside him a deep, gruff voice whispered, "Don't be a fool, Loot. Want to end up like Clyde Branson? Let them go for now. Once they get out there in the wilds, there won't be nothing to keep us from killing them."

"Yeah, Loot," the voice of Hank Phipps whispered, "Tarksel's right. They're not going to get very far. I've got news for Mr. Danny Duggin, and his two look-alike brothers. . . . There ain't none of the three going to live to see their next birthday."

"I like your attitude, Phipps," said Al Tarksel. "See if you can get Loot here to settle down before I have to backhand him into the next county." Al Tarksel was a big man, weighing over two hundred fifty pounds, all of it hard muscle and bone. He spread a flat smile at the other men in the darkness. "Boys, I know that since Axel Eldridge got himself killed last month, there ain't been nobody to really take charge of this gang." He let his eyes cut from one to the other as he spoke. "But just to keep things well organized, I've decided that from here on, I'm taking over." His smile faded as he added, "Any objections?"

The four men looked at one another, then turned back to Al Tarksel as he said in his deep voice, "If there is, let's get it settled here and now." He called each of them by name, looking them square in the face. "Loot, any problem with me taking over?"

Loot Harkens shook his head, saying, "No. Far as I'm concerned, you're the boss."

"Hank?" Tarksel asked.

"Fine by me," Hank Phipps replied, sounding a bit nervous.

"Hector?" Al Tarksel stared coldly at Hector Sabio.

After a pause, Hector shrugged, looking sullen. "*Sí*, you are in charge. But I say to you the same thing I say to Axel back when I join." He thumbed himself on the chest. "I am a free man. I come and go as I choose. If I decide to quit and return to *Méjico*, I do so without asking anyone's permission."

"I can't run this bunch if everybody does as they damn well please, Hector," said Al Tarksel. "Are you sure that's your final say on it?"

"*Sí*, I say nothing more," said Hector in a firm tone.

"All right, then."

Al Tarksel reached out a big hand, clamped it around Hector's throat, and lifted him nearly off the ground. Hector's boot toes scrapped back and forth in the dirt as he was if running in place. His eyes bulged, both hands clamping around Tarksel's thick wrist. Al Tarksel only stood smiling, flat and cold. Hector reached down with his right hand and tried to snatch his pistol from his holster. But as he raised the gun, Al Tarksel slapped it away and kept squeezing.

"God Almighty!" said Jack Pearl. "Let him go, Al. You're killing him!"

But Al Tarksel didn't let go until Hector Sabio hung limp as a wet towel. Then he dropped Hector to the ground and looked at Jack Pearl. "What about you, Pearl? Any objections to me taking over as boss?"

"Hell, no. What do I care?" Jack Pearl looked down at the Mexican. "You didn't have to kill ole Hector, though. He was a damn good man. He was just running his jaw some. He wouldn't have quit us and gone back to Mexico. Hell, he's wanted in every province down there! They've been wanting to cleave his head off for years."

"Then I just saved everybody a lot of trouble," said Al Tarksel. "Now, are we all through here?" He stared at Jack Pearl as the others nodded in agreement.

"I told you, I've got no problem with who's in charge," said Jack Pearl. "I just want my part of that two thousand dollars when we kill this Danny Duggin."

"Don't worry, Jack," said Al Tarksel. "Anybody who rides with me, I'll see to it they get what's coming to them."

Jack Pearl only stared at Tarksel, realizing what Tarksel had just said could have been taken a couple of different ways. But Jack

Pearl didn't need to have it spelled out for him. He knew that two thousand dollars was worth more to one man than it was to five. For the time being, Jack Pearl thought, the best thing for him to do was to keep a close watch on his back and keep his mouth shut.

"Are we ready to ride?" Tarksel asked, still staring at Jack Pearl.

"Yep." Jack Pearl smiled. "I'm just waiting on you to make the first move, boss."

"Then let's get going."

Al Tarksel stepped over Hector Sabio's body and walked toward the horses that were hitched back at the far end of the alley. In minutes the four men were mounted and riding along the dirt street as the first rays of sunlight seeped upward on the eastern horizon.

The young U.S. federal marshal's name was Charles Fox Mc-Cord, but most of the other marshals called him C. F. for short. The outlaws along the Cherokee Strip had taken to calling him the Fox. It was a name they used with a great deal of respect, if not with much affection. During the brief 2.5 years that C. F. McCord had been riding for the federal district court out of Fort Smith, Arkansas, his reputation as a lawman had become almost legendary. When folks who had only heard of C. F. McCord met him for the first time, they had a hard time believing that this thin, clean-jawed young man could be the same marshal who had brought in some of the most hardened killers in Indian Territory.

But C. F. McCord had learned to take it all in stride. Whatever work he had done in his short life, he had always tried to do his best at it. Law work was no different, he thought, riding his line-back dun at a walk along the center of Newton's main street. Mid-morning sunlight fell glaring and harsh on the passing wagons, buggies, and foot traffic.

At the hitch rail out front of the sheriff's office, McCord stepped down from his saddle, stretched his back, hitched his sweat-streaked dun, and stepped up onto the boardwalk. As he swung the creaking door open and stepped inside the small dusty sheriff's office, Sheriff Bart Lynch looked up from the stack of papers and wanted posters atop his desk. The sheriff's expression was stiff at first, but when he saw who'd just walked in, his expression changed. A slight smile even came to his lips as he spoke.

"Come in, Marshal McCord," Sheriff Lynch said. "To what do I owe this honor?" He rose from his chair and gestured a hand toward the empty chair in front of his desk.

"I'm here to see a man by the name of Danny Duggin," said McCord, "the young fellow who got shot out front of the saloon here a while back."

"Yep, I know him," said Lynch. "What can I tell you about him?"

"For starters," said McCord, "does he happen to ride a chestnut?"

"Yes, I believe his mount is a big chestnut mare, come to think of it. Why? Lots of people ride a similar mount, I reckon."

"Yeah, just curious," said McCord. "Word has it he's been laid up in the room atop the doctor's office."

"Yep, that's right," said Sheriff Lynch. "He has been. But he ain't now. I went by to see him earlier to talk some about a shooting he was involved in last night. But he's gone. Him and his brothers, too. The liveryman said they left before daylight, headed toward Dodge City."

"Gone?" McCord gave the sheriff a look of surprise. "After being involved in another shooting here?"

"That's right. He was innocent of any wrongdoing. A paid assassin by the name of Clyde Branson tried to ambush him through a window. Danny Duggin shot him from across the street . . . in the dark, mind you." Sheriff Lynch cocked a bushy eyebrow. "I mention that fact in case you and Duggin have anything to settle between yas. It appears this young Danny Duggin has nine lives, like a cat, and can see through the night just like one, too."

"Nope," said the young marshal, "there's nothing that needs settling between him and me." McCord shook his head, pulled the empty chair back, and slumped down in it, dropping his dusty hat on his lap. "The judge sent me out to clear up some things for the record."

"Yeah? What's that?" Sheriff Lynch asked. "Can't the judge keep busy enough in Indian Territory? Now he's gonna start telling us how to run Kansas?"

Lynch grinned, but C. F. McCord heard him loud and clear. No local sheriff wanted federal marshals interfering with how they ran their towns.

"You know how Judge Parker is, Sheriff. He can't stand not knowing what's going on—says he loves a good riddle." McCord smiled. "This Danny Duggin sort of popped up out of nowhere this past summer. He was in the Territory when Parker sent in a posse to clean up a gang of outlaws. The next day or so, Duggin gets in a shoot-out here with some of the same bunch who were fleeing the posse. You have to admit, it makes you wonder who this boy is and what he's out to do. The judge takes a dim view of vigilantism."

"Vigilantism . . ." Sheriff Lynch considered it, then said, "Well, I ran a check on him the best I could after the first shooting here. Nobody was holding wanted papers on him that I could find. I'm not big on vigilantism myself. But no innocent bystanders were harmed. The only gripe I've got about the ones he shot is that the town had to foot the bill for their coffins. If I'd had time, I'd liked to have given him a list of a few others that needed killing, since the federal law can't seem to keep the riffraff from converging on my town."

C. F. McCord chuckled, then said, "I might *personally* agree with you, Sheriff, except Judge Parker is a curious man. He called me in all the way from the strip just to find out more about this man Duggin. I've been scratching around all the way from St. Joseph, Missouri, finding out what I can about him and his brothers."

"Anything interesting?" Lynch asked.

McCord shrugged. "Nothing much out of the ordinary. These so-called brothers of his are Tim and Jed *Strange*, the best I can figure. I found no family with twins in it by the name of Duggin. The only twins in the area around those boys ages are the Stranges.

"Maybe they're stepbrothers, then," Lynch offered.

"That's what I wondered at first," said McCord, "but then I checked around town, couldn't find a soul who ever even heard of a Danny Duggin being from there, let alone of him being any kin to the Strange brothers."

"Hmmm," said Lynch, looking puzzled.

McCord continued. "I did hear about a young man named Daniel Strange who killed some gunmen last summer over in Texas. Rumor has it they killed his father, and he went on a vengeance trail after them. But then, he supposedly got himself killed in a knife fight last winter." McCord gave Lynch a knowing look. "Now, this summer, here comes Danny Duggin, doing the same thing, and he just happens to be traveling with the Strange twins, Tim and Jed."

"So, you think Duggin is really this Daniel Strange, the one who was supposed to have gotten killed?" Lynch rubbed his chin. "I can see where you might think that." He thought about it for another second, then asked, "What about Tim and Jed Strange's family? Were you able to talk to anybody kin to them?"

"Here's the real trump card," said McCord, leaning a bit closer to the edge of the desk. "Tim and Jed Strange's folks are both dead. The mother only died last spring . . . but the father, whose name just happens to also be Daniel Strange, mind you, was killed over a year ago down in the Territory. Now, do you see why Parker considers this quite a riddle? What do *you* make of it?"

"It's confusing all right," said Sheriff Lynch, still rubbing his chin. "And these boys, Tim and Jed, have no brother named Daniel?"

"Nope," said C. F. McCord in a flat tone, carefully phrasing his words, "they have no other *brothers* at all." He watched Sheriff Lynch's eyes as Lynch tried sorting it out to some reasonable conclusion.

"Well, they *do* have a brother somewhere, or a cousin, somebody that nobody knew about, and he was going by the name Daniel

Strange till he got knifed. He lived through the knifing, then took on another name. That name is Danny Duggin."

"You think that's it?" McCord asked, a faint smile on his face.

"It has to be," said Lynch. "There has to be a brother, a cousin, or something."

"What if this Tim and Jed managed to find themselves a hired gunman?" McCord asked, just to introduce the possibility. "Maybe he was just going by their father's name to rattle the killers?"

"Naw, that ain't the way Missouri boys do things. They settle their own trouble."

"Yeah, that's the way I figured it, too," said McCord. He stood up, raised his hat, and dropped it on his head. "But whatever the case, Parker wants to know, so I'm on Duggin's trail until I can find something out. Do you suppose the doctor is in this time of day?"

"Our doctor's in at all times of day or night," said Sheriff Lynch. He started to rise up from his chair, saying, "Hold up. I'll get my hat and go with you."

"No, you've been plenty of help already, Sheriff. I'll talk to him alone."

"He might be more helpful if I'm there," said Lynch.

"Or," said McCord, "he might be more helpful if you're not."

"Suit yourself, then," said Sheriff Lynch, dropping back into his chair. "I've got plenty to do here anyway. Somebody damn near choked a Mex to death last night and left him for dead in an alley."

"Where is he?" McCord asked, seeming interested.

"He's back there in a cell. Tried to leave him at the doctor's to recuperate, but all the danged fool could do was try to break away and run off. I figured he'd be better off here for a few days, least-wise till he can talk and tell us what happened to him."

"Care if I take a look at him?" McCord asked.

"Help yourself," said Lynch. "He's a handful, though. Something sure has got him awfully upset."

McCord and Sheriff Lynch walked back along a row of cells to the last one. Lynch kicked his boot against the bars until Hector

Sabio rose up from beneath a blanket on a sagging cot, looking at them through puffy bloodshot eyes.

"What's his name?" McCord asked.

"Beats me," said Lynch. "Like I told you, he can't say a word. Lordy, look at his throat!"

McCord winced and whistled low under his breath. "Did somebody hang him?"

"No . . . those aren't rope burns," said Lynch. "If there were any claw marks, I'd swear he got snatched up by a grizzly bear."

McCord nodded, then turned to Hector Sabio. *"Habla Inglés?"*

Hector groaned, trying to nod, and cupped a hand to his swollen throat.

"Good," said McCord, "you understand English. Then listen to me. The man who did this to you . . . was he about this tall?" McCord held a hand above his head.

Hector only looked up, giving no acknowledgment.

"Was he a big man named Al Tarksel, used to ride with the Axel Eldridge Gang?" McCord saw that the man was not going to tell him anything, but he watched Hector's dark eyes as he spoke, seeing if they revealed anything.

"See, he's a knothead," said Sheriff Lynch. "I can't say that I blame him, though. If somebody done me that way, I wouldn't want nobody going after them but me and a smoking shotgun."

"Is he charged with anything, Sheriff?" McCord asked, staring through the bars at Hector.

"No, he's not. I was hoping he'd tell us something before I let him go. But it doesn't look like he's going to. The poor devil can't eat . . . nothing but soup and broth, that is. Can't hardly manage even that."

"Let me take him off your hands, Sheriff," said McCord.

"Suits me if it's all right with him," said Sheriff Lynch. "I can't hold him here much longer."

McCord looked back at Hector, seeing that he had been listening close to everything they were saying, a look of distrust shadowing his dark eyes. "You heard him," said McCord. "You want to ride south with me, see if we can round up the man who did this to you, maybe let you and him settle things between you?"

Hector's expression changed. He stood the rest of the way up and walked over to the bars, his eyes turning to black fire as he leaned close with a hand cupped to his throat. He motioned Marshal McCord closer until McCord held his ear between the bars. Then with all his effort, Hector struggled until he managed to whisper in a strained rasp, "*Sí, por favor!*"

"What did he say?" Sheriff Lynch said, leaning in closer.

McCord smiled. "He said, 'Yes, please!' Seems he's real interested in running into whoever did this to him."

"Well, I'll just go get the key and be right back," said Lynch.

"No," said McCord. "Just wait until I get back from the doctor's." He turned to Hector Sabio. "Is that all right with you, mister?"

Hector nodded with murder smoldering in his eyes.

C. F. McCord left the sheriff's office and walked the length of the boardwalk until he came to the doctor's office. Inside, McCord took off his hat and stepped over to a divan, where he waited until a woman and a young boy wearing a sling around his right arm came out of the next room. After the doctor had walked the woman and boy to the door and closed it behind them, he turned to McCord and, seeing the badge on McCord's chest, said, "Now, then, Marshal, what seems to be your problem?"

McCord smiled, standing up, gesturing the doctor toward the other room. "I seem to have an identification problem, Doctor. I sure hope you can give me something for it."

In the other room, McCord declined taking a seat when the doctor offered it to him. Instead, McCord stood restless and waited until the doctor seated himself.

"Now, then, Marshal"—Dr. Lannahan smiled cordially—"since identification has never been a serious ailment, what *really* is the problem?"

C. F. McCord stepped in close and leaned down in front of the doctor. "I'm not going to beat around the bush, Doctor," McCord said. "Tell me what you know about this patient of yours, Danny Duggin."

Dr. Lannahan was taken aback. He tried to collect himself as he spoke. "Well, he—that is, Mr. Duggin—was severely wounded in a gunfight. He left here against my advice. He has no business being on horseback. He'll likely kill himself if he's not careful. Other than that, I'm not really at liberty to discuss any particulars with you."

"Then don't," said McCord. "But you said his wounds were severe. Then tell me this—did you have to perform surgery and take any bullets out of him?"

"Well, yes, in fact, I did," the doctor said reluctantly.

"So you took his shirt off of him, maybe even his trousers?"

"I don't see why you're asking me this, Marshal. Of course I had to remove the patient's shirt . . . trousers, too—"

"All right," said McCord, cutting him off. "Now tell me an honest yes or no to this next question. Then I'll be on my way."

Dr. Lannahan stared at McCord, feeling pressed and nervous as if already knowing what that question would be.

"Is Danny Duggin a woman?" McCord asked bluntly.

Dr. Lannahan shifted his eyes away from McCord and tried to look unruffled by the marshal's abrupt manner. "Now, see here, Marshal," Lannahan said, "has Mr. Duggin broken the law? Because unless this question has some relevance to—"

"No, I don't think he has broken any laws," said McCord, again cutting the doctor off. "But unless I can stop him, he might very well end up dead. Now let me ask you again—"

"You might as well not ask," said the doctor. "When I give my word to a patient, Marshal, I keep it."

McCord relented and took a step back; the doctor's eyes had given away any secret he'd promised to keep. "I respect you for that, Doctor," McCord said. "When I give my word, I'm the same way. Nobody can make me break it. So you've got my word right now that whatever you tell me about Danny Duggin, I'll never repeat. Fair enough?"

The doctor stared at him. "No, I'm not going to discuss this with you. If Danny Duggin is indeed a woman, you'll have to hear it from someone else. . . . I gave my word."

Marshal C. F. McCord smiled. "Thank you, Doctor. That's all I wanted to know. The secret's safe with me."

He put his hat on and walked out the door. Outside, C. F. McCord walked along the boardwalk until he reached the hitch rail where his dun stood with its muzzle raised, sniffing toward him. McCord stepped down into the street and ran his hand along the dun's neck.

"Don't worry," McCord said. "We're not going anywhere till we get fed and rested." He turned his gaze southwest toward the trail leading out to Dodge City. "I know where they're headed," he said to himself and the horse. "We'll catch up to them quick enough." He paused as if thinking of something. "I hope you're as tough as you think you are, Miss Danny Duggin," he said quietly to the distant sky. "We've never met . . . but from what I'm hearing, I like you already."

CHAPTER 2

Shortly after noon, Marshal C. F. McCord walked into the undertaker's parlor and back to a small room in the rear where the undertaker's assistant, Martin Cobb, had just poured a fresh bucket of ice into the pine coffin that lay flat between two sawhorses. Cold water dripped steadily from the bottom of the pine coffin onto a cushion of wet sawdust. Martin Cobb set the ice bucket on the floor, keeping a small chunk of ice in his hand. He looked up at Marshal C. F. McCord as he wiped the ice across his sweaty forehead.

"It's about time you got here, Marshal," said Cobb, perplexed. "Sheriff Lynch said you'd be here over two hours ago. We've been keeping his man iced down so's you can recognize him."

"I appreciate it," said McCord.

"Well, I hope so," said Cobb. "Do you realize what a premium ice is at, having it shipped by rail all the way from St. Louis?"

McCord didn't answer, instead only looking down at the naked body of Clyde Branson and the gaping bullet hole in his chest. Clyde Branson lay naked save for the wet towel thrown over his privates.

Flustered, Cobb answered himself, saying, "Well, it's very, *very* expensive. I can tell you that!"

"I bet it is," McCord murmured, looking at the parchmentlike face of the corpse. His eyes went to the pale folded hands on Branson's belly and saw that the man's trigger finger was missing.

"Well?" said Cobb while McCord studied the dead face with the drops of cold water on its cheeks and brow. "What do you say, Marshal? Is that Clyde Branson or not?"

"If I said it wasn't Branson, would whoever bought the trigger finger get their money back?" McCord asked.

Cobb's face reddened in embarrassment. "I don't make the rules here. I'm only an assistant. Is it him, though? Is it Clyde Branson? Sheriff Lynch said he'd never seen him in person, but that you had."

"It's Branson all right," said McCord. "If you need me to sign something, give it here."

"I'll just be a moment!" Cobb's voice grew excited at the good news. He scurried from the room, wiping his hands dry on his mortician's apron.

Alone with the corpse, McCord cocked his head sideways and studied the bullet hole dead center of Branson's chest.

"Good shooting, Danny Duggin," McCord whispered to himself. Yet knowing the circumstances, with the gunfight having taken place in the dark and Duggin having shot from a window, McCord couldn't help but think that luck had played its role in this shot.

"Here we are, Marshal!" said Cobb, returning with an affidavit and an ink pen and dipping bottle. "Just sign right here on the bottom and we put this matter to rest."

"Tell me something, undertaker," said McCord as he dipped the pen and scrawled his name across the bottom line. "Who's claiming this body?" He nodded at the shipping tag tied to Clyde Branson's big toe.

"Well, now that we have a signed identification, our Mr. Branson here will be packed in ice, hauled to the railhead, and shipped to Chicago on the first available train!" He reached out and patted Branson's stiff foot as he spoke. "My boss, Mr. Tull, has had an open arrangement with a traveling show for them to purchase an unclaimed body of any outlaw of notoriety. Mr. Branson here came along at just the right time!"

McCord looked down at the cold, wet body and shook his head, saying, "Sorry, Clyde. Hope you enjoy the show."

In his excitement, Cobb continued to babble. "Thank heavens it wasn't one of those awful deals where they only want the bones after the deceased has been boiled and stripped and—"

"I get the idea," said McCord, interrupting him. McCord turned to leave but found himself staring into the red-bearded face of the bounty hunter Bob Dennard.

"It's a terrible end, ain't it, Marshal McCord?" said Dennard, nodding at Branson's body. "But one that befits the life he lived, nevertheless."

"You slipped in here awfully quiet, mister," said McCord. "Do I know you?"

"No, you do not, sir," said Dennard, hooking a thumb in his vest as he turned facing McCord. "That is, we've never met. But I've certainly heard a lot about you. Down on the Cherokee Strip the outlaws all call you the Fox, I believe."

"So I've heard," said McCord. "Now that's me. . . . Who are you?"

"Dennard, sir . . . Bob Dennard, at your service." Dennard beamed as he spoke. "I saw you in Fort Smith a few months back whilst I was delivering the bodies of a couple of cattle rustlers."

"A bounty hunter, huh?" McCord said flatly. "Now I recognize the name. You used to be a preacher of some kind or other."

"Yes, it's true I was at one time a minister of the Gospel," said Dennard. "But now I am a private lawman or, as you so distastefully put it, a *bounty hunter.*"

McCord turned to Cobb and said, "We're all through here, right?"

"Yes indeed, Marshal." Cobb nodded, wiggling the signed affidavit in his hand.

"Wait, Marshal McCord," Bob Dennard called out as McCord turned to leave. "I have a proposition for you. . . . Don't you want to hear it?"

"Whatever it is, Dennard, I've heard it before," said McCord without turning around.

Dennard spoke hurriedly. "McCord, I know who you after—you're after the Delmanos, and you've been after them for a long time! I can help you. Danny Duggin and his brothers are after them, too. I know Duggin. I know all about him!"

C. F. McCord stopped with his hand on the doorknob and turned it slowly. "What do you know about Danny Duggin?"

"First things first," said Dennard, seeing if he could get the upper hand on the conversation. "You are looking for the Delmanos, aren't you?"

McCord gave him only a flat stare, not wanting to let his expression give anything away about whom he was after or why. "You said you know about Danny Duggin," McCord said. "Now what exactly do you know?"

"Well, I know he's on the vengeance trail looking for the Delmanos," Dennard said, not knowing much else to say. "I know if I'm riding with you, we'll catch up to him and his brothers. . . . I know where they're headed!"

"So do I. They're headed for Dodge," said McCord.

"No, I mean after Dodge. I know where they're headed and what they're gonna do once they get there," Dennard responded.

McCord stared even harder at him. "Is there anything else you know about Danny Duggin? Anything that I might find *real* interesting?"

Dennard squirmed in place, searching for something. Finally he had to shrug in submission. "I just know you're gonna need my help, McCord."

"You don't know nothing, Dennard." McCord started to turn back to the door, satisfied that Dennard had no idea about Danny Duggin's secret.

"I know that two guns are always better than one!" Dennard called out in a last attempt.

"That's a good thing for you to remember, Dennard," McCord said, looking back over his shoulder, "because if I catch you out there fanning my trail, that *one* little gun you're carrying won't do nothing more than get you killed."

When C. F. McCord had left, Bob Dennard turned to Martin

Cobb with his fists clenched at his sides. "Damn his hide! Damn them all! We'll see who comes out on top of this thing! We'll see!"

Martin Cobb eased back a step from Dennard in his rage and said in a guarded tone, "I hope this doesn't change anything as far as our agreement?"

Dennard calmed himself, picked up a chunk of ice from inside Clyde Branson's coffin, and ran it across his forehead. "No, this doesn't change our agreement. Where is it?"

"Twenty dollars first," said Cobb, his wet hand outstretched toward Dennard.

Bob Dennard grumbled under his breath as he took out a wallet from his inside coat pocket. He riffled through his money until he snatched out twenty dollars and flung it down on Clyde Branson's icy leg. "There's you damn money. Where's the finger?"

"I'll get it," said Cobb. "It's in a jar in ice, just like you wanted it."

"Hurry up, then," Dennard barked. "I haven't got all day. I've got to get it shipped to Cleveland, Ohio, before it turns rank!"

As Cobb hurried to a wooden cupboard and swung its door open, Dennard looked down at Clyde Branson and said under his breath, "Damned outlaws. It's getting to where they're worth more in parts than they are whole."

Leaving the undertaker's parlor, C. F. McCord walked to the livery stable and bought Clyde Branson's horse, complete with its California saddle and fancy bridle. Once he'd looked the horse over—a solid little roan barb gelding with a white blaze on its forehead—he saddled it, tacked it out, and led it to the hitch rail outside the sheriff's office. Inside the sheriff's office door, McCord looked at Sheriff Lynch and Hector Sabio, who both sat sipping hot coffee at Lynch's desk, Hector having a hard time getting the coffee down.

"Are you ready to ride, mister?" McCord asked Hector, still not knowing his name.

"For crying out loud, C. F.!" said Sheriff Lynch. "Let the man get something in his belly first."

But Hector rose up and set his cup on the desk, raising a hand toward Sheriff Lynch, letting him know it was all right.

"See? He's eager." McCord smiled. "Ready to get under way." He looked at Hector. "Aren't you, mister?"

Hector cupped his hand to his bruised, swollen throat, "*Sí.*" He gasped with much agony and effort.

At the hitch rail, Hector was surprised to see Clyde Branson's horse standing beside C. F. McCord's.

"It's yours for now," said McCord. "Ole Clyde never rode nothing but the best. I'll say that for him."

Hector looked around nervously as if to make sure it was all right. Then he unhitched the roan's fancy reins and swung up into the saddle. Beside him, C. F. McCord swung atop his dun and together they turned the horses to the street.

On the boardwalk, Bob Dennard appeared and called out, "This beats every damn thing I ever saw, McCord! That man is nothing but a heathen outlaw! He rode with the Eldridge Gang!"

Marshal C. F. McCord stopped his horse and swung it around, facing Bob Dennard. "You watch your language, bounty hunter." McCord seethed. "This man is riding with me. I might even deputize him before it's over." He looked at Hector Sabio. "You're not an outlaw, are you, mister?"

Hector Sabio shook his head slowly, cupping a hand to his sore throat.

"There, you see, Dennard? This man is not an outlaw. He just said so. He's an innocent victim who wants to see justice done."

Hector Sabio gave McCord a strange look, his hand still cupped to his throat as he nodded slowly in agreement.

"You damn fool," Bob Dennard cursed under his breath, seeing the two men turn their horses and heel them out along the rutted dirt street. "I hope he kills you in your sleep."

At the edge of town, McCord slowed his dun to a walk and reached over and caught the roan barb by its bridle, bringing it over near him. "Just so we don't get off on the wrong foot, mister," he said to Hector, "I think I'd best tell you now. We're going after Al

Tarksel and what's left of the Eldridge Gang, because they're going to lead us to the Delmanos. What you do with Al is your business. But make no mistake, if you cross me in any way, shape, or
form, I'm bound to kill you graveyard dead. *Comprende?*"

"*Comprendo,*" Hector managed to croak.

THE DODGE CITY TRAIL. SEPTEMBER 9, 1871

Owing to the pain in Danielle's wounded side, the ride to
Dodge City was taking longer than it should have. The first
day they had ridden across the flatland and made a camp in a dry
wash surrounded by waist-high prairie grass. The autumn grass
stood brittle in its shoots and served as a good guard against anybody approaching the camp unannounced. Jed boiled a small pot
of coffee and turned some jerked beef above the low flame to work
some of the stiffness out of it. Once the coffee was ready and the
jerked beef hung from the ends of their knife blades, Danielle and
the twins sat around the fire having their supper.

Seeing the pained expression on Danielle's face, Tim asked his
sister, "Are you doing all right? You look pale and feverish."

"I'll do," said Danielle, forcing down a bite of warm jerky. "I
knew I'd be stiff and sore the first day or two."

Tim and Jed looked at each other, then back at their sister.

"I brought along a bottle of whiskey if you need it for the pain,"
Jed offered.

"Maybe just a short sip," said Danielle. "But I'll use some to
clean this wound and change the dressing soon as I rest some and
get my strength back."

"We could always lie up a day or two once we get to Dodge,"
said Tim. "We don't want to travel hell-for-leather, you know."

"I know, Tim," said Danielle, "but you can feel in the air that
winter's coming early. I want to settle all accounts with Saul Delmano
aforehand. Once he's dead, I'll take all the time I need to heal up
properly."

"If we had to," said Tim, "Jed and I could finish this thing out. We'd come back for you afterward—you know that."

"I know," said Danielle, sipping her coffee, "but it's something I've got to do—I made a promise at Pa's grave marker. I started with ten names on my list and crossed them off one at a time. I'll stop when I crossed off the last name, not before."

A silence passed as the night wind rustled through the wild grass. Then Jed spoke in a lowered voice as he gazed into the low flames. "Sometimes I wonder if there ever will be an end to it. Seems like the more of these kind of men you kill, the more spring up in their place. We thought we had only Saul Delmano left to deal with. Now it turns out he's got his pa and whoever works for him on his side, not to mention that hired killer Branson. Are you sure you're going to be able to let it all stop when Delmano's dead?"

"It'll stop," Danielle said with conviction. "I haven't developed a taste for killing if that's what you're asking, Jed."

"I needed to ask," Jed said softly, still staring down into the flames.

"And now you have," said Danielle.

After their meal, Tim and Jed brought her the whiskey along with the fresh bandages she'd brought in her saddlebags. As Danielle dabbed the whiskey on a wad of gauze and carefully touched it to the wound in her side, Jed and Tim led the horses a few feet from the camp and picketed them to graze.

"I'm awfully worried about her," Tim said, the two of them stopping on their way back to the campfire.

"Both of us, brother," Jed replied. "I believe she'd keep on going on this even if she knew it would kill her."

"Yeah, and I'm afraid it just might," said Tim. "We'll be in Dodge tomorrow evening. If she's not looking any better, we've got to find a way to make her stay there till she's well."

"She won't take kindly to it," Jed warned.

"I know," said Tim, "but it's something we'll have to do if we don't want to end up burying her."

"We'll see," Jed whispered, as the two of them walked into the camp as Danielle looked up at them from tending her wound.

SEPTEMBER 10, 1871

Tim and Jed noticed the way their sister had begun to slump to one side in her saddle, her hand pressed to her side. But when Tim sidled his horse close to Danielle's chestnut mare, she looked up at him from beneath her hat brim through fevered eyes and waved him away.

"I just need to catch my breath, is all," she said. "I'm feeling lots better." Beads of sweat stood on her cheeks. Her face looked pasty and pale.

Tim let his horse fall back beside Jed with a worried look on his face. "That does it," he said to Jed, keeping his voice low so Danielle wouldn't hear him. "We'll be at the Arkansas River this afternoon. As soon as she's rested some, we're pushing on into Dodge tonight and getting her some help whether she likes it or not."

"I agree," Jed replied, nudging his horse forward.

Behind him, Tim had started to do the same, but then he stopped short when he caught a glimpse of a hat moving through the tall grass fifty yards to his right.

Jed, hearing Tim's horse jerk to a halt, looked back at his brother, saying, "What's wrong, Tim?"

Tim Strange kicked his horse forward a step, speaking under his breath. "Don't look over there, but we've got somebody watching us."

"What should we do?" Jed resisted the urge to look all around the flat grassland.

"Get up there and tell Danielle," Tim whispered. "We don't want to get caught by surprise out here. I'll lag back some, keep anybody from riding in on you two."

"But what about you, Tim?" Jed asked.

"Just do it, Jed," Tim hissed. "I'll be all right. You get past that low rise," he added, nodding toward a short upward roll in the land ahead of them. "Both of you get moving as fast as you can to the river. There's plenty of cover there. Don't worry about me. I'll find you."

Fifty yards to the right, Jack Pearl watched Jed bolt forward as Tim stayed back and drew his rifle from his saddle boot. "Well, they're onto us," Pearl said, scooting back down the side of a low natural cutbank. He looked at Al Tarksel. "It can get real bloody out here with sparse cover. Since you're in charge now, what do you want to do?"

"Damn it!" Tarksel cursed under his breath. He shot a harsh gaze at Loot Harkens, saying, "You had to raise your ugly head up and see what was going on, didn't you?"

"I only did it for a split second," said Loot, feeling the hard eyes of the other men on him, making him nervous. "We could go ahead and rush them."

"For two cents I'd make you go rush them by yourself, you slab-sided fool!" Al Tarksel growled, trying to keep his deep voice from carrying across the flatland. "Pearl's right. . . . This is bloody land for a gun battle. The whole idea of shooting somebody for money is to not get shot yourself—Clyde Branson wishes he was here to agree with that notion."

"We could take this one," Jack Pearl said, jerking his head in Tim Strange's direction. "It'd be one less to deal with."

"That would be real smart, Pearl," Tarksel said in sarcastic tone. "We'll shoot the one that's not worth shooting, then let the one worth two thousand dollars hear it and get away. Are you sure you're smart enough to carry a loaded firearm?"

Jack Pearl bristled, but remained silent.

Hank Phipps rose high in his saddle, looked across the tops of the swaying grass, then dropped back down. "They'll probably take cover and spend the night along the Arkansas. We can close them up and hit them first thing in the morning. . . . What do you say?"

Al Tarksel sat atop his horse, brooding for a moment. Then he nodded, saying, "Yeah, that's our best shot." He looked around at each man in turn, then added, "The next son of a bitch who messes up, I'm going to grab by his head and his ankles and snap him across my knee for kindling."

Meanwhile, Tim Strange took his time, carefully moving forward, keeping a good distance back from Jed and Danielle and swinging his horse slightly to his right, keeping an eye along the grassy horizon.

Once out of sight across the roll of the grasslands, Jed and Danielle pushed their horses up into a fast pace. Jed stayed a few feet behind Danielle, seeing the difficulty she had keeping to her saddle. By the time they reached the low banks of the Arkansas River, Danielle was hunched down low, fighting the pain.

Jumping down from his saddle when they reined their horses to a halt, Jed reached forward just in time to catch his sister as she swayed and toppled out of her saddle.

"Easy, easy!" Jed said to her, cradling her in his arms and lowering her to the ground on his lap. He pulled her hat off and ran his hand across her forehead. "Lord, you're burning up with fever!"

"No," Danielle said, nearly delirious, her voice trembling in a chill, "I'm freezing . . . freezing cold. Where's Tim?"

"He'll be here. Just lie still. I'll get a blanket and some water."

"Don't leave him here!" Danielle cried, her voice strained and weak.

"Oh, Lord," Jed whispered, looking down at the fresh bloodstain seeping through her bandages and through her shirt. "Don't worry. We won't leave Tim behind."

But as Danielle spoke, Jed could see she wasn't even talking about Tim "Ma? Pa . . . ?" Danielle's eyes rolled back and forth aimlessly across the sky. "Where are they, Jed . . . ?"

"Oh, Danielle, Danielle, please!" Jed cried out, holding her shivering body against him. "Don't you dare slip away on me, you hear?"

"I—I won't," she whispered, her voice sounding more distant.

Jed hurried to the horses, then raced back with a canteen and a blanket. He wrapped her in the blanket and poured tepid water over her face, swabbing it with the tail of his shirt. He splashed water across her burning lips, then into her mouth, much of it gushing back up as she swallowed. Then he waited, holding her against him, clutching her as chills racked her body.

When Tim rode in, he found the two of them there in the long evening shadows. Leaping down from his horse, his rifle in hand, he slid down beside Jed and looked at Danielle's sweaty face. "How is she?" he asked.

"Better, I think, for now," Jed replied, sounding spent and worried. "But if we don't get her to Dodge, I'm afraid she ain't going to make it."

"You're right," said Tim. "Be ready to ride as soon as I water the horses."

He hurried to the river's edge, loosened the horses' cinches, and let them draw water while he stood among them, wishing he could hurry them, but knowing he couldn't. Once the horses had their fill, Tim hurriedly drew their cinches and led them over beside Jed and Danielle.

"Let's ride," he said.

"What about them back there?" Jed jerked his head in the direction of their back trail.

"They know I saw them," said Tim. "They stayed back. I figure they'll hit us tonight or first thing in the morning. We've got to get out of here."

"I'm with you, brother," said Jed, rising to his feet with his sister in his arms. "I'll carry her on my lap. You lead Sundown."

DODGE CITY, KANSAS. SEPTEMBER 11, 1871

It was deep into the night when the three Stranges rode into Dodge City. Lights along Front Street formed pale circles on the ground and along the edge of the boardwalks. The sound of cattle lowing resounded from the holding pens, their musky smell looming heavily in the darkness. The sound of a twangy piano danced upon the nearly empty street where a few late-night drinkers, cigars glowing in one of their hands and a whiskey bottle or a beer mug hanging from their other, staggered from one saloon to the next.

Tim and Jed reined up out front of a doctor's office, recognizing the painted wooden sign hanging above the door. A dim light glowed in the window. Beyond the light, a silhouette moved toward the door.

"Thank God, he's in," Tim said, stepping down from his saddle and letting Jed hand Danielle down into this arms.

The light in the window turned dark; then the door creaked open and a man stepped out onto the boardwalk, pulling his coat on. He looked around at the faces of Tim and Jed Strange as he began to lock the front door.

"My goodness, gentlemen," he said, looking from the twins to Danielle. "What have we here?"

"It's our brother! He's fevered up real bad, Doctor," said Tim. "He got shot three weeks back up in Newton. I reckon he tried to get up too soon."

"I see," the doctor said, putting his key back in the lock and swinging the door open. "Watch your step back through there until I light the lamp. I was just on my way home. Luckily I stayed late to do some paperwork."

By the time the doctor had lit the lamp and turned it up, Tim had already stepped across the dark parlor and into the adjoining room. Jed followed and, taking out a match, found another lamp and lit it as well. In the glow of light, Tim saw the gurney standing in the middle of the floor and laid Danielle down upon it.

"Fellows, I'm Dr. McFee," the doctor said, already out of his coat and rolling up his sleeves. "Since this happened in Newton, I assume it was Dr. Lannahan who treated your brother?"

"Yes, it was," said Tim. "Dr. Lannahan tried every way in the world to keep him from leaving. But our brother Danny is pretty headstrong sometimes."

"I see," said Dr. McFee, stepping in close and leaning down near

Danielle's face. "Well, from the looks of him, he won't be putting up much of an argument about leaving this time." He turned to Tim and Jed and looked them up and down. "There's nothing you two can do here for now. Why don't you go get yourselves something to eat and drink? Looks like you could both use it. I'll take over now."

"Doctor," Tim said, hesitantly, "there's something maybe I ought to tell you about our brother. . . . It's sort of a secret."

"Unless it pertains to his health, you can tell me later. This young man needs treatment quickly."

The twins nodded, Jed saying, "Thank you, Doctor. We'll be waiting right outside."

Tim and Jed weren't about to leave Danielle unprotected, knowing the men on their trail were probably not far behind. Tim stood back in the shadow of the boardwalk overhang with his rifle in his arms and kept watch on the street while Jed led the horses around the side of the building, out of sight in the darkness. Then he hurried off to an open saloon halfway up the long boardwalk. When Jed came back, he carried a bar towel with a half dozen boiled eggs and sour pickles wrapped in it. In his other hand he carried a small tin bucket of foamy beer and two empty mugs.

"Is everything all right?" he asked, laying the food down on a wooden chair sitting against the front of the building.

"So far, so good," said Tim, scanning the dark street. He then looked down at the eggs and pickles as Jed unfolded the bar towel. "I haven't seen anything that looked so bad and smelled so good in my life," Tim said, reaching down, picking up a boiled egg and popping it whole into his mouth.

"I know," said Jed, filling the beer mugs. "It's all I could rustle up this time of night. The bartender said he wants this towel back. I ran into the sheriff and he asked what was going on up here—reckon he saw the horses. I told him what had happened, about our brother Danny getting shot a while back."

"What did he have to say?" Tim asked, chewing on the boiled egg as he spoke.

Jed sucked back a mouthful of beer foam, then spoke. "He said he'll drop by in a few minutes just to see how things are going."

"Yeah," said Tim, "he probably thinks we're up to something we shouldn't be up to."

"Well, that's his job," said Jed. "It might be good, him being here for a while, in case we need him."

"Maybe," said Tim, taking the beer-filled mug Jed handed up to him. "But it's also a sheriff's job to ask, and we don't need to be answering a lot of questions."

"Why?" Jed asked. "We've got nothing to hide from the law."

Tim didn't answer. His eyes had gone to the single line of horsemen riding their horses in at a walk on the far end of Front Street.

Jed saw them, too, and he set his beer mug down and stood up slowly, wiping his left hand across his mouth. His right hand went down to the Colt on his hip and rested there.

"Do you think that's them?" Jed whispered.

"I don't know," Tim replied. "There's nothing we can do but wait and see." His thumb reached across the rifle hammer and pulled it back quietly. "Ease inside, Jed," he added in a whisper. "See how much longer that doctor's going to be."

At the hitch rail out front of the dirty and less frequented Aces High Saloon, Al Tarksel swung his big frame down from the saddle, the horse beneath him blowing out a long breath and straightening its back. He looked around at the others, who stepped down as well.

"Check around, boys. They're here somewhere. I know they are."

"Yeah," Jack Pearl grumbled half aloud, "you knew they were on the riverbank, too."

"What's that, Jack? Speak up," said Tarksel, "I didn't hear you."

"Nothing," said Jack Pearl. "I just want to get this job done and go on to something else."

"Well, so do we, Jack," Al Tarksel said, stepping past Loot Harkens and shoving him aside to get closer to Jack Pearl. "So do like I said and start looking for them."

"And where will you be?" Jack Pearl asked, tired and irritated from the long, hard ride.

Al Tarksel motioned with his hand toward the darkened front of the Aces High Saloon. "I'll be right inside. . . . Any objections?"

"No," said Jack Pearl, "except the place is closed." He looked closer at the faded sign hanging by one rusty chain, the other chain broken and dangling from the overhead ceiling. "It looks like it's out of business."

A sheet of corrugated tin stood covering a large broken window. In the closed doorway, a thin gray cat lay coiled in a ball, asleep.

Al Tarksel stepped closer to Jack Pearl, saying, "I happen to know the owner, Jack. He'll open up for me. Any other questions?"

Jack Pearl stepped back, looking at the dilapidated saloon, shaking his head.

"Come on, Pearl," said Loot Harkens. "We'll check along the other side of the street. Hank and Al can take care of this side. Does that sound all right to you, boss?" he asked Al Tarksel.

"Yeah," said Tarksel. "If you find them, don't do nothing till you come and get me."

He stepped up onto the rickety boardwalk and kicked the cat away with a sweep of his boot. The cat let out a shriek and shot off into the darkness. Jack Pearl and Loot Harkens walked across the street toward the row of all-night saloons and gaming houses.

"Pearl is right about this place," said Al Tarksel, looking through the dusty window at the dark, cluttered insides of the Aces High Saloon. "How does Bernie Odell make a living in a place like this?"

Al Tarksel knocked on the door, then shook it, then rapped again, louder this time. "Open up, Odell. It's me, Al!" he shouted.

He shook the door again, stepped back, and lunged against it with his shoulder, crashing it open as Bernie Odell came walking through the bar, hooking his galluses up onto his shoulders. Odell jumped back in surprise as the door barely missed hitting his face. Al Tarksel came charging through and stopped, seeing Bernie Odell in the darkness.

"I was coming!" Odell said, looking at the splinters on the floor and the busted wooden door latch. "Damn it, Al, you've ruint my door!"

"It couldn't be helped, Bernie," said Al Tarksel, chuckling as he brushed splinters off his shoulder. "We're passing through on the trail of an ole boy Saul Delmano wants dead. I knew you would want us to stop by and say howdy." He looked around in the darkness, smelling the musty air full of stale whiskey and cigar smoke. "So this is your Aces High Saloon. . . . Well, well, ain't she something?"

"It was when I first bought it," said Bernie Odell, walking around behind the bar and striking a match to a lantern. "But I've fallen on hard times the past couple of months. I haven't been able to compete with the big saloons here. To tell you the truth, I've done more drinking than my customers."

"Well, I reckon a couple of friends can still get a bottle of rye and a beer here, can't they?" asked Tarksel as he and Hank Phipps stepped over to the bar.

"Yep, but just barely," said Bernie Odell, fishing a hand along beneath the bar until he came up with a half bottle of rye whiskey and set it on the bar. "I've been thinking about closing this place long enough to go out on the trail and make myself some operating capital."

"Have you, sure enough?" Al Tarksel grinned. "In that case you're lucky we came along when we did. I could use a good man like yourself to replace a soreheaded Mexican I left lying dead back in Newton."

"Yeah?" said Bernie Odell, getting interested, rubbing his hands together. "What kind of money is Delmano paying?"

Al Tarksel pulled the cork from the bottle with his teeth and blew it away. "Two thousand dollars," he said. "Your end of it will come to four hundred dollars for just a quick piece of work."

Bernie Odell leaned forward, saying, "For four hundred dollars, I'll help you shoot a whole string of people. Tell me more."

While Al Tarksel, Hank Phipps, and Bernie Odell talked at the bar of the Aces High Saloon, Jack Pearl and Loot Harkens made their way along the other side of the dark street, stopping first at the livery barn, where a sleeping hostler rose up from a bale of hay and met them, looking at them through bleary bloodshot eyes.

"Has three men come by here in the past few hours?" Jack Pearl asked, looking past the old hostler and along the row of stables for any sign of Tim, Jed, and Daniel Duggin's horses.

"Nope, business has been slow here since before noon. You needing to leave your horses here for tending?" the old hostler asked.

"Not right now," Jack Pearl replied. "We'll let you know."

He and Loot Harkens turned and left. They made their way along the nearly deserted street, looking at horses lined up at the hitch rails out front of saloons, looking closely at the faces of cowboys as they staggered by.

"I wonder if our new boss, Al, ever stopped to consider that those three might have kept on riding," said Jack Pearl, his voice sounding a bit sarcastic.

"We followed their tracks right to the main trail leading here," said Loot Harkens.

"Yeah, and once on that heavily traveled trail, they could have cut off anywhere. We'd never have seen it," said Pearl.

Inside the saloon where Jed had purchased the beer and food, Jack Pearl and Loot Harkens walked up to the bar, where three cowboys stood leaning with their faces lowered over their whiskey glasses. When the bartender came forward to them, he asked, "What can I get you?"

"Two whiskeys," said Jack Pearl. Then he said as the bartender set two glasses up and filled them, "We're looking for three young men who might have come by here earlier. One of them is limping from a gunshot wound. Have you seen anybody like that?"

"Nope, I haven't. All's I've seen here today are these same ugly faces." The bartender pushed the two shot glasses forward and considered it while Pearl and Harkens tossed back their drinks and set the glasses back on the bar. "A young fellow came in here a while ago, though, bought some eggs and pickles, said he was taken 'em to the doctor's office for his brothers. Do you suppose that might be them?"

Jack Pearl grinned, running his hand across his mouth. "I'd bet on it," he said, pushing his empty glass forward. "Give us one more quick one, ole buddy."

"Hadn't we better hurry over and tell Al?" said Loot Harkens.

"You heard the bartender," said Jack Pearl. "They're at the doctor's office. We've got time to wet our whistles first. That's what our new boss is doing right about now."

Inside the doctor's office, Tim and Jed hurried, picking up the gurney with Danielle on it and heading toward the rear of the building.

"Watch your step, boys," the doctor cautioned them, moving ahead of them to open the back door.

"Are you sure you can trust the woman you were talking about, Dr. McFee?" Tim asked, almost stumbling in the dark.

"Sarah Sims is as steady as a rock, boys. She'll tend to young Danny and never tell a soul he's there."

Dr. McFee moved quickly. As soon as the gurney passed though the door, he closed the door and locked it. Then, as Tim and Jed stood anxiously waiting with their sister on the gurney between them, the doctor ran around the corner of the building, unhitched their horses, and returned, leading them behind him.

"This way, boys," he said.

Tim and Jed rushed along behind the doctor and the horses until they reached a small white cottage sitting back on a quiet side street.

Dr. McFee hitched the horses to a white picket fence, swung the gate open, and held it as the twins passed through. Then he hurried ahead of them again up onto the small porch, where a dim light glowed in the window. He knocked softly and kept his voice lowered.

"Miss Sarah, it's Dr. McFee. Please hurry!"

"Dr. McFee?" The door opened an inch, then swung open all the way as Tim and Jed slipped in quickly with the gurney. "My goodness, Doctor, what's going on?" said the spinster Sarah Sims, stepping back and reaching for the lamp in the window.

"Don't turn the light up, Sarah," said the doctor. "These boys need some help. I'll explain it all later. I thought you might be willing to look after a patient of mine for a while."

Sarah Sims hesitated, but only for a second. "Why, of course, Doctor," she said, picking up the lamp from the small table at the window. "Just follow me."

Inside the Aces High Saloon, Loot Harkens stood back by the broken door and said to Al Tarksel, "We found them, boss. They're down the street at the doctor's office."

"Where's Jack Pearl?" Tarksel asked, setting his glass down, then turning from the bar with Hank Phipps and walking to the door.

"Pearl is headed there now. Said to meet him," Loot Harkens replied.

"He said to meet him?" Al Tarksel bristled. "I told you both to come get me before you did anything."

"I know, boss," said Harkens. "Don't blame me. I'm right here, ain't I?"

Behind them, Bernie Odell hurriedly shoved the cork back into the rye bottle and snatched a gun belt from beneath the bar. "Wait for me," he said, strapping on the gun belt as he walked across the dirty floor.

"Who's this?" asked Loot Harkens.

"This is Bernie Odell, a friend of mine," said Al Tarksel, lifting his pistol from his tied-down holster and checking it as he spoke. "Bernie's going to be riding with us."

"For a share of the reward?" Harkens asked, looking Bernie Odell up and down. "But, boss, that's going to mean less money in all our pockets."

"You're not a bookkeeper, Loot," said Al Tarksel, "so let me handle how the reward gets split up." He tapped the pistol barrel against Loot Harkens's chest as he spoke. "Any objections?"

Harkens shrugged and turned to the door with a begrudging look on his face.

"Al, if my being here is one too many," said Bernie Odell, "I can always shoot one of these peckerwoods."

"See?" Al Tarksel grinned, headed out the door. "That's what I always liked about Bernie here. He'll work with you any way he can."

Dr. McFee had barely made it through the back door of his office when he heard the footsteps on the boardwalk out front. He quickly snatched up the bloodstained cloth and the old dressing gauze that he'd left lying on a table beside the gurney while he'd cleaned Danielle's wound. When he heard loud knocking on the front door, he called out, "Just a minute." Then he threw the telltale items into a trash basket and went through the dark front parlor as the loud knocking resounded once again. "Hold your horses!" he said, ruffling his hand through his hair and loosening his necktie.

"Open it, or I'll kick it down," Jack Pearl demanded, rattling the doorknob.

Dr. McFee opened the door, giving the appearance of a man who'd been asleep. "What on earth is going on?" he asked, looking right into the bore of Jack Pearl's pistol. In the street beyond, Dr. McFee saw the other four men arriving, Al Tarksel's head and shoulders towering above his companions.

Jack Pearl shoved the doctor back and stepped inside the office as the other four men hastened their steps to join him. "Where are they, sawbones?" Jack Pearl asked in a threatening tone. "Try lying to me and see what you get." He cocked the pistol loudly.

"Who in the world are you talking about, sir?" McFee asked indignantly, buying as much time as he could for Tim and Jed Strange, who'd left town only moments before the doctor had returned to his office.

"You know damned well who I'm talking about." Pearl sneered.

He stepped sideways to the lamp in the window and raised the wick, bringing a circle of light into the dark parlor. Before he could say anything more, Al Tarksel and the others came through the door. Tarksel shoved Jack Pearl aside.

"I told you to come get me first, Jack!" Tarksel growled. He turned to the doctor. "Where are they, Doc?"

Dr. McFee looked back and forth at the faces of the men, holding out as long as he could. "I have no idea what you're talking—"

"We'll see!" said Tarksel, cutting the doctor off, shoving him backward to the other room.

The men followed, advancing on McFee until he stood with his back against the wall, his hands up as if to protect his face.

"Please, gentlemen, I was sound asleep," McFee pleaded. "I don't know who you're looking for!"

"Yeah, take a look at this, Al," said Jack Pearl to Tarksel. Pearl reached down and picked up the bloodstained gauze from the trash can, then dropped it and wiped his fingers on his dirty trousers. "Let me pistol-whip it out of him," Pearl hissed, stepping forward, his hand on his pistol butt.

"Easy now, young man," said the voice of Sheriff Harrington as he stepped into the room, a shotgun pointed at the five men, both hammers cocked. "Dr. McFee is the only doctor we've got. If you hurt him, who's gonna dig all this buckshot out of your bellies?"

Thinking quickly, Al Tarksel said, "Sheriff, we're not breaking any law here. I'm looking for a gunman named Danny Duggin. I'm a bounty hunter, you see."

"You've broken two laws that I can name," said Sheriff Harrington. "First of all, you barged in here against the doctor's will. Second of all, you've made me cock this shotgun." He stared coldly at Al Tarksel.

"All right, Sheriff," said Tarksel, giving a nasty smile. "We'll play this your way. You've got two loads of buckshot. But two loads ain't going to get you out of here alive."

"I know that," said Harrington. "That's why I asked Harvey here to join me." He took a step to one side of the door, and a short man moved into the room with another double-barreled cocked and pointed at them. "Harvey, no matter what happens, you make sure this big sucker gets both barrels, all right?"

"Sure enough, Sheriff," Harvey said in a tense, quiet tone.

A nerve twitched in Al Tarksel's jaw. A sheen of sweat glistened on his brow. "You know what, Sheriff? I can't help think this is all just some sort of misunderstanding. We meant the doctor no harm. Hell, I always liked doctors, always thought they did a lot of good. If I had it to do over again, I might even—"

"Shut up, mister," said Harrington. He looked at Dr. McFee, saying, "Doc, where are those three young men who were here earlier?"

Dr. McFee let out a breath, hoping Tim and Jed were well on their way by now. "All right, I did treat a patient here a while ago for an infected gunshot wound. But they moved on. They headed southwest out of town."

"See, Sheriff, a gunshot wound," said Al Tarksel. "That's the gunman we're after. We really are bounty hunters. We're just doing what the law abides."

"So am I," said Sheriff Harrington, jiggling the shotgun in his hands. "I'd jail the lot of yas, but then I'd have to feed you and have the whole jail fumigated." He slid a glance over at Bernie Odell, who stood beside Loot Harkens with his face ducked a bit in an effort to go unnoticed. "What about you, Odell? Are you a bounty hunter now after poisoning half the town with your rat-tail rye?"

"Rat-tail rye?" said Hank Phipps, swallowing back a sudden bitter taste in his mouth.

"Weren't nothing wrong with my whiskey," said Bernie Odell, "but yes, sir, I'm bounty hunting now—this town never appreciated my drinking establishment."

Sheriff Harrington turned his gaze back to Al Tarksel. "It's worth letting you go just to get this two-bit grifter out of town. Doc, you bringing any charges against this bunch?"

Dr. McFee looked the men over. Seeing how bad things could get all of a sudden, with two shotguns and five pistols all firing at once in a small room, he said, "No, Sheriff, I just want them out of here."

"You heard the doctor," said Harrington, motioning with his shotgun barrel. "Get your ragged asses out of here and don't come back. Harvey, keep these buzzards covered till their knees are in the wind."

"Sure enough, Sheriff," said Harvey, his finger tight across the triggers.

Filing out the door, Bernie Odell grumbled toward Sheriff Harrington, "I can't leave this town quick enough to suit me. I hope everybody who ever drank at my place dies with the bleeding runs."

"I'll tell them you said so," said the sheriff.

Once the men had left town, and Sheriff Harrington and Harvey had lowered their shotguns across their forearms, the sheriff stepped up onto the boardwalk where Dr. McFee stood. "Now, what went on here, Doc? Why was you protecting those three boys?"

"They just looked like hardworking farm boys to me, Sheriff. I felt like they needed protecting." McFee shook his head. "This was a most peculiar situation."

"Yeah, how's that?" the sheriff asked.

Dr. McFee seemed to consider something for a second, then said, "Well, it doesn't matter. The main thing is that there was no bloodshed here tonight. Right, Sheriff?"

"Yes, that's the main thing, Doc. Come morning I'll be leaving town for a couple weeks to give testimony in a murder trail in Abilene. I don't like leaving here with bad dust hanging in the air. Is there something you ain't telling me, Doc?" Sheriff Harrington asked, lifting a bushy eyebrow.

"Why, no, Sheriff, not at all." The doctor smiled.

CHAPTER 3

Three miles out of town where the trail swung southward into a stretch of rocky brushland, Tim drew up his horse and looked back through the moonlight toward Dodge City. Jed reined down beside him and brought Danielle's chestnut mare to a halt between them.

"I hate leaving Danielle unguarded back there, Jed," Tim said. "It's too risky."

"It's the best we could do for now, Tim," Jed replied. He reached over and adjusted the heavy sack of feed across the chestnut mare's saddle, placed there so its tracks would look like it was carrying a rider. "We'll let them follow us around out here. Then the first chance we get, we'll shake them off of our trail and head back for her. The best thing for Danielle is a few more days' rest to get rid of that fever and infection."

"She's going to throw a fit," said Tim, inching his horse forward into the brush.

"Yep, but at least she'll be alive to throw it," Jed replied.

While the twins headed off into the brush, a mile past the outskirts of Dodge City, Bernie Odell sidled his horse close to Al Tarksel and motioned him away from the other three men.

Al Tarksel let Jack Pearl, Hank Phipps, and Loot Harkens drift past them. Then Tarksel checked his horse down and said in a lowered tone, "Yeah, Bernie, what is it?"

Bernie nodded at the backs of the three men riding on ahead of them. "How close are you and these boys?" he asked in the same low voice of secrecy.

Al Tarksel just looked at him for a moment, then replied, "I'm two thousand dollars close to them. Why?"

Bernie Odell nodded at the three fresh sets of hoofprints they'd been following. "I didn't want to say it in front of the others, but what we're doing here is fool's play, Al."

"Oh, really?" said Tarksel, his tone turning cold, offended. "And now you're going to start right off telling me how to run things?"

"Hell, no, but I've been living in Dodge. I know more about the doctor than you do."

"What are you getting at?" Al Tarksel asked.

"Listen to me, Al. . . . Suppose I told you we could split that reward two ways between us and not have to ride all over creation to do it? Would you be opposed to it?"

"I'm listening," said Tarksel, "but you'd better tell it quick before these boys look around and wonder what we're talking about back here."

Again Bernie Odell nodded at the prints on the ground. "There's only two men we're following, Al. One horse ain't carrying no rider."

"It looks to me like it is, Bernie," said Tarksel.

"I know it looks like it, but it ain't," Bernie replied. "These boys are being real cagey. Did you notice anything out of the ordinary back at the doctor's office?"

"No. What?" Tarksel asked, getting a little put out.

"There was no gurney there." Bernie smiled. "Ever seen a doctor who doesn't keep a gurney set up for emergencies?"

Tarksel didn't answer.

Bernie Odell continued. "No, you've haven't, and neither have I. It's a known fact that Dr. McFee always keeps one set up. I saw it there one night when one of my customers got to upheaving and couldn't stop."

"What was wrong with him?" asked Tarksel.

"Something he et or drank I reckon, but that's not important. The thing is, those two boys moved Danny Duggin on that gurney. They took him somewhere and laid him up back in Dodge. Alls we're doing out here is chasing wind."

Realization lit up Al Tarksel's eyes. "I'll be damned. Now I get you. These two are only leading us away from Duggin."

"Exactly," said Bernie Odell. "I didn't have to tell you this, Al. I could've stayed back there and collected that reward from the Delmanos myself. I'm doing it because you and I have known each other a long time. Now the question is, are me and you going to split that two thousand between us and let these three peckerwoods whistle for their supper?"

Before Al Tarksel could answer, Harkens, Phipps, and Pearl turned in their saddles and looked back at Tarksel and Odell in the moonlight.

"What's the holdup?" Pearl called back to them.

"Nothing," All Tarksel called back to them, kicking his horse forward. "Me and Bernie here were talking. It makes no sense, all of us bunched up together. We might need to split up."

"What for?" asked Jack Pearl. "Hell, we can see they're all three riding together!"

"Yeah, they were when they made these tracks," said Tarksel, "but that means they haven't rode apart since then. I'm thinking we need to spread out some as we go forward here." He gestured a hand at the dark land in front of them. "You three stay on their tracks here, and me and Bernie will ride over to the right a mile or so. We'll all meet inside of Texas if we haven't caught up to Danny Duggin first."

The three men looked at one another, baffled.

"I don't like it," said Jack Pearl.

"I don't recall asking if you like it or not, Jack," said Tarksel. "I'm the boss, and that's what we're going to do!"

"I understand," said Jack Pearl, "but why are you two going

over there and us three are staying here? Why not you, your friend Bernie, and me over there, and Hank and Loot over here?"

Al Tarksel jerked his horse close to Jack and drew back his big hand. "I'm tired of your mouth, Pearl!"

He moved to backhand Jack Pearl out of his saddle as Pearl shied back with his forearm raised for protection. But Bernie Odell jumped his horse forward, stopping Tarksel.

"Hold it, Al," Bernie Odell said. "This ain't worth arguing over. Let this knothead ride with us. We're wasting time here."

"Who are you calling a knothead?" asked Jack Pearl.

Bernie Odell raised his hands chest high in a show of peace, saying to Jack Pearl and the others, "Look, boys, I know I'm a stranger to you all, except for Al here. Al knows I rode with the Axel Eldridge Gang long before any of you came along. All I'm wanting to do is see us get that money, four hundred each. If nobody wants me here, that's too bad. But as long as I am here, I'm going to do my part. If Al Tarksel's in charge, then by God, I'm going to do what he says without any back talk. I don't know how this looks to any of you, but I'd be damned ashamed to face the Delmanos and admit that five of us couldn't run down one wounded gunslinger and a couple of his buddies and smoke all three of them out without raising a sweat."

"Listen to him, boys. He's got a point," said Al Tarksel.

Bernie Odell continued, saying, "Four hundred dollars apiece ain't the biggest chunk of money in the world, but it's damn good pocket change. Now, I'm sorry as hell that ole Axel Eldridge got his brains blown all over his shirt. If you can't do something this simple without him along, how are you ever going to rob another bank or railcar or payroll?" He looked at each of them in turn, watching them lower their eyes in shame. "Now Axel Eldridge did a good job leading this gang, robbing, killing, pillaging, and I say God bless him for it. But he's gone and ain't coming back. The question is, can you men pull together, act like you've got some sense, and go on with the fine work he started?"

A silence set in. Then Jack Pearl said in a humble voice to Al Tarksel, "Al, I'm sorry. . . . You just tell me how you want to do this, and that's what I'll do."

"That's more like it," Bernie Odell said, looking down and nodding his head. "I know that's what Axel would want to hear."

In a few moments, as the three men rode forward following the three sets of horse's hooves, Al Tarksel and Bernie Odell cut off to the right, seeing Jack Pearl and Loot Harkens look back at him in the moonlight.

"As soon as we get out of sight," said Bernie Odell, "we'll circle, find this Danny Duggin, and make a quick piece of work out of him." He chuckled, adding, "The only thing those boys needed was a little rallying speech, Al. I'm surprised you hadn't already given them one. You know, sometimes a good talking-to goes a long ways."

"I figured choking Hector Sabio might make them straighten up and follow my lead," said Al Tarksel. "I've never had a way with words like you do, Bernie. To tell the truth, that might be why I came and got you."

"Then that was a smart move on your part," Bernie Odell said in a smug voice.

Al Tarksel gave him a solemn look and asked, "You're not thinking about taking this gang over, are you, Bernie? Because I'll not stand for it. I'm warning you."

"What gang?" Bernie Odell laughed, heeling his horse forward. "I just need some money fast. We can't help it if we followed this Danny Duggin back to Dodge while they're out there looking for the other two, can we? We'll tell them that's how it happened. They can't expect a share of the money if they had no hand in the work. As far as I'm concerned, after it's over, if you want to ride with these boys again, that's your business. I'll go somewhere else and start me a gang of my own if I take a notion."

"What about that shotgun-toting sheriff?" asked Tarksel. "He ain't going to stand still for us snooping around town, looking for Danny Duggin."

"Don't worry about Sheriff Harrington," said Bernie Odell. "I happen to know he ain't going to be in town for the next couple of weeks. As far as Harvey Bain or any of Harrington's half-wit deputies, they'll back off without the sheriff around. Besides, there's a couple of cousins named Clem and Otis Gooden in Dodge that'll help us out. We'll let them do most of the work." He grinned.

"For part of the reward?" Tarksel asked.

"Hell, no," said Bernie Odell, his grin disappearing. "These boys will do it just because I asked them to. They both owe me bar bills. We won't tell them why we're killing Danny Duggin. We'll just say it's personal business of yours. We might give them twenty or thirty dollars apiece when it's over."

"Sounds good to me," said Tarksel, "but just out of curiosity, what would you have done if Jack Pearl had've rode over with us instead of with Hank and Loot?"

Bernie Odell grinned and ran a finger across his throat. "What do you think I would've done for half of two thousand dollars?"

Al Tarksel laughed and said, "That's what I figured you'd have done. You're still the same ole Bernie—nothing's changed a bit that I can see."

"That's right," said Bernie Odell. "Now that I'm back in the saddle and getting the smell of other people's whiskey off my shirt, I'm fixin' to make up for some lost time."

Tim and Jed Strange had ridden farther south than they'd intended to, but with the gunmen close on their trail, they wanted to be sure they'd completely lost them before turning back to Dodge City. After two more hours of riding, the twins stopped at the crest of a higher land swell and looked back through the clear gray moonlight.

"What do you think?" Jed asked, leading the chestnut mare by its reins.

"I think it's safe for us to circle around now," Tim replied. He looked ahead of them at a wide stand of cottonwood and juniper.

In the moonlight, the black outlines of the trees swayed on a night wind. "Let's drop the bag of feed in there, then stay in the trees for a half mile or so to our left, then head back."

"That's fine by me," Jed said, booting his horse forward.

A few yards inside the cover of the trees, Jed dropped the heavy bag of feed from the mare's back. They turned east, staying deep inside the trees, hoping to leave very few tracks for the gunmen to follow. When they'd gone a half mile or more and started to turn back toward Dodge City, Tim stopped his horse and raised a hand to have Jed do the same.

After a second of sitting in silence, Tim looked back at his brother, saying in a whisper, "Did you hear that?"

Jed quietly stepped his horse up beside Tim, leading the chestnut mare. "I might have heard something, but I don't know what it was," he whispered in reply, his hand poised on the butt of his Colt.

"It sounded like a wheel creaking," Tim whispered.

They sat in silence, listening, until the faint sound came again. They looked at each other, then inched their horses forward to a sapling. They stepped down from their saddles without making a sound, and hitching the horses, they moved forward on foot. The sound came again, this time more clearly, followed by a horse blowing out a deep breath in the darkness.

Looking past the trunk of a cottonwood, Tim made out the dark form of a horse and the outline of a tall wagon behind it. "I don't know what it's doing here, but I don't like it," Tim whispered. He backed away a step. "We'd best get out of here. I think that's the posse that rode through the Territory and chased everybody out."

"That's good thinking," a voice said, breaking the deathlike quietness. "Now get your hands in the air before we open fire."

In the second that Tim and Jed stood stunned in surprise, the sound of rifles cocking filled the close space around them. Tim and Jed hesitated, their hands ready to snatch their pistols from their holsters.

But the voice said, "Don't even think about it. There's five armed U.S. federal marshals surrounding you. You're both under arrest."

The twins slowly raised their hands chest high, but stayed poised to make a grab for their Colts.

"If you're lawmen, we'd better see some badges," said Tim.

A lantern flared in the small clearing, then grew into a corona of light. The man held the lantern out from himself at arm's length to his side, not making himself a target for them.

The voice chuckled, saying, "You damned outlaws are all alike. The first thing you do is start trying to call the shots."

"We're not outlaws," said Jed Strange, "and we still haven't seen any badges."

"Then look around real easy-like," said the voice. "You'll see more badges than you ever wanted to."

Taking a cautious look around, Tim and Jed saw the lantern light glint on badges and rifle barrels. Tim let out a breath of relief as the two of them raised their hands a few more inches.

"All right, you really are lawmen," Tim said. "But you've no reason to arrest us. We're not wanted for anything."

"Maybe, maybe not," said the man holding the lantern. He stepped closer, the riflemen doing the same, closing the already small circle. "I'm U.S. Marshal Christian Dane," he continued, "and we heard every word you said a moment ago."

Hands reached in and lifted the twins' Colts from their holsters; then they stepped back, the barrels of cocked rifles leveled on them less then three feet away.

Marshal Dane looked at the twins with a flat smile, his tired eyes going up and down them. "And you were right. . . . We *are* the posse that swept through Indian Territory a while back."

"Chris, I found their horses," said another voice. An older deputy stepped into the light behind Marshal Dane, leading all three horses.

"Good work, Seals," said Marshal Dane over his shoulder. "Take them over and hitch them to the back of the jail wagon. We're headed back to Fort Smith at the crack of dawn." He looked back at Tim and Jed, saying, "We're plumb tuckered out, rounding all you boys up. If we had missed you two tonight, you'd have gotten away free and clear for a while longer."

"Marshal Dane," said Tim, "listen to me, please. We were in the Territory when your posse hit there . . . but we're not outlaws. I'm Tim Strange. This is my brother, Jed. If you want some real outlaws, there's some on our trail right now, about an hour or two behind us. If you arrest us, you're arresting innocent men."

"You might find this hard to believe, Tim Strange, if that really is your name," said Dane, "but in my whole career, all I've ever arrested is *innocent* men."

The other lawmen stifled their laughter. Two of them stepped in behind Tim and Jed, drew their arms down roughly behind their backs, and handcuffed them. When Tim stiffened and started to resist, the man behind him said, "Take it easy, young man. We'll remove these cuffs once you're in the wagon."

"You men are making a big mistake!" Jed hissed, struggling as two pairs of hands turned him and Tim around and shoved them toward the wagon in the larger clearing ahead.

"Settle down," Marshal Dane demanded behind him. "If you boys aren't wanted, we'll soon find out. If we've made a mistake, you'll have our sincerest apologies."

"But you don't understand, Marshal!" Jed insisted. "We've got to get back to Dodge City before—"

"Shut up, Jed," Tim hissed under his breath. "You heard the marshal. We're innocent. . . . We've got nothing to worry about."

One of the deputies swung open the door to the jail wagon and helped Tim and Jed take a step upward and inside. When the door slammed shut and a deputy locked it, Marshal Dane said, "You two back up against the bars. We'll take the cuffs off . . . and we'll leave them off so long as you can behave yourselves."

On the floor in the darkness, an old man looked up, his face almost entirely covered by a gray tangle of beard. He chuckled and said to the twins, "Good to get some company for a change. Ole Cooley and Sipes here are too cross to converse with." He stretched his leg out and nudged his boot against one of the two figures lying against the wall of the wagon wrapped in blankets.

One of the figures growled, "Keep your boot to yourself, Alley Cat, or I'll rip your leg off."

"See what I mean?" the old man snickered. "They're both salty as hell." He rose up slightly, looking the twins over. Seeing to his surprise that they were twins, his eyes widened a bit. "Say now. You boys are look-alikes, ain't yas?"

Neither of the twins answered. Instead they slid down to the floor of the wagon and watched one of the deputies hitch their three horses to the rear of the wagon. Marshal Dane stepped close to the wagon, asking Alley Cat Catlin, "Do you recognize these two, Alley?"

"Yep, I sure do," said Catlin. "They was there all right. Do I get some extra beans for breakfast for identifying them?"

"Sure, why not?" said Marshal Dane. He turned and said to one of the deputies as he walked away, "Paris, you get up in the seat for a while, give Dooley a rest. We're going to push on tonight while we've got good moonlight. Once you get back on the trail, it'll be easy going."

Tim turned to Alley Cat Catlin as the men prepared to get under way. "You're a liar, mister. You didn't see us in Indian Territory."

Alley Cat Catlin shrugged and laughed. "What's the difference? Hell, I weren't there myself! But these boys feed good. If you stand the heat, this wagon ain't a bad way to travel."

"Shut up, Alley," a muffled voice growled from within one of the blankets. "You keep running your jaw, I'm going to twist your head around backward."

"That's Lon Cooley," said Alley Cat, lowering his voice. "Him and Lawrence Sipes weren't in the Territory either, but the marshals come upon them leading a string of stolen Indian horses three days ago."

"Keep it up, Alley Cat," Lon Cooley warned. "See if I don't kill you."

"We've got to get out of here, Jed," Tim whispered to his brother as the wagon made a short lurch forward and began to roll. "What's going to become of Danielle if we don't get back there to her?"

"I know," Jed whispered in reply. "I started to tell the marshal everything a while ago. It's a good thing you cut me off. They wouldn't understand, would they?"

"No, they wouldn't," said Tim. He looked around in the darkness at the passing black outlines of trees and brush swaying in the night wind. "It's up to us to get back there and look after her. Lord help her if those gunmen figure out where she's at."

CHAPTER 4

THE ARKANSAS RIVER. SEPTEMBER 13, 1871

Without pushing their horses too hard, Marshal C. F. Mc-Cord and Hector Sabio reached the banks of the Arkansas River at the end of a two-day ride from Newton, Kansas. Along the way they'd picked up the tracks of four riders. One of the horses left the distinct print of a Double Diamond brand horseshoe, which Hector said belonged to the big lineback dun Al Tarksel had been riding. Hector's voice began coming around by the end of the first day on the trail, with the help of honey-laced whiskey and a hot poultice of cayenne oil wrapped around his throat. Although his voice was still raspy and strained and he still cupped his hand near his throat, once Hector started talking, C. F. McCord had no problem finding out anything he wanted to know about the Axel Eldridge Gang and the bounty the Delmanos had placed on Danny Duggin's head.

"This Danny Duggin is one bad hombre, *sí?*" Hector said as they rode along the trail, seeing where the three sets of hooves ran along the trail. A few yards to the left and off the path, four other sets followed. "Why else would Saul Delmano and his family pay so much to have someone else do their killing for them? I think they are afraid of him."

"It would appear so," said Marshal C. F. McCord. McCord wasn't about to tell Hector that he suspected Danny Duggin was really a woman. That was one piece of information the marshal wasn't about to reveal to anyone. "My main concern is finding the Delmanos and putting them out of business. It just happens that Danny Duggin's interests and mine are the same in that regard."

"So you mean what you say, McCord," Hector asked, "about letting me settle with Al Tarksel on my own?"

"Yes, I meant it, Hector. So long as it's on the other side of the border, it's out of my jurisdiction."

"You *Americano* lawmen," Hector said, a crafty smile forming on his lips as he tapped a finger to his forehead. "I have never understood how this jurisdiction works. When I meet this Tarksel on a street in *Méjico* and shoot him like the pig that he is, you will not interfere because it has nothing to do with your American law. Yet you go into *Méjico* to hunt these Delmanos, and when you find them, you will feel justified in shooting them, *sí*?"

C. F. McCord grinned, saying, "You promised to lead me to the Delmanos' place in Mexico. As soon as we cross the border, this badge comes off my chest and goes into my vest pocket, Hector. The Delmanos have taken advantage of the border too long. I don't think the *federales* or the U.S. federal law will either one shed any tears over the Delmanos."

Hector nodded. "Nor will the world be worse off when I kill this dog Tarksel and spit in his dead face." Hector's expression turned to stone just thinking about it.

McCord gazed off along the riverbank to where the three sets of horses' hooves bunched up. Stepping his horse over amid the tracks, he looked down at scrapings in the dirt where boot prints and knee prints sank deep, picturing in his mind how one person had lain in the dirt, perhaps being cradled in the arms of another. Surrounding the area were the four other sets of hoofprints, one of them bearing the Double Diamond marking.

"Looks like Danny Duggin's wound wasn't as healed as he might've thought it was," McCord said. His eyes followed the tracks down into the water. "They left here, one of them leading a horse and two of them riding double, Hector. Now what do you make of that?"

"I do not know." Hector shrugged. "But perhaps it is time you give me a pistol in case we run into trouble across the river?"

"Don't push things, Hector," McCord replied. "We're still a long way from Mexico."

"This is so," said Hector in his raspy voice, "but you had the sheriff in Newton check and see that I was telling you the truth. I am not a wanted man, nor am I a dangerous man. I think for my protection you should give me a pistol now."

"Soon, Hector," said McCord, nudging his horse down the bank to the edge of the water. "First let's see how things shape up in Dodge City."

"Why do you hunt so hard for the Delmanos?" Hector asked, gigging his horse along behind him. "Is there not enough desperadoes to keep you busy?"

McCord looked along the rippling water, then out across the sky as if recounting an event in his mind. Then, letting out a long breath, he said, "Right after the war, there was a young sailor who came all the way from the port of New Orleans to El Paso to ask for a young lady's hand in marriage. He'd saved himself six hundred dollars before leaving the navy. The night before he was to travel out to talk to the young lady's father, he got into a poker game in town and won himself another three hundred dollars before he quit. But one of the men he'd won the money from was Saul Delmano. The next morning someone found the young sailor's body in a rubbish heap with his throat cut and his pockets empty. Dogs were licking at his blood."

"This is a terrible thing that happened," Hector said, shaking his head slowly. "I have done many things that I am not proud of, but never have I stooped to such a low thing as this." He paused as if thinking about it, then added, "Well . . . I did once stick a man for grabbing the behind of a woman I was dancing with. But I stick him only a couple of times, just to make him apologize. But I never would do such a thing as this."

McCord sat staring out across the river, his expression slack and unchanged, yet his hand clenched his reins tightly.

After another moment of silence, Hector said, "And this man's killer was Saul Delmano?"

"Yep," said McCord.

"But how do you know he did it?" Hector asked.

"It wasn't hard to find out. Saul Delmano bragged about it—after he left Texas of course," said McCord.

"This young sailor?" Hector asked, his raspy voice lowered. "You knew him, *sí*?"

"Yes, I knew him," said McCord. "He was my kid brother."

"Oh, I see," said Hector. "So there is bad blood between you and Saul Delmano, the same as it is between him and this Danny Duggin."

"The very same," McCord said in a firm tone, nudging his horse into the rippling water.

DODGE CITY, KANSAS. SEPTEMBER 14, 1871

C. F. McCord and Hector Sabio swung wide of the main trail leading onto Front Street and circled around onto a narrow path leading into Dodge through an assortment of shacks, small houses, and tents. At a small private stable behind the cattle pens, McCord swung down from his saddle and handed a young boy the reins to his horse.

"Grain them short. Then wait two hours and grain them again," McCord instructed as Hector stepped down and also gave the boy his reins. McCord handed the boy a dollar, saying, "Don't let me come back here in a hour and find they haven't been rubbed down real good."

"Right away, Marshal," the boy said, snatching the dollar from McCord's gloved hand.

"Now, then, Hector, let's take it one alley at time, see who we come up with on the streets," said McCord.

"So this is how you do things," said Hector, falling in beside the marshal, keeping up with him across the rutted ground. "You do not ride boldly down the middle of the street the way some law-men do."

"I always found that to be a foolish practice," McCord said, "especially if you want to look things over and find out what's going on first. I prefer to go unnoticed until I'm ready to make a move."

"I see," said Hector. "No wonder all those outlaws on the strip call you the Fox, eh?"

C. F. McCord just looked at him.

Hector added quickly, "Or so I have heard. I myself have never ridden with those cattle rustlers and stagecoach robbers along the strip."

"What exactly have you done that rates you an outlaw, Hector?" McCord asked, turning his gaze straight ahead with a trace of a wry smile. "Are you telling me that all those times you rode with Axel Eldridge you never committed any crimes?"

Hector didn't answer as they walked on through rubble and broken bottles, past garbage barrels and stray dogs that crept along the backs of the row of buildings facing Front Street. "Where do we start looking for this Danny Duggin and his brothers if they are still here?" Hector asked as they entered a littered alley.

"Knowing he's wounded, seeing how they started riding double at the river crossing," said McCord, "my best hunch would be to start at the doctor's office. From there I'll go to the sheriff's office, let him know what I'm doing here."

"*Sí*, that would be wise," said Hector, "and let the sheriff know that I am with you so he will know I am on the side of the law, eh?"

Stopping at the front corner of the alley and looking out along the busy street, C. F. McCord said over his shoulder, "But I'm going to see the doctor and the sheriff alone, Hector. I want you to start here and work your way one alley at a time, looking for Al Tarksel or any of the others. I've got a feeling they'll be doing the same thing we're doing, looking for Danny Duggin."

"Then you must give me a gun!" cried Hector, cupping his hand to this throat. "If I see Tarksel, I will shoot him many times and be done with it!"

"That's exactly what I *don't* want you to do, Hector," said McCord. "You're leading me to the Delmanos, remember?"

"*Sí*, I gave you my word that I will take you to the Delmanos, and I will keep it. But how can I lay eyes on Al Tarksel and not blow his brains out? What kind of man would I be to not do so after he does this to me?"

McCord turned to Hector with a cold gaze. "You're not going to disappoint me, are you?"

Hector relented grudgingly, rubbing his boot back and forth in the dirt as he looked down. "No, I will work the alleys as you say. But you must hurry, because if I see this pig Tarksel, I don't know if I can keep myself from killing him with my bare hands!"

"Do the best you can, Hector," said McCord, taking his badge from his chest and slipping it down into his vest pocket. "I'm counting on you." He moved forward, up onto the boardwalk, blending into the passing crowd with his hat brim low on his forehead.

McCord took his time, working his way along the boardwalk until a few yards ahead he saw people milling about in front of the doctor's office. Among the group a small restless boy stood with a sling around his arm, a woman beside him jerking his other arm to make him settle down. Across the street from the doctor's office, two rough-looking men wearing low-slung gun belts stood lounging against a striped barber pole, one of them picking his teeth with a matchstick. Upon seeing the men, McCord stopped for a second and pretended to look into a shopwindow. After a moment, he slipped sideways a couple of steps and cut back through an alley to the back of the doctor's office.

Before knocking on the rear door, McCord tried turning the knob to see if it was locked. Before he could let go of the knob, a tense voice called out from inside, "Go away! The office is closed! I'm armed, I'm warning you!"

McCord stepped to one side of the door, took his badge from his vest, and pinned it on. "Doctor, this is U.S. Federal Marshal C. F. McCord speaking. I'm here to help you."

After a short pause, the door opened an inch and Dr. McFee

eyed McCord up and down. McCord saw the small pistol in the doctor's hand.

"A marshal, huh?" said the doctor, letting out a sigh of relief. "Thank God you're here." He swung the door open, then shot a glance both ways along the alley before closing and locking it. "My office is being watched by some gunmen! I haven't even been able to slip away and go for help. The sheriff's out of town, but he has a couple of deputies. Yet from the looks of things, I'm afraid I'll only get the deputies killed!"

"I understand," said McCord. "I saw two men across the street. Do you recognize them?"

"Yes, they're the Goodens," said the doctor, wiping a hand across his forehead, "a couple of hard cases who've been hanging around town for the past three or four months. I don't know why Sheriff Harrington has allowed it."

"Settle down, Doctor," said McCord in a calming voice. "If they've broken no law, your sheriff can't do much about them being here." He looked the doctor up and down. "What do they want from you?" McCord had a pretty good idea already.

"There are two others involved," said Dr. McFee. "A fellow named Al Tarksel and a local thug named Bernie Odell, who owns a saloon here. I treated a young man here the other night for a gunshot wound. This Al Tarksel wants the young man dead. He thinks they can pressure me into telling them where the young man's staying. Bernie Odell met me out front yesterday evening. Said if I didn't tell them what they wanted to know, they'd be back this afternoon. Said I'd tell them one way or the other."

"I see," said McCord, "but you *won't* tell them because you've given your word, right?"

"In a nutshell, yes." The doctor slipped the small pistol into his pocket as he continued. "What kind of doctor would I be to turn these wolves loose on a wounded man?"

"Not much of one, I suppose." McCord considered things, then said, "Doctor, which is the most important to you: keeping your word or saving this Danny Duggin's life?"

The doctor looked surprised. "How do you know his name?"

"Because I'm looking for him, too."

"To kill him? Is he wanted by the law?"

"No, he's not wanted for breaking the law. I've got a feeling he's been on a vengeance rampage. I want to bring it to an end before some innocent people get hurt—one of them being him. Are you going to help me?"

The doctor eyed McCord closely, suspicious of the marshal's intentions. Then he said, "There's something about this young man that I don't think anybody knows. Can you tell me what that is?"

"I could," said McCord, "but I'm not going to. If there comes a time when Danny Duggin wants to reveal his secret, it'll be up to him. Until that time, I don't care *who* he is or *what* he is. I'm only here to do some good whether Danny Duggin wants me to or not."

The doctor wrestled with it in his mind. McCord watched, not offering another word. Finally coming to a decision, McFee let out a breath and said, "All right, Marshal. It looks like I'm going to have to play this your way."

When McCord left the doctor's office, he walked along the long alley behind the building, looking around the corner of each smaller alley in turn until he spotted Hector watching the horse and foot traffic on Front Street. He approached Hector quietly from the rear, seeing him reach down and pull a wooden slate from an abandoned packing crate. McCord realized what was about to happen, and hurrying forward, he grabbed Hector by the back of his collar and yanked him back just as Hector started to bolt out of the alley.

"You gave me your word, Hector!" McCord said, turning the Mexican around and pinning him to a clapboard wall. He jerked the wooden slat from Hector's hand and pitched it away.

"I know, Marshal! But there is that pig!" He gestured a hand toward the other side of Front Street, where Al Tarksel stood in the doorway of the Aces High Saloon with a bottle of whiskey hanging from his hand. "I am sorry, but when I see him, I lose all control. I want to kill him so badly!" Hector said in a voice still strained and raspy.

McCord held him against the wall with one hand and stood watching Al Tarksel for a moment. "You're going to have to pull yourself together, Hector," he demanded. "I've got some things set up for us. If you do like I ask, you might get a chance at Al Tarksel right here in Dodge tonight. But I won't let you mess things up. *Comprende?*" He stared into Hector's eyes, letting him see the warning there.

"*Sí, comprendo,*" said Hector with resolve, easing down and calming himself. "Tell me what you want me to do."

McCord loosened his grip on Hector's shirt and patted his shoulder, saying, "That's more like it. I spoke to the doctor. He told me where Danny Duggin is staying. This evening he's also going to tell Tarksel. There's three men in this with Tarksel. When they come to kill Danny Duggin, we'll be waiting for them. If you bring down Tarksel, it'll be in self-defense, but only if you still take me to the Delmanos. Do we understand each other?"

"Ahhh, I see!" Hector grinned. "This is how you work, eh, the Fox? You do not step out and call these men into the street like some big *pistolero*. Instead you use your head, eh?" Hector tapped a finger against his temple and winked. "I think I like this way you do things."

"Boot hill is plumb full of big *pistoleros*," said McCord. "I don't plan on being one of them. I want you to go to the stables and keep out of sight until I come and get you."

"Oh? And where will you be?" Hector asked.

"I'll be going to see Danny Duggin, make sure he doesn't shoot at us by mistake. Then I'm going to keep an eye on the doctor until the time comes. I don't want this riffraff getting carried away and hurting him."

"You are sure they will come tonight and try to kill this Danny Duggin?"

"Yes, I'm sure," said McCord. "If these men know Duggin, they know they've got to get him while he's still recuperating. Otherwise they won't stand a chance." McCord looked across the street and saw Al Tarksel turn and step back inside the Aces High Saloon. "They're probably talking it over right now."

"I think it is time you gave me a pistol, eh, Fox?"

"Not yet, Hector," said McCord. "But don't worry. Tonight, when the time comes, I'll see to it you're armed."

CHAPTER 5

Inside the small wood-framed house surrounded by its picket fence, Sarah Sims stood in the bedroom door, tying the strings of a fresh clean apron around her waist. She looked over at the sleeping form on the bed and cleared her throat, not too loudly, but just loud enough to cause Danielle to open her eyes.

"Oh, dear, I hope I didn't wake you, Mr. Duggin," she said.

"No," Danielle replied drowsily, "I was only dozing." She rose up on one elbow and started to swing her feet down to the floor.

"No, no," said Sarah Sims, "you lie still now." She moved forward as if prepared to press Danielle back down onto the feather mattress. "I'm going over to the restaurant to help prepare the evening meal. I wanted to know if there was anything you needed while I was out."

"No, ma'am, not that I can think of." Danielle lay over on her side, and Sarah Sims pulled the thin white sheet back over her, tucking her in like a child. "I haven't been this well cared for since I was a little—" Danielle caught herself on the verge of saying *little girl*. But then she stopped herself and added quickly, "a little *boy*."

Sarah Sims glanced away with a knowing look in her eyes, saying, "Well, it doesn't hurt to be cared for now and then. I'm glad to see you're feeling better."

"I'm feeling just fine," Danielle said, patting her bandaged side.

"The swelling is down. My fever has broken. I don't how to thank you and the doctor."

"But see?" Sarah Sims smiled. "You just did." She pressed her palm to Danielle's forehead, then said with relief, "Yes, your fever is all but gone." She glanced at the empty bowl on the tray beside the bed. "I'm glad to say you're appetite is much improved, too. For two days you didn't eat a thing."

Danielle relaxed, easing her head back onto the pillow. "Two days? I can barely even remember coming here."

She looked up at Sarah Sims and was reminded of her mother, and of home, and of countless memories of her family. Then her eyes went around the room, to the chair back where her clean washed trousers hung beneath her pistol belt. Her boots sat on the floor beside the chair.

"I need to get up and on my way," she said.

"Nonsense," Sarah Sims said firmly, a look of motherly authority on her face. "You need to spend at least another day or two in bed. Gunshot infections may appear to be gone, but as you saw before, they have a way of springing back up on you."

"I—I know," said Danielle, "but I have to get going and find my brothers."

"Dr. McFee explained all that to you, young man," said Sarah Sims. "They told him they would be back for you, and I'm certain they will."

Danielle decided not to pursue it. There was no way of explaining to this gentle woman what a harsh destiny life had forced upon her and her brothers. "Yes, ma'am, you're right. Another day or two would be wise, I suppose. But I have to say, the treatment you and the doctor have been giving me has worked. My mind is cleared more than it has been since all of this happened. I feel stronger, too."

Before Sarah Sims could reply, a voice behind her in the doorway said, "That's good to hear, Danny Duggin, because you and I have a lot to talk about."

Danielle's first reaction was to bolt upright, ready to flee, but seeing the badge on the young marshal's chest caused her to hesitate for a second.

In that second, C. F. McCord stepped in between her and the chair and looked down at her. "There's nothing to get excited about, Danny. I'm U.S. Federal Marshal C. F. McCord." A trace of a smile flickered. "I'm one of the good guys."

"But . . ." Sarah Sims was lost for words.

McCord turned to her, seeing the look of apprehension on her face. "Don't worry, ma'am. The doctor knows I'm here. He told me you worked evenings at Delmonico's restaurant. I started to wait until after you left for work, but I decided it best to come on in now, make sure you understand what's going on." He swept his battered Stetson from atop his head and continued. "I'll be spending the evening here with Danny. Some men are coming to kill him. I intend to see to it they don't."

As the marshal spoke to Sarah Sims, Danielle lay watching him, his calm manner, the way he seemed to keep an eye on everything around him, yet looking Sarah Sims squarely and gently in the eyes. Sarah seemed flustered, confused, and frightened, her fingertips pressed to her lips as she spoke.

"Then perhaps I shouldn't leave," said Sarah. "I have an old ten-gauge shotgun behind the pantry . . . some shells somewhere."

"No, ma'am," said McCord, "but much obliged anyway. What I'd really like for you to do is to go on about your business the same as you do every day."

Danielle noted how the young marshal's voice remained calm and soft as he spoke to Sarah Sims as if it were only the two of them in the room, as if he might have just as easily been talking about the weather.

"Don't you worry about Danny and me. We'll both be just fine." His gaze cut back to Danielle. "Won't we, Danny?"

It took a conscious effort for Danielle to look into his slate gray eyes and speak at the same time. "It's fine, Sarah," she said at length, not taking her eyes from McCord's. "The marshal's right. If someone is coming here to kill me, we'd best make them think today's the same as any other."

Sarah Sims calmed down, looked back and forth between the two of them, then said as she turned toward the door, "Then I'll just take down my grandmother's mirror from the wall before I leave. I wouldn't want to see it broken."

"We'll do our best not to leave a mess here, ma'am," McCord said to Sarah Sims without taking his eyes from Danielle's.

No sooner had Sarah Sims left the house than C. F. McCord picked up Danielle's gun belt from the chair back, slipped one of her Colts from its holster, and said to her as he turned the pistol back and forth in his hand, inspecting it, "This is some set of pistols you have here . . . shaved barrels, raised hammers . . . looks like the grips were custom-fit for a smaller hand than usual. I bet if I spun a cylinder these babies would tick as quietly as a Swiss clock." McCord raised his eyes to Danielle beneath his lowered brow. "Bet your pa must've done all this custom work back in St. Joe?"

Danielle didn't answer, but she could see he'd done his job well, checking her out, probably her brothers, too. No lawman had done such a thorough job before that she knew of.

McCord shoved the big Colt back down into the holster and hung the belt back on the chair. "You know something, Danny," he said, taking a deep breath and letting it out patiently, "if I've learned anything at all about you, I figure you've got a derringer or some such small pistol under that sheet somewhere, figuring if I'm not who I say I am, or if I'm here for any reason than to help you, all you've got to do is pull the trigger and be up and on your way. Am I right?"

Danielle only stared at him, her hand steady and poised beneath the sheet, her palm dry, her strength and senses sharp. She held a poker face, not revealing a thing.

Yet the young marshal shook his head and smiled, saying, "Yep, that's what I thought." In no hurry, he stepped over to one side of the partly opened window, turning his back to Danielle. Pulling back a lace curtain with one fingertip, he peered out and toward the front yard. "If you think you need that pistol cocked and pointed, it's okay with me, so long as you don't sneeze and set it off accidentally. I've found out enough about you to know I can trust you. Do you think you'll learn enough about me in the next couple of hours to say the same?"

Beneath the sheet, Danielle let the hammer down and let the small pistol she indeed had hidden lie against the side of her thigh. "I've broken no law, Marshal," she said.

"I know it," McCord replied, turning back from the window and walking over to the side of the bed. "Like I said, I've done some thinking and some checking. If I was to pull out a few names of outlaws reported dead or missing over the past year, I'd bet those names would match up well with where you've been."

"Any killing I've done has been in self-defense," Danielle offered.

"Well, we won't get into that," said McCord. "It'd be your word against the word of outlaws. . . . Since they're dead, it'd be hard for them to dispute you."

"What's your stake in this, Marshal?" Danielle asked. "If you were already after these men who are coming to kill me, why didn't you take them down when you got here? Why all the cat-and-mouse games?"

"It's the way I work," said McCord. "I hate shooting up a town, taking a chance on getting some innocent folks killed. Back here, we're out of the way. If there's going to be shooting, this is the best place for it, don't you think?"

"What I think, Marshal," Danielle said, "is that you're beating around the bush."

"Well, maybe a little," McCord admitted, "but I reckon it's because I don't know yet how to act around you, Danny Duggin. I know all about your secret, and maybe I just didn't know how to approach the subject."

Danielle felt her chest tighten. "Marshal, you don't know nothing about me."

McCord raised a hand slightly to try to calm her. "Now don't get upset. . . . I've only done my job. The fact is, it doesn't matter at all to me how a person wants to present themselves. But call me curious," he said as he shrugged. "I can't help wondering why."

Danielle lay in silence for a moment, deciding how far to trust this man. Finally she said grudgingly, "It's a man's world, Marshal. I had a job to do and I figured this was the best way to get it done. You've got your way of doing things. . . . I've got mine." She raised her brow in question. "Is there any need to talk about it further?"

"No, none at all," said McCord. "I wanted only to clear the air before we get down to business tonight." He gestured a hand toward her gun belt. "Are you able to ride after we finish up with these men?"

"Yes, I can. Why?" Danielle asked.

"Because with a bounty on your head, there'll be more gunmen coming to collect it. I figure the best thing for you to do is to head south of the border and cut this trouble off at the source."

"You mean, ride with you when I go looking for Saul Delmano? Sorry, Marshal. When I get to Delmano, I want it to be just the two of us face-to-face. Don't concern yourself about me, Marshal. I can take care of myself. I want to see myself in Saul Delmano's eyes when they close for the last time."

C. F. McCord looked at Danielle as if running something through his mind. "We'll see," he said. "Let's take it one step at a time. A lot can happen between here and the border. . . . Maybe I'll grow on you by then." He sat down in the chair, took his pistol from its holster, checked it, and let it lie across his lap. "We might as well get comfortable. This could be a long evening."

As a slivered moon touched the horizon, McCord left Sarah Sims's house long enough to go to the stable, where Hector Sabio was waiting.

"What has taken you so long?" Hector asked, reaching out and snatching the rifle McCord held out to him. "I started to go over to the saloon and beat that pig Tarksel to death with a rake handle." He raised a finger for emphasis. "It is only because I gave you my word that I have not already done so."

"And I'm proud of you for that, Hector," said McCord. "I told Danny Duggin that you'll be behind Tarksel and the others, making sure they don't escape."

"What? Behind them? But I want to be in front of Tarksel! I want to call out his name and watch my bullets nail him to the ground!" Hector's raspy voice grew louder as he spoke.

"Take it easy, Hector," said McCord. "If he comes into your sights, he's all yours. But keep in mind I've got a job to do here. Work with me."

"*Sí*, I will do as you say," said Hector, a bit crestfallen.

"Good man," said McCord. "I'm going past the doctor's to see what's going on. Then I'll get back to the house and take cover outside somewhere. Be careful you don't have me in your sights once this gets under way."

Leaving the stable, McCord kept to the shadows and crept up across the alley from the rear door to the doctor's office. He saw that the door was ajar, and without approaching any closer, he caught a glimpse of the two men he'd seen earlier standing outside of the barbershop.

"You'd better not be lying to me, sawbones," warned a voice. "Come on, boys, let's go."

McCord hurried away before the door opened all the way. He had disappeared up the alley by the time Al Tarksel, Bernie Odell, and the Gooden cousins walked out into the clear night.

Al Tarksel pulled a leather glove from his right hand and opened and closed his fist a few times, loosening up. "Boys, we're going to wait here a few minutes, let it get good and dark, make sure this doctor don't try to go warn him. Then we'll go open this Danny Duggin up with some forty-five slugs and see what he had for supper."

Clem Gooden looked at his cousin Otis, then turned and asked Al Tarksel, "So you've taken over the Axel Eldridge Gang?"

"Yeah. What of it?" Tarksel replied gruffly. He reached over, took a bag of chopped tobacco from Bernie Odell's shirt pocket, and began rolling himself a smoke.

"Nothing," said Clem Gooden, "except Otis and me are looking for somebody to throw in with full-time. Pickings are a little slim around here. We figured if we did a good job for you killing this Duggin fellow, maybe we'd be able to ride on with you?"

Al Tarksel ran the cigarette in and out of his mouth, licking it, then looked them both up and down, saying, "We'll see how it goes. Bernie here vouched for both of you or you wouldn't be here. It takes some top-notch men to ride with me. I've got big plans for the Axel Eldridge Gang. What do you say, Bernie? Do these boys have what it takes?" He struck a match and lit the cigarette.

"We're fixin' to find out, ain't we?" Bernie Odell grinned, the palm of his right hand rubbing back and forth on the butt of his holstered pistol.

Darkness covered the town like a black shroud by the time Al Tarksel finished smoking his cigarette, then dropped it to the ground and crushed it beneath his bootheel. Without a word he started walking in the direction of the picket-fenced house where the light of a dimmed lamp glowed in the front window. Bernie Odell and the Gooden cousins followed, spreading out and halting as Tarksel did at a distance of thirty yards.

"Get ready, boys," Bernie Odell said. "Both of you circle around, hit the house from the rear. Al and me will take the front. Right, Al?"

"Right," said Tarksel, lifting his pistol from its holster and letting it hang down his side. "Bernie, you get over at the other front corner. Anybody inside will never know what hit them."

Tarksel stood only a few feet from the side door of the stable, where Hector Sabio had taken cover behind a large pile of used straw. Hearing Al Tarksel's voice, Hector felt his hands tighten on the rifle stock. He watched and listened as the other three figures moved away into the darkness. Then he cursed silently to himself and raised the rifle butt to his shoulder.

His thumb across the rifle hammer ready to cock it back and let it fall, Hector stared at his target for a full ten seconds, thinking how good it would be to feel the kick of the rifle butt against his shoulder and watch Tarksel sink to the ground. Yet there was something incomplete, almost unsatisfying in the deed. He wanted Al Tarksel to know who was going to kill him. This wouldn't do at all, he thought, lowering the rifle the second that Al Tarksel began walking slowly toward the house.

Hector turned the rifle around, gripping the barrel in both hands, hefting it like a club. Yes, this was more like it. He made a couple of short practice swings and moved forward, falling into Tarksel's footsteps, stalking him closely.

From his position behind a short bush in the corner of the picket fence, C. F. McCord sat hunched down in his riding duster, his Colt already cocked as he watched the dark shadow of Bernie Odell approach the right front corner of the house. The other two men had passed the front yard and were headed for the rear. Just as Mc-Cord started to stand up and aim his Colt toward the unsuspecting Odell, the sound of a loud thump and a deep grunt came from the direction of Al Tarksel, followed by Hector's hoarse voice.

"It is I, *Hector*, back from the dead, you *pig*! Now *you* die!"

In the split second of distraction, C. F. McCord caught only a glimpse of Bernie Odell dropping down out of sight. The next thing McCord saw of Bernie Odell was him running along the picket fence in a crouch. McCord's shots followed him, pieces of fencing flying into the air with each explosion of McCord's Colt.

At the rear of the house, fire from Danielle's blazing Colts flashed in the night. As McCord raced along the front yard, he heard the loud thumping sound of Hector's rifle stock, followed by the cries of pain from Al Tarksel. Now Bernie Odell had found cover behind a pile of firewood. Two shots whistled past McCord's head. But rather than duck for cover himself, McCord ran straight toward the muzzle flash of Odell's shots, firing back repeatedly until he caught sight of Odell breaking from cover and making a run for it. McCord halted, raised his Colt out at arm's length, took aim on the fleeing dark figure, and watched it fall as his pistol bucked violently in his hand.

Without hesitation, McCord ran to the back corner of the house, then sprang out with his pistol ready, fanning it back and forth, looking for a target. But he stopped and lowered his pistol as he heard the sound of six spent pistol shells fall to the wooden porch, and saw Danielle standing in a drift of smoke, reloading.

"I got two," she said, her voice tight and flat. "Where's the others?"

"I got one out front," said McCord, stepping forward, looking down at the body near Danielle's feet. A bullet hole above Clem Gooden's right eye oozed blood into a widening puddle on the wooden porch. "It sounds like Hector's got the fourth one taken care of."

Danielle clicked her Colt shut with the snap of her wrist and stepped down off the porch to where the body of Otis Gooden lay facedown in the dirt. "It didn't go quite as smooth as you wanted, did it, Marshal?"

McCord felt a twinge of embarrassment. "Hector got a little carried away," he said, looking down at the body on the ground. "I meant to be here before these two doubled up on you. But apparently you had it under control."

"Like I told you earlier, I can take care of myself. I've been doing it for a long time now."

McCord heard the defiant self-confidence in her voice, but he also heard weariness, perhaps even loneliness there. "I know you can, Danny," he offered gently, "but now and then all of us need somebody we can—"

His words stopped short at a rustling sound from the side of the house. Both he and Danielle swung their pistols toward it at the same time.

"Don't shoot!" Hector Sabio shouted. "It is me!"

His hands went up, the stub of the broken rifle butt trembling above his head. Danielle and McCord lowered their pistols as one. McCord stepped forward, took the rifle from Hector, and looked at it, shaking his head.

"Well, you've ruint a good rifle, Hector," McCord said, seeing that even the barrel was slightly bent. He tossed the rifle to the ground. "Do you mind telling us why you didn't do the way you were supposed to?"

Hector squirmed in place, saying, "The rifle jammed, I think."

"The rifle didn't jam, Hector," McCord said, sounding clearly put out with him.

Hector shrugged. "It might have, I think. But what does it matter? We have killed them all, *sí*?" He clenched his fists as he spoke and held them close to his throat. "I killed that pig who did this to me!"

Danielle just watched.

"Did you make sure he was dead, Hector?" McCord asked.

"Of course he is dead," said Hector. He patted the pistol in his waist belt. "I even take back the pistol he took from me."

McCord shot Danielle a glance. "We'd better go check."

CHAPTER 6

Danielle, C. F. McCord, and Hector Sabio walked to the spot where Hector had left Al Tarksel lying bloody on the ground. Hector stood back with a gasp, seeing that Al Tarksel was not only still alive, but from the markings on the ground had managed to drag himself through the side door of the stable.

"This cannot be!" Hector said.

"Wait here," McCord said over his shoulder, running forward with his pistol drawn.

Hurriedly but with caution, McCord made his way through the length of the barn and out the open front door. At the far end of the street, the sound of hoofbeats pounded away in the night. McCord didn't even raise his pistol, for already people were rushing from the saloons toward the sound of earlier gunshots. McCord slumped and lowered his Colt into his holster as the townsfolk slowed to halt before him.

"It's all over, folks," he said, raising his voice to them. "This was law work. . . . Everybody go on with what you were doing."

But the townsfolk wouldn't hear of it. They slipped past McCord and through the barn, looking all around curiously.

McCord made his way through the gathering crowd, finally spotting Danielle and Hector. McCord hurried and caught up to them just as they stopped and looked down at Bernie Odell's body on the ground.

"At least you managed to hit something," Danielle said, dropping her Colt back into her holster.

"I usually do," McCord replied, catching the touch of sarcasm in her voice.

"*Sí*, it is true," said Hector in McCord's defense. "If you have ever heard of the Fox, you would know that he is—"

"The Fox?" Danielle snapped her eyes to McCord, cutting Hector off. "Is that who you are?"

McCord looked a bit embarrassed, saying, "That's what some of the outlaws along the strip call me. My name is Charles Fox McCord. I mostly go by C. F. I thought I told you that."

"No, you didn't tell me." Danielle looked him up and down as if having just seen him for the first time. "I've heard of you, C. F.," said Danielle. "There was a story about you in the *Carver's Illustrated* a few months back about how you had cleaned up the strip single-handed!"

"Well, don't make a lot of it, Danny," said McCord. "Somebody cleans up the strip every year or two." He smiled. "It just gets dirty again."

"*Mi amigo bueno* is being too modest now," said Hector, butting in on McCord's behalf.

McCord noted with a wry smile how all of a sudden he had become Hector's *good friend*.

Before McCord could say anything, Hector continued in his hoarse voice. "It is true he has sent many outlaws fleeing for their lives! Now the two of us go face a gang of outlaws below the border!"

Danielle looked at Hector closely, then asked McCord, "Who is this, and what's he talking about, going to Mexico with you?"

"This is Hector," said McCord, "the man I told you I had waiting back at the stables. I ran into him after Tarksel almost choked him to death. He used to ride with Tarksel and some others, and he knows where the Delmanos' place is below the border."

Danielle narrowed her gaze at Hector, saying, "So you were after the reward the Delmanos are paying for me?"

"No, no!" Hector said, lying quickly. "I was riding with Al

Tarksel because I needed to make some money. When he said there was a price on your head, I told him I wanted nothing to do with it!"

"I bet you did," said Danielle coldly. She turned back to C. F. McCord and said, "I'll ride with you, Marshal, but only because it'll be quicker finding the Delmanos' spread. Then I'll be on my own. But before I do anything, I've got to know what's happened to my brothers. The doctor said they were coming back. I figure they've run into trouble or else they would have been back here by now."

"Good enough for me," said McCord. "We'll look for them on our way."

Sarah Sims ran forward out of the milling crowd, and coming up to Danielle, she looked at the body on the ground and gasped. Then she turned to Danielle, saying, "Merciful heaven! Danny, are you all right?"

"Yes, ma'am, I'm fine," said Danielle, clasping Sarah's shaking hands. "I'm sorry for this happening at your home, but we'll get everything in order before we leave. I'm afraid part of your picket fence will have to be replaced."

"Oh, I'm not concerned with picket fences," said Sarah, tossing the matter aside. "The main thing is that neither of you are hurt." Her glance went to McCord. "Marshal, are you all right?"

"Yes, ma'am," said McCord, stepping in between Sarah Sims and the body on the ground to block her view of it.

"And so am I," Hector said without being asked.

Sarah Sims gave Hector only a curious glance.

"He's with us," said Danielle.

"Oh, then, I'm glad you're all right, too, Mr. . . . . ?"

"Allow me to introduce myself," said Hector, trying to soften his rough voice. "I am Hector Sabio. . . . I work with the Fox." He gestured a nod toward McCord.

"The Fox?" Sarah Sims looked puzzled.

"It's a long story, ma'am," McCord said. He looked at Danielle and added, "If we're going to be looking for your brothers on the way, we'd best get a move on."

"Then let's get to it," said Danielle. "We'll see if we come across this Al Tarksel on our way." She shot Hector a cold glance, saying to him, "Maybe you'd better stay in front of me, mister, until we get to know each other a little better."

Hearing Danielle and seeing the look on Hector's face when Danielle shoved him ahead of her, McCord smiled to himself as the three of them walked back toward Sarah Sims's house. "I think we're going to like working together, Danny Duggin," he said.

"With a bounty on my head, every two-bit gunman on the trail will be out to make himself some money," Danielle said. "I hope you know what you're getting yourself into, Marshal."

"If I had any doubts, I wouldn't be here, Danny." McCord smiled without facing her. "From now on why don't you just call me C. F.?"

"All right, *C. F.*," Danielle said, liking the way the young marshal tried to hide his smile from her. She even smiled herself, feeling better, her wound not bothering her any longer as she walked along in the pale moonlight at McCord's side.

Outside the Dodge City limits, Al Tarksel rode hard, not slowing the horse down until the town lights grew small and dim behind him. In the gunfire and confusion, he'd headed east out of Dodge, going the wrong way. But that didn't matter. Once he put some distance between himself and the shooting, he could swing wide, circle past the town, and ride south. The main thing was that he was still alive. He'd grabbed the horse from the first stall he'd dragged himself into, luckily finding one that was already saddled and ready for the road. It was only when he'd stopped the horse and sat, feeling himself over carefully to assess the damage Hector had done to him with the rifle, that Tarksel looked down at the fancy reins and saddle and realized the horse he was riding was none other than Clyde Branson's roan barb.

"Jesus!" Al Tarksel said through swollen lips, leaning down, looking the horse over in surprise.

What were the odds on this? he thought. But he didn't have time to wonder about it. He continued checking himself over, wiping blood from the gashes and lumps on his head, neck, back, chest, and shoulders. Hector had given him a terrible beating, catching him off guard. For a second, when he'd heard Hector's voice and seen his face twisted in rage in the darkness, it stunned Tarksel so badly, he hadn't been able to think, let alone defend himself.

The whole thing had happened so fast and his senses had been so dulled from the rifle clubbing him over and over, as he looked back on it now, most of it was still a blur. Tarksel blinked his swollen eyes and took a few deep breaths, trying to get a better grip on what had really happened. In his foggy state of mind, it appeared that he'd just been beaten half to death by one dead man and was now fleeing on another dead man's horse.

"Jes-*us!*" he said again, this time feeling an eerie chill run the length of his spine.

His hands shook as he lifted the canteen from the saddle horn by its strap, uncapped it, and poured out a palmful of tepid water. He dashed water on his battered face and rubbed it around gently, tasting blood as some of it seeped through his split lips. In a moment he reached down and felt the horse's mane as if to make sure the animal was alive and not some ghostly creature. He turned up a mouthful of water, then sat for another full minute, slumping in the saddle, trying to make sense of it all.

"Damn you, Hector," he said finally, capping the canteen as realization set in and the events of this night became more real to him.

He touched his wet palm to the pistol at his hip, glad that he'd at least managed to scrape it up off the ground before dragging himself to the stables. He shot a nervous glimpse back over his shoulder along the dark trail. Then he batted his boots to the horse's sides and brought it up into a quick trot, still headed east for the time being, his pain causing him to bow forward unsteadily in the saddle.

Before Tarksel had gone two miles, he caught sight of a dark figure on horseback rise up in the moonlight ten yards ahead of him. Before he could even get his pistol up from his holster, he saw the flash of a pistol and braced himself as the roan reared and whinnied, the dirt from the shot hitting the ground too close to the horse's hooves. As the roan touched back down and twisted sideways beneath him, Tarksel struggled with the reins, trying to right both himself and the horse, his right hand still wrapped around the holstered pistol.

"Raise it and die," said a gruff voice. The dark figure had stopped his horse and turned it crosswise in the trail.

Tarksel weighed his chances quickly, then raised his right hand chest high as his left hand wrestled the reins and settled the roan. "Mister, I don't know who you are, but if it's money you're after, you're lost out of luck," said Tarksel.

"Pipe down," said Bob Dennard, stepping his horse forward. "This is no robbery. I just don't like to be come upon at a gallop this time of a night. What's your big hurry, mister?" But as Dennard drew closer and sidled his horse three feet from Al Tarksel, he squinted and recognized the big man even through the blood on Tarksel's battered face. "Well, my, my, look who we have here," Dennard said under his breath, hardly believing his eyes.

"Bob Dennard?" Tarksel asked, almost as stunned as he'd been at the sight of Hector Sabio. But recognizing Dennard, Tarksel had already begun wondering how to get himself into a better position. Now that the roan wasn't working against him, Al Tarksel knew he would have to make a grab for his pistol.

"Don't even think about it," said Dennard as if reading his mind. Dennard kept him covered with the cocked pistol as he reached out and snatched Tarksel's Colt from his holster. He winced, looking closely at the knots and cuts on the big man's face. "From the looks of you, I'd say you've had one hell of a day."

Al Tarksel allowed himself a deep breath, and he exhaled slowly. "I'm not wanted for anything, Dennard. All you're doing is committing murder if you let that hammer fall."

"So?" Dennard chuckled, his eyes agleam, his bristly red beard lending him a look of pure evil.

"You used to be a preacher, Dennard," Tarksel said, his voice nearly pleading. "Doesn't that mean anything?"

"It don't to me if it don't to you," Dennard said, his voice going low and menacing. "All those years I preached . . . gave sinners like you a chance to atone themselves, and none of you ever did. I just call this getting back the time I wasted on you heathens."

As Al Tarksel spoke, he gave the appearance of resting his right forearm across his lap, getting into position for a good swing. But again, Bob Dennard was a step ahead of him.

"If you try backhanding me, Tarksel," Dennard said, "you might get it half done. But then I'll spend the rest of the night shooting chunks off of you a little bit at a time. You won't weigh fifty pounds by the time I let you die."

Tarksel eased down, looked away into the darkness for a moment, then said, "You know what, Dennard?"

"What?" Dennard grinned.

"I think if you was really going to kill me, you already would have," said Tarksel.

"You're not as stupid as you look, Tarksel." Dennard backed up his horse a step, looked the roan barb up and down, noting the fancy saddle and reins, then said to Tarksel, "I'm going to ask you a question that I might already know the answer to . . . so whether I kill you or not depends entirely on the next words coming out of your mouth." He wagged his pistol barrel at the roan. "How'd you end up on Clyde Branson's horse?"

Al Tarksel stared at him with a bewildered expression, shaking his big swollen head back and forth slowly. "To tell you the God's honest truth, Dennard . . . I don't have any idea in the world how it came about. The last I saw of Clyde Branson, he was deader than a gob of chicken fat. I took this horse because it was the first one I could grab after Hector Sabio beat me into the ground with a rifle. If my life depends on explaining this horse to you, you might as well drop that hammer."

"Hector Sabio, eh?" Dennard jerked his pistol barrel upward and saw Tarksel breathe a sigh of relief. "See, Tarksel? This is one time the truth has set you free. I saw Hector leave Newton on that horse."

"You did?" Tarksel gave him a strange look, partly amazed that

Hector really was alive and partly relieved that what had happened in Dodge was not the work of some unearthly demon.

"That's right," said Dennard. "I heard about somebody almost choking a Mexican to death. Then, when I saw Hector leave Newton with the Fox, I put two and two together."

"Hector is riding with the Fox? That's who it was with him back in town?" Tarksel still looked baffled.

"Yep," said Dennard. "Ain't you glad you didn't lie to me just now?"

Tarksel sat speechless, raising his free hand and rubbing his forehead.

"What happened in Dodge?" asked Dennard.

"Oh, Lord, you don't even want to know," Tarksel said, his jumbled thoughts trying to piece everything together. "I don't suppose you have a bottle of whiskey, do you, somewhere under your Bible maybe?"

"I might have," said Dennard. "Step down off the horse easy-like and let's see if the two of us can't do some business together."

Al Tarksel hesitated. "What kind of business?"

Dennard said, "I'm interested in the two thousand dollars on Danny Duggin's head, Tarksel, same as you are."

Tarksel stared at him for a second. "Is this a trick? I never heard of you taking an interest in collecting for anything but dead outlaws."

"Well, I tried to throw in with Danny Duggin and his brothers, but they wouldn't hear of it. I tried to ride with the Fox, but he wouldn't go for it either." Dennard shrugged. "A man has to make his living some way."

Tarksel's cracked and swollen lips spread into a painful-looking grin. He swung down slowly from the saddle and stood with a forearm pressed to his aching ribs. "Hell, Dennard, it sounds to me like you was after the two thousand all along."

"It doesn't matter now what I was after," said Dennard without answering one way or the other. "It's what I'm after now that counts." He reached over and took the reins to the roan barb and pulled the horse around behind him. "Start walking, Tarksel," said Dennard.

"Walk?" Tarksel looked up at him, pain etching his bruised and lumpy face. "Dennard, I was doing all I could to stay in the saddle. I'm beat to a pulp here."

"Hush now," said Dennard. "A big ole boy like you? It would take three Hector Sabios to do any serious damage."

"I might have some broken ribs," Tarksel offered, almost pleading.

"You'll have worse than that if you try my patience. Now get going. Walking is the best thing for them broken ribs. It'll keep you from stiffening up."

Tarksel turned reluctantly and staggered forward along the trail, heading back in the direction of Dodge City.

Bob Dennard nudged his horse along at a walk behind him. "What happened to the men you were riding with?" Dennard asked.

Tarksel thought about it quickly. Somewhere out there were Pearl, Harkens, and Phipps. It might work to Tarksel's advantage if Dennard didn't know about them. "What men, Dennard? I was riding alone," Tarksel said over his shoulder.

A shot rang out. The dirt kicked up by the bullet hitting the ground an inch from Tarksel's boot caused him to jump sideways, the movement causing pain to shred throughout his sore body.

"Lord, Dennard! Give a man a chance to explain!" Tarksel shrieked.

"Do you think I'm just making conversation here?" yelled Bob Dennard. "I won't tolerate any lying!"

"All right! What I meant was, I've been riding alone ever since my men got separated out there while we were tracking Danny Duggin! Me and a buddy of mine couldn't find them, so we circled back to Dodge. That's when we got ambushed!"

Bob Dennard fell silent for a second, considering it. Then he said, "So what it sounds like is you and your buddy decided to cut the others out of the reward. The two of yas must've had an idea that Danny Duggin was somewhere in Dodge?"

"No, it was *nothing* like that, Dennard," said Tarksel. As soon as he spoke, he heard Bob Dennard cock his pistol behind him, and he said quickly, "Wait, Dennard. Let me finish! What I mean is, it wasn't *exactly* like that! But it was close. We figured since the others weren't around, if we ran into Danny Duggin, we'd go ahead and kill him ourselves! That's the way I meant it!"

"Well, I reckon that's about as straight an answer as I'll get out of you," said Dennard. The pistol uncocked and Tarksel let go of a tense breath. But then Tarksel braced up again as Dennard said, "Stop at the first tree or tall stand of grass you come to."

"You're not going to kill me, are you, Dennard? I thought you said you wouldn't—"

"Shut up, Tarksel," said Dennard. "We're going to stop and talk awhile, figure out what move to make. I'm not going to kill you. We're partners now."

"We are?" Tarksel stopped short, Dennard's horse bumping into him before it stopped, too. "You mean, fifty-fifty on the Danny Duggin bounty?"

"That's right," said Dennard, "unless you'd rather I leave you lie out here and feed the buzzards."

"But how about collecting the money, Dennard?" Tarksel asked, already figuring out how to use Dennard, then cut him out of the reward. "If you showed up at the Delmanos', they'd kill you before you could say howdy. Then they'd kill me for bringing you there."

"Then I expect I'll have to trust you, Al," said Dennard, getting on a first-name basis now. "Once we kill Duggin, you'll have to collect the money and bring it back to me. You'll do that, won't you, *partner*?"

"Why, sure I'll do that," said Tarksel as he started walking forward again. "But I want you to promise me one thing."

"Yeah, what's that?" Dennard asked, already knowing that Tarksel had no intention of sharing the reward with him.

"If we run into Hector Sabio . . . let *me* have him."

"You've got my word on it, Al," Dennard agreed, nudging his horse forward.

CHAPTER 7

Marshal Christian Dane sat close to the low campfire, sipping coffee from a tin cup. The other marshals had pitched their saddles and blankets in a wide circle surrounding the jail wagon. In planned rotation, each man would stand a two-hour watch throughout the night, then awaken the next man to his right to take his place.

When Lowell Metcalf—the newest marshal of the group—had finished walking a wide, quiet circle around the camp, he came back to the fire and looked at Marshal Dane, saying, "What's the matter, Chris? Can't you sleep?"

Dane looked up at him from beneath his hat brim and shook his head. "There's something about taking those look-alikes into custody that don't sit right with me.

"I know what you mean," said Metcalf. "Dooley and Ryan says the same thing. But Seals says they're right out here where all the outlaw action has been going on, so they must've be involved. Besides, Alley Cat identified them from being with that bunch we routed."

"Seals might be right," said Dane, "but as far as Alley Cat Catlin goes, he would identify his own mother as an outlaw if it benefited him some way."

Dane looked out across the darkness, then said, "Go get yourself some sleep, Metcalf. I'll stand the rest of this watch for you."

From a thousand yards away, Hank Phipps, Loot Harkens, and Jack Pearl had been tracking the jail wagon ever since the hoofprints of Jed and Tim Strange's horses had led them to the spot where the posse had taken the pair into custody. Now, deep in the night, Harkens and Phipps lay listening quietly to the sound of bending brush as Jack Pearl worked his way back to them in a low crouch.

"What'd you find out?" Harkens asked in a hushed tone.

Jack Pearl took a few breaths before answering. "Boys, I'll tell you. Getting close to that jail rig gives me the jitters."

Phipps and Harkens looked at each other in the moonlight. "Damn your jitters," said Phipps. "What did you find out? Is Danny Duggin in there?"

"Yep, he's there," said Pearl.

"You saw him?" asked Harkens.

"No, not exactly," said Pearl, still catching his breath.

Harkens and Phipps looked at each other again. "What do you mean, not exactly?" said Phipps. "Either you saw him or you didn't!"

"I didn't see Duggin," said Jack Pearl, "but I saw the other two's faces plain as day when a deputy took a lantern over near the bars. There was others in the wagon wrapped in blankets. I figure one of them has to be Duggin."

"We've got no way of knowing that," said Phipps. "I wish we could have gotten a closer look during the daylight. It could be that Duggin got away."

"We saw all three of their horses, Hank!" said Jack Pearl, getting a little testy. "If he got away, he did it on foot. If he was on foot, where's his boot prints? We've covered every inch of ground! I'm telling you, unless he flew away like a bird, he's got to be in that wagon!"

"All right, then," Phipps said, giving in. He rubbed his jaw. "I just wish Al was here. He's supposed to be running this gang, not us."

"Hank," said Jack Pearl in a flat, impatient tone, "we *are* the gang and we *are* running it. If we can't figure things out for ourselves, what are we doing out here?" He looked back and forth between Phipps and Harkens, then said, "I don't know why you can't get it through your heads that Tarksel and his pal Bernie Odell has run out on us."

"Maybe so, maybe not," said Hank Phipps. "But if we're the ones who kill Danny Duggin, we still get the money. I don't know about you boys, but I *need* that money bad. Winter ain't far off, and I don't have a dollar put away. I don't have to tell you how hard it's been making a living since ole Axel got himself killed."

"Yeah, good ole Axel," said Loot Harkens in a reverent tone. "I still miss him something fierce."

"Me, too," said Hank Phipps.

They sat for a second in silent reflection until at length Jack Pearl gave them each a curious look and said, "Well? Are we going to hit that jail wagon or not?"

"Yep, why not?" said Loot Harkens. "We'll catch them at breakfast before they's good and awake."

All three stood up, dusted off their trousers, checked their rifles and pistols, and swung up into their saddles. Jack Pearl took the lead, heeling his horse forward into the brush.

SEPTEMBER 16, 1871

A t dawn, Marshal Tom Seals loudly raked a stick back and forth across the bars of the jail wagon. "Rise and shine! Everybody up!"

Tim and Jed Strange were the first two on their feet. The other three men groaned, coughed, and cursed to themselves as they tossed their blankets aside and pulled themselves up to the bars.

"Get over here and get your jewelry on so's I take you to the bushes," Seals said to them. "Honest men would have been up two hours ago."

"Yeah, how long have you been up, Marshal?" Alley Cat Catlin asked in a sleepy voice.

"The law never sleeps, Alley Cat." Seals chuckled.

Marshals Curtis Dooley and Tom Seals reached through the

bars with sets of ankle cuffs and snapped them into place on each of the prisoners. The prisoners' boots sat lined along the wall, where they had left them overnight. Anytime the men left the security of the wagon, they did so barefoot in chains. Marshal Dooley took the ring of keys from his belt, unlocked the iron door, and swung it open. The five prisoners filed down and walked to the edge of the small clearing at the bottom of a sloping hillside.

As soon as the men lined up to relieve themselves, Tim Strange caught the glint of morning sunlight streak from a rifle barrel. Tim's eyes fixed on it just in time to see the rifleman rise up from behind a rock on the hillside and level down on Marshal Dooley, who stood next to Tim, looking back toward the camp.

"Look out, Marshal!" Tim shouted.

Seeing the marshal would not have time to respond, Tim shoved him hard with his left hand. As he did, Tim's right hand snatched the marshal's pistol up from his holster. He cocked it and swung it up toward the rifleman. Tim fired two rapid shots, the first hitting Loot Harkens in the shoulder, causing him to throw his arms open as he rocked back. The second shot hit Harkens squarely in his chest.

On the ground, Marshal Dooley rolled up to his knees. Because he had not seen what Tim had just done, the sawed-off shotgun in Dooley's hand instinctively aimed at Tim and fired just as Tim leaped out of the way.

"Dooley, don't shoot him!" shouted Marshal Christian Dane, having seen the whole thing.

He and the other marshals ran forward just as two more riflemen opened fire.

The prisoners scurried back a few feet, taking cover as best they could on the rocky ground. Tim lay flat in the grass on the edge of the clearing. Jed Strange dived over to his brother, seeing the blood on Tim's shoulder. Gunfire exploded back and forth, shattering the quiet of morning.

"Tim! Are you hit bad?" Jed shouted above the melee.

"Just a couple of buckshot nicks," Tim answered, jerking Jed down to safe cover beside him as a bullet whistled past his head.

Tim still held Marshal Dooley's pistol, but he didn't fire just yet. Instead, he looked around and saw Marshal Dooley taking cover behind a rock next to Marshal Dane, a few feet back near the wagon. He also saw the ring of keys on the ground where they had fallen from Marshal Dooley's belt.

Bullets from the hillside stitched up dirt all across the campsite. The other three prisoners lay pressed to the ground.

Tim jerked his head toward the ring of keys on the ground behind them and said to Jed, "We've got to get out of here. Can you get to those keys?"

"I can try," Jed replied. "Keep me covered."

Jed hurried, turning and crawling on his belly, shots whizzing dangerously close to his back. He snatched the ring of keys and scurried back across the ground. Tim fired two shots from the marshal's pistol toward Jack Pearl, who rose up and fired down the hillside at Jed. Pearl ducked down as Tim's bullets sent chips of rock slicing into his forearm.

"Damn! That kid can shoot," said Pearl to Hank Phipps, who lay a few feet away. Pearl grasped his forearm, then levered another round into his rifle chamber, rose up, and continued firing.

"I got them, Tim," Jed said, his breath pumping short and fast as he crawled back to his brother's side.

He shot a glance back at the marshals in the clearing and saw that they were too busy firing to pay any attention to the prisoners. He drew into a ball on his side, unlocked the cuffs on his ankles, and let them fall. Quickly he rolled over and did the same for Tim.

"I've got only two shots left in this pistol, Jed," Tim said, glancing around at the prisoners, then at the marshals, then back to the hillside. "Stay close to me."

"I'm right beside you," Jed said.

They crawled faster now, rifle shots thumping the ground near their bare feet. At the edge of the clearing, the brothers sprang up, running wide of the marshals' position and around the clearing until they jumped behind the wagon. At the other end of the wagon, the horses had shied around. At the horses' hooves lay Marshal Seals, his dead eyes staring up at the morning sky.

"Come on, Jed! Get the horses!" Tim said, dropping down beside the dead marshal, unbuckling the gun belt from around his waist, and slinging it over his shoulder. The gunfire continued, hard and steady. Tim grabbed the dead marshal's rifle from the ground and turned to the horses in time to catch the reins Jed threw to him.

As they mounted and turned the frightened horses, Marshal Dooley caught a glimpse of them, turned, and fired. "The prisoners are getting away!" he shouted.

Marshal Dane turned and fired as well, seeing the rest of the horses scatter and race down out of sight, following the Strange twins. But the marshals' shots hit only the bars of the jail wagon and ricocheted away. On the ground a few feet to Dane and Dooley's left, Marshal Metcalf rose up and fired at the hillside, but a bullet from Jack Pearl's rifle slammed into his shoulder and spun him around in the dirt.

"Cover me!" Marshal Dane shouted, seeing Metcalf sprawled out bleeding in the dirt. He ran in a crouch, grabbed Metcalf by his boots, and dragged him back to safety from the stinging lead cutting the air all around them.

On the hillside, Jack Pearl and Hank Phipps both dropped back down behind their cover at the same time.

"Did you see what I saw?" Pearl asked, levering a round into his rifle chamber.

"Yeah, I saw the look-alikes," Phipps replied, his breath heaving in his chest. "I didn't see Danny Duggin, though."

"If we didn't see him, he's either dead or not there," said Pearl. "They're leading a spare horse."

"Maybe he crawled away and they're taking his horse to him?" said Phipps.

"Maybe," said Pearl. "Either way, we need to get out of here and run them down." Shots spat past overhead. "What kind of shape is Loot in?"

"I thought he was dead, but I saw him wiggle around a little," said Phipps.

"Leave him," said Pearl. "We'll be lucky to get ourselves out of here."

"We can't just leave him!" said Phipps.

"I can." Jack Pearl hissed, already lowering onto his belly and crawling away back up the hillside toward their horses. "You do what suits you."

"Damn it, Jack!" Phipps tried to raise his head enough to look over at Loot Harkens, but a rifle shot sliced past his nose. "Wait for me!" He dropped flat and hurried along behind Jack Pearl up the hillside, sticking his rifle barrel back behind himself one-handed and firing a wild shot down at the lawmen.

From his position in the clearing, Marshal Dane raised a gloved hand after the firing from the hillside had ceased. "Hold your fire, men. They're gone!" he shouted. Marshal Dane stood up and levered another round into his rifle as he scanned the hillside, saying, "Dooley, Seals, the two of you scout up there from the right. Ryan and I will take the left."

"Seals is dead, Chris," Metcalf said in a strained voice. "I saw him get shot down."

Marshal Dane glanced around, now seeing Seals's legs lying limp past the edge of the wagon. "Dooley, give me a hand!" he shouted.

Helping Metcalf to his feet, Dane and Dooley propped the wounded marshal between them and walked back to the edge of the wagon, where Ryan had already arrived and stooped down beside Seals's body.

"Damn it, Chris," said Marshal Dooley, looking up at Christian Dane with watery eyes. "Tom didn't deserve this! He always gave a man a fair shake."

Marshal Dane helped Metcalf seat himself on the ground and lean back against the wagon wheel. "Come on, Dooley, let's get this bleeding stopped. Tom Seals was one of the best . . . but he's dead now. We'll take care of him later."

"I understand," said Marshal Dooley, wiping a hand across his face. "I'll get the prisoners back inside and go round up the horses."

"Good man," said Dane. "Ryan will help you. I'll get the medical bag and take care of Metcalf."

Dooley managed to put his grief and anger aside as he and Marshal Ryan closed the door behind the three prisoners and walked off into the distance where the horses had gathered, milling among clumps of grass. Once he and Ryan had led the horses back to the camp and hitched them to the wagon, Dooley looked down and saw that Marshal Dane had slowed the bleeding and pressed a bandage into place on Metcalf's shoulder.

"As soon as we get Seals's body wrapped up and aboard, I'm heading after them look-alikes, Chris," he said in a resolved tone. "I won't stop till I've got those two facedown over their saddles. I reckon if there was any doubt before about them being outlaws, it's pretty clear now."

"Wait a minute, Dooley," said Marshal Dane, standing up and stepping back as he capped the canteen in his hand. "Don't go running off half-cocked. You didn't see how this started, did you?"

"I saw enough," said Dooley. "I heard my pistol fire four times while the fight was going on."

"Yeah, but if you'd've looked toward those twins, you'd have seen they were firing at the riflemen, same as we were."

"It's true," Metcalf said through his pain. "It looked like the riflemen were firing on them more than us."

"All's I know right now is that Tom Seals is dead, and somebody's got to face his woman and his daughter and break it to them. I want to at least be able to tell them that the buzzards who did it are dead."

Marshal Dane studied Dooley's eyes for a moment, considering everything. Then he looked at Marshal Ryan and said, "Eddie, why don't you two go see about the one we shot up there?"

He nodded toward the hillside. "When we get caught up here, we'll decide who's going after the others and who's going to get Metcalf and these prisoners back to Fort Smith."

"Come on, Dooley," said Marshal Eddie Ryan. "It'll give you time to cool down some."

Dooley seethed and cursed under his breath. But then he turned and walked off with Ryan up the hillside, the two of them with their rifles cocked and poised before them.

"He'll be all right, Chris," said Metcalf, seeing the concerned look on Marshal Dane's face as he stared after Dooley.

"I know," said Marshal Dane. "I've seen him like this before. But he'll have to settle down a whole lot before we can let him go off after those twins."

Alley Cat Catlin had been listening to the conversation, and wrapping his hands around the iron bars, he pressed his face between the bars as deep as he could and said, "Don't leave that wild-eyed fool here guarding us, Marshal Dane!"

"Shut up and sit down, Alley Cat," said Dane. "This is none of your business. I believe you were lying about those boys to begin with."

Alley Cat shrank back and slid down onto the wagon floor. "Hell, I just said what I thought you wanted to hear, Marshal. I meant no harm by it."

Dane rose up to his feet and stared at Alley Cat through the bars. "You mean they weren't with that bunch down on the other end of the Nations?"

"Marshal," said Alley Cat, "to be honest with you, I wasn't there myself."

"Then, for God sakes, man," Marshal Dane hissed, "why didn't you say so?"

Alley Cat looked worried, casting a glance at the two other prisoners, then back at Marshal Dane. "I knew you boys always feed good—I was headed to Fort Smith anyway! Why not throw in with yas?"

Dane just stared at him.

One of the other two prisoners rose partly to his feet, saying, "Just give me the say-so, Marshal. I'll stomp his head till something squirts out both ears."

"Sit down!" Marshal Dane barked.

As the prisoner dropped back to the floor, four rifle shots exploded steadily from the hillside, causing Marshal Dane to spin toward the sound with his pistol coming up cocked and ready.

Silence followed the shots until Marshal Dane took a step forward and called out, "Dooley? Ryan? Is everything all right up there?"

Ryan replied in a shaken voice, "It's all right, Chris. We're coming down."

Marshal Dane stood at the edge of the clearing as the two marshals worked their way down to him, Marshal Dooley dragging the body of Loot Harkens by the shirt collar. Ryan arrived behind Dooley with a shocked look still on his face.

"There's one of 'em," said Dooley, slinging the body forward on the ground.

"What happened up there?" Dane asked in a firm voice, looking past Dooley at Ryan.

But it was Dooley who answered. "He was still alive. He made a move for his gun and I nailed him."

Marshal Dane looked down at the four exit wounds in Harkens's back. "It took four shots?" he asked.

"One shot, four shots, or a dozen," said Dooley, "what's the difference? It might have been his bullet that killed Tom Seals."

"And it might not have," said Marshal Dane.

"Yep, you're right," said Dooley. "It might not have been. That's why I want to hurry up and get after the others."

"Dooley, you ain't acting right," Marshal Dane said. "Now get a grip on yourself. We're men of the law."

"Oh? You don't believe me?" Dooley asked, jerking his head back toward Ryan, who was standing behind him. "Then ask Eddie about it."

Before Dane could say a word, Ryan cut in, saying, "I wasn't watching when the man went for his gun, but there was a gun on the ground—"

"I don't need to hear it," said Marshal Dane, cutting Ryan off to keep him from lying for Dooley. "Men, I'm as sorry as you are about losing Tom Seals. But let's not forget who we are and what we represent."

"Save it, Chris," said Dooley. "I don't know what's going on between those look-alikes and the ones who ambushed us, but they're all to blame for Seals's death."

"I'm warning you, you'd better calm down, Dooley," said Marshal Dane. "Acting like this ain't doing nobody any good."

Dooley had started to walk forward, past Dane toward the horses. But he stopped short and turned, facing Marshal Dane. "You're *warning* me?" he said, his voice dropping low and taking on a menacing tone.

"That's right," said Dane, "if that's what it takes. I'm the senior marshal here. If you make me pull rank on you, I will. I'm afraid there was a mistake made, us taking those boys prisoners. It was my mistake and I stand responsible for it. Let's not make another one between you and me."

Dooley studied Marshal Dane's eyes and took a deep breath. "You might have pinned a badge on a couple of months before I did, Chris, but if you think that'll stop me from going after those boys, you're badly mistaken." As he spoke, he reached up slowly with his left hand, unpinned his badge from his chest, and pitched it to the dirt at Marshal Dane's feet. "We're all square now, Chris. Don't warn me again unless you're prepared to make it stick."

"Dooley, get back here!" Ryan called out as Dooley angrily turned his back on Christian Dane and walked to the horses. "Come on, now, pick this badge up and settle down! You hear me?"

"Let him go, Eddie," said Marshal Dane in a lowered tone, taking Ryan by the forearm, stopping him from running forward. "There's no talking to him right now."

They watched Dooley sling a saddle up over his horse's back and ready it for the trail. When he stepped up into his saddle, Dooley took off his hat and looked at the body of Tom Seals on the ground for a brief moment. Then he put on his hat, jerked his reins, turned his horse, and booted it off in the direction the twins had taken.

"We've got to stop him somehow," said Ryan to Dane as they walked back to the wagon.

"I'll catch up to him once he's cleared his mind a little," said Marshal Dane. "You'll have to get Metcalf and the prisoners back to Fort Smith on your own. Metcalf will need some real doctoring. More than what we can give him out here."

"I'll do it, Chris," said Ryan. "Don't worry about us getting to Fort Smith."

Metcalf managed to struggle to his feet and lean back against the wagon as the two approached him. "Chris," he said, "why didn't you tell him old Alley Cat was lying on those look-alikes?"

"Because the shape his mind is in right now, he'd have likely killed Alley Cat," said Dane. "I couldn't take that chance." Dane unhitched his horse and pulled it away from the others. "I'm going to get saddled up and get after him." Dane looked off up the hillside and cursed under his breath. "Meanwhile, there goes two killers on the loose."

Metcalf said in a weak voice, "Get me up on the wagon seat. I can roll this rig into Fort Smith with a bullet hole in me. You two split up, one go after Dooley, the other after the gunmen."

"Look at you, Metcalf," said Dane, reaching down, pulling his saddle up from the ground, and tossing it atop his horse. "You're barely on your feet." Dane then turned to Ryan. "Get Seals's body wrapped up and get this wagon going." He nodded at Metcalf. "If he keeps talking foolish, crack him across the head with something. I'll take care of the rest of this mess. Those look-alikes are innocent from the looks of things."

"You be careful out there, Chris," said Marshal Ryan. "I don't know about the other one, but the one called Tim is a crack shot. I saw what he did to that rifleman."

"So did I," said Marshal Dane. "All the more reason to catch up with Dooley. Those boys took Seals's gun belt and rifle with them. If they are innocent now, I don't want Dooley to end up making killers out of them."

CHAPTER 8

Tim and Jed Strange rode hard, straight south, deeper into Indian Territory. After a full hour, they pulled their exhausted horses up alongside the shallow drop of a creek bank and looked back along their horses' hoofprints. "We're awfully easy to follow, riding across country that way," said Tim. They had not taken the hoof-worn trail—instead, they had cut off through the desolate, brushy rock land, needing to put as much distance behind them as possible in the shortest amount of time. "You can bet they're on our tails right now."

"Yes," Jed agreed, "both the law and the outlaws if one bunch hasn't killed the other by now. I hated leaving the lawmen there, fighting our battle for us."

"They gave us no choice, Jed. We tried explaining our situation. They didn't believe us."

The two of them stepped their horses down the natural cutbank to the narrow stream of water and swung down from their saddles, loosening the cinches to let the horses drink.

"If we ever live through all of this, we'll make it a point to go to Fort Smith and clear ourselves. Meanwhile, we'll do whatever we've got to do."

He ran a hand across the chestnut mare's sweaty rump as she drew water. Looking at their sister's mare painfully reminded them both of Danielle and the dangerous situation they'd left her in back in Dodge City.

"What about Danielle?" Jed asked. "Is there no way we can double back and see what's become of her?"

"None that I can see right now," said Tim as he swung Seals's pistol belt down off his shoulder and strapped it on.

He pitched Jed the dead marshal's rifle. Jed checked the rifle over while Tim lifted the Colt from the holster. The pistol Dooley had dropped on the ground now stuck up from Jed's waist belt. Jed had fully loaded it with cartridges from Seals's gun belt as they'd ridden away from the battle.

"Wherever we go, we'll be bringing gunmen behind us. As long as it's been, if Danielle got back on her feet, she's gone by now. The best we can hope for is to meet up with her along the border."

"But if she didn't get back on her feet . . ." Jed offered in an air of doom.

He didn't finish his words, for he couldn't bring himself to say what they knew would be the truth. By now Danielle was either on the trail, or else she was dead. Neither of them wanted to think it. They stared back toward the north for a silent moment as the horses drew the sandy water.

"I reckon going on to the border is all we can do, Jed," Tim said somberly. "If Danielle's there, she'll be going with us. If she's not there . . . well, it's what she'd have wanted us to do."

They gathered the three horses, tightened the cinches, and swung up into their saddles without another word on the subject.

A half hour after the twins rode away from the narrow creek bank, Jack Pearl and Hank Phipps rode in off of the trail two miles to the west. Seeing the hoofprints of the three horses, Phipps nodded and said, "Trail or no trail, I told you they'd have to come in somewhere along this creek. It's the nearest water to the trail." He swung down from his horse's back, looking all around, wary of an ambush.

"We've got no time to waste here," said Jack Pearl, looking back at the distant line of land and sky without stepping down from his horse. "We've got law on us."

Phipps looked closely at the hoofprints on the ground. "One thing's for sure: They haven't met up with Danny Duggin. There's still no rider on that third horse."

Jack Pearl let out an exasperated breath, saying, "Damn it. It looks like we caused ourselves all that trouble for nothing."

"Maybe so," said Phipps, "but it's trouble we'll easily fix once we get into some hill country. I know for a fact that I put one marshal down back there. There's another one wounded. They can't leave the wagon sitting there alone. So that means there can't be no more than two on our trail. As soon as we get some good cover, we can take care of them when they come along."

"Then what?" asked Jack Pearl. "Keep on following these two look-alikes, hoping somewhere we'll run into Duggin?"

"Have you got any better ideas?" Phipps asked in a sharp tone of voice.

Jack Pearl thought about it, then grumbled. "Hell, no, I reckon not. Let's get moving."

"You'd better water that horse," Phipps cautioned him; his own horse was eagerly drawing water from the creek.

"I told you, we've got no time to waste," said Jack Pearl, jerking his reins to keep the horse from bending its muzzle down into the running water. "This horse is fine until we get to the next water."

"You'll think it ain't so fine," said Phipps, "when that horse is blown and you're afoot out here. I'm not leaving here till this horse is tanked up."

"Yeah? You'll think *not leaving* when you're lying there face-down in the water with a rifle bullet through your belly." Pearl yanked harder on his reins, kicking his tired horse forward. "I'm going on."

"What about yourself?" Phipps asked as Pearl gigged his horse up the low bank. "Ain't you going to at least fill your canteen?"

"I ain't thirsty," Jack Pearl called back to him. "Catch up to me if you ain't shot from a half mile away."

"Stupid as a mud hen," Phipps said under his breath, watching Jack Pearl ride away.

Shaking his head, Phipps took his canteen down from his saddle and filled it as his horse continued drinking. When his canteen was filled, Phipps capped it and laid it by his feet. He took off his hat and held it down in the shallow creek bed, letting water run into it. Then he raised the hat and poured the water down over his head, cooling himself. Standing up, he slung his wet hair back and forth and put his hat on.

He chuckled to himself. "Damn fool gets thirsty enough, I reckon I'll let him lick my shirt collar."

Within ten minutes, Hank Phipps was back in his saddle and on his way. Within another five minutes, he'd caught up to Jack Pearl and sidled his horse up close to him. Seeing the way Jack Pearl's horse had slowed down almost to a walk in spite of Pearl batting his boots against the horse's sides, Phipps said, "Don't be a fool! Turn back and water that animal while there's still time, damn you! He'll be blown before we reach those low hills." He nodded toward the higher rise of purple land in the distance ahead of them.

"He's just winded is all," said Pearl, ceasing to goad the tired horse. "He'll catch his breath here in a minute." He looked at Phipps with a tight expression. "Did you fill your canteen?"

"Yes, I did, but you didn't, remember? You wasn't at all thirsty at the time." He heeled his horse ahead of Phipps by five yards and looked back. "Are you sure you don't want to go back and water that animal, you ignorant peckerwood?"

"I'll manage somehow. I ain't going back," said Pearl.

"Suit yourself, Jack." Hank Phipps chuckled.

But seeing the distance between them grow, Jack Pearl cursed under his breath and called out, "Wait up, Hank! Give me one little drink . . . just a sip!"

But Hank Phipps ignored him and rode his horse forward another fifty yards, then reined it down and waited until Jack Pearl drew nearer. "What's wrong, Jack? Ain't it hot enough for you out here? That poor horse looks plumb tuckered out."

"Damn it, Hank. Wait up a minute," Pearl called out in a dry, hoarse voice. "All I want is a sip! How many times have I given you a shot of whiskey when you had none?"

"Not as many times as you should have," Phipps said, laughing and slapping his leg.

"This ain't funny, Hank! Quit fooling around!" Jack Pearl bellowed.

Phipps grinned and waited until Jack Pearl got within twenty feet of him. Then he spurred his horse, causing it to bolt forward, saying, "Ooops! This horse is just too strong to hold back!" He called out over his shoulder, "Next time you ask, you'd better remember to say, 'Pretty please.'"

"Son of a bitch," Jack Pearl growled to himself, running a hand across his parched lips. He gigged the horse forward hard.

But for all its effort, the hot, tired animal could barely hold a weak trot. In another five minutes, the animal had slowed to a loose walk, even with Pearl spurring and slapping his reins to its rump.

Over a low rise, Jack Pearl saw Hank Phipps sitting atop his horse, waiting for him. When Pearl got within fifty feet of him, Hank Phipps raised the canteen in his hand, took a mouthful, and spat it out in a long stream. He held the canteen out toward Phipps and said, "I've just been teasing with you, Jack. Sorry. Come on up here and get you a good long drink."

"It's about damn time," Jack Pearl said, trying to show a friendly smile on his hot dry lips. He coaxed the exhausted animal forward, the horse almost staggering beneath him. "You're lucky I've got a sense of humor, Hank."

But when Pearl got within twenty feet, Hank shook the canteen toward Pearl and said, "Sorry. You waited too long. You should have come quicker when I called you!" He spun his horse and batted it forward, calling out over his shoulder, "When you get to hell, tell the devil I said howdy!" Laughing, he waved a hand and rode on.

This time Hank Phipps had made it only a few feet when a shot rang out behind him. He stiffened forward in his saddle, his laughter falling silent in his throat. As he rocked back in his saddle, a second shot rang out. Hank Phipps's canteen slumped onto his lap, then clattered to the ground. He managed to turn his horse around, facing Jack Pearl with a startled look on his distorted face.

"I—I was only . . . fooling."

The third shot lifted Phipps from his saddle.

"I wasn't fooling, though," said Jack Pearl, his pistol smoking in his hand. "That'll teach you to make light of me at a time like this, you dumb bastard. I've shot more men in the back than you've got fingers and toes."

He stepped down from his saddle and ran forward on foot, catching the horse's reins and drawing the animal to him. He walked the horse back to where the canteen lay in the dirt. He picked the canteen up and uncapped it on his way back to Hank Phipps's body, lying dead on the rocky ground.

Raising a long drink, then lowering the canteen, Pearl said to the lifeless eyes staring up at the sky, "There, now, Hank, I told you I'd manage somehow."

U p in the low hills, Tim and Jed Strange had turned at the distant sound of the first pistol shot. By the time the third shot echoed across the land to them, they had pinpointed the tiny figures of men and horses through the wavering heat. They stared as one figure stepped onto a horse and rode forward, leaving the other man stretched out on the ground.

"I don't know who it is," said Jed Strange, "but it looks like one just killed the other."

"Come on," said Tim, pushing his horse upward on the narrow path, leading the chestnut mare, "we don't need to stick around and see."

"Hold it, brother," said Jed, still looking back. "Maybe we should. There's somebody farther back, one rider pushing hard."

Tim stopped his horse. Again they looked back across the land, this time seeing a single black speck at the head of a low rise of drifting dust.

"I figure that one's the law, Tim," Jed said in a firm tone. "If this one in front makes it into the bottom of the hills, the next rider will be a sitting duck."

"If he's any kind of lawman, he knows that already," Tim said. "Come on, let's go. Whatever they do down there just buys us more time."

"Uh-uh," Jed replied. "I don't feel right about it." He pulled the rifle from his saddle boot.

"You don't feel *right* about it?" Tim spun his horse toward him, saying, "Then you can feel *wrong* about it while we clear these hills and get out of here!"

"You don't mean that, Tim." Jed levered a round into the rifle chamber and slipped down from his saddle. "It might not bother you now, but it will later if we find out one of those deputies got killed, especially if he's supposed to be hunting us."

Tim bit his lip, knowing Jed was right. "Gawd dang it! Give me your reins," he said, reaching down and snatching the reins from Jed's hands. "I'll hide the horses out of sight."

Leading the other two horses behind him, Tim guided his own horse around a shoulder-high stand of rock. When he came back on foot, Tim joined his brother a few yards off the trail, where Jed lay wiping his shirtsleeve along the rifle barrel.

"How many shots are in the rifle?" Tim asked.

"Just three," said Jed. He raised the rifle butt to his shoulder and steadied it out across the exposed half of a boulder sticking out of the ground in front of them.

"Then all we've got is a dozen rounds between us, counting what's in the pistol belt," said Tim. "If you shoot him, you'd best do it the first time."

"I aim to," Jed answered without looking around at Tim. "I'm not going to shoot until I have to."

He clicked the long-range sight up on the rifle barrel, then adjusted it carefully with his thumb and finger.

On the land below them, Jack Pearl pushed the horse up onto the slope reaching into the low hills. At the first upthrust of rock,

Pearl reined the horse down, slipped out of his saddle with a rifle in his hands, and led the horse out of sight. When he returned, he carried the canteen strapped over his shoulder.

"Yep, it's an ambush sure enough," Tim said, scooting in close beside his brother.

Not answering, Jed concentrated on his target, slowing his breathing down, getting a feel for the wind across the hillside.

Jack Pearl looked out across the stretch of flatland at the distant rider and smiled to himself. The rider was coming on fast, too fast for caution, Pearl thought. He leveled the rifle out across the rock, adjusting the canteen behind his back safely out of the way. He watched and waited.

Following the tracks of five horses ever since he'd left the creek bank, Marshal Curtis Dooley had time to run things through his mind. Up ahead in the low hills, there were a thousand perfect spots for an ambush. But he didn't think that would happen until he was farther up along the crest of the ridges. The men had met at the creek bank and ridden out as one, he figured. Now that they were four guns strong, they wouldn't be so careful about watching their back trail.

As he pushed on, Dooley caught sight of the worn-out horse standing near the body on the ground. He reined down and circled wide, looking the situation over before riding in. Once he arrived at the spot where Hank Phipps's dead eyes looked skyward, Dooley stepped down and ventured closer with his rifle in his hand.

"Easy, boy," he whispered to the spent horse as the tired animal sawed its weary head up and down and scraped a tired hoof on the dirt.

Dooley uncinched the saddle from the horse's wet back and let it drop to the ground. Looking all around, mostly toward the low hills ahead of him, he dropped the bit from the horse's mouth and gave the animal a shove. But the blown horse only drifted away slowly a few feet, then stopped and stood looking back at him. Dooley had no idea why one of the men lay dead with three bullets in him. What did it matter? he asked himself. The main thing was that the men were on the run. All of the tracks leading away from the body on the ground were stretched out in the length of a run, the four sets of prints lighting out at about the same speed. These boys weren't wasting any time. Neither was he.

When a few minutes had passed, Jed saw the figure below them tense up and aim his rifle out at the closing figure in the low rise of dust. "He's getting ready," Jed said, taking aim himself. Yet, as his finger started its slow squeeze on the trigger, a flash of sunlight off the rim of the canteen below stabbed his eyes, just enough to cause Jed to hesitate for an instant. But in that short slice of time, as Jed recovered and fired, the rifle in Jack Pearl's hands bucked in a blast of fire and smoke. Then the bullet from Jed's rifle blew a hole through the canteen, nailing it to Pearl's back, causing the water to spill in a long, clear stream that soon turned bloodred.

Beside Jed, Tim Strange looked down and saw Jack Pearl slump forward against the rock, almost as if he had fallen asleep. Then his eyes rose out across the stretch of flatland and saw the rider veer slightly in his saddle and sink to the ground.

"You got your man, Jed, but not soon enough." He pointed. "Look out there!"

Jed stood up, looking out as Curtis Dooley dropped sideways off his horse and sat on his haunches in the dirt. "Dang it, Tim, we've got to go help him."

Tim grimaced and said, "I know it. We can't leave a lawman there to die. . . . Besides, if he does, we'll get the blame sure enough."

They hurried back to their horses, mounted, and booted the animals down the path to the flatland. In passing the body of Jack Pearl, they looked over only long enough to assure themselves that he was dead. Then they heeled the horses up into a run.

On the ground, Marshal Curtis Dooley struggled to lift his pistol from his holster with one hand, his other hand pressed against his ribs to try to stop the steady flow of blood. He raised the pistol shoulder high, but the weight of it in his weak, blood-slick hand kept him from being able to cock it.

"Stay back," he managed to say in a halting voice as the twins stepped wide of the pistol.

"Marshal, don't shoot," Tim called out. "We're here to help you."

The pistol dropped to the lawman's lap. "Hell . . . I can't do nothing . . . with it anyway," said Dooley.

The twins stepped down from their saddles and ran to him, Jed carrying a canteen in his hand. "Take it easy, Marshal."

"Why?" Dooley asked, his voice going weak and shallow. "I'm done for."

"We didn't do this to you, Marshal," Jed said, stooping down beside him, reaching over with his hand to take a look at the wound.

Dooley shoved his hand away. "I know you didn't. . . . I heard the shot. Did you get him?"

"Yep, he's dead, Marshal," said Jed.

"Good . . . Now leave me in peace. I've got . . . some things to reconcile."

"Let us help you," said Jed. He started to reach out again, but seeing Tim shake his head slowly, Jed drew his hand back and sat silently watching Dooley struggle to catch his breath. "Can you drink some water?" Jed asked quietly.

"Water . . . would be good," said Dooley. He tried to take the canteen, but after two attempts, Jed raised it to his lips for him. "Much obliged," Dooley said, water running pink from the corner of his lips. "When . . . Dane catches up to you, tell him . . . things are fine . . . in Clay County. He'll know you didn't . . . do this to me."

Tim and Jed looked at each other; then Tim said to Dooley, "We don't aim for him to catch up to us, Marshal. If he does, we won't be having time to deliver any messages."

"In my saddlebags . . . there's a pencil," said Dooley. "Take it. Write down what I said. Pin it on the dead outlaw's back. Hurry on now. I want to be alone."

"We're sorry for what happened, Marshal," said Jed, standing up, capping the canteen.

Behind him, Tim went through the dying marshal's saddlebags and took out a pencil stub and a scrap of paper.

"Hell . . . it weren't your fault, I reckon." Dooley looked off toward the low hills and shook his head slowly. "Damn them out-laws. . . . I wish I could have shot him . . . for Tom Seals's sake."

The twins waited, standing back a ways while Marshal Dooley lay silent in the dirt. After a while, when they stepped over to the marshal again, Jed reached down and checked for a pulse, finding none. He stepped back and said, "I wish we had time to bury him."

"So do I," said Tim, "but we don't. There'll be somebody else along. We'd best get on out of here. It's a long ride across Texas."

They mounted and rode to where Jack Pearl's body lay against the rock. As Jed took off Jack Pearl's gun belt and strapped it around his waist, Tim sat atop his horse, staring back along the trail. "If his boots will fit, you ought to take them, Jed."

"I already checked," said Jed. "Neither his nor the marshal's ei-ther one are close enough to our size."

"Looks like we'll keep riding barefoot, then," said Tim. "Let's get moving."

Jed stepped in and put the note Tim had written halfway down in the dead outlaw's shirt collar. "I hope this will square us of kill-ing the marshal." Then he backed away and swung up into his sad-dle, and the two of them heeled upward along the trail, leading the chestnut mare behind them.

CHAPTER 9

It was afternoon when Marshal Christian Dane stepped his horse down to the creek bank and watered it. Leaving the creek, he saw low-circling buzzards, and following the tracks across the stretch of flatlands, he soon came upon the body of Hank Phipps. By then the worn-out horse had wandered off, leaving a meandering path of hoofprints behind it. Marshal Dane didn't even step down from his saddle. Instead, he looked skyward in the direction of the low hills and saw the next group of circling buzzards. He nudged his horse onward until he saw the body of Marshal Curtis Dooley on the ground.

"Damn it, Curtis," he whispered to himself, stepping down, looking all around on the ground, trying to get a picture of what had gone on.

Curtis's saddle lay beside his body. His horse had not wandered far. Marshal Dane walked to the horse with his rifle hanging from his hand. He brought Dooley's horse back, bridled it, and saddled it. Then he took Curtis Dooley's bedroll from behind the saddle, shook it out, and wrapped Curtis in it.

"You just wouldn't listen, would you?" he said to the dead face.

With Curtis Dooley facedown over his saddle, Marshal Dane led the fallen lawman's horse, moving his own horse forward across the flatland at a steady but cautious pace. At the spot where Jack Pearl's body lay against the rock, Christian Dane stepped down again, this time with less caution. He pulled the scrap of paper loose from the dead outlaw's shirt, read the penciled words on it, then folded it in his gloved hands and put it inside his duster.

"Everything's fine in Clay County, huh?" he said under his breath. "Well, Curtis, let's see if we can get you back there."

He scanned the upward-sloping hillside for a moment as evening shadows stretched long across the land. As a wind licked in from the west, he tugged his hat down on his forehead, stepped back up into his saddle, and turned his horse north, leading Dooley's horse behind him.

By nightfall, Marshal Dane had traveled along the creek bank a half mile to the east of where the twins, the outlaws, and the dead marshal had all watered their horses. He built a small fire down in between the cover of the natural cutbanks and spent the night. By midmorning the next day, he had traveled only a few miles when he spotted the three riders rise above a crest of rolling land, spreading out abreast as they approached. Dane lifted his rifle from his lap and propped the butt of it on his thigh, his thumb across the hammer. But he relaxed as he saw the familiar face of Marshal C. F. McCord at the center of the riders. Bobbing closer at a trot atop his big dun, McCord raised a hand slightly, then checked his horse down and turned it sideways to Marshal Dane as the three riders stopped.

"Chris, what are you doing over this way?" McCord asked, his eyes already on Marshal Curtis Dooley's horse and the blanket-wrapped corpse.

"We had a run-in a few miles east of here," said Dane, looking Danielle and Hector over as he spoke to McCord.

Danielle stepped her horse closer for a better look at the blanketed corpse.

Marshal Dane stopped her in a respectful yet firm tone, saying, "That's close enough, young man. I don't believe I know you."

"This is Danny Duggin and Hector Sabio," said McCord to Marshal Dane. "Danny here is concerned it might be one of his brothers."

"One of your brothers?" Dane asked, looking Danielle in the eye. "Are they a couple of look-alikes?"

"Yes, they're twins," said Danielle. "Have you run into them out here?"

"I'm sorry to say it, but yes, I have." Seeing the anxious look come upon Danielle's face, Marshal Dane added quickly, "They're all right, though. I just left their trail yesterday evening."

"Who is that?" asked C. F. McCord, nodding at the body.

Christian Dane let out a regretful breath, saying, "It's Curtis Dooley. Some outlaws hit our jail wagon farther back along the breaks trail. We lost Seals. . . . Then Dooley went mule-head stubborn, thought those look-alikes were responsible. He got himself killed."

"Where are my brothers?" asked Danielle.

Dane jerked his head southwest. "They're headed for Texas if I guessed right. You can almost follow the bodies from here to the hills."

"My brothers aren't killers, Marshal," Danielle said firmly. "If they had to shoot somebody, it wasn't because they wanted to. I can tell you that much."

"Settle down, young man," said Marshal Dane. "I'll admit I misjudged your brothers at first. I don't know what they've got stuck in their craws or why those outlaws are after them. They've done no wrong back there as far as I can see. But they did break loose from custody." He looked at Marshal McCord. "Will you be meeting up with those two?"

McCord had stepped his horse around, raised a corner of the blanket, and looked at Dooley's face. He dropped the blanket now and said to Marshal Dane, "We're going to try our best to meet up with them between here and the border."

"Then tell them they're cleared," said Dane. "Dooley had them leave a note for me back there. There's no charges on them. We still have their gun belts. They can pick them up in Fort Smith. I'll square things for them as far as them breaking loose from custody." He shook his head. "I just wish our paths had never crossed. It's cost the lives of two good men, Seals and Dooley. Metcalf's wounded pretty bad. Ryan's with him. I'm going to try to catch up to them on the trail."

"I'm sorry to hear it," said McCord. He stepped his horse back around beside Danielle.

Hector Sabio sat watching in silence with his wrists crossed on the fancy saddle horn.

"What are you boys up to anyway, McCord?" Dane asked, eyeing Hector Sabio as if trying to recognize him.

"It's a long story, Chris," said McCord. "But we're headed down below the border, looking for the Delmanos."

"Hunting the Delmanos is nothing new for you, C. F.," said Marshal Dane. "You've been looking for Saul Delmano ever since I can remember."

"That's right," said McCord. "Only this time I've got a good guide who knows the country and a man here who wants that bunch as bad as I do." He nodded toward Hector, then Danielle. "The Delmanos have a two-thousand-dollar bounty on Danny's head. Hector knows where their spread is. He's going to lead us there."

"For two cents I'd go with you," said Dane. "It's time somebody took off their badge and crossed the border. The Delmanos have had it too good for too long."

"You'd be welcome along," said McCord, "but you'd best get on back to Ryan and Metcalf, get to Fort Smith, and get ole Dooley here in the ground."

"I know it," said Dane. He turned his attention to Hector Sabio and said, "You look familiar."

"*Sí*, everybody tells me that," said Hector. "I have one of those faces everybody thinks they have seen." He shrugged. "But no, we have never met."

Marshal Dane studied Hector's face for a moment, then looked at McCord, saying, "The Delmanos again, huh?"

"That's right." McCord nodded. "This time for sure."

"Will you be crossing the border at El Paso?" Dane asked.

"Yep, we intend to," said McCord.

"The Delmanos have lots of men working for them. El Paso is their stomping ground, this side of the border." Dane looked the three over as he spoke. Then, focusing on Danielle, he added, "You boys watch yourselves down there. Two thousand dollars is a lot of money."

CABALLO SANGRIENTO PASA, MEXICO. SEPTEMBER 25, 1871

Lewis Delmano stood over six feet tall, lean, but broad across his shoulders. He carried himself with the confidence and swagger of a younger man, of a man used to enforcing his will on all things within a world he'd created for himself. No sign of his age showed except for his wiry salt-and-pepper beard and hair and the deep lines burned into his weathered face after years under the harsh Mexican sun. On the stone porch of his hacienda, Lewis Delmano struck a match to his first cigar of the morning and looked off toward the south and the entrance to Bloody Horse Pass. Beside him, the government emissary from Mexico City, Raul Hernandez, stood quietly, his hand supporting his saucer and coffee cup. They had taken breakfast together while discussing their business. Now Hernandez waited for some sort of reply, something he could take back to his superiors.

After moments of silent consideration, Lewis Delmano said without taking his eyes off of the distant surrounding hills, "Tell them I'll pay the extra money this time. But if they keep gouging me, I'll pull up stakes and give Bloody Horse Pass back to the Apache." He turned slowly now, spreading a flat smile. "That should make for an interesting situation. They leased me this land because they couldn't handle Victorio and his warriors. Maybe I'll tell Victorio he can have this place, house and all."

"I will tell them," said Raul, "but I will soften the words so that they sound more diplomatic, eh?"

"No, Raul, not this time," said Lewis Delmano. "This time you say it word for word the way I tell you to. I'm through fattening up every two-bit official in Mexico City."

"But we do so well here, you, me, and those who support our interests. Let us not say something hastily that we might regret later." He raised a finger for emphasis. "Don't forget, *mi amigo*, I am on your side as always."

"You should be." Lewis Delmano stared at him. "I've made you a wealthy man since I brought my cattle operation here, not to mention that now you can travel here by buggy with no fear of getting your scalp lifted or your wallet emptied."

Raul shrugged. "All of this is true. When you and your sons came to Caballo Sangriento Pasa, it was nothing but a killing ground for the Apache and a hiding place for desperadoes." He swept his arm across the surrounding land. "You and your men have all of this. You are free of the gringo law here, and my government turns its eyes from what you do across the border. So why not pay these greedy *político* officials what they want and keep them happy? You and me, we can grow old in comfort here, eh?"

"Maybe you, Raul," said Lewis Delmano, "but not me, not if the price keeps going up. Besides, I've got enough political connections back across the border that I don't have to fear the law there anymore either. I'm rich now, Raul. Money buys power and respectability on either side of the river. If the boys in Mexico City don't realize that, maybe it's time I move on. They might need me more than I need them now." He shrugged a shoulder and gazed back out across the land. "I send them money all the time. What do I ever get in return?"

Raul studied Lewis Delmano's face, starting to realize that this whole conversation hadn't been about money at all. Something else was bothering Lewis Delmano. After a moment, Raul said, "What is it, *mi amigo*? Why do you stare off toward Caballo Sangriento Pasa as if you expect to see the devil?"

"Say it in English, Raul," Lewis Delmano demanded. "It's Bloody Horse Pass. As much sweat and guts as I've put into this godforsaken furnace, I deserve to hear it said in my own damn language."

"All right," said Raul reluctantly. "Why do you stare off at Bloody Horse Pass?"

Lewis Delmano drew long on the cigar and blew the smoke in a slow, steady stream, taking his time before finally saying, "Did I tell you my older boy, Saul, is back?"

"No, you did not mention it," replied Raul. Hearing Saul Delmano's name prepared Raul. Whenever Saul Delmano came to Bloody Horse Pass, trouble was always close behind him.

"Yep," said Lewis Delmano, without facing him, "he's been here a little while now. He's over in the canyon, helping his brother with the branding. Maybe you'd like to go say hello to him?"

Raul Hernandez felt his chest tighten at the thought of being around Saul Delmano. He'd as soon wrestle with a rattlesnake. But he wasn't about to say so. Instead he said casually, "Not today, they are busy . . . and so am I. Soon I must return to the city and conduct our business. Please tell Saul I will see him the next time I am here perhaps."

Lewis chuckled under his breath, saying, "He'll be disappointed I'm sure." He drew another long pull from his cigar and blew smoke out across the dusty land. "The fact is, Saul has a gunman on his tail, Raul. I'd consider it an act of respect if your pals in Mexico City would offer me their services, help me get rid of Saul's problem for him."

"Oh?" Raul looked surprised that Lewis Delmano would ask for help of this nature. "What is it that my government can do for you?"

Lewis Delmano caught the surprised tone in Raul's voice and turned to him, saying, "You've known me well enough to know that I don't back away from a fight, Raul. But something tells me that this time I need to bring in somebody special who has lots of experience dealing with these kinds of situations."

"*Sí*, I know my contacts in the city will be glad to help, but who has more experience in these matters than you and your men?" asked Raul. "As you have said, you have fought Apache, desperadoes, American lawmen."

"I know," said Lewis Delmano, "and I'll fight this gunman and whoever is riding with him if it comes to that. But I'd like to think that I've gotten to a point in life where I can turn the dirty work over to somebody else when I feel like it. If your pals in the city did this for me, it would sure make me feel better about all the money I dish out to them every month. Do you see what I mean?"

Raul saw exactly what Lewis Delmano was asking. This was Delmano's way of seeing what power and control he might be able to wield for himself. What would be next? Raul thought. If this favor was done, how long would it be before Lewis Delmano began asking for more and more until one day he might even have part of the military at his beck and call?

Raul considered it for a second, then said, "There are men that I and my friends know who are good at this kind of work. Perhaps we can call them in for you?"

"Military men?" Lewis Delmano asked.

Raul smiled, knowing he was right. Lewis Delmano needed no help in this matter. Delmano was just seeing how far he could take this, testing the power of his American dollar. "Oh, but these men I speak of are far better than soldiers! These are the men our leaders turn to when they have things they want done that they cannot ask the *federales* to do."

Lewis Delmano thought about it. This wasn't quite what he wanted, but it might be good to see what Raul and his officials had to offer. "These are mercenaries, I take it?" Delmano asked.

"*Sí*, mercenaries who show no mercy," said Raul, grinning, wagging a finger. "Not often do we call on these men, but when we do, they act quickly and fiercely."

"Yeah?" Delmano worked the cigar back and forth in his mouth, appearing to consider it. "Well, I'd rather have army troops on my side. . . ." He let his words trail, still hoping to get Raul to commit some government power to him.

But Raul held firm. "You will like these men much better, I promise."

"The thing is, Raul, I've got twenty good gunmen working right here for me. I'd just feel good knowing you and your friends think highly enough of me to put a fighting force out there between my son and his enemies."

"Oh, but that is exactly what I am doing," said Raul. "I would not trust our *federales* the way I trust these mercenaries. In political circles, these men are called *la escuadra de la muerte*."

Hearing the name, Lewis Delmano drew on his cigar and afforded himself a slight smile. "The death squad, eh? I've heard of them. Some of them are from the U.S., some are Frenchmen and German, and some are from here. A real mean bunch as I recall."

"*Sí*, a real mean bunch of hombres. They are the *generalissimo*'s personal fighting force, and they are far better at the craft of killing than our young soldiers, most of whom are simple peasants who have not fired a rifle until we take them into the army."

"And you think you can get this death squad for me?" Lewis Delmano asked.

This was a good start, he thought. Delmano had all the guns he needed. But this would be interesting. The *generalissimo*'s personal assassins, Lewis Delmano thought to himself, liking the idea more and more as he thought about it.

"I can have them here within a day. Just say the word, *mi amigo*, and they will set up a defense between here and the border. Nobody will get past them. You have my word."

"I don't know," said Delmano, trying to appear hesitant. "Would this death squad follow my orders, do everything the way I tell them to do without question?"

"They obey *only* the orders of the *generalissimo*. But if I send them to you, he will have told them to do what you say until the job is done. What more can you ask than that?"

Lewis Delmano's mind was already at work, seeing the great possibilities before him if he could win over the *generalissimo*'s death squad. This might even be better than having some control over a column of *federale* troops.

"All right, Raul," Delmano said at length as if he had to give it a lot of careful consideration, "you've talked me into it. Send them as soon as you can." He reached inside his linen suit coat and took out a thick brown envelope. "This is for you, Raul, my friend, a little something extra that your officials needn't know about."

Raul smiled, taking the envelope and hefting it in his hand before putting it away. "As always, you are too kind, *mi amigo*," he said.

Lewis Delmano returned the smile, turning away to once again look out toward Bloody Horse Pass. "Yep, that's me all right, generous to a fault."

CHAPTER 10

Amid the dust and the cattle in the corral, Saul and Ramon Delmano stood up from the fire and looked toward the hacienda, where their father stood talking to Raul Hernandez. Saul pitched the end of a branding iron down into the licking flames and pulled off his leather gloves.

"Want to know what they're talking about, little brother?" He swabbed his brow with a damp bandanna.

"I do not care what they talk about," said the younger Ramon. "I have too many cattle to brand." There was a bitter snap to his voice.

"Yeah? Well, they're talking about me," said Saul, ignoring the tone of his brother's voice. "Pa's telling Raul about the trouble I'm causing him. He wants Raul and his politicians to make it all go away. What do you want to bet?"

Ramon looked toward the hacienda for a second longer, then shrugged and reached down and turned the branding iron in the fire, checking the color of the hot metal. "I would not bet against a sure thing."

Ramon looked at the two men who stood waiting, one of them coiling his lariat and shaking it free of dust. He nodded at the two men, then turned to Saul as the men walked toward the milling cattle, unwinding a coil from their lariats.

"If you resent him interfering in your trouble, why do you bring your trouble to him?"

Saul looked at his brother. "I don't resent his help, Ramon. What I don't like is his high-and-mighty attitude of late. He acts like he's better than me. I reckon he's forgotten how it was when I was just a boy. He made his living then doing the same things I do now. I robbed my first bank riding with that old man. Now that he's rich and got others doing his robbing for him, he acts like he thinks there's something wrong with the way I live."

Ramon spat and ran a hand across his dust-caked lips. "He tells me he wants a better life for me than he has had."

"Sure," said Saul, "but how much money does this better life put in your pocket? Enough to pay for all the dirt you swallow in a day's time?"

Ramon didn't answer. Instead he gave his brother a sour look as he reached down and picked up the hot branding iron. He hurried over to where the two ropers had taken down a longhorn steer. He expertly placed the tip of the iron over the older brand on the steer's rump, then stamped the iron down, cross-branding it. When he walked back to the fire and shoved the iron into the bed of glowing coals, he looked back at Saul Delmano and said, "Do you think I handle stolen cattle because I like it? This is all I get, Saul. This is all I'll ever get hanging around here, staying under his thumb. I'm not much more than a hired hand."

"Then what's stopping you from doing something about it?" Saul asked. "You used to say it was because of your mother. Now that she's dead, what's your excuse?"

"After my mother's death," said Ramon, "I thought I should stay here until he got over his grief." He spat again as if to rid a bad taste from his mouth. "But I was wrong. Before my mother was in the ground two weeks, he brought the young German nurse Greta into his bed."

Saul chuckled, saying, "So he's gone from Irish to Mexican, now to German. Sort of working his way around the world, woman-wise. But don't be bitter, little brother. That's the same thing that happened when my own dear Irish mother disappeared. He took right up with your ma within a week. Some say he had it all planned.

Some even say it weren't the Apache who took my ma if you know what I mean."

"And this does not bother you?" Ramon stared at him.

"Naw, I was too young to think about it at the time," said Saul, taking a bag of tobacco from his shirt pocket and rolling himself a smoke. "After I grew up some, I figured, 'What the hell?' It wasn't nothing to me. He taught me that whatever happens twixt a man and a woman is their business and nobody else's." He lifted the branding iron and lit his cigarette, then shucked the iron back into the glowing coals. "By then I was long riding, robbing, running wild with him and his men. I didn't care for nothing . . . and I haven't since." He drew on the cigarette and let go a gray stream of smoke. "Now that I am what I am, he's acting like it ain't good enough for him." He looked off toward the hacienda. "That old son of a bitch. I'd give anything to know what he's thinking right now."

"He told you he would defend you against this gunman who is on your trail. He has placed a bounty on the man's head. What more would you have him do?"

Saul thought about it, blowing out a breath of smoke. "He's doing all that, sure enough. But don't ever think it's for me he's doing it. Our dear ole daddy ain't never done nothing for anybody unless he gets more back than he puts in. You watch. Somehow he plans on gaining something from all this."

"Yes, maybe so," said Ramon, looking over at the two ropers, then stooping down and picking up the branding iron. "Either way, no matter the outcome, I will still be doing what I do, handling stolen cattle for hired-hand wages." He stood up with the iron glowing in his gloved hand.

"Like I said, Ramon, what's your excuse now? Why don't you do something about it?"

"Like what?" Ramon asked.

"Oh, I don't know," Saul said in a cagey tone. "Me and a couple of the boys are planning to rob ourselves a little stagecoach outside of El Paso. Maybe you'd like to tag along? It ought to be worth a few hundred dollars to you."

Ramon didn't answer. He lingered for a moment, staring at his brother. Then he hurried over to the downed steer. When he came back and raked the burned hair from the branding iron across the sole of his boot, he stuck the iron back into the coals and said in a lowered voice, "He'll skin you alive if he finds out."

"Naw, I'm too old for a skinning anymore. He'll throw a fit, maybe try to pistol-whip me. But that ain't going to happen either. I'm thirty-three years old, Ramon. If it came down to a serious tussle, I'd put a bullet or two in him, and he knows it." Saul grinned, then added, "But forget I said anything about it, little brother. Maybe it's best you stay here eating dust and spitting cow hair. Hell, you might get to like it after a few more years. Not everybody gets to know the ways of the world, see the big cities, and taste the finer things in life."

"Do not tease me as if I am a fool who knows nothing," said Ramon, his face glowering beneath a sheen of sweat. "While you have drifted here and there, I have spent my time fighting Apache and taking care of business. I have been to Juárez, Mexico City, and even El Paso. If you have done so well, why do you come sneaking in off the trail with men wanting to kill you?"

"Easy, little brother," said Saul Delmano, a bit of a warning in his voice. "No point in getting all riled up in the heat of the day. I'm heading out around midnight tonight with Joe Tully and Kid Jeffrey. Tomorrow, we're going to hit a stage or two, then duck back across the border. If you want to ride with us, meet us out back of the barn. If you don't, then forget I mentioned it."

"Tully and Jeffrey?" Ramon looked surprised. "I never knew they were bandits. I only knew they run cattle across the border."

Saul grinned. "There's probably lots more you don't know, little brother. Hell, Kid Jeffrey rode with the Blue Star Gang nearly a year. Joe Tully still rides with Los Pistoleros every chance he gets. If you think you can keep up with that kind of company, grab your bedroll tonight and be ready. We'll make us some quick money and get back here before Pa gets back from Sonora. He's leaving today before noon."

"I will think about it," said Ramon.

"Yeah, you do that, little brother," said Saul. "We've all got to grow up and get on our own sooner or later."

They worked until noon, neither one mentioning the proposed stage robbery. When Saul Delmano walked back to the fire from branding a downed yearling calf, he looked over past the hacienda and saw their father and two of his gunmen riding out toward the main trail.

"Let's take a break," Saul said, stripping his sweat-moistened gloves from his hands and slapping them against his leather chaps. "I'm going to the cellar and crack open a bottle of wine, cool myself off a little."

"There is still much to do here," said Ramon.

"There always is," said Saul. "Let these boys do it. They're the hired hands. I told you my plans for tonight. I aim to rest up first." Saul stooped enough to untie his chaps and drop them to the ground.

"You go ahead," said Ramon. "I will take the irons and our tools to the barn." He reached down, picked up his brother's chaps, and draped them over his dusty forearm.

"Suit yourself, little brother," said Saul, walking away.

Ramon walked to the barn behind the hacienda, propped the branding irons against a tool bin, and hung both his and his brother's chaps on a wall peg. As he did so, he felt Greta's arms slip around him as she pressed herself to his back.

"You must tell him soon," she whispered in his ear, only a trace of a German accent in her voice.

Ramon turned to her, casting a cautious glance through the open barn door, then reaching out and swinging it shut. "Greta, you have to be careful doing this," he said in a hushed tone. Even as he said it, he put his arms around her and nestled his face into her soft golden hair.

"I know," she said, "but he's gone, and the others are too busy to notice anything. I came here as soon as I saw you walking over from the corrals. I can't stand it when you're not near me." She pressed her lips to Ramon's.

Yet, as they kissed long and deep, Ramon opened an eye and kept watch on the barn door.

Greta felt his reluctance and ended the kiss with a sigh and laid her face against his chest. "We can't go on like this. We've got to get away from here."

Ramon gently freed himself from her embrace. "This is too risky, Greta. I'm sorry."

He took a side step to the dusty window and looked out. On the rear porch of the hacienda, he watched Saul raise a water-gourd dipper to his mouth, take a mouthful of water, swish it around, and spit it out.

"You shouldn't have came back here," Ramon whispered over his shoulder. "My brother has the soul of a wolf. He can *sense* when something is going on."

"I—I had to see you, Ramon. If I have to hide in the shadows, that's what I'll do."

He turned to her and held her.

"We have to tell your father. . . . We *have* to. Only last night, he told me I was to become his wife."

"No!" Ramon said, holding her closer. "He cannot *tell* you what you must do! He has no right!" In his desperation, his voice trembled, and she cupped a hand to his dust-streaked cheek.

"Perhaps if we told him the truth, that you and I have been lovers since I came to take care of your mother. Maybe he would understand."

"He understands nothing." Ramon hissed. "He does not care. He knew what the outcome would be when he brought you here. He doesn't think like normal men. My father knew my mother would not live much longer. He hired you to take care of her, knowing that when she died he would take you for his wife! He is a devil, my father! He would never leave us in peace! We can only flee from here and make a new life for ourselves."

"But when, Ramon?" she whispered. "I can't stand for him to touch me. When I am in his bed all I can think of is—"

"Please!" Ramon said, cutting her off. "Don't tell me about such things. I do not want to hear about you and my father. We must get away from here and never speak of or even *think* of what has happened here."

"I have seven dollars, Ramon," Greta said. "It is money I have saved since your mother's death."

"Seven dollars won't get us very far, Greta. But don't worry. I think we'll soon have enough money to get far, far away, maybe to New Orleans or even the Southern shores."

She leaned back slightly in his arms and studied his eyes, saying, "Oh? And where will you get this much money? I know your father pays you nothing until the cattle sell across the border. That will be weeks from now. Even then you'll get no more than his hired hands."

Ramon nodded through the dusty barn window toward Saul. "My brother has a way for me to make some quick money. He's going to rob a stagecoach. He told me about it while we were branding."

"But he is a thief and a killer!" Greta said, shocked at the idea. "There are men wanting to come here and kill him for the terrible things he has done. You told me so yourself!"

"It's only this one time, Greta, for us, for you and me . . . and the baby."

"No, no!" she shook her head. "Your brother will get you killed! We can take the seven dollars and run as far as it takes us! Or if we must steal, we can take the money your father keeps in his safe!"

"Listen to me, Greta," Ramon said, holding her shoulders gently yet firmly. "I must do this. It won't be long until you cannot hide your condition. We have to get away from here while you are still able to travel. I'm leaving here tonight with Saul, and when I return, you be ready to leave with me."

"And if your father returns before you do? What then?" she asked.

"We slip away in the night and get as far away as we can before he comes after us. That's all we can do," he said.

"And if he finds us? If he forces me back to him? What will we do then?" she asked in a lowered tone.

"Then I will do what I dread even *thinking* about doing," said Ramon. "God forbid . . . I will have to kill him."

———

L eaving the barn through the back door half an hour later, Greta walked wide across the sand, then turned back toward the hacienda as if coming back from direction of the corrals. Saul Delmano stood up from his chair on the back porch with one of his father's cigars between his fingers and a bottle of wine hanging on his hand.

"Well, now," he said to Greta, stepping in front of her, blocking her way, "where have you been, out gathering jackrabbit eggs?"

She stopped, and seeing his eyes were lit and shiny from the wine, she said, "I went to the corral to tell you and Ramon that your father has left on his trip. Let me pass, please."

"Why, sure, you little yellow-haired filly you." He leered drunkenly, stepping to one side with an exaggerated sweep of his free hand. "Oops, wait a minute," he said, reaching up to her hair, running his fingers through it. "Looks like you've picked up some straw here." He winked knowingly and let a stem of straw fall from his fingertips. "Must be quite a wind out by the corrals."

She walked on into the hacienda without responding, Saul Delmano's low laughter following her through the door.

"Nothing like keeping it in the family, I reckon," Saul Delmano said to himself, sinking back down into his chair and propping his boots up on the iron porch railing. He drank wine and smoked the cigar, his hat brim pulled low on his forehead.

In a few minutes, Ramon came walking from the barn, and Saul only tipped his head enough to get a glimpse of his younger brother as Ramon stepped onto the porch.

"That barn is a busy place, little brother," said Saul, holding the bottle of wine out to Ramon without looking at him. "I'm going to have to get out there one of these times, see what the attraction is."

"What are you talking about?" Ramon took the bottle of wine and looked at it.

Saul shrugged, saying from under his lowered hat brim, "It ain't no sweat off of my neck, little brother. I'm just here for the dry air and sunshine."

"That is one of his favorite wines," said Ramon. "He's going to throw a fit when he sees you've drunk it."

"His wine ain't all that's being tasted," said Saul, letting out a relaxed sigh, "but that's no sweat off my neck either. I just hope you know what you're doing. There are things in this world even your blood kin will kill you over."

"Do you think I don't know that?" Ramon said bitterly. "There are also things in this world that men should leave alone when they see it does not belong to them."

"Well . . ." Saul Delmano let his words trail as he seemed to be considering something. Then he reached out for the bottle of wine, took a long sip from it, then said without raising his face, "Since I don't have an idea in the world what *else* you might be talking about, I'm just going to figure you're talking about taking money from stagecoaches."

"Yes, then that is what I am talking about," said Ramon.

"So I take it you won't be riding out with me tonight?" Saul asked. "I kind of figured you wouldn't be."

"Then you have figured wrong, my brother. Yes, I will ride with you. But only until I raise some money for myself. I will not become an outlaw."

Saul Delmano chuckled and drew on the cigar. "Now that brings up an interesting question. How many robberies does it take to make a man an outlaw?"

"Don't tease me," said Ramon, snatching the wine bottle from his brother's hand and throwing back a long drink.

Saul Delmano raised his hat brim and looked up at Ramon in surprise. "I'll be damned. You're really riding out with me tonight?" He smiled with satisfaction. "It's about time we done something together besides stick a hot iron on a steer's backside."

Ramon allowed himself a trace of a smile, handing the wine bottle back to his brother. "I think I know what stage we rob, and I think I know why."

"Oh, really, now?" Saul said, cocking his head slightly in curiosity.

"Yes, the stage that runs from Pecos to El Paso, because you know there will be money on it that our father has had sent to him from his attorney there."

"That's good thinking, little brother," said Saul. "You might really have a knack for this kind of work."

"But if I have figured out that you are going to steal the very money our father has sent for to pay the bounty for whoever kills the gunman Danny Duggin, do you not suppose our father will figure it out also? He is not a fool, and he knows how you are, my brother."

Saul raised a finger toward Ramon, saying, "See, that kind of thinking must run in our blood. We had different mothers, but damned if we both didn't get the old man's way of thinking." He grinned. "As soon as Pa hears the stage was robbed, the first thing he'll think is that I done it. But I've got that taken care of."

"How?" Ramon asked.

"Never mind how, little brother," said Saul, standing up, leveling his hat brim. "You just be ready to leave here after dark. I'll show *how* once the time comes. Until then, don't you worry about a thing."

"But what happens if someone kills this Danny Duggin and shows up here to collect the bounty and the money is not here for them?"

"That ain't my problem." Saul grinned. "Once Duggin's dead, what do I care if Pa pays the bounty or not? Besides, Pa's got plenty more money. He didn't have to send off for more anyway. He's just strutting his stuff, wanting us to see how rich he is."

"And what about this Danny Duggin?" Ramon asked. "What if he shows up? What if we run into him while we are out there?"

"We won't," said Saul with confidence. "Hell, as many men as there are between here and Kansas after that bounty money, Duggin's probably dead already."

"You cannot be sure of that," said Ramon.

"I know. But there's got to be some risk in anything we do, little brother," Saul Delmano said. "That's what makes life interesting."

CHAPTER 11

NEW MEXICO TERRITORY. SEPTEMBER 25, 1871

Danielle, C. F. McCord, and Hector Sabio had ridden hard across Northwestern Texas. They had dropped down across the sand flats and rock country of New Mexico, stopping only long enough to take on supplies as they needed to and to look around for any signs of her brothers at the relay stations and small desert settlements. Hector Sabio's knowledge of the land and its rocky twists and turns had proved invaluable. Once they had crossed the Pecos River and picked up the long trail toward Las Cruces, they rode southwest across the salt basin, then on toward the Hueco Tanks.

"Does this Danny Duggin ever slow down?" Hector Sabio asked McCord as they rode a few yards behind Danielle in the hot afternoon sun.

"If he does, I haven't seen it," McCord answered.

"I fear he will cause us to run these horses to death," Hector said grimly. "Never have I seen a man so driven."

"Don't worry about the horses," said McCord. "I've noticed that no matter how hard he pushes himself, he never overworks the animals. He knows what he's doing," McCord added with confidence, smiling slightly as he watched Danielle from behind. "Our Danny Duggin seems to have just the right touch."

"*Our* Danny Duggin? Perhaps you admire this man, but I cannot say that I do," said Hector Sabio.

"That's because you don't understand him like I do, Hector." McCord smiled.

"No, it is because he does not trust me . . . and he does not like me," said Hector.

"Well, Hector, after all, you were riding with men who wanted to kill him." McCord looked at him. "You have to admit a thing like that does knock a dent in any budding friendship." McCord chuckled to himself.

"*Sí*, but still . . ." Hector started to say more, but seeing the knowing look in C. F. McCord's eyes, he shrugged, plainly puzzled. Hector scratched his head and heeled his horse forward beside McCord, both of them having to work at keeping close to Danielle.

Atop a sandy rise five hundred yards across the sand and mesquite, the gunman Cleery White lowered the telescope from his eye and scooted back a few feet before standing up and dusting himself off.

"What's the doings out there?" asked one of the three other riders who had sat atop their horses while Cleery White scanned the three distant horsemen.

"You ain't going to believe this, Curly," said White. "That's Hector Sabio out there!"

Curly York stiffened in surprise at first, but then a knowing smile spread across his face. "Well, I'll be. Talk about luck! He's one of the men who was riding with Tarksel, going after that bounty money. Are you sure that's him?" As he asked, Curly York reached down for the telescope, took it from Cleery White, and raised it to his eye.

"Yep, it's Hector," said White. "I'd recognize that weasel through a hailstorm. He and Tarksel and the others were going to try to hook up with Clyde Branson if Branson would stand still for it."

"Hook up with who?" one of the other riders asked, a matchstick dropping from his mouth.

"Don't soil yourself, Duff," said Cleery White. "Branson ain't out there . . . just Sabio."

"I wasn't worried," Duff mumbled, his face reddening in embarrassment.

"Like hell you wasn't." The man beside him laughed. "You lost your matchstick just hearing Branson's name!"

"Shut up, Hale, I was through with it anyway," said Duff. He nudged his horse up beside Curly York. "Let me take a look, Curly." As Duff spoke, he fished a fresh matchstick from his shirt pocket and stuck it between his teeth.

"Just a damn minute," said Curly York, not giving up the telescope. He scanned for another few seconds, then said, "Boys, what does Delmano's pal Billy Sherman say this Danny Duggin fellow looks like?"

Donald Hale moved his horse closer, saying, "Billy said he's tall, slim, wears a brace of Colts . . . rides a chestnut mare, he said."

"Well, there's no chestnut out there, but otherwise this fellow fits the description." Curly hesitated, then added, "Guess who the third man is."

Donald Hale, Cleery White, and Joe Duff all looked at one another, but didn't offer a guess.

Curly York said in a wary tone, "It's none other than U.S. Federal Marshal Charles McCord . . . in the flesh!"

"The *Fox*?" said Duff. "You don't mean it!" The fresh matchstick flew from his lips. Duff fumbled, trying to catch it, but missed.

Donald Hale gave Duff a goading grin, saying, "Guess you was through with that one, too."

"Shut up, Hale. I mean it!" said Duff. Frowning, he sidled his horse against Curly's. "Come on, Curly, let *me* see!"

Curly York shoved him away with his free elbow, still staring through the telescope. "If you want one of these things so bad, why don't you buy yourself one?" he hissed.

Duff brooded, hearing Donald Hale stifle a laugh behind him. A moment later, Curly York lowered the telescope and handed it to Duff. "There, take a look if it'll cool your fever."

Joe Duff raised the lens to his eye and searched for the three riders. Just as he found them in the tight circle of vision, Danielle,

Hector, and C. F. McCord disappeared around a rocky bluff, leaving only a drift of dust in their wake. "Damn it, missed them!" Duff said, lowering the telescope and poking it back toward Curly York.

Donald Hale snickered and put a hand to his mouth, hoping to keep himself from laughing out loud.

"What do you make of it, Curly?" Cleery White asked, stepping back up into his saddle.

Curly York sat in silence for a moment, feeling the men's eyes on him as he considered it. Finally he said, "Here's what I get from it." He raised a finger for emphasis and rubbed his chin as he spoke. "Hector Sabio is McCord's prisoner, which means the rest of the old Axel Eldridge Gang is either dead or in jail."

"Serves them right, then," said Cleery White. "They had no business going after that bounty. They were always just thieves, and a man ought to stick to what he knows."

Curly York nodded in agreement. "The thing is, McCord has been after Saul Delmano for the longest time. . . ." His words trailed as if he had just stated the obvious.

"So?" said Donald Hale. "What's that got to do with the bounty money?"

"Explain it to him, White," said Curly York, sounding impatient.

"Because, you damn Georgia cracker neck!" said White. "Delmano wants this Duggin dead . . . and the Fox wants Delmano dead! Does that spark any thought at all in your mind?"

"Yeah, I get it," Hale said grudgingly, backing his horse a step away from the others. "You don't have to act that way."

Listening, Duff rolled his eyes skyward, took out a fresh matchstick, and bit down on it. "So what do you want to do, Curly? McCord ain't no short piece of work. Neither is this Danny Duggin, from what we've heard."

Curly York turned his horse quarter-wise and looked at Duff with a flat stare, saying, "Don't blow your matchstick over this, Joe. But we're going to ride over there and kill them."

"What if that ain't Danny Duggin?" asked Hale.

"So what if it ain't?" Curly York snapped in reply, jerking his horse around and heeling it away. "If we're wrong, all it'll cost us is a handful of bullets."

When Danielle first caught a thin distant glint of sunlight off metal, she decided not to mention it to Hector and McCord right then. Instead, she slowed her horse for a few yards, enough to let the two catch up to her.

"What's wrong?" McCord asked, coming up on her right while Hector slipped his horse up on her left.

"Nothing," said Danielle, patting her gloved hand on her horse's sweaty neck. "Thought I'd walk this horse down and rest him for a couple of miles."

There was something in her tone of voice that McCord picked up on right away. Danielle gave the slightest nod in the direction where she'd seen the flash of light. She let her eyes move to Hector, then back to McCord.

McCord caught on, but he saw that Hector had no idea what Danielle was doing. "It's about time you slowed down for a while, Danny," McCord said. He managed to let his gaze drift back out across the sandy stretch of mesquite and cholla. He saw nothing.

They rode on in silence for another half mile. Suddenly Hector straightened in his saddle and turned his horse sidelong to the right. "Riders are coming!" he said.

"Yep, they sure are," said McCord, giving Danielle a look. He stopped his horse short and raised his rifle from his saddle boot.

Hector looked back and forth quickly between the two of them, then said, "What? You already saw them coming? You were testing me? But that was foolish, letting them get so close!"

"This is open country, Hector. There's no place to run even if we wanted to."

Danielle had also stopped her horse and stepped it sideways, putting a few feet between her and the other two. "Get ready," she said, "in case this is no social call."

"Hello the trail," Curly York called out as the four riders came into full sight from around an upthrust of rock. As the riders drew nearer, checking their horses down to a slow walk, they spread out a few feet apart. "I thought we saw some riders over here a while ago." York forced a stiff, cordial smile. "Reckon I was right." He spoke above a hot licking wind.

"I reckon you were," said McCord. He sat facing the four men with his rifle propped up on his thigh. "What can we do for you?"

Danielle sat with her right palm resting on her holstered Colt.

Hector felt sweat run down the back of his neck and kept his hand near the pistol that was shoved down in his waist belt.

Curly York looked taken aback by McCord's firm tone of voice. He almost completely stopped his horse. But then, cutting a glance to White and the others, he inched the horse forward, saying, "We just saw yas and thought we ought to come say howdy."

"Howdy," said McCord, his tone of voice not changing. "Now stop that horse right there."

"Well, boys," Curly said to the others, "looks like we've come upon some inhospitable pilgrims today."

"Cut it short, Curly York," said McCord, letting York know that he recognized him. "It's too hot to sit here and pretend we don't know what you're after."

York feigned a surprised look, saying, "Now what in the world are you talking about, Fox? We're just headed over toward Kansas, wanting to see what the weather's like."

Without taking his eyes off Curly York, McCord said over his shoulder, "Hector, do these boys know about the reward money?"

"Sí," said Hector Sabio, his gaze narrowed on Curly York. "He heard about it from Billy Sherman, the same one who told Al Tarksel and the rest of us."

"That's what I thought," said McCord, his thumb cocking the rifle hammer as he spoke. "Well, Curly, that pretty much stops the need for any further conversation, wouldn't you say?"

Curly York ignored McCord and turned his attention to Danielle, saying, "So you're Danny Duggin, huh? You don't look like much to me—not two thousand dollars anyway. How come the Fox does all your talking for you?"

Danielle lifted her face slowly and said from beneath her lowered hat brim, "Did you come here to talk or fight, mister? So far you're doing a whole lot of one and none of the other."

Feeling something unsettling in the calm, cold voice, Curly York called out to Hector Sabio, "What about you, Hector? What's your stake in this? Are you going to stand with them or us? We've known you a lot longer than they have."

"You see where I stand, you *hijo de perra*!" Hector spat.

"What'd he say, White?" Curly York asked over his shoulder.

"He . . . uh . . . called you a son of a bitch, Curly," Cleery White said cautiously. "Maybe this ain't a good time or place," he added, seeing no sign of weakness in the eyes of the three who stood before them.

Curly York bristled and said to Hector Sabio, "It's a long trail you're on, *amigo*. A lot can happen between here and the border."

"Back your horses and turn them, or by the saints, you will die here." Hector hissed. Hot wind whirred across the sand.

"Tomorrow's another day, Curly," Cleery White said, sounding worried.

Curly York sat staring for a second longer. Then he let out a tense breath and said as he backed his horse and began turning it slowly, "I'll be seeing you farther down the trail, Mr. Danny Duggin."

As Curly York turned away, his hand suddenly snatched for his pistol. He heard the voice call out behind him, "York—!"

Swinging his horse quickly, bringing his pistol up, York looked into the barrel of Danielle's cocked Colt.

"You won't be seeing anything more."

The first shot lifted Curly York from his saddle before he could get his shot off. The second hit Joe Duff as the tip of his pistol cleared his holster. Beside Danielle, Hector Sabio nailed Donald Hale in the chest, Hale's drawn pistol flying from his hand as he twisted sidelong out of his saddle. Cleery White's horse reared up as he drew and cocked his big Smith & Wesson, but one shot from

C. F. McCord's rifle sent both White and his horse backward in a spray of dust.

In a matter of seconds, the fight was over. Dust stood high and drifted on the wind. Three of the men's horses scattered. Cleery White's horse rolled back up onto its hooves, shaking off dust, its saddle hanging down around its side. Danielle was the first to step off her horse, walking forward with her Colt pointing down from one man to the next. On the ground, Cleery White looked up at her pistol barrel, blood running down both corners of his mouth.

"Don't shoot," Cleery pleaded in a pained voice. "It . . . weren't my idea."

"Then you should have ridden away," said Danielle.

Stepping down from his horse as well, McCord hurried forward beside Danielle as she cocked her Colt toward Cleery White. "Don't do it, Danny. . . . He's dead anyway!"

"Listen to the marshal!" Hector said, running up on Danielle's other side.

Danielle turned slowly toward Hector Sabio as if in a trance. It seemed to take all of her effort to lower the Colt and let the hammer down.

As she stood staring at Hector with a glazed and distant look in her eyes, McCord said quietly, "There, you see. This one's dead now, too."

Danielle turned back to the blank face of Cleery White, who had slumped down on his side, his cheek pressed to the ground. It took her a moment to snap out of it. Hector and McCord looked at each other as Danielle lowered her Colt back into the holster.

"See why I'm in a hurry?" she said in a hushed tone. "I want to put an end to it."

"*Sí*," said Hector, "and you will very soon." He stepped between Danielle and the bodies on the ground as if to shield her view of them. "Go to the horses, *por favor*, while the marshal and I bury these men."

"No," said McCord as he stepped over to White's horse, loosened its cinch, dropped its saddle and bridle, and slapped its rump, sending it out across the sand. "Let's ride on." Looking around at the four bodies sprawled in the dirt, he said, "Let the sand do all the burying."

After they had mounted and ridden away, with Danielle in front of Hector Sabio and C. F. McCord by ten yards, Hector sidled his horse close to the marshal and said, "You saw what he did. . . . They were already leaving. This Danny Duggin is a cold killer, I think."

"It was too close to call, Hector," said McCord, shaking his head. "I saw Curly York go for his gun the same time as Danny called out his name. One thing's for sure, though. It's all starting to take its toll. The sooner we settle with the Delmanos, the better."

They rode on in the stinging wind.

No sooner than they were out of sight, Al Tarksel and Bob Dennard ventured forward around the crest of a long rise of sand. Dennard stepped his horse over to the bodies on the ground and looked down at them, holding his hat down on his head against the wind.

"We lost a good chance there," he said, sounding disappointed. "I was hoping these boys would take care of things for us. We could have ambushed them afterward." A dusty pair of binoculars hung around his neck on a long strip of rawhide.

"Damn it." Al Tarksel spat and ran a hand across his mouth. "I never seen men come on so strong, then lose their nerve so quick in my life."

Bob Dennard reined his horse away from the bodies, the blowing sand already heaping up along the dead men's sides. "Let's get out of the wind before it skins our hides off us." He nudged the horse forward, still holding his hat down on his head.

"What about them?" Al Tarksel asked, nodding toward the windblown trail ahead.

"Don't worry," said Dennard. "They've still got a ways to go. We ain't lost them yet."

CHAPTER 12

LITTLE HUECO PASS, TEXAS. SEPTEMBER 26, 1871

At a small run-down trade station west of the mountain line, Tim and Jed Strange had spent the night beneath the shelter of a canvas-covered lean-to, where three burros grudgingly made room for them and their horses. The owner of the station, a grizzled old peddler named Martin Wheatley, had no room for the twins inside his small tent. But at the sign of distant sunlight, he came to the lean-to, carrying a hot skillet full of flat biscuits, and set it on a cleared spot on the ground.

"Here you go, boys, same as last night, only fresher. I would've had us some brush-deer steak to go with them, but none came up during the night. Danged Mescaleros must be on the prowl, keeping the deer scared, I reckon."

"Are you expecting any trouble?" Tim asked, raking up a hot biscuit with his fingertips and bouncing it in his cupped hands, blowing on it to cool it.

"From the Apache? Naw, sir," said Wheatley, stooping down beside the twins. "This ain't their stomping grounds nohow. They're just roaming through, on the dodge, like most everybody else who comes this way lately." He eyed the gun belts lying on a blanket, then nodded at the twins' bare feet. "I reckon wherever you boys came from, you left in a hurry? Meant to ask yas last night but I figured you was too tired to talk."

"We're not outlaws if that's what you think," said Jed, friendly but firm.

"It wouldn't make me no difference if you are outlaws," said Wheatley. "So long as a man ain't shooting at me, I ain't shooting at him neither." He patted a weathered hand on the big saddle-style Walker Colt strapped across his belly beneath a wide wool sash. "I've shot this ole hand cannon once every Christmas for the past ten years just to hear it bark, make sure she ain't died on me. Otherwise, it's as quiet as death here. Nobody comes this way anymore unless they ain't wanting to be seen or smelt."

"That's us," said Jed, offering a thin smile. "We're not outlaws, but we don't want to be seen or smelt."

"If you don't use your Walker," asked Tim, "how do you kill your brush deer?"

"Bow and arrow," said the old man. "I learnt to use it years ago. A man lives in the wilds, he learns to separate himself from all mechanisms of man's device."

"What about your trade goods?" asked Jed. "How do make your living if nobody comes this way?"

"Trade goods, ha!" The old man cackled. "I ain't traded nothing since I can remember. I call this a trade station just to keep my hand into something—reminds me that I'm still alive."

"Then I guess there's no point in asking if you'd have any boots for sale, is there?" said Tim. As he asked, he looked at the old man's feet, at the worn-out boot on his right foot and the floppy moccasin on his left.

"No, there's not," said Wheatley. "Nearest boots will be in El Paso if you can stand all the noise there."

"How much farther are we from there?" asked Jed.

"Half a day hard . . . all day easy," said Wheatley. "If you stumbled from here, you'd roll in there by nightfall."

"Much obliged for the biscuits," said Tim. "Can we pay you for breakfast?"

"I don't see why." The old man shrugged. "I was going to eat anyway."

Jed gave the old man a level gaze and said, "We saw some fresh hoofprints coming in last evening. Has there been anybody else come through here lately who didn't want to be seen or smelt?"

The old man had to think about it as he scratched his bearded neck. "Yep, now that you mention it. Three men came past here day before yesterday. They didn't stay long, though. Said they was doing some private bounty hunting." He looked away from the twins as he spoke. "Asked me had I seen any strangers passing through. I told them everybody I've seen in the past ten years has been a stranger."

"I see," said Tim. He stood up, took the last bite of his biscuit, and swung his holster belt around his waist and strapped it into place. "We'll be getting along now, thanking you for your hospitality."

"I'm still eating," Jed protested over a mouthful of hot biscuit.

"Eat on the way," said Tim, giving his brother a level stare. "I want to get into town and get me some boots."

Jed caught the look in Tim's eyes and offered no more hesitancy. He stood up, taking his gun belt from the blanket and putting it on, still chewing his food.

"Don't know what's your hurry," Martin Wheatley said, standing up with them, brushing the ragged seat of his trousers.

"He's always in a hurry," Jed said, nodding toward Tim as he took the pistol from his holster, checked it, then put it away. "I can hardly keep up with him sometime."

Martin Wheatley watched them closely while they saddled their horses and made ready for the trail. He followed them out from beneath the lean-to, saying as they stepped up into their saddles and turned their horses, "Adios, fellers. If you come back through, bring some tobacco."

"We sure will, mister," said Tim, drawing the chestnut mare up close beside him.

He tugged his hat brim down onto his head, making a quick sweep with his eyes before heeling his horse forward to the narrow trail. Beside him, Jed did the same. Neither of them spoke or looked back until they had rounded the trail past a large split boulder fifty yards away.

Then Tim sidled his horse and the mare off the trail in between two tall rocks and turned to Jed, saying, "Something wasn't right, was it?"

"I didn't notice until you got anxious to leave," said Jed, "but you're right. There was something wrong, sure enough. I just can't put my finger on it."

"Me neither," said Tim.

"Then what do you want to do?" Jed asked.

"I say we need to circle around, get above the place, and watch him a while. I believe there's somebody back there with him. If there is, I want to know who. Danielle might be coming this way. We don't want her getting bushwhacked."

They stepped down from their saddles and led the horses up off the trail through rock and brush until they had moved to a point above the old man's run-down shack. Hitching the horses to a deadfall tangle of juniper, the twins eased out onto a rock overhang and looked down just in time to see two men step out through the door of the shack and walk toward Martin Wheatley. Beside Wheatley stood another man, this one wearing a long riding duster and carrying a rifle in his gloved hand. From sixty feet above them, Tim and Jed listened closely to make out their words.

"Hey, Carl," the man in the long riding duster called out to one of the men walking toward him, "this ole geezer wants to know if he did all right. What do you think?"

The one he spoke to was Carl Zabow, and the man walking beside Carl was his brother, Lucas. "He did all right, Ellis," said Carl Zabow. "If he hadn't he wouldn't be standing there. Right, Lucas?"

Lucas Zabow only nodded. In his hands he held a short bow and a thin crooked arrow, trying to get the arrow to seat onto the bowstring. "How the hell does a man shoot one of these things?"

As they neared Ellis Short and Martin Wheatley, Lucas managed to get the arrow seated and draw it back a couple of inches.

When he let the arrow go, it arched slowly and stuck in the ground between Ellis's and Martin Wheatley's feet.

"Hey! Take it easy!" old man Wheatley shouted. "That ain't no toy! I've killed deer and elk bigger than you are with it."

Lucas Zabow laughed. "I don't believe it," he said, taking another crooked arrow from the rawhide quiver under his arm. He looked the arrow over and notched it to the bowstring. "You couldn't knock wet wind out of a sick chicken with this thing."

"What do you think, Carl?" Martin Wheatley asked. "You think they're the ones you told me about, the look-alikes who travel with the man you're looking for?"

"I'd bet on it," said Carl Zabow. "How many twins can you remember ever coming through here?"

"None that I recall," said Wheatley. "Notice how I didn't mention it to them, about them being twins?"

"Yeah, I noticed," said Carl Zabow.

On their rocky perch, Jed turned to Tim and whispered, "*That's* what didn't feel right. Everywhere we go, somebody always comments on us being look-alikes."

Tim only nodded, still listening intently to the men below.

"Does this get me part of that bounty money once you kill this Duggin feller?" old man Wheatley asked. "I did it just like you asked me to."

"Sure, old man. Why not?" said Carl Zabow.

Beside him another arrow streaked from the bow, this one a little stronger.

"Dang it, Lucas!" Wheatley said. "I told you to be careful with that thing!"

"I'm getting better," said Lucas Zabow. "Don't talk cross to me, old man. I'm apt to put one of these in your chest."

Martin Wheatley looked worried. Beside him, Ellis Short only chuckled and glanced at the arrow that had pinned itself to one of the supports of the lean-to. "You ought to know better than to leave something like this lying around. You never know when some idiot is going to take it up."

"Who are you calling an idiot?" Lucas Zabow said, grinning, stringing the arrow and pointing it at Ellis Short.

Ellis Short raised a hand toward him, smiling, saying, "I take it back. Don't shoot."

Lucas swung the arrow tip toward Martin Wheatley, saying, "What do you think, old man? Do you think I'm an idiot?"

Martin Wheatley ignored him and said to Carl Zabow, "What do you think about giving me a few dollars right now, Zabow? Call it an advance. You said yourself, I did a fine job lying to them boys. They never guessed anybody was here."

"No," said Carl Zabow, "no advance. When we take care of Danny Duggin, I'll remember that you're in for a couple of dollars, but that's as far as I go."

"A couple of dollars?" Martin Wheatley looked stunned. "Hell's fire, I wouldn't have wasted my time for a couple of dollars! Maybe I'll just slip atop one of the burrows and catch up to those look-alikes, see how much they'll pay me for telling them you're here."

Carl eyed him closely. "You'd do that to us?"

"I need some whiskey awfully bad," said Wheatley. "I'm apt to do what benefits me. Can you blame a man for that?"

"I reckon not," said Carl Zabow. He turned to his brother, Lucas, and said, "Have you got the hang of that yet?"

"I'm getting there." Lucas pulled the arrow back from the bow and looked it up and down.

"Then shoot some arrows in this old buzzard," said Carl. "That'll teach him to keep his mouth shut."

"Now just one dang minute!" said Martin Wheatley. "I was only testing you, Carl!"

"Testing me?" Carl grinned. "Well, I hope I passed."

The twang of the bowstring was followed by a deep grunt as Martin Wheatley clutched the arrow shaft sticking out of his left shoulder with both hands. "Dang!" he managed to say in a strained voice.

Another arrow hit him, this one in his thigh, causing him to buckle down onto his knee. "Boys . . . this ain't right!"

Another arrow sliced deep into his right shoulder. "Cut it out, boys, please," said Martin Wheatley, catching his breath.

"Nope, I'm just getting started," said Lucas Zabow. "Now that I got the hang of it, I could do this all day long." He grinned, stringing another arrow. "Do you hear me, old man? I said, all . . . day . . . long." Lucas aimed the arrow low and let it fly, nailing Martin Wheatley's foot to the dirt. The old man bellowed and cursed.

"I got to get me one of these," said Lucas Zabow, taking another arrow and stringing it. "I bet I can put this one right smack in the middle of his forehead."

On the overhang, Tim stood up, saying to his brother, "I can't stand here and watch this."

"Neither can I." Jed jumped to his feet beside him.

Lucas Zabow took careful aim this time, drawing the arrow back its full length. "Ten dollars says I can do it." He chuckled.

"You're on," said Ellis Short, stepping farther away from the old man.

But before Lucas Zabow could let the arrow go, a shot from Tim's pistol exploded, the bullet slicing through Lucas's hand and shattering the bow shaft. The arrow dropped down and skidded across the dirt.

"What the—?" Carl Zabow spun around, his pistol coming up out of his holster as Lucas fell to the ground, screaming, clasping his bloody hand, seeing the stub where his middle finger used to be. Ellis Short ducked back behind the lean-to pole, his pistol coming up cocked and ready.

"Up here," Tim Strange called down to them.

Carl Zabow's eyes went up toward the sound of Tim's voice, his pistol following his gaze. But before he got more than a glimpse of Tim standing on the overhang above him, the second shot from Tim's pistol hit Zabow high in the chest and sent him flying backward. Jed saw Ellis Short's pistol swing around the pole and try to take aim upward. The pistol in Jed's hand exploded twice, each shot nailing Ellis Short and walking him backward into the frightened burrows. As Short fell to the ground, the burrows brayed and kicked and stomped him beneath their sharp little hooves.

"Don't shoot!" Lucas Zabow cried out from his knees, his right hand gripping his left wrist, trying to slow the flow of blood. "You shot my damned finger off!"

Ten feet away, Martin Wheatley shouted through his pain, "Shoot him again! Look what he did to me!"

"Everybody stay real still till I get there," Tim called down to them. He looked at Jed, saying, "Keep them covered while I climb down. Once I get there, you bring the horses and ride on around."

"All right, be careful," said Jed.

He turned to his horse, slipped the rifle from his saddle boot, cocked it, and held it poised downward toward Wheatley and Lucas Zabow while Tim began a slow descent down the steep rocky slope.

At the bottom of the slope, Tim drew his pistol and cocked it. He kept the two wounded men covered as he walked first to the body of Carl Zabow, then to the body of Ellis Short lying broken and bloody amid the burrows' nervous hooves.

Walking back from beneath the canvas lean-to, he asked Martin Wheatley, "What kind of heads do you have on those arrows?"

"They're Comanche heads," said Wheatley, giving Lucas Zabow a cold stare. "They'll have to be cut out if that's what you want to know." He tried to walk toward Zabow on his bloody knees, one hand reaching out toward him like eagle talons. "All I ask is that you kill this dirty lousy—"

"No, you don't," said Tim, stepping in between the two men, stopping Martin Wheatley. "There'll be no more killing here." He looked at Zabow and nodded toward a bucket of water sitting at one end of the lean-to. "Get that water bucket and bring it over here. We're going to need some hot water and bandages."

"Like hell," said Zabow. "I can't get that bucket! Look at my hand! My finger's blown off!"

"You've got another hand," said Tim. "Now do like I tell you."

By the time Jed came down around the trail, leading Tim's

horse and the chestnut mare, Zabow had dragged the water bucket over, poured water into a battered coffeepot, and scraped together some kindling for a small fire. With a bloody bandanna wrapped around the stub of his finger, Zabow kneeled down and blew onto the smoldering kindling to raise a flame.

"Have they told you anything?" Jed asked, stepping down from his horse and leading all three horses to a hitch rail.

"Nope, not yet," said Tim. "I'm more interested in getting those arrows out of the old man before an infection sets in."

"Hear that, you rotten jackass!" Martin Wheatley raged at Lucas Zabow. "I'll be lucky if these things don't kill me!"

Zabow ignored him and cursed under his breath.

"I figure there's not much to tell us anyway," said Tim. "These gunmen were out for the bounty. Lucky Daniel—I mean, *Danny Duggin*—wasn't with us. We'd all three've been bushwhacked."

With the flames starting to stand and grow, Zabow rose up on his knees and fanned the fire with his good hand, saying, "We was going to stay on your trail. Brother Carl said it wouldn't be long till this Duggin showed up. We heard he traveled with a couple of look-alikes. You boys ain't exactly hard to spot, you know." His eyes went to the hand-tooled gun belt on Jed Strange. "Say, that's Jack Pearl's holster and pistol. What are you doing wearing it?"

"What do you think I'm doing wearing it?" Jed challenged.

"The man it belonged to is dead," Tim cut in. "When the Delmanos put the word out about that reward, they must've forgot to tell all of you it would be the hardest money you ever tried to earn."

"Don't count on your friend Duggin being safe just yet." Lucas Zabow sneered. "There's plenty more guns aimed at you between here and the Delmanos."

"Yes," Tim said, offering a trace of a harsh smile, "but if they are all as smart as you all are, we've nothing to worry about."

Lucas Zabow grumbled to himself, looked down at the bloody bandanna on his hand, and shook his head in contemplation. Then he raised his eyes back up to Tim and Jed as Tim walked over and put the pot of water on the fire. "Hey, can I get something done about this hand? It's bleeding pretty bad."

Tim looked at Jed, saying, "You want to take care of him while I cut these arrows out of Wheatley?"

"Yep," said Jed, "I'll do it—"

"Look out, he's got a gun!" Martin Wheatley shouted, cutting Jed off.

Even as Jed spun toward him, the derringer in Zabow's hand leveled out toward him, Zabow's thumb cocking it quickly. But he was not quick enough. Jed's pistol exploded twice on the upswing from his holster, hammering Zabow backward and down, the shot from the derringer going wild and skyward, the gun falling to the dirt. Smoke curled up from the short barrel. Jed stepped in close and kicked the derringer away, looking down at Zabow's blank dead face.

"That was the stupidest move I ever saw." Old man Wheatley gasped. "That fool was dead before he hit the ground!"

The two bullet holes in Zabow's chest lay less than an inch apart, centered on his left shirt pocket at heart level. Jed punched out the two spent cartridges from his pistol and replaced them as he spoke. "We might not get all the men out to collect that bounty, but one thing's for sure: We're thinning them out as we go."

It was afternoon when Tim finished removing the arrows from Martin Wheatley's wounds, wrapping the crude gashes in strips of cloth torn from a white shirt they found in the saddlebags of one of the dead gunmen. When Tim was finished and he and Jed had dragged the bodies of the outlaws out of sight behind the canvas lean-to, the twins walked back and found that Martin Wheatley had raised himself up from a blanket on the ground, and now sat on the single wooden step out front of the shack. He'd picked up the blanket and wrapped it around his shoulders even in the heat of the day. Sweat streamed down his weathered, whiskered cheeks.

"I feel real ashamed, lying to you boys earlier," old man Wheatley said. "I reckon the idea of big money makes fools of all us if we let it. How can I thank yas for what you've done for me?"

"You can keep an eye out for our pal Danny Duggin if he passes this way. If you see him, let him know we're in El Paso waiting for him."

"I'll sure do it," Wheatley said.

"And don't go trying to collect that reward or telling anybody else about it, old man," Jed warned him. "If you do you'll likely end up dead."

"Hell, don't worry. I've learnt my lesson," said Wheatley. He nodded at his bandaged wounds. "Every time I move a muscle, it feels like a fire runs through my bones. What made that jackass do something like this? Seems like if he wanted to kill me, he could've had the decency to put a bullet in me! Why this?"

"You'll have to figure that one out for yourself," said Jed, stepping over to the hitch rail and loosening the horses' reins.

"Are you going to be all right here alone?" Tim asked as Jed brought the horses over to him.

"Yeah, I always do better alone, it seems like." Wheatley looked off across the sky. "Ya'll go on. Don't worry about me."

The twins mounted and rode away, looking back only once at the solitary figure in the afternoon shadows before rounding the turn out of sight.

"He's right about something," Tim said. "We are easy to spot, looking alike the way we do. We need to do something, since the word's out that Danny Duggin travels with a pair of twins."

"What do you want to do?" Jed asked.

"I think before we ride into El Paso, I'll shave and change my appearance as much as I can." He rubbed a hand up and down on his week-old beard stubble. "You can even take your boot knife and cut my hair real short. Do you think that'll work?"

"It's worth a try," said Jed. "Another thing we need to do is put this mare somewhere out of sight for a while. There's too many people who remember it. We'll split up before we ride into El Paso. Once we're in town, we'll listen around the saloons and see what we hear. Then we'll meet up and camp somewhere outside the town limits till we hear something from Danielle."

CHAPTER 13

The open-sided Spanish-style coach was one of the last of its kind to provide transportation across the flats and rock lands of West Texas. It rolled around the turn in the dusty trail with its canvas covers tied down to protect its passengers from the blazing sunlight. At one time, the canvas side covers had displayed bright hand-painted flowers and scenes of cherubs serenely above the earth. Tassels had danced on the breeze from the corners of the canvases. But now, after the coach had performed years of service across the harsh terrain, the sand and sun had stripped away all of the garishness. Green and gold paint that had once glistened in sunlight had now faded to the color of the arid land around it.

"There she is, boys," said Saul Delmano, looking down at the coach from a sandy bluff.

Beside him, Ramon rose up in his stirrups and watched the stage straighten out of the turn, its four sweat-streaked black stage horses forging ahead at a strong gallop.

"They have no one riding shotgun," Ramon said in surprise.

Saul grinned, saying, "I know. . . . It's pretty foolish of them, huh?" He raised his bandanna and adjusted it over his face.

"Why are they moving so fast?" Ramon asked. "Have they spotted us?" He pulled his own bandanna up and smoothed it down over the bridge of his nose.

Saul chuckled behind his mask. "No, little brother, they just ain't taking no chances for the next few miles. There's too many blind spots along the stretch of trail. Most times when somebody has robbed a stage along here, it's been while the stage was traveling slow. A man would just step out into the trail with a shotgun and stop it cold. But the stage company has gotten wise to that tactic. So we're going to do something a little different today. Right, Tully?" he called out to his left, where Joe Tully sat atop his horse with a rifle cradled in his arm.

"That's right," replied Joe Tully. "Anytime you're ready."

"Come on, little brother," said Saul Delmano. "Let's get headed down there with Kid Jeffrey."

"But what are we doing?" asked Ramon.

"I'll show you." Saul grinned. "Just don't go getting nervous on me."

He gigged his horse down the path toward the trail, Ramon following close behind him. Halfway down the sloping path, a shot rang out from Joe Tully's rifle. Ramon watched stunned as the driver down on the stagecoach melted from his seat, fell to the dirt, and rolled away, his arms flapping like the broken blades of a windmill.

"He got that sucker on the first shot!" Saul Delmano bellowed, laughing aloud, spurring his horse harder.

"Holy saints!" Ramon gasped, seeing the stage veer off the trail, the horses spooked now and pounding into a run.

"Don't worry," Saul called out. "Kid Jeffrey's got it."

From out of nowhere, Kid Jeffrey bolted forward below them on a big silver dapple stallion. Overtaking the runaway stage horses, Kid Jeffrey reached out from his saddle, grabbed the lead horse, and began checking the stage down. From inside the canvas covers came the sound of a woman screaming. A bald head poked out through the canvas, looked all around at the riders descending on the stage, then withdrew quickly back inside.

Once the stage was halted, Kid Jeffrey backstepped his horse and called out to the passengers with his pistol drawn, "All right, everybody out!"

The canvas cover flew up enough for the portly bald man to jump out to the ground, shouting in a frenzy, "Don't shoot!" as he ran out across the sand and brush with his stubby arms raised high.

Beside Ramon came the sound of Saul Delmano's pistol, and the man spilled to the ground in a puff of dust. "Stupid bastard," Saul Delmano growled.

"You said there would be no killing!" Ramon shouted at his brother, jerking his horse into a sidelong canter as they approached the stage.

"Well, that one couldn't be helped," said Saul. "Now don't lose your head over it! This is robbery most foul, little brother. Get used to it."

Joe Tully rode in hard, joining them at the stage, where a woman and an old man had stepped down from behind the canvas flaps, their hands high above their heads.

"Climb on up there and get the box," Saul Delmano said to Kid Jeffrey, keeping his smoking pistol aimed down at the two passengers.

Kid Jeffrey sidled his horse to the stage and swung up out of his saddle into the driver's seat. In a second, the small iron box fell to the dirt. Saul Delmano stepped down from his saddle, staring coldly at the two terror-stricken passengers.

"Bet this is your first robbery, huh?" he asked them.

The woman stood staring wild-eyed and trembling.

The old man glanced away at the body on the ground, then spoke in a shaky voice. "Ye ain't going to shoot us, too, are ye?"

"That all depends, old man," said Saul Delmano, pointing his pistol down at the lock on the iron safe box. A shot exploded and the lock blew open. "Have you got any money on you?" Saul kneeled down and flipped the lid open.

"I've got about fourteen dollars . . . and a pocket watch," the old man offered, nodding at the gold watch fob on his vest.

"Well, get it out and give it to us, fool!" said Saul Delmano.

He reached inside the box, took a handful of letters, and slung them away on the breeze while the old man drew a worn leather wallet from his coat pocket and fished out the money with quaking fingers.

"Leave the passengers alone," said Ramon Delmano. "Take what we came here for and let's go."

Ignoring Ramon, Saul Delmano lifted a cloth bag from the box, opened it, and took three stacks of bound dollar bills.

"You brother's awfully skittish," said Kid Jeffrey, jumping down from atop the coach. "Are you sure he's cut out for this kind of work?"

Ramon shot him a harsh stare.

"Aw, don't judge him harshly," said Saul Delmano. "You know how it is, his first time and all." He stepped over and snatched the money from the old man's hand, then jerked the watch from his vest pocket, looked at it, and held it to his ear. "What are you trying to pull, old man? This watch don't work!" He slung the watch to the ground and stuck the tip of his pistol barrel beneath the man's chin.

"No, please!" the old man pleaded. "It was working earlier! I swear it was!"

"Saul, leave him alone!" Ramon shouted, jumping down from his saddle.

Kid Jeffrey and Joe Tully looked at each other in surprise above their bandanna masks.

Saul Delmano turned, slowly facing Ramon. "Damn it, why'd you have to go and say my name?"

He pulled his mask down and spat lint from his lips. Kid Jeffrey and Joe Tully both slumped in disgust and lowered their bandannas as well.

"Wait, no!" said Ramon. "There must be a way to—"

His words were cut short beneath the sound of pistol fire. The old man and the woman crumpled to the ground like spent puppets. Ramon stood stunned, not believing his eyes.

Saul Delmano shrugged, stuffing the money inside his shirt. "It couldn't be helped, little brother. What more can I say? Things happen in this line of business."

Ramon's hand tightened on his pistol butt, yet he stood speechless.

"Easy now," said Saul Delmano. "Don't do something stupid. This is your first job. . . . It'll get easier, I promise." He smiled and stooped down to the woman's body, lifting a small silk purse from her limp wrist. As he stood up, opening it, his fingers rifling inside it, he said to Kid Jeffrey and Joe Tully, "You boys cut out in different directions. Ride three or four miles, then circle around through a creek bed. Meet us tonight at the old mission. We'll split this up and get on to something else."

"Why not split it up now," Kid Jeffrey asked, "the way we always do?"

"Are you going to get picky on me, Kid?" Saul gave him an exasperated look, reaching back inside his shirt. "Because if you feel that way, here!" He jerked out the money and held it up to him. "You hang on to all of it! Hell, I trust you!"

Kid Jeffrey looked ashamed. "I was just asking, is all."

"Then you *don't* want to hold on to it?" Saul Delmano put the money away and shook his head, saying, "Damn, Kid, as long as you've known me, you have to ask me something like that?"

"I meant no harm," Kid Jeffrey offered in a submissive voice.

"I understand," said Saul Delmano. "Now both of yas go on. We've been here too long as it is."

Ramon Delmano stood silently looking at the two bodies on the ground until he felt Saul push him toward his horse. Only when he had mounted and taken the reins in his hands did Ramon notice that Kid Jeffrey and Joe Tully had already spurred their horses out in opposite directions through the brush and rock lands.

"You're going to have to get a grip on yourself, little brother," Saul Delmano said. "This job ain't over till we tie up some loose ends."

"I—I don't want any part of this," Ramon said, shaking his head.

"Well, you're a part of it now whether you want to be or not.

The only question is, do you want to hang from the gallows pole for murder and robbery?" He grinned. "See? All that time you thought I was just out here having myself a grand ole hoedown . . . bet you never realized how hard this work can get."

He slapped his gloved hand on Ramon's horse's rump, laughing as they both rode away.

"Where are we headed?" Ramon called out above the sound of the horse's hooves.

"Into town, just as quick as we can cut across some rock and hide our tracks," Saul replied. "We want to be seen around town like we've been there all day. Tonight we'll build ourselves an even better alibi."

"What do you mean?" Ramon asked.

"You'll see." Saul Delmano grinned.

At the edge of town, Saul and Ramon slipped in along a back trail, stepped down from their saddles, and led their horses through a narrow alley to a hitch rail out front of a crowded saloon. Then they mingled among the many passersby in the dusty street until they made their way to the next saloon a block away. Once inside the saloon, the day gamblers and drinkers looked up and some of the men who were friends of the Delmanos made room for them at the bar. A gunman called Thurman Pratt waved them forward and slapped Saul on his back as he summoned the bartender to bring them both a shot glass.

"How the hell have you boys been?" Thurman asked, snatching a bottle of rye and filling the two glasses for them. "I'm surprised to see you out and around, Saul."

"We're both fine," said Saul Delmano, answering for himself and Ramon. "We just come from Mama Rosa's up the street. Saw all the horses out front and thought we'd drop by here before heading back across the border."

"You're taking an awful big chance, ain't you," said Thurman Pratt, "what with this Danny Duggin looking for you?"

Saul Delmano smiled. "You know me, Thurman. I don't scare

real easy. To tell the truth, I wished the ole man had never put that bounty up on Duggin. I'd kind of like to meet him myself face-to-face." He raised his shot glass in a salute to the men along the bar and tossed back his drink.

A red-faced young man named Reggie Weil, who stood leaning on the bar next to Thurman, looked over at Saul and Ramon and said, "I hope to hell you don't meet him face-to-face. Me and Thurman are counting on making that two thousand for ourselves so's we can chase whores all winter on it."

Saul poured himself another shot of rye and replied, "Reggie, if you're interested in that bounty, why ain't you out fanning the trails for Duggin right now?"

Before Reggie Weil could answer, Thurman Pratt cut in, saying, "Reggie talks too damn much."

He cut a glance along the bar to make sure the other men weren't listening. Seeing the crowd had turned their attention to a woman dancing with her skirt raised above her waist, Thurman continued in a lowered voice beneath the sound of a twangy piano.

"The only way to collect that reward, I figure, is to let this Danny Duggin come through here looking for you. Then Reggie and me will walk out into the street, pop a few shots in him, and bring you his head in a flour sack." Thurman shrugged. "It makes more sense than to be out there eating dust in the hot sun, don't it?"

"It sounds good to me," Saul answered. He threw back another shot of rye, nodded toward Ramon beside him, then asked Thurman Pratt, "You haven't seen Kid Jeffrey or Joe Tully around, have you? We've looked for them all day in every saloon around here."

"No, we haven't seen them," said Reggie Weil, "but you don't look drunk enough to have been in every saloon in town."

Saul Delmano's expression turned dead serious. "What's that supposed to mean?"

"Nothing," said Reggie Weil, looking stuck for a response.

Thurman Pratt looked Saul and Ramon up and down. "Pipe down, Reggie," he said. "I reckon these boys know if they've been in town all day or not." He gave Saul a knowing look, adding, "Hell,

Saul, you've been drinking most of the day with me and Reggie if anybody asks. Is this something important?"

"Much obliged," Saul Delmano said under his breath. "Yeah, it might be important. Seems like the law hereabouts has a pick on me. Least little thing happens, I always expect to get blamed for it."

Thurman Pratt leaned a little closer, saying between the two of them, "You think maybe Kid Jeffrey and Tully have done something and you and your brother might catch the blame for it?"

"Yeah, something like that," Saul responded, looking a bit concerned. "Kid Jeffrey has been talking lately about hitting a stagecoach. He asked me to join him, but I'm lying low for a while."

"Don't worry," said Thurman. "I'll put the word out among these men. If anybody comes asking, you two have been in town with us since morning."

Saul nodded and threw back his shot of rye. "I knew I could count on you, Thurman." He raised his shot glass toward the bartender and called out, "Bring us all a mug of beer, something to wash down the taste of snake heads."

Ramon had been listening, puzzled, wondering what his brother had in mind. He nudged Saul, asking him in a whisper while the bartender slid beer mugs along the bar, "What are you trying to do, Saul?"

Without facing him, Saul Delmano answered in lowered voice, "I told you we was going to build ourselves an alibi. Now drink up. Leave all the thinking to me."

The drinking crowd grew as the afternoon wore on. When the evening sunlight cut black slashes of shade across the dirt street, Saul Delmano nudged Ramon with his elbow and nodded at a few men who had stepped away from the bar and headed out the back door toward the outhouses.

"Come on, little brother, it's time we meet Kid Jeffrey and Tully." He stepped back from the bar and said to Thurman Pratt as Thurman and Reggie stood with their arms draped around two young women, "Hey, Thurman, we're going to the jake. Keep an eye on our beers."

"Sure thing," said Thurman Pratt in a drunken voice, barely raising a drooping eye from the young woman's bare shoulder.

Once out the back door, Saul and Ramon hurried along the backs of the buildings to their horses a block up the street. Once atop their horses, they raced out on the east road to the old mission three miles out of town. It was dark by the time they slid their horses to a halt and stepped down from their saddles. Ramon saw the outlines of two horses standing back at the rear edge of the old adobe church building.

Kid Jeffrey called out quietly in the darkness, "Hey, Saul, we're back here."

"Hope you haven't been waiting too long," said Saul Delmano.

He and Ramon led their horses back into the darkness and joined Kid Jeffrey and Joe Tully.

"No, just got here ourselves," said Joe Tully, holding an open canteen in his hand, wiping a wet bandanna across his forehead.

"There's been nobody on your trail?" asked Saul Delmano.

"Not a soul," said Kid Jeffrey. "We've been real careful. We shook off our tracks three or four different times through creek beds and rocks. Besides, it might be sometime tomorrow before anybody finds that stagecoach."

"Let's settle up and get moving," said Joe Tully. "It's been hotter than hell out there. I'm ready to go drink myself into a blind stupor."

"Good idea," said Saul Delmano, "I'm in a hurry myself."

He reached inside for what Kid Jeffrey and Joe Tully thought would be the stacks of money. They leaned in, watching him eagerly, but then stood taken aback when Saul Delmano pulled out the dead woman's small silk purse and tossed it on the ground at their feet.

"Hey," said Kid Jeffrey, "what's going on here? What are you doing with that?"

But as Kid Jeffrey spoke, Joe Tully caught onto Saul Delmano's intentions and jumped back a step, saying, "It's a setup, Kid! Kill them!"

Tully's hand went for his pistol, but it was too late. Saul Delmano had already drawn his Colt and cocked it. He dropped the hammer on Joe Tully first, then quickly turned the pistol on Kid Jeffrey and put a bullet through his heart. Saul took a step back, kicked the silk purse up between the two bodies on the ground, and turned to Ramon.

"Let's ride fast, little brother. Our beer's getting warm."

"My God!" said Ramon Delmano, looking down at the dead men. "What kind of low monster are you? These men were your partners, your *amigos!*"

"Yeah, well, that was their mistake, I reckon. We got the money, and once the law sees that purse, they'll get the blame." He grinned, taking a stack of the money from inside his shirt. "Ain't that the best kind of partners to have?" He reached out and shoved the money down into Ramon's shirt pocket. "There's a thousand dollars for a day's work, little brother. If you don't trust me, you're free to count it."

Ramon wasn't about to count the money. He didn't even want to look at it. Something told him to keep his mouth shut and go along with his brother until he found a chance to make his getaway.

Saul must have read the look on his face. He turned away laughing and stepped up into his saddle. "As far as what kind of monster I am, little brother . . . I've been wondering about that my whole damn life."

CHAPTER 14

What the hell took yas so long?" Thurman Pratt asked Saul Delmano when Saul and Ramon slipped in through the back door and into their places at the crowded bar. "I've already been drunk and sobered back up since you boys went to the jake! Thought I'd have to cleave the bartender's fingers off to keep him from pitching your beer out."

Next to Thurman Pratt, Reggie Weil hung facedown on the bar, passed out cold, a fly walking boldly across his chin.

Saul Delmano spoke for himself and Ramon, saying, "We walked back and got our horses from out front of the cantina. Then we ran into a couple of ole boys we knew on our way here and got to talking." He sipped his beer, set the mug down, and pushed it across the bar, saying to the busy bartender, "What's it take to get a couple of beers livened up?"

Thurman Pratt eyed Ramon, then said to Saul, "What's wrong with your brother? He looks like he's seen a ghost!"

"He looks like that all the time." Saul chuckled. "I always said his ma shoulda weaned him sooner."

Ramon seethed in silence and drank his beer.

By the time Saul and Ramon Delmano had finished their beers, the young woman was back at the bar with Thurman Pratt's face buried in her sweaty bodice. Saul Delmano set his empty mug on the bar top beside Ramon's and patted Thurman on his shoulder.

"I can see you're in love, ole pard. I reckon me and little brother will head back across the line. Don't forget we was with you all day."

"What's your hurry?" Thurman Pratt asked in a muffled voice without raising his face. But Saul and Ramon turned and left without answering.

Leaving the saloon, the Delmano brothers crossed the border under the cover of darkness and rode in a wandering trail across rocks and through thick brush. More than once they doubled back and followed their own tracks, just to confuse any would-be followers. Dawn churned orange and hazy in the eastern sky as they made their way along the last stretch of trail toward Bloody Horse Pass.

"You've been awfully damn quiet, little brother," Saul said, riding along with his pistol out of his holster, idly twirling it on his finger.

For the past mile Ramon had been wary of the sound of his brother cocking and uncocking the big pistol.

"I have nothing to say," Ramon replied. "I only want to return home and put this thing out of my mind." He'd considered lifting his own pistol, just as a precaution, yet he realized that doing so might only progress whatever dark thoughts Saul Delmano was already harboring.

"Sorry, little brother," said Saul Delmano in a quiet tone, riding up close beside him. Ramon tensed at the sound of the pistol cocking. "But you won't be going home this morning."

Ramon jerked his eyes toward Saul, his hand clutching around the butt of his holstered pistol. But he saw his brother uncock the pistol and twirl it, giving him a bemused look.

"Take it easy now, Ramon." Saul chuckled in taunting voice. "You're strung tighter than a cheap fiddle." He slipped his pistol into his holster and let out a breath of regret. "Things went bad for us back at the stagecoach . . . you mistakenly saying my name before those people, us having to kill them. Not that I'm holding it against you. We all make mistakes. But to be on the safe side, we might want to ride on through Bloody Horse Pass and take to the hideout for a few days."

"Why?" Ramon asked bluntly, not trusting anything Saul had to say. "We are already across the border. . . . You set up our alibi. What are we hiding from now, this Danny Duggin who is looking to kill you? I thought you were not afraid of him."

Saul reined his horse to a halt. Ramon did the same.

"Listen to me, little brother. I ain't afraid of man, beast, nor reptile. In all likelihood Kid Jeffrey and Joe Tully are going to wear that stage robbery. But don't forget there are four sets of tracks there. The sheriff is going to know there are two others involved if he pushes it—and he *will* push it since people died, especially one of them an old codger and another being a woman!" He shook his head. "Don't ask me why, but for some reason, the law gets plumb doubled over at the death of a woman or an old person. We might have done wrong killing them. Even with Pa and the sheriff being good friends, this could get real stiff before it's over."

Ramon only stared at him for a moment, beginning to realize just how wild and bloodthirsty his brother was. "It was not we who killed them, Saul. It was *you*! Do you feel nothing at taking their lives? Does it not bother you in any way?"

"Damn it, Ramon! I just told you I might have done wrong! What do you want from me? We went to do a job, and we had to kill them. Not everything in life goes perfect, you know!" He eased down, took a deep breath to calm himself, then said, "The thing is, I've seen posses get so riled up, they forget all about that border and ride right in here. So, just to be safe, we're going to lie up in the hideout for a while and cool off. There's a few others up there doing the same thing, wanted men who'll back us if something goes wrong. You never know when we might get—"

His words stopped short at the close sound of a horse nickering low in the dim morning light. His hand snapped to the pistol in his holster as his eyes cut through the darkness to the outlines of figures sitting atop their horses in a half circle around them.

A deep voice said quietly, "Take your hand from the pistol, or you will both die hard."

As if to state the seriousness of the man's words, six rifles levered almost as one, the metal on metal sounding harsh in the stillness of morning.

"Who are you, and what are you doing in Bloody Horse Pass?" The voice had a trace of a French accent, and somehow hearing it caused Saul Delmano to sigh in relief.

"I'm Saul Delmano. . . . This is my brother, Ramon. I'm guessing you men work for our pa, Lewis Delmano?"

"Stand down, men," the voice said to those surrounding the Delmano brothers. "These are his sons."

The sound of rifles uncocking brought a smile to Saul Delmano's face.

"Hear that, little brother? These boys work for us." Saul chuckled. He looked back at the ghostly-looking figures in the grainy light. "Boys, you are a sight for troubled eyes," he continued. "I knew ole Daddy was getting some extra help, but I reckon he must've forgot to tell—"

The voice cut him off. "We do not work for the Delmanos. I am Henri LaBourge. We were sent here by an emissary of the *generalissimo* simply to do a small job. Then we leave. Let us be clear on that."

"Hey, that's good as gold, far as we're concerned. Right, little brother?" He grinned at Ramon, who sat silent. Then he added, looking from one dark figure to the next, "We was just discussing whether or not to go hide out for a few days. Reckon there's no need in it now, eh, boys?"

A silence passed; then the voice said, "Perhaps it is still best that you go there. I have more men out a half a mile or more, surrounding the place. Until I meet your father, it is best we all know who we are shooting at out here."

"You get no argument from me," said Saul Delmano. "We might stop by the house and grab something to drink. Then we'll be out of your hair until this is all over. Fair enough?"

"Fair enough," Henri LaBourge answered. "Ride quickly. If anyone stops you, tell them you have already met with me."

"You've got it all, mister," said Saul Delmano, collecting his horse beneath him and raising the ends of his reins to slap it forward. "I believe I could get used to this, having my killing done for me without me lifting a finger." He laughed aloud and batted his heels to his horse's sides. "Let's ride, little brother!"

"Two idiots," said Henri LaBourge as the Delmano brothers rode away. "This is the fool Raul Hernandez was asked to protect? It is incredible, is it not?"

The men closed in together. A ripple of dark laughter rose and fell.

"Come, men, back to your positions," he said.

Daylight had spread across the land by the time Ramon and Saul Delmano rode into the front yard of the hacienda. Buck Benton and Gus Latimer, two of Lewis Delmano's old outlaw partners, had heard the horses approaching at a gallop. They came running from the bunkhouse, both of them strapping their gun belts around their waists.

"Take it easy. It's only us," Saul Delmano called out to them, sounding less than respectful to the two older men as he skidded his horse down almost onto its haunches and swung down from his saddle.

"What's wrong, Saul?" asked Latimer, looking back along the trail. "Is somebody dogging you?"

Saul Delmano gave the two old men a smirk. "What would you do if there was?"

The two men caught the bluntness of his sarcasm, but didn't respond.

"Leave them alone, Saul!" said Ramon, reining up his mount. He looked at the two old outlaws, saying in a friendlier manner, "There is no one dogging us. But there are men out there that our father has hired to keep watch for this Danny Duggin."

"Then we'll grab our rifles and go join them," said Buck Benton.

"No, wait," said Ramon. "These men are hired to do the job. They asked that everyone stay back and let them do it."

Gus Latimer grumbled, "I don't see why. . . . There's plenty of guns here. Nobody ever had to—"

"Because that's the way we're going to do it!" Saul Delmano

shouted. "You old geezers stay the hell out of the way! Go cross-brand some stolen cattle! Leave the fighting for the ones who still know how!"

He stepped close to Gus Latimer as if he were going to push the old man backward. But Ramon stepped quickly in between them.

"Let's go get what we're taking with us," Ramon said. "I will meet you back here as fast as I can."

Saul Delmano backed up a step and spread a knowing smile. "Don't bring nothing you can't tote in your saddlebags, little brother," he warned with a wink. "Those boys up at the hideout can turn randy real quick if you get my meaning."

Ramon spun away and stomped off toward the front porch of the hacienda, where Greta stood watching through the partially open door.

Gus Latimer and Buck Benton backed away from Saul Delmano, giving him a bitter look, and they both walked back to the bunkhouse.

"Don't slow down on getting the branding done today, old-timers!" Saul called after them. "Somebody's got to tend the steers while us *men* take care of business." He stood watching them leave with a nasty look on his face. "Worthless old dogs."

"That rips it for me," Gus Latimer said to Buck Benton under his breath. "I don't care who shoots him. . . . I just hope to hell somebody does."

"Something went wrong, I can tell!" Greta gasped, seeing the look on Ramon's face as he stepped inside the hacienda, closing the door behind himself and leaning back against it. He took the first calm breath he'd drawn since leaving her the day before.

"Yes, things went very wrong. I have made a terrible mistake, thinking I could do something like this and walk away." He leaned forward from against the door and took her in his arms. "Greta, people have died! Three men and a woman. It is only a matter of time until their bodies are found."

"God, no!" Greta gasped again. "Ramon, you didn't . . . ?"

"No, I did not," he said. "But it makes no difference. I was there. I was a part of it. I am as guilty as my brother. If ever we are caught, we will both hang for it."

"What must we do now?" she asked, her eyes turning misty in fear and desperation.

Ramon held his hands on her shoulders. "I will leave the money with you, and I will ride up to the hideout with my brother. He is caught up in his own craziness right now, but I will wait until he settles down. Then I will come back for you and we will leave." He took out the stack of money and pressed it into her hands. "There are many dangerous things going on out there," he said, nodding toward the land beyond the window. "If I do not return by tomorrow night—"

"Don't talk like that, Ramon!" she said, cutting him off in a trembling voice. "If anything happens to you, I don't think I could go on living."

He shook her gently. "Listen to me. You must be strong. If I do not return, you must think of yourself and our baby. You must take this money and leave right away. Take the best horse in the stables and flee this place. My soul would find no rest, knowing that our child would grow up in this place the same as I did."

"But where would I go?" Greta asked.

"Go far from here. Go to Fort Smith, near the Territory. It is a town where there are many lawmen. My father will not follow you there."

"Fort Smith . . ." she said to herself, committing the name to memory. She looked back into his eyes. "But you will return. I know you will! I will pray for it!"

"Yes, I will return to you," said Ramon, seeing he had to give her some hope to cling to. "But you must be gone before my father comes back. If I come here and you are gone, I will meet you in Fort Smith. Do you understand?"

She collected herself and leveled her gaze. Summoning up her courage, she said, "Yes, don't worry. I will do as you say. Be careful, Ramon. . . . God be with you."

EL PASO, TEXAS. SEPTEMBER 28, 1871

At daylight, Sheriff Lloyd Deweese and his two deputies stormed along the narrow hall above the saloon, room by room, kicking open doors and dragging blurry-eyed men out of their beds. Saloon girls screamed and cursed, grabbing whatever sheets or towels they could to throw around themselves. Once the men were downstairs, Sheriff Deweese stood in the middle of the floor with his palms resting on the pair of pistol butts sticking up from his high-riding holsters.

Behind the bar, Ned Lynnly, the bartender, wiped a wet bar towel across his face and tried to wake himself up. At a table sat five men the deputies had herded in off the street. One of them was Tim Strange, who had just stepped down from his horse and hitched it to the rail out front when the deputies approached him. Tim kept quiet, watching the lawmen force the half-naked men down the stairs and line them up along the bar.

The men grumbled and staggered, looking at Sheriff Deweese as he started at one end of the line, speaking to the bartender as he went.

"All right, Ned, what about Freddie Coats?" the sheriff asked, looking the first man up and down.

"Freddie was here all day, Sheriff," the bartender replied. "Him and Norvel Yates, too. You never see one without seeing the other."

Sheriff Deweese looked the next man up and down, saying, "Is that true, Norvel? You and your pard here spent the whole day drinking? Neither of yas was out on the east trail? Neither of yas was over at the old Spanish mission?"

Norvel Yates slung his stringy hair back out of his bloodshot eyes and said, "Me and Freddie at a church? Hell, no, Sheriff Deweese!" He leaned forward an inch, keeping one steadying hand on the bar top. "We've been blind drunk ever since we hit town three days ago. You heard the barkeep. We was here all day, far as I remember."

"I needed to hear it from you," said Sheriff Deweese, shoving Norvel back against the bar. He stepped in front of Reggie Weil and asked, "What about you, Reggie? Have you and your pal Thurman here been out and around, stirring up trouble along the stage route?"

Before Reggie could gather himself enough to give an answer, Thurman Pratt cut in, saying, "Sheriff, you know damn well me and Reggie was here. If you can't take Ned's word, then why don't you just—"

His words were cut short in a puff of breath as Sheriff Deweese slammed a hard right into his naked stomach, lifting him up onto his toes.

"Now, everybody, listen up!" said the sheriff, turning to the others while Thurman Pratt struggled to catch his breath, both arms thrown across his stomach. "I don't want to repeat one damn word I say here." He turned back to Thurman Pratt. "Was you and Reggie out on the east road yesterday at any time?"

"No," Thurman Pratt replied in a strained wheeze, "we wasn't, Sheriff. We . . . spent the whole day here."

"That's good," said Sheriff Deweese, patting a hand on Thurman's shoulder. "Now, who were the two boys I heard you was drinking with last night?"

"Sheriff, you knew who they was," Thurman rasped.

"All the same, you'd best tell me, Thurman Pratt," said Sheriff Deweese, "else I'll keep cracking you in the ribs till you do." He drew back a fist.

"All right, Sheriff," Thurman Pratt said, raising a hand in a show of submission. "It was the Delmano brothers, Saul and Ramon."

Hearing the name Saul Delmano, Tim Strange felt his pulse quicken. But he sat still, listening closely.

"So you remembered the Delmano brothers being here," said the sheriff. He turned his eyes to Reggie Weil. "I reckon you remember it, too, don't you, Reggie, even as blind drunk as you was?"

Reggie nodded, saying, "I do remember them being here, Sheriff. That's a fact. We drank with 'em most of the day."

Sheriff Deweese turned his gaze to Ned Lynnly behind the bar and asked, "Does that sound about right, Ned?"

"I remember them being here, Sheriff," Ned Lynnly replied.

"All day?" asked Deweese.

"I can't say, Sheriff," said the bartender. "It got awfully busy in here."

"They was here all day, for sure, Sheriff," Thurman Pratt lied, his stomach settling now. "They left for only a few minutes, is all, just long enough to go to the jake and get their horses from out front of Mama Rosa's. Saul Delmano has enough trouble as it is right now. . . . He wasn't looking for more."

"Yeah, I know all about his trouble," said Deweese. "I heard there's a gunman dogging him. I heard all about the bounty, too." Sheriff Deweese looked around at the other men along the bar and the ones seated at the table. "I'm going to tell every one of you: There'd better not be any gunplay in my town over that bounty money. I won't stand for it. If you boys want to collect some money for killing, there's plenty of *legal* bounty on Saul Delmano. Anything that ain't legal, you'd best leave it alone. Does everybody hear me good and plain?"

Some of the men nodded. Thurman Pratt cut in, saying, "Then why didn't you come get Saul last night, Sheriff, if you heard he was here?"

Sheriff Deweese glared at him. "Am I going have to hit you again, Thurman?"

"No, Sheriff," said Thurman, "but the fact is, we all know you and old man Delmano have something worked out between yourselves. Saul Delmano was here if you wanted him."

Sheriff Deweese let it pass. "Boys, Saul Delmano is not wanted for breaking any law in my jurisdiction, or anywhere in Texas for that matter. Leastwise not yet anyway." He looked back at Thurman Pratt. "I'm giving you boys ten minutes to get your clothes on and get out of town. I see you here after that, there'll be trouble between us."

"What's this about, Sheriff?" Thurman Pratt asked.

"What's it about?" the sheriff said, turning his level gaze to each man in turn as he spoke. "I'll tell you what this is about. Yesterday the stagecoach was hit out on the east trail. The driver and passengers were killed—one of them was a poor young woman. She was even robbed of her purse!" He had to keep his anger in check as he spoke. "I found that purse this morning on the way back. Found it beside the bodies of Kid Jeffrey and Joe Tully, two men who work for Lewis Delmano." His gaze went right back to Thurman Pratt. "But of course working for the Delmanos doesn't mean his sons were involved, does it, Thurman?" He speared a thin knowing smile. "I mean, knowing they was both here drinking with you all day?"

Thurman Pratt winced. "A young woman was killed?"

"Yep," said the sheriff, studying the look in Thurman's red-rimmed eyes. "Are you still sure the Delmano brothers was with you all day?"

Thurman swallowed as if something was caught in his throat. He glanced at Reggie Weil, then back to the sheriff, saying, "Well, it seemed like they were."

"It seemed like?" Sheriff Deweese asked, stepping in closer with a deep piercing stare. "You just said they was *for sure*. Now you're saying it *seemed like* they were? Do you need to talk to me in private, Thurman?"

Thurman shot a nervous glance around at the others, then shook his head, saying, "No, Sheriff, I told you all I can."

"All right, then," said Sheriff Deweese to the four men along the bar, "you four men get dressed and get moving. My watch is already ticking."

Thurman Pratt, Reggie Weil, Norvel Yates, and Freddie Coats filed away from the bar and back up the stairs, the two deputies close behind them. Sheriff Deweese stepped over to the table and looked down at the first of the five men sitting there.

"Stanley Bush?" he said out loud as if surprised to see the man cowering there at the table. Deweese turned to the third deputy, who stood guarding the men with a shotgun. "Hell, Wayne," he said to the deputy, "Stanley ain't got enough sense to find the east road, let along a stagecoach." He nodded toward the door, saying, "Get out of here, Stanley, before I arrest you for being stupid."

Stanley Bush scurried up from the table and out the door.

The new deputy, Wayne Connick, looked embarrassed. "You said round up everybody out front, so I did."

"I understand," said Deweese, looking down at the next man, a quiet stranger with a flat-brim Stetson sitting low on his forehead. "What about you, mister?" Deweese asked, looking the stranger up and down.

"What about me?" the stranger replied, not giving an inch.

"What's your name? What are you doing here in El Paso?" Deweese asked.

"My name's Jack Smith, but you can call me *Mr.* Smith. I'm here to meet a friend. I don't rob stagecoaches, I don't steal purses . . . and I don't answer a hell of a lot questions." He gave the sheriff a flat, level stare. A pistol butt shone at the edge of his black linen coat, close to his right hand. "I was on my way to breakfast when this deputy showed up. I only came in here out of courtesy. I spent yesterday and last night playing cards with two town councilmen and a Texas judge. Go ask them if you feel like it."

"Sheriff, I already asked one of the councilmen on the way in here," Wayne Connick said, cutting in. "It's true that's where he was all right."

The sheriff looked taken aback for a second. He said to the deputy, "Then what the hell is this man doing in here, Wayne?" Deweese glanced at the pistols still strapped on the remaining four men at the table. "And why are these men still armed?"

Wayne Connick squirmed in place, his face turning red in embarrassment. "I asked Smith here for his gun. He wouldn't give it to me. I reckon these others just followed suit."

Sheriff Deweese looked stunned. "Damn it, Wayne! I know you're new, but don't ever do something like this again!"

Smith stood up slowly, adjusted his hat, and said, "I'll be leaving now, Sheriff, unless you have another question."

"Get out, *Mr.* Smith," Deweese snapped.

But the stranger stopped for a second and pointed down at Tim Strange. "One thing before I go, Sheriff," he said. "That man ain't one of the ones you're looking for either."

"Oh? And what makes you say that?" asked Deweese.

"Because your deputy checked his horse's shoes before we came in. They're worn thin. The deputy said the tracks you found were made by new shoes, hardly worn."

Tim Strange sat watching in silence.

"Just thought I'd mention that to you, Sheriff," said Smith, turning and walking out the door.

Sheriff Deweese turned his attention to Tim Strange, noting the Colt on his hip. "All right, young man, what's your story?"

"I've got no story, Sheriff," said Tim. "I'm here looking for my brother. He's supposed to meet me here today." Tim guarded his words, cutting a quick glance at the two remaining men at the table.

"What's your name?" Deweese asked, getting a bit testy with his job.

"Tim Coffax," said Tim, picking the first name that came to his mind. "My brother's name is Jed Coffax. I got here late last night. I don't know nothing about any stagecoach robbery."

"Yeah?" Sheriff Deweese looked him up and down. "I don't suppose you know anything about a bounty on a gunman who's supposed to be coming this way either?"

"I heard about it, Sheriff," Tim admitted. "Everybody from here to Kansas has heard about it. But I'm not here for it. If I was, I wouldn't be sitting here on my rump. I'd be out there collecting it." He stared up at Deweese and said, "Can I go now?"

Sheriff Deweese didn't answer. Instead, he turned to the other two men, saying, "Dee Philpot and Early Brown, don't even try to tell me you two ain't here looking to collect that bounty."

Dee Philpot, a young gunman with a surly smile, said, "We ain't denying it, Sheriff. Killing for bounty money is what we do. We'll keep it outside of your town. But that's all we can promise."

"That's right," said Early Brown, a heavy young man missing

his right ear. "We ain't innocent lambs, Sheriff, but don't try to tell us you didn't chop off a head or two for bounty before you pinned on a badge."

"Get out, all three of you!" yelled Deweese, jerking a thumb toward the door. "Get out of my town and stay out! If you're smart, you'll get out of this part of the country. From what I've heard, this Danny Duggin ain't going to be an easy day's work."

"We'll see, Sheriff," said Dee Philpot, standing up along with Tim Strange and Early Brown.

Sheriff Deweese and Deputy Wayne Connick stood in the middle of the saloon floor and watched the three men leave.

Behind the bar, Ned the bartender cleared his throat and said in a sarcastic tone of voice, "Are we all through, Sheriff, or is there a few more paying customers you'd like to chase away from here?"

Sheriff Deweese spun to face him, his anger screwing up his reddening face. "Don't give me a hard time doing my job, Ned. I'll board this place up and have the town condemn it! I believe the Delmanos had something to do with that stagecoach robbery. And I believe you and Thurman Pratt are lying for them!"

"Hold it, Sheriff," said Ned Lynnly. "I told you I was too busy to pay attention to everybody's comings and goings yesterday. If you want to know more about the Delmanos, go ask their father. You and him are always on good speaking terms from what I hear."

Just outside the saloon doors, Tim Strange heard what the bartender said, but he didn't let on. He felt the eyes of Early Brown and Dee Philpot on him as he stepped down to his horse at the hitch rail. He took his time unhitching his horse. Tim knew they wanted to say something. He wanted to give them the opportunity.

"Hey, you, Coffax, hold up a minute," said Early Brown as he and Dee Philpot stepped over to the hitch rail, keeping a few feet distance between themselves and Tim Strange. "What's your hurry?"

Tim turned just enough to acknowledge them with a trace of a flat smile. "You heard the sheriff," he said. "I wouldn't want to get myself in any trouble with the law." His nervous tone of voice implied that getting in trouble with the law would be a new experience for him.

Early Brown and Dee Philpot shared a short laugh. "Right," said Dee Philpot, "that's our thoughts, too." He and Early Brown looked at each other. Then Philpot continued. "What you told the sheriff in there about not being here for the bounty? I'm betting my pard here that it wasn't quite true, was it?" He spread a knowing grin.

"I hope you boys aren't calling me a liar," said Tim calmly. He looked them up and down, taking his time adjusting his saddle.

"Naw, it's nothing like that," said Dee Philpot, backstepping the tone of his voice a little, keeping it friendly. "We're looking for this Danny Duggin . . . thought a three-way split might be worth making if a man knew something about Duggin that we don't."

Tim Strange took a deep breath and let it out, shaking his head slowly. "Fellows, why would I want to split a bounty with anybody if I *really* was after Danny Duggin? I doubt either of you even know what he looks like, do you?"

"Well, no," said Early Brown. "Do you?"

"Yep," said Tim. "I've seen him more than a few times in Kansas."

Early Brown looked interested. "Really, now? All we know is that he's young, rides a chestnut mare, and carries a brace of Colt pistols."

"So what?" Tim said. "Look at me. I'm young. I wear two pistols—*one* of them is a Colt. I don't ride a chestnut mare, but I might have changed horses along the trail. For all you know, I could be Danny Duggin."

Early Brown looked puzzled for a second, then said, "You're not, are you?"

"No. If I was, I expect you'd both be dead by now," Tim said. He turned back as if to step into his saddle. "Sorry, boys, but I don't need any partners. All I need to know is where to take this Duggin's head once I kill him."

"That's easy enough," said Dee Philpot. "We know how to get

to the Delmano spread. We'd gladly show you if we was in on this together."

Tim stopped, appearing to give it some thought. Then he nodded at the doors of the saloon. "What about that Thurman Pratt and his partner? I figure if they're friends of the Delmanos, they'll be after Duggin, too. There's only so many ways to split two thousand dollars before it turns into nothing more than pocket change."

Early Brown and Dee Philpot stepped in closer. Dee Philpot lowered his voice and said, "See? That's the thing about this bounty. Everybody in this part of the country is out to collect it. We figured we could catch Thurman and Reggie off to themselves and do away with part of the competition, so to speak."

"You might have something there," said Tim. "How do you know which way they'll be headed when they leave here?"

"They get on across the border," said Dee Philpot. "They'll be easy to take care of. What do you think? Have we got ourselves a deal?"

Tim looked back and forth between the two of them, knowing that whatever deal he struck with these men would be worthless. If there was a bounty to be collected, they would shoot him in the back as soon as they were through with him.

"Why not?" he said finally. "It would be better splitting something with you two than being cut out altogether by this Thurman Pratt and his pal." Tim stepped up into his saddle. "Come on, let's go somewhere and talk about it."

"We're right behind you," said Dee Philpot.

He and Early Brown smiled at each other and reached for their horses' reins.

CHAPTER 15

J ed Strange had just boarded the chestnut mare at the livery barn
and led his own horse out to the street when he saw the deputy
round up Tim along with some other men out front of the saloon.
Their intentions had been to keep a distance between themselves
and work their way around town, finding out what they could about
the Delmanos and about how many men were out to collect the
bounty money. But as soon as he'd seen his brother walk into the
saloon under the cover of a shotgun, Jed had backed inside the livery
barn and stood watching through a crack in the door.

He'd stood tense for a few minutes and breathed a sigh of relief
when he'd seen the first man come out and hurry away. He'd
breathed even easier when another walked out, stepped into his
saddle, and rode away. Now, seeing Tim and the two other men
ride their horses at a walk along the street, Jed stepped out of the
door to let his brother get a look at him and hopefully give him
some sign of what was going on.

As Tim and the two men came past him, Jed lowered his hat
brim slightly and saw his brother nod ever so slightly toward the
road leading out of town. Jed got the message. He moved back
inside the barn, waiting until the three riders were past him and
on the road toward the border. Then he went back to the hitch rail,
swung up into his saddle, and heeled the horse forward.

Outside of the town limits, Tim Strange, Dee Philpot, and Early

Brown swung off the road, found an old path leading to the shallows of the Rio Grande, and stepped their horses down into the river. As soon as they had stepped up on the Mexico side of the river and moved away through some brush, Jed Strange nudged his horse forward, down into the river, following them. When his horse stepped out on the other side of the bank, dripping water, Jed nudged it forward, but stayed to the left of Tim and the others' hoofprints, keeping in the brush and hidden from sight. From his position, Jed could also look back on the Rio Grande, where he soon saw Thurman Pratt and Reggie Weil slip down into the shallows and come across.

"Lord, Tim, what have you gotten us into now?" he asked himself in a whispered breath. Before the two men stepped their horses up onto the low banks, Jed had heeled his horse away, staying wide of the fresh hoofprints in front of him.

Two miles farther up the trail, Tim, Dee Philpot, and Early Brown had taken cover behind a low shelf of rock. Tim sipped water from his canteen and listened as Dee Philpot spoke to him. Early Brown slipped a rifle from his saddle boot and moved in a crouch to the edge of the rock.

"Don't worry, pard. Early will spot them as soon as they make the bend in the trail," said Dee Philpot.

"Do I look worried?" Tim replied. "I can't say I cotton much to ambushing, though. I always figured a man who'll ambush another will someday ambush me if I ain't careful."

It seemed to take a moment for his words to sink in as Dee Philpot stood staring blank faced. But finally Dee got it and laughed, tapping a finger to his forehead. "I see what you mean, Coffax. But you don't have to worry about me and Early double-crossing you."

"Like I said," Tim repeated, "do I *look* worried?" He gazed off along the trail into Mexico and said, "How far is it to the Delmano spread?"

"It's a day's ride straight ahead," said Dee Philpot.

Tim smiled, saying, "If it's straight ahead, why do I need you and Early to show me?"

"Because there's more to it than just finding the Delmano spread. Most times you have to get past the spread and up into the rock country. The Delmanos keep a hideout up there. You could search for days and never find it on your own. Early and I spent the winter up there a couple of years ago, lying low after killing a Mexican land baron. Once you're there, you can see anybody coming at you for miles below."

"I see," said Tim. He turned his eyes back to Early Brown as he continued speaking to Dee Philpot. "Did you ever hear why Danny Duggin is hunting Saul Delmano?"

"Not really," said Philpot. "It had something to do with Saul and some friends of his killing this Duggin's father, is what I heard. But it doesn't matter none. Alls I know is there is two thousand dollars in it for us." He grinned. "Everybody's daddy dies sooner or later, I reckon."

"Yeah," said Tim, barely able to keep his anger from showing on his face, "I reckon so."

"Here they come!" Early Brown said in a lowered voice, sounding excited at the prospect of killing men from behind his cover of rock. "You'd best get ready, boys!"

Dee Philpot snatched his rifle from his saddle boot and hurried over in a crouch, slipping down beside Early Brown and saying over his shoulder to Tim, "Come on, Coffax. This ought to be good practice for when we get to Danny Duggin!"

"Yep," said Tim, walking over to the edge without so much as bending down as Thurman Pratt and Reggie Weil rode around the turn in the trail.

"Damn it, Coffax!" Dee Philpot hissed. "Get down here before they see you!"

But Tim only stood staring at the two riders, his hand resting on the pistol at his hip. "Thurman Pratt," he called out loudly.

"Jesus! What's he doing?" Early Brown bellowed.

"Damned if I know!"

Dee Philpot tried to swing his rifle barrel up toward Tim, but seeing him make the move, Tim clamped a boot down on it, pinning it to the rock shelf. At the same time Tim drew and cocked his Colt, pointing it down at both Philpot and Brown.

On the road, Thurman Pratt and Reggie Weil reined their horses to a sudden halt at the sound of Tim's voice. They looked up at him standing seven feet above them, twenty feet ahead, the cocked pistols in his hands.

"Who is it? The hell do you want?" Thurman Pratt called out, his hand going to the revolver on his hip.

"I'm Coffax," Tim called out. "I was in the saloon when the sheriff busted you in the gut. There's a couple of boys here wanting to ambush you. I thought I'd put you all in the same circle and see which ones fall out."

"Coffax, you fool!" Dee Philpot said in a harsh growl. "We're supposed to be partners! Damn you!"

"Oh?" said Thurman Pratt. "And who might that be?" As he spoke, he and Reggie Weil stepped slowly down from their horses, dropping their reins to the ground.

"Dee Philpot and Early Brown," said Tim. "They've been waiting here to shoot you out of your saddles when you came around the turn. Are you ready to face off with them?"

"You're mighty damn right we are!" shouted Thurman Pratt. "We was friends once. Rode together! Hell, Dee still owes me seven dollars from two years ago, and I never hounded him for it! Come on out here, Dee, you sneaking son of a bitch!"

Tim stepped back, keeping his pistol pointed down at Philpot and Brown. "Come on up, *partners*," he said. "Here's you a chance to prove what kind of gunmen you are."

"You've lost your mind, Coffax." Dee Philpot hissed, standing up, unable to lift his rifle with Tim's boot standing on it. "When this is over, you'd better hope to God I don't come up here and—"

"Shut your mouth," Tim snapped, cutting him off. "Get on down there. Don't keep these men waiting."

"What's your interest in this, Coffax?" Thurman Pratt called out to Tim, watching Philpot and Brown pick their way down from the rock shelf to the middle of the dusty road.

"I just don't like back shooters and bushwhackers," said Tim, keeping his pistol pointed at the two men, watching them stop twenty feet from Thurman Pratt and Reggie Weil and plant their feet a shoulder's width apart.

"Why was you boys doing this, Dee?" Thurman asked, already opening and closing his fingers to loosen them up. "I never treated either one of you any way but right."

"It's for that bounty money, Thurman," said Dee Philpot. He shot a sidelong glance up at Tim, then settled himself toward Thurman and Reggie. "We might just as well get on with it. Soon as we kill you both, me and Early is going to have to kill this jack-potting peckerwood, too."

"Don't count us dead yet!" Reggie Weil shouted, his hand going for his pistol.

"Wait, Reggie!" shouted Thurman Pratt.

But it was too late. Reggie Weil's move brought the tension to a head. Dee Philpot's pistol came up from his holster, cocked and firing. Beside him, Early Brown did the same. Both of their first shots went toward Thurman, whose draw was slower than Reggie Weil's, but whose aim was known to be more deadly. Reggie Weil fired repeatedly, his shots whistling past Philpot and Brown like mad hornets, the two men flinching at the sound yet still firing.

A shot hit Thurman Pratt in the chest, driving him back a staggering step, but not taking him off his feet. He struggled, getting a good bead on Early Brown, his shot punching through Brown's right shoulder and exiting in a long ribbon of blood. Early Brown flew backward, getting off another shot, which caught Thurman Pratt in the leg, making him drop to his knees as he returned fire.

"Son of a—!" Reggie Weil screamed, his words cut short when he felt two bullets hit him at almost the same time. His pistol exploded twice, one shot clipping Dee Philpot's hat from his head, the other shot nailing Early Brown as Brown struggled back to his feet, still firing, staggering sidelong as blood sprayed upward from his collarbone.

Dee Philpot managed to get off two more shots, both of them

hitting Thurman Pratt in his chest. This time Thurman was done for. He twisted back and forth as he sank from his knees to the ground, his gun going off one last time, the shot going wild as his face hit the dirt. On his knees beside his fallen partner, Reggie Weil fired until his hammer fell on an empty chamber. He tried punching out his spent rounds to reload. Twenty feet away, Dee Philpot did the same, seeing Early Brown stagger back and forth, his pistol hanging limp in his hand.

Before Reggie Weil could snap the cylinder shut on his reloaded pistol, Dee Philpot had reloaded and cocked his Colt and stalked forward with it out at arm's length, pointing at Reggie's face.

Reggie screamed, "You rotten bastard, I never dreamed it was you who'd kill me!"

The shot from Dee Philpot's pistol kicked him backward into the dirt like a limp bundle of rags. Philpot stopped and turned, looking back at Early Brown, then up to the edge of the rock shelf, where he saw no sign of Tim.

"Come on, Early! We're going to kill that peckerwood!"

Early Brown shook himself out like a horse, blood streaming from his wounds. "Look at me, Dee! Look what he caused here!" Brown cried out. He staggered as he ran toward the path leading upward.

"Don't let him get away, Early!" Dee Philpot yelled, scrambling upward over stones and loose sand and gravel.

At the top of the rock shelf, they looked toward the horses, their pistols still cocked and ready.

"It's two agin one, Early. Let's find him!"

"Over here, boys," said Tim in a quiet voice.

They spun to their right and saw Tim with his Colt holstered, his hand poised near the handle. But before they could fire, another voice called out from their left.

"No, over here!" said Jed Strange. They spun in Jed's direction, seeing the rifle in his hands.

Dee Philpot felt cold fear run through him, seeing these two men were ready and determined and had caught them completely off guard. "Who are you people?" Dee Philpot demanded. "What's this all about?" His eyes went to Jed Strange, seeing the resemblance. "Are you Danny Duggin? Is that it? You're Duggin and you two are brothers?" His eyes flashed back and forth.

Beside him, Early Brown stood frozen in place, waiting for Philpot to make the first move.

"We're neither one Danny Duggin," said Tim Strange. "But we're kin of hers."

"Kin of *hers*? What the hell are you talking about, *hers*?" Philpot shouted.

"That's right, Philpot," said Tim. "Danny Duggin is our sister."

Philpot looked baffled, but only for a second. Rage took over as he swung his pistol toward Tim Strange. "Why, you crazy damn fool!" he screamed.

Three shots rang out, two from Tim's Colt and one from Jed's rifle. In the silence that followed, Tim stepped forward and looked down at Dee Philpot's wide-open eyes beneath the bullet hole in his forehead. He cut his gaze to the bodies of Thurman Pratt and Reggie Weil lying down below them in the middle of the road.

Opening his pistol and dropping out the spent cartridges, he said to Jed, "Four down . . . but how many more to go?"

"That's anybody's guess, brother," said Jed. "Come on. Let's get them bodies out of the road and get moving."

It was almost noon when Danielle walked out of the livery barn, leading the chestnut mare behind her. She walked the mare over to where C. F. McCord and Hector Sabio stood watering the horses at a trough. "They've been here," Danielle said, patting Sundown's muzzle. "The hostler said a young man named Jed paid for a week's board in advance. Said if his brother, Danny, showed up to let him take the mare with him."

C. F. McCord ran his sweaty bandanna across his forehead beneath his hat brim. "When was this?" he asked.

"This morning, not long after sunup," said Danielle. "He also told me there's been a stage robbery and four killings. The sheriff questioned some men in the saloon this morning."

McCord poured himself a mouthful of water from his canteen, swished it around, and spat it out. "Saul Delmano," he said, wiping a hand across his mouth. "I'd bet on it."

Danielle reached beneath the belly of the horse she'd been riding. She loosened its saddle, taking it off as the horse drank from the water trough. She turned and laid the saddle atop Sundown and cinched it tight. Then she pulled the drinking horse's muzzle up from the trough, unfastened the bridle, and slipped the bit from its mouth. The horse slung its head and stuck its muzzle back down into the water.

"What are you doing?" McCord asked, watching her slip the bit into Sundown's mouth and string the bridle up behind the mare's ears.

"What does it look like I'm doing?" Danielle said. "I'm getting this gal ready for the road."

"But everybody who's out to collect that bounty knows that Danny Duggin rides a chestnut mare," McCord said.

"*Sí,*" said Hector Sabio, "you are asking for trouble, Danny. This is not a good idea."

"Good idea or not, I'm riding her," said Danielle. "If we're in the Delmanos' stomping ground, why not let everybody know I'm here? They're out to kill me. . . . I'm out to kill Saul Delmano. I've got nothing to hide."

C. F. McCord had trouble with it for a second, but then, after thinking it over, he tossed Hector a quick glance and saw the worried look on his face. Then he said to Danielle, "You're right. . . . Why not?" He lifted his horse's muzzle from the water trough and retightened its cinch. "Let's go to the sheriff's office and see what he can tell us about the stage robbery or Saul Delmano."

"Why?" asked Danielle. "It's got nothing to do with what we're here for."

"Call it my courtesy call as a lawman," said McCord. "I still wear a badge, you know. He might also be able to tell us something about your brothers. Let's find out what we can before we move on."

"I don't know, *amigos*," said Hector Sabio. He looked greatly concerned, rubbing his chin. "I think we should go on and get into Mexico. I know this sheriff. I don't think he likes me so much."

"Is there any charge against you, Hector?" McCord asked.

"No, it is nothing like that," Hector replied.

"Then don't worry," said McCord. "You're with me now, Hector. Unless he has an outstanding charge against you, you're in good hands."

"Even so," Hector said with great reluctance, "I think it is best that I stay here and take care of the horses."

"All right, then," said McCord, "you stay here and watch the horses. We won't be long." McCord turned to Danielle and together they walked along the dirt street toward the sheriff's office.

Glancing back over her shoulder, Danielle said to McCord, "I hope you're not trusting him too much, Marshal. Don't forget: He didn't exactly come into this thing with clean hands."

McCord offered a thin smile, staring straight ahead. "You have to learn to have more faith in people."

"Maybe," said Danielle, "but so far it's been my *lack* of faith in outlaws like Hector that's kept me alive."

McCord shook his head, still wearing the same thin smile. "Why, Danny, what a terrible thing to say."

Hector Sabio watched Danielle and C. F. McCord walk away until they both stepped inside the door to the sheriff's office.

"Aw, *amigos*," he whispered to himself, "you do not know how *big* two thousand dollars is to a man such as me." He rubbed his palm back and forth on the butt of the pistol shoved down in his waist belt. "But forgive me," he added under his breath, making a quick sign of the cross on his chest as his eyes darted to heaven. "I must not think such things." He leaned back against the hitch rail and let out a long breath.

CHAPTER 16

Riding into town, Al Tarksel was the first to spot Hector Sabio. As soon as he saw Hector, Tarksel grabbed the reins to Bob Dennard's horse and jerked them sideways, leading them out of the street and into an alley before Hector had a chance to see them.

"What's going on?" Dennard said, wrestling for control of his horse. "Have you gone mad?"

Dennard's hand had just dropped to his pistol butt when Al Tarksel let go of his reins and spoke in excitement.

"There's that snake, Hector!" said Tarksel. "Up by the livery barn! I saw him!"

Bob Dennard eased down, moving his hand away from his pistol. He slipped down from his horse and pitched Al Tarksel his reins. "Wait here," he said. "I'll make sure."

He inched out of the alley past the edge of the boardwalk and peeped around a post toward the livery barn. Then he stepped back inside the alley, looking back and forth along the dirt street. "You're right. It's him. Danny Duggin must be close at hand."

"All right, then," said Tarksel, slipping down from his saddle, "I say we gun Duggin down right here in the street, then grab his body and make a run for it." Tarksel fell silent, then added, "But damn it! What about the Fox?"

Dennard looked at him. "Settle down, Tarksel. You're getting too anxious."

"Anxious, hell!" Tarksel growled. "If we wait until Duggin gets to the Delmanos', there'll be no bounty. . . . They'll kill him themselves and save two thousand dollars. We've got to make our move!"

"Of course we have to," Dennard agreed. He nodded toward the livery barn. "But the Mexican is holding their horses. So wherever Duggin is, he'll have to go back there to get his horse. We're not going to start blazing away in the middle of the street! We'll wait until Duggin gets inside the livery barn, kill him nice and quiet-like, then get out of town."

"What about the Fox?" asked Al Tarksel.

"McCord will have to die, too," said Dennard.

"That might not be so easy to get away with," said Tarksel.

"Have you got any better idea?" Dennard asked, getting impatient.

Tarksel winced, trying to think of one. "Damn, I reckon not."

"Then don't argue with me." Dennard hissed. "Come on, bring the horses."

"All right, but I have some serious misgivings about killing a lawman right here in town," Tarksel grumbled. He snatched the reins to both horses and followed Dennard back to end of the alley, which led to the rear of the livery barn.

Inside the sheriff's office, C. F. McCord and Danielle poured a cup of coffee and spoke to the new deputy, Wayne Connick, who sat behind Sheriff Deweese's big desk with both hands firmly clutching the chair arms. The deputy was plainly nervous after McCord had introduced both himself and Danny Duggin to him.

"Heck, Fox—I mean, Marshal McCord—it could be all day before the sheriff gets back. He left me here because I'm the newest man he's got. I'd tell you whatever I could, except I just don't *know* much." He nodded at Danielle. "I do know that Mr. Duggin here had better watch himself. All we've heard the past week is how every gunman and two-bit outlaw around is planning on collecting that bounty money."

Danielle shrugged it off. "What about this young fellow you told us about, this Tim Coffax?" she asked, already certain it was her brother.

"What about him?" Wayne Connick asked. "I took him into the saloon, Sheriff Deweese questioned him, and then he let him go. He didn't seem to be interested in the bounty money . . . but then he did leave town with a couple of backstabbing rascals named Early Brown and Dee Philpot. Is that any help to you?"

"Yep, quite a bit," Danielle said, sipping her coffee. "Which way did they head out?"

"I heard the three of them headed for the border," said the deputy. "I hope he's not hooked up with those two. They're both killers."

"He's not. That boy is one of my brothers. You did the right thing letting him go. I've got two brothers. . . . Neither one of them had anything to do with a stage robbery. I can promise you that much."

Leaning against the hitch rail, Hector Sabio gave no thought to the sound of the livery barn door creaking open behind him. The street out front of the livery barn was empty except for a skinny spotted dog that stood with its nose to the hard ground. No one saw Al Tarksel slip up quietly behind Hector, throw a big arm around his neck, and drag him backward into the barn. Hector tried to let out a yell, but Tarksel's forearm cut off his air.

"I'll just take that pistol, you rotten little worm!" Tarksel slammed Hector against a barn pole and snatched the gun from his waist.

Hector caught a quick breath and started to lunge forward with his bare hands toward Al Tarksel's throat. But the cold bite of Bob Dennard's pistol cocking against Hector's temple stopped him and kept him frozen in place.

"Make a decision fast, Mex," Dennard growled in Hector's ear. "Either help us kill Danny Duggin or die alongside him."

Hector stalled, saying, "What are you talking about? I am not out to kill Danny Duggin for the bounty money! He has become my friend! I would not betray an *amigo!*"

"You lying weasel!" said Tarksel. "I know you, and I know how you think! You've been after that bounty money all along!" Tarksel grabbed Hector by his hair and banged his head against the pole. "Let me kill him, Dennard!" Tarksel sneered. "We don't need this little rat to lure them in here."

Dennard looked deep into Hector's eyes and said to Tarksel with a nasty grin, "Be my guest, Al. But take him back there somewhere and do it. Let's keep things quiet in here." He lowered the pistol from Hector's temple and walked to the front door, peeping out through a crack between the planks.

Al Tarksel slung the much smaller Hector Sabio toward the back of the barn. As Hector sprawled on the floor, Tarksel sprang forward beside him and kicked him in the ribs, raising Hector a foot off the dirt floor, leaving him gagging and choking for air.

"We can keep it quiet all right, *Hec—tor*! But I owe you something fierce for that beating I took in Dodge. Your last minutes are going to be the worst you ever had!" He snatched Hector up from the floor and backhanded him back and forth into an empty stall.

At the front of the barn, Bob Dennard looked around and called out in a harsh whisper, "Here they come! Hurry up and finish him off."

Al Tarksel held Hector up by the front of his shirt with one hand. Hector struggled to keep his head from swaying limply.

"*Sí*," he said, managing to straighten himself and spread a battered crooked smile, "finish me off, you big tough *pig* of a man!" He spat a spray of blood into Al Tarksel's face. "Break my neck with your *cerdo* hands!"

Tarksel snatched his pistol from his holster, cocked it, and jammed it into Hector's belly, wiping blood from his face with his free shirt cuff. "Uh-uh, Hec—tor," Tarksel said in a taunting voice. "You ain't getting off that easy."

"Take that blasted gun out of his belly and kill him quietly, damn it!" Bob Dennard hissed from the front door.

"No, Bob, I'm keeping him alive till this is over. I want to take my time on this little border trash!"

"Shut up, then!" Dennard hissed. "They're almost here! Get ready!"

Hector looked down at the cocked pistol jammed against his stomach and shook his bloody head. "You are such a stupid man, Al Tarksel," he whispered. "I will never allow you to kill me."

Then before Al Tarksel could stop him, Hector reached down, grabbed the pistol with both hands, and forced Tarksel's finger to pull the trigger. The explosion lifted Hector off the ground; then he slumped against Al Tarksel with smoke and fire rising from the open wound in the back of his shirt.

Tarksel shrieked, "This crazy son of a bitch!" He jumped back from the torrent of Hector Sabio's blood as he hit the floor. Somehow, Hector was still alive and managed to start crawling toward the rear door.

"Damn you to hell!" Bob Dennard shouted at Tarksel. Seeing the element of surprise was now gone, Dennard swung the door open and sprang forward with his pistol blazing.

The warning shot that Hector Sabio had caused was all the time C. F. McCord and Danielle needed to get ready. Bob Dennard ran headlong into four shots that exploded almost as one, spinning him in place, then hammering him back inside the barn doors. As Dennard spun off a barn pole, his pistol exploded wildly in his hand. The shot hit Al Tarksel as tried to lift the latch on the rear door and make a run for it. Tarksel staggered backward and slumped down by the open stall door, where he'd left Hector Sabio lying in the dirt and straw.

Outside, C. F. McCord called out, "Drop your guns and step out here with your hands raised high!"

By the time Hector Sabio had dragged his shattered body across the stall and halfway out the open gate, Al Tarksel was flat on his back, a hand pressed to the gaping exit wound in his lower stomach. He heard Hector's weak gurgling breath and turned sideways on the dirt to face him. Only inches of dirt and straw lay between them.

"This is your last chance in there!" C. F. McCord called out again.

"What . . . are you . . . grinning about?" Al Tarksel asked, his words getting hard to come by.

Hector Sabio could not answer past the thick, dark blood in his mouth, nor did he even try to. With all of his effort, he reached out and clasped both bloody hands around Tarksel's pistol lying on the dirt between them. The back of Hector's bloody shirt still smoldered in a widening circle around the gaping bullet hole.

"If you don't come out, we're coming in," C. F. McCord yelled into the barn.

He and Danielle moved up closer, Danielle taking position with her back flat against the barn, her pistol raised, ready to swing around into the open door and fire.

Al Tarksel choked and said in a halting voice to Hector Sabio, "I reckon . . . you really . . . won't . . ."

Hector managed a weak nod, crawling up onto Al Tarksel's large body like a dark spirit until he lay full atop him. With the hammer cocked, Hector raised up the pistol and pointed it at Tarksel, letting all of his weight press down on it. The tip of the barrel was rooted down on Tarksel's heart as he pulled the trigger.

"Hector? Are you in there?" Danielle said into the darkness of the barn as she stepped inside with McCord. "Speak to us, Hector. We heard the shot."

McCord stepped over to Bob Dennard's body and nudged it with his boot. Danielle made out the two shapes on the floor out front of the rear stall and quickened her steps. She heard a moan as she reached down atop Al Tarksel and rolled Hector off him. Hector Sabio looked up at her with glazed eyes. She bent down, seeing the large hole blown through him, bits of straw clinging deep inside his open stomach.

"Oh, God, Hector—no!" So severe was his wound, she saw no way to even cradle him on her lap without causing more torment. Biting her lip, she held her hands down close to his wound as if that was all she could do to comfort him. "You did this, didn't you, Hector? You did it to warn us!" She sobbed. She felt C. F. McCord's hand rest on her shoulder as he bent down beside her.

"*Sí . . .*" Hector somehow managed to gasp. His bloody right hand found hers and tried to squeeze it, his eyes drifting between hers and McCord's. "*Amigos*, eh . . . ?"

"*Sí, amigos,*" Danielle whispered, holding his hand to her face,

McCord nodding with her as he reached a hand out and placed it on Hector's shoulder in confirmation.

Hector's last breath came out softly like a child at rest, and his open eyes stared blankly into the rafters overhead.

"He's gone," McCord said gently. "Let him go."

Danielle looked up at McCord with tears streaming down her cheeks, her pistol lying loosely across her lap. Without reserve she fell forward into his outstretched arms and wept shamelessly against his chest.

"I know," McCord whispered. "It's all right. Let it out. It's time you got rid of it. I'm here. I'm not leaving you . . . and nobody's going to kill us. You have my word."

For the following few moments, McCord held her pressed to his chest, knowing that Danielle had seen far too many people die to let it affect her this way. Yet there was something at work here that he knew she had to get out of her system. He, too, was remorseful about Hector Sabio's death rightly enough. He'd brought Hector with him on a manhunt. He'd known the risk and so had Hector Sabio. But there was far deeper sorrow inside this woman than even she realized. McCord had seen it coming since the day they'd met. Nobody could remain so tough for so long without it spilling out somewhere—nobody should ever have to, he thought.

When Wayne Connick ran to the open door with a shotgun in his hand, followed by some onlookers who ventured forth to see what the shooting was about, McCord separated from Danielle and waved them all away.

"Stay back, Deputy. We need a few minutes here to sort things out."

Wayne Connick turned to the gathering crowd, shouting, "All right, you heard the marshal. Stay back! This is a law matter. Let us handle it!"

"Come on," McCord whispered in Danielle's ear, seeing that her tears had subsided. "Let's get up."

Together they rose to their feet, Danielle's Colt falling to the dirt. McCord bent down, picked it up, and shoved it down into her holster.

"It—it needs to be reloaded," Danielle whispered. She started to reach for the pistol, but McCord's hand closed gently on hers, stopping her.

"Not this second, it doesn't. I've got you covered, Danny Duggin, for as long as you need me. Wipe your face and straighten yourself up. We'll get out of here, make a camp somewhere, and head out first thing come morning. We both need some rest."

They walked toward the door, Danielle leaning against McCord's side for strength. But before they reached the eyes of the onlookers, Danielle stood straight on her own and lowered her hat brim on her forehead.

"The Mexican's name is Hector Sabio, Deputy," McCord said as they walked to the hitch rail through the parting crowd. "See that he's buried proper. He's our *amigo*."

Danielle and McCord mounted up and rode out of town. Once across the Rio Grande, they found the fresh tracks along the Mexican side of the shallows and made a camp under the canopy of an ancient piñon, out of the afternoon heat.

"It could be hard finding the Delmanos' hideout without Hector along to show us," said McCord.

"My brothers are ahead somewhere," Danielle replied. "If there's any way to find the hideout, they will. But we can't let them get too far ahead of us."

"We won't," said McCord. "After we've rested, we can travel all this evening and through the night if you want to. After what happened back there, I just thought we ought to take ourselves a breather. We've pushed hard these past few days."

"I've been pushing hard this whole past year," Danielle said, spreading her blanket on the ground. She took off her hat and boots and lay down, crossing a forearm over her face. "Sometimes I have a hard time remembering what life was like before I started down the vengeance trail."

McCord came over and sat down on the corner of her blanket. "It was good," he said with a tired smile.

"How would you know my life was good?" Danielle asked.

"Anything compared to *this* kind of life had to be good." McCord reached out, pulled a long stem of wild grass, and stuck it between his teeth. "I wish I'd known you then."

"You say it like you think it might have made a difference of some kind," Danielle said.

"It might have," McCord said.

She sighed. "No, it wouldn't have. I know for a fact it wouldn't."

McCord chuckled under his breath. "Funny how I can't know it *might* have . . . but you know *for a fact* that it wouldn't."

Danielle smiled with her forearm across her eyes. "You couldn't have kept me from doing what I had to do. That's the part I know for a fact."

"But knowing you, maybe I could've helped. That's the part that I think might have made a difference."

"Well, you know me now," said Danielle. A silence passed. Then Danielle added in a softer tone, "I think having you with me has made a difference. It hasn't been as lonely." She smiled playfully. "And you don't eat much. . . . It's been cheaper than buying a dog."

"Thanks," said McCord. He took the stem of grass from his mouth and studied it, twirling it back and forth between his fingers. His voice turned more serious. "Once this is all over, what will you do?" he asked. "Where will you go?"

"I don't know," Danielle said. "I've tried not to ask myself that question."

"It needs asking," McCord said.

"I know." Danielle turned onto her side, facing him.

"But I haven't had the time to think about it. I haven't *allowed* myself to think about it."

"I understand," said McCord, "because it scares a person sometimes to make plans . . . knowing there's a good possibility they won't be around long enough to carry them out. I've caught myself feeling the same way."

She studied his face as he looked away, back toward the border, the river, and beyond. "You're not like most lawmen I've met," said Danielle.

"Really?" McCord smiled. "Well, you're not like any gunmen I've ever met."

"You got me there." They shared a short laugh. "I get the idea that when we're finished down here, you're not going to go back to marshaling," Danielle said, "in spite of your big reputation."

"A reputation never meant that much to me," said McCord. "I've just done my job the best I can." He shrugged. "I'd hate to think this is all there's ever going to be to life, shooting and getting shot at. . . . Wouldn't you?"

"Yes, I would." Her voice softened as if in concern. "Maybe that's another reason I haven't thought much about what comes next. Maybe I'm afraid this is all there is to it."

They sat for a silent moment in the hot Mexican wind while McCord thought things over. When he did speak again, his voice was almost a whisper.

"I think it's time I told you . . . Saul Delmano killed my brother. I've been looking for him far longer than you have."

Danielle let out a breath. "I figured it was something like that. There had to be some reason for you to want to come down here with me."

"No, there didn't *have* to be a reason, not after I met you, not after I got to know you. But it turns out there *is* a reason. I suppose I just should have told you sooner."

Danielle sat up on her blanket and folded her arms around her knees. "You don't have to explain yourself to me. When it's over, we'll go our own way."

"But I don't want that," said McCord. "I want us to stay together."

Danielle abruptly stood up and pushed her hair back without facing him. She then picked up her boots and hat and looked over at the horses. "They're rested enough. Let's move out. I want to catch up to my brothers before they reach the Delmano spread."

With a slight sigh, McCord got to his feet and followed her over to the horses.

CHAPTER 17

CABALLO SANGRIENTO PASA, MEXICO. SEPTEMBER 30, 1871

Tim and Jed Strange had been watching three riflemen from a dark, shadowed spot beneath a deep cliff overhang when they saw Sheriff Deweese ride toward them. Two of the riflemen stood no more than ten feet from the sheriff, while the other one sat in his saddle, discussing something with the sheriff, Tim thought. Then all of a sudden, the man backstepped his horse a few inches as the rifles blasted Sheriff Deweese out of his saddle and left him lying bloody and dead on the ground.

"My God," Tim whispered. They were a good quarter of a mile from the grisly scene, and he and Jed stood transfixed, watching as one of the riflemen stepped forward and viciously kicked the dead sheriff in the face.

"We ought to do something," said Jed. "It ain't right standing here doing nothing while they kill a lawman in cold blood."

"We had no idea they was going to do it till it was already done," Tim retorted. He stared at the riflemen and at the tall rocky passageway through the rock land behind them, where more rifle barrels glinted from hidden perches. "I hate to say it, but we were fortunate the sheriff rode in there before we did. He must've rode straight here when he left town—else how did he get ahead of us on the trail?"

"Beats me," said Jed, "but from the looks of that bunch of gunmen, I'd say it makes them no difference who they kill so long as they're killing somebody."

"I know," said Tim, studying the men, trying to get an idea how many were out there. "They must be some extra hired guns the Delmanos brought in. They sure don't dress like cowhands."

"What's puzzling," said Jed, "is the way Sheriff Deweese was sitting there talking to that one as if they knew each other or as if the sheriff thought he might have been expected here or something."

"I heard talk while I was sitting in the saloon waiting for the sheriff to question me," said Tim. "It sounded like Sheriff Deweese and Lewis Delmano might have known each other pretty well. Since Deweese's badge ain't worth the tin it's made of this side of the border, he might have been coming here just to talk to Lewis Delmano."

Jed gave his twin brother a curious look. "You suppose the sheriff was on Delmano's side?"

"I won't try to guess," Tim replied, "but if he was, he sure ain't now. We're going to have to pull back out of here and wait for Danielle somewhere farther back along the trail. I know she can handle herself, but we can't let her ride into this bunch without some kind of warning."

They turned with their reins in their hands, leading the horses over to the upward path at the far end of the cliff overhang. Following the path to a stretch of flatland, both Tim and Jed were taken by complete surprise when they looked into the faces of two gunmen who had apparently been awaiting them.

One of the gunmen spoke in French, telling Tim and Jed to raise their hands. But not understanding a word the man had said, Tim and Jed only stared for a tense second, noting the way these men were dressed very much like the men who had just shot the sheriff. The man repeated the order—*"Levez les mains!"*—his tone of voice sounding more demanding. Tim and Jed stood frozen, watching, listening warily, until the sound of the other man cocking his pistol caused the twins to move as one, their hands snatching their pistols from their holsters with blinding speed.

The men responded quickly, but not quickly enough. Three shots erupted from Tim's and Jed's pistols before the gunmen had time to take aim. The two men fell backward in a heap, a shot from one of their pistols firing wildly in the air. While Jed stood with his pistol covering the bodies on the ground, Tim swung a glance out across the land below toward the spot where the other men had shot Sheriff Deweese.

"They're mounting and heading this way!" said Tim. "We'd better pull back fast!"

They jumped up into their saddles and batted their heels to their horses' sides, racing back along the trail they'd come in on. When they had ridden a half mile, Tim slowed his horse enough to turn and look back at the cliff where they had shot the two gunmen. There was no sign of riders on their trail, not even a rise of dust except for their own. Tim could barely make out the few men and horses standing atop the cliffs, looking toward them.

"Hold up, Jed," Tim shouted. "They're not following us!"

Jed slowed his horse and turned it back to his brother in a short circle. "Why not? You know they heard the shooting. You saw them riding toward us."

"And I still see them now," said Tim, pointing a finger at the tiny figures atop the cliff overhang. "But you tell me if I'm mistaken. It looks like all they're doing is sitting there watching us ride away."

Jed looked at the distant figures, then glanced all around warily. "There's something not right about this."

"What do you think it is?" asked Tim, also looking all around.

"I don't know, but I don't trust it," said Jed. "Maybe they know there's more of them between us and the way out of here, so they're in no hurry to chase us down."

"Could be," said Tim. "But I don't think that's it. It looks to me like their job is to guard that pass, and they ain't letting nothing or nobody draw them away from it."

"Then it's going to be even harder than we thought to get through there," Jed replied. He turned his horse back along the trail leading away from Bloody Horse Pass and nudged it forward. "Come on, Tim, let's find us a good place along the trail to wait for Danielle."

They didn't have to wait very long. Danielle Strange and C. F. McCord had ridden hard throughout the night, stopping only long enough to rest their horses every few miles. When they'd heard the pistol shots moments earlier, they'd moved forward quickly yet carefully. At the sight of the twins' trail dust, Danielle and McCord had split up, the marshal making a wide half circle flanking the trail, then closing around behind Tim and Jed as the distance between them and Danielle grew shorter and shorter.

At a hundred yards, Danielle and her brothers spotted one another and raced forward the rest of the way. Danielle hugged Tim and Jed in turn without the three of them leaving their saddles. After an affectionate embrace, the three sat atop their horses in the middle of the narrow trail.

"We're glad you're feeling better, Danielle," said Tim, "but I hope you ain't slipping a little, us riding up on you like that. What if it hadn't been us? A hundred yards ain't a lot of room to correct a mistake if there's rifles involved."

"Maybe you're the ones who are slipping," she said, smiling. She raised an arm and waved it back and forth, summoning C. F. McCord down from the rocky hills alongside the trail. "You've let a U.S. federal marshal get all the way around you and fan your trail."

"What the—?" said Tim.

The twins both looked around in surprise at C. F. McCord as the young marshal stepped his horse down toward them with his rifle propped up from his lap.

"Boys, meet Federal Marshal C. F. McCord." Danielle smiled, gesturing a hand toward McCord.

As McCord worked his way closer, Jed exclaimed, "He's the one they call the Fox! Everybody's heard of him!"

"Well," said Tim, tipping his hat to McCord as McCord's horse stopped a few feet back, "I reckon if we had to get ourselves surrounded that way, at least it was by one of the best."

"C. F., these are my brothers I've told you so much about, Tim and Jed, the family twins."

McCord looked at them and blinked as if seeing double. Then he smiled and tipped his hat. "Your sister has said lots of good things about you two," said McCord. "I feel like I already know you both."

"Sister?" Tim and Jed gave Danielle a guarded look.

"It's all right. He knows," said Danielle.

"I thought you weren't going to tell anybody until all this was over," said Tim.

"I didn't tell him," said Danielle. "He figured it out. McCord here went all the way to St. Joseph to find out what he could about me and my family. Somewhere along the line he was able to put two and two together."

Tim and Jed passed each other a knowing glance, noting the affection in C. F. McCord's eyes as he listened to Danielle's words.

"Well, Mr. McCord, you're mighty welcome along on this trip. From the looks of things, we're going to need all the help we can get," said Jed.

"We heard the gunfire earlier," said Danielle. "What's wrong?"

"The pass is guarded by a passel of riflemen," said Tim. "We had a run-in with a couple of them. It looks like their sole purpose is to keep anybody and everybody out of Bloody Horse Pass. We're pretty sure Saul Delmano and his brother are in there. The sheriff from El Paso was on their trail for a stagecoach robbery, and those riflemen just shot him dead!"

McCord asked, "You mean, Sheriff Deweese is dead?"

"We saw them do it," said Jed, nodding. "It looked like he was just talking to them. Then the next thing we knew, he was dead on the ground."

McCord winced and shook his head. "Poor Deweese," he said. "He played both sides of the law when it came to the Delmanos.

Now it looks like it all caught up to him. What do these riflemen look like?"

"The ones we ran into spoke a foreign language. It sounded like French," said Tim, "but I wouldn't swear to it."

"Yep," said McCord, "it sounds like the *generalissimo*'s private bodyguards. They're a bunch of mercenaries who call themselves the death squad." McCord looked back and forth between the three of them. "We're lucky you spotted them," he said to Tim. "We'd have been in some serious trouble if we'd run into them out there all of a sudden. Once the *generalissimo* sends them out to do something, they don't stop until they get it done."

"Now that we know they're there, does anybody have any ideas how we ought to deal with them?" asked Jed. He and Tim looked at Danielle for advice.

"Let's slip in and get a look at them," Danielle said. "Then we'll come up with something." She tapped her boots to Sundown's sides and moved the chestnut mare forward at a trot.

The four of them stayed back a safe distance in the cover of rocks until evening sunlight stretched long across the flatland. With the riflemen scattered out along the high walls of Bloody Horse Pass, it was next to impossible to get an accurate count of how many men were out there.

"One thing's for sure," C. F. McCord said. "As soon as some shooting starts, every man they've got between here and the Delmano spread is going to come running."

He lay beside Danielle behind an upthrust of rock where they could see one of the men on horseback ride forward from the mouth of the pass, peering back and forth across the flatland. Then the man turned his horse and rode back out of sight.

A few feet away, Tim called out in a whisper, "Another thing is for sure. They're not about to let anybody through that pass unless we blast our way through."

Hearing Tim's words, Danielle asked McCord, "What if we rode around them? Is there any other way in?"

"Not that I know of," said McCord. "If there was, once a person got on the other side of the pass, they would be spotted awfully easy making their way toward the Delmanos' spread. Hector Sabio said the hideout is even harder to get to."

"Then we've got to make a rush and take our chances getting through," said Danielle.

McCord shook his head. "Even if a couple of us made it through, these men would be on our tails. The Delmanos would be tipped off. I'm afraid it would destroy any chances of getting to them."

"I've got to hand it to the Delmanos," said Danielle. "They've made themselves a safe little nest here in Mexico. No wonder they've operated so long without getting caught." She looked back and forth across the flatlands.

McCord considered things as he lay studying Danielle's face while she scanned the high walls to the pass. "We need to wait until it's good and dark. What we've got to do is create a diversion long enough for one of us to slip through the pass," he said after a few moments of thought on the matter.

"That makes sense," said Danielle, looking into his eyes, waiting to hear the rest of his plan. "I suppose you figure you'll be the one to slip through."

McCord didn't respond to Danielle's question. Instead, he continued as if he had not heard her. "Whoever gets through is going to have to go on alone and find the Delmanos' hideout while the rest of us hold these men back here and keep them busy."

"You didn't answer me," Danielle said. "Do you plan on it being *you* who rides through and takes down Saul Delmano?"

C. F. McCord fell silent for a second, then said in a quiet, resolved tone, "It's going to be awfully dangerous for whoever goes in. But no, I've thought it out. You'll never see any peace until you've faced your father's killer yourself. If you want to be the one to slip though and get Saul Delmano . . . I won't try to stop you."

Danielle looked surprised. "But what about your brother? What about all these years you've wanted to avenge his death the same as I want to avenge my pa?"

"I've had plenty of time to think about it," said McCord, "and watching you, seeing what wanting revenge so badly has cost you, I think I've lost my thirst for it."

Danielle started to object to McCord's words, but he stopped her before she got the chance. "Don't take it the wrong way," McCord said. "I'm not judging you. I'm just saying, so long as Saul Delmano gets what's coming to him, it doesn't have to be me who delivers the justice. I'll let go of my revenge if it'll help you get shed of yours."

Danielle thought about it for a second, then said, "Thanks, McCord. I won't forget you doing this for me."

"It's not a favor, Danielle," McCord said. He offered a slight smile. "I just figure the sooner you get this out of your craw, the sooner you and I can talk about our future together."

Danielle looked over at her brothers a few feet away, making sure they hadn't heard what McCord had said to her. Then she lifted her pistol from her holster and checked it as she asked, "What makes you think we have a future together? For all we know, neither one of us might live through this."

"I know," said McCord. "That's why I wanted to get it said now."

Danielle looked around at the harsh land in the setting sunlight, then said, "You sure picked a romantic time and place to talk about it, McCord."

"This place wouldn't have been my first choice," McCord said, "but I wanted to tell you before we split up out here. After our talk the other day, you haven't given me much of a chance to tell you how I feel about you. I'm hoping that my stepping back and letting you and Saul Delmano settle up will let you know that you're more important to me than my revenge."

Danielle nodded, slipping her pistol back into her holster. "Do you remember telling me how you'd never leave me . . . and you weren't about to get killed and be taken away from me, McCord?"

"I remember," McCord said.

"Good," said Danielle, "because I'm holding you to it."

She stood up in a crouch and moved over to her brothers. McCord studied the darkening terrain as Danielle told Tim and Jed about the plan. By the time Danielle slid back in beside him, darkness had settled in for the night.

"I told them," Danielle said. "They wanted to ride with me, but I told them no."

McCord nodded. "Here's the way I've got it worked out in my mind. You get about fifty yards ahead of us and lie low till we start shooting. We'll be shooting in your direction, but don't worry. We'll keep a high aim on the rocks. While we keep them attending to us, you slip though without firing a shot. We'll keep them shooting at us for an hour, giving you plenty of time to slip through the pass. Then we'll fall back a little at a time, letting them think they've turned us back. That way, you'll have none of them on your trail—provided you don't leave them a clear set of tracks to follow."

"I'll keep to the rocks," Danielle said. "They won't find any tracks."

"Then get yourself ready," said McCord. He stared at her in the darkness.

Danielle could tell he wanted to say more to her. But she knew as well as he did that there was nothing more to say. *Not now,* she thought.

Before scooting back toward the horses, Danielle laid a hand on McCord's forearm, saying, "I know how much facing the man who killed your brother must have meant to you, C. F." She paused for a second, then added, "Thanks for stepping back."

"The only thanks I want is for you to come back to me in one piece," McCord said almost in a whisper. He watched her slip away into the darkness without another word.

CHAPTER 18

Danielle slipped out across the dark flatlands, leading Sundown behind her from cover to cover until she kneeled down behind a low spreading juniper and waited for C. F. McCord and her brothers to start shooting. At the sound of the first rifle shot, Danielle felt the chestnut mare jerk against the reins, startled, yet keeping obediently quiet as if she understood the situation and what was required of her. Danielle stood up and ran a hand down Sundown's muzzle, settling her.

"Easy, girl," Danielle whispered close to the mare's ear. "We'll soon be out of the firing."

Danielle waited until the return fire from the rocky walls of Bloody Horse Pass blossomed steadily in the darkness. Then she eased forward, leading the mare, knowing that she was reasonably safe, provided the riflemen in the high pass kept their sights aimed on the muzzle flashes fifty yards behind her. When she had drawn nearer to the riflemen's positions, Danielle slipped up atop the mare. Lying low in her saddle, she pressed the animal onward, searching for hard footing to keep from leaving hoofprints.

Feeling the tall, dark walls of Bloody Horse Pass close around her, Danielle rode on slowly as quiet as a ghost beneath the constant barrage of rifle fire. A full half hour had passed by the time Danielle saw the black shadows of steep rock give way to the midnight blue of the night's sky. The firing was behind her now and she breathed a little easier. She looked back over her shoulder for a second, then heeled the mare up into a trot.

"Come on, Sundown," she whispered, "they're doing their part. Now let's get to doing ours."

The mare carried her swiftly farther and farther away from the noise of battle.

Atop a hidden cliff in the rockwork of Bloody Horse Pass, Henri LaBourge watched the muzzle flashes of rifles explode on the dark flatlands below.

Beside him, a wiry German gunman known only as Vesp asked in a bemused voice, "What do these fools think they accomplish by this? Do they think they will overpower us and force their way through the pass?"

Henri LaBourge studied the darkness, tiny bursts of gunfire reflecting in his eyes. "I have stayed alive many years by never venturing a guess at what other men think."

"Yes, I know," said Vesp, "but for the sake of curiosity, do you believe that this is Danny Duggin, the one who has Lewis Delmano so upset?"

"The one Lewis Delmano would like us to kill for him?" A thin smile came to Henri LaBourge's face. "Yes, perhaps it is him." A silence passed; then Henri added, "But if this Danny Duggin *was* down there before, it is unlikely that he is down there now." His eyes scanned the darkness below where the trail snaked though the pass like a black ribbon of silk. "If I were Danny Duggin, I would have created this little skirmish to cover me as I slipped through the pass."

Vesp looked taken aback at the thought of Danny Duggin having ridden right past them in the darkness. "Shall I send some men immediately to make sure this has not happened?"

"No, I don't think so." Henri LaBourge chuckled under his breath. "My orders from the *generalissimo* are quite clear. I will do nothing until I have met with Lewis Delmano face-to-face."

"But meanwhile," said Vesp, "we are being attacked. Do we only sit here and hope they cannot hit us?"

"No," said Henri LaBourge, "we will not be treated like help-less fools, not even for the *generalissimo*. I have already sent some riders out to surround these riflemen. Let them shoot at these rocks all night if they wish. When morning comes, our men will move in so swiftly, these poor imbeciles will not know what hit them." He gazed out across the darkness as two shots blossomed at once on the flatland.

From his position behind an upthrust of rock, C. F. McCord looked over at Tim's and Jed's black silhouettes against the purple sky.

Jed whispered over to McCord, asking, "How far do you want us to pull back now?"

"Not too far," McCord replied, "fifteen or twenty yards. If we pull back too far at once, it might tip them off what we've done and send them after Danny," McCord said. "I figure by now Danny has made it through the pass, so let's cut down on our shooting, save our ammunition in case we need it later on."

"What are you expecting?" Tim asked in a lowered voice as he and his brother moved closer to McCord on their way back to a new position.

"If I was them," said McCord, "I'd be sending some men out to circle us in the dark. Come morning I'd have them sweep in for the kill."

"Do you think that's their plan?" asked Jed.

"Just my speculation," said McCord. "But to be on the safe side, by morning there'll only be one of us here on the flatland. I want you two back in those rocks behind us by then. If they circle in on me, you'll have them covered from behind."

"Uh-uh, McCord," said Tim. "That's too risky. We can't leave you down here by yourself."

"You told your sister that you'd do what I asked. Well, that's what I'm asking," McCord said firmly. "I'm going to move back and forth, firing from different positions. Now that they've seen three rifle flashes, they'll figure we're all three still here. Just be ready to throw down some long fire if they're dogging me when I light out of here in the morning."

"I don't like it," said Tim. "You're taking an awfully big chance sitting down here alone, McCord."

"Not if you boys can shoot those rifles as well as your sister thinks you can." He smiled to himself in the darkness.

"Don't worry about that, Marshal," said Jed barely above a whisper as the two of them moved back past McCord toward the black outline of scattered rock. "If you're crazy enough to stay here by yourself . . . we're crazy enough to hold the back door open once you make a run for it." Jed paused, then asked, "You do plan to make a run for it at the last minute, don't you?"

"That's exactly what I plan on doing," McCord said over his shoulder to the darkness, levering a fresh cartridge up into his rifle chamber.

Upon seeing the distant glow of light in the window of the Delmano hacienda, Danielle reined the mare toward it. She rode quickly until she knew the hacienda was within a mile; then she slowed the mare to a walk, silencing the hoofbeats and keeping down any rise of dust that might show against the night sky. At two hundred yards, Danielle stepped down from her saddle and led Sundown the rest of the way, into the dark shadows of a small adobe building facing the east side of the hacienda. Danielle stood in silence as three men stepped off the back porch, talking quietly among themselves as they walked over to a long bunkhouse. When a glow of light rose and fell as the men stepped through the door and closed it, Danielle laid the mare's reins up across the saddle. Knowing that Sundown would not move until Danielle once again took the reins in her hand, Danielle slipped forward in a crouch toward a partially open window.

Danielle reached up, eased the window open a few inches higher, then slipped inside. Taking care to look back toward the bunkhouse to make sure she hadn't been seen, Danielle eased the window back down to where it was originally. Standing for a moment in the darkness, listening to the tomblike silence of the hacienda, Danielle knew that Saul Delmano was not there. Saul Delmano would be in the hideout up there somewhere in the rock land just like Hector had said.

Drawing her Colt, Danielle eased her way from one dimly lit room to the next until she heard the sound of soft sobbing coming through an open bedroom door. She stepped to the side of the bedroom door for a second, then took a breath and moved inside. When she saw a woman lying facedown across the bed, her face buried in a handkerchief, Danielle's first thought was to sneak closer and throw a hand across the woman's mouth to keep her quiet. Yet, before Danielle could make it all the way to the bed, a squeaking floor plank beneath her boots betrayed her, and she stopped short.

"Who—who's there?" said Greta's frightened voice, turning her eyes to Danielle in the darkness.

Danielle moved quickly now, seeing Greta reach for a small pistol on the nightstand beside the bed. Her hand clamped down on Greta's wrist in time to keep her from arming herself. "Take it easy, ma'am," said Danielle, using her man's tone of voice. "I'm not here to harm you. I'm looking for Saul Delmano."

"I know who you are! You're Danny Duggin! You're here to kill Ramon!" Greta responded in a harsh whisper, bordering on desperation. She tried to wrestle her hand free of Danielle's grip, but Danielle held firmly and pulled her back away from the nightstand.

"You're wrong," Danielle said. "I came here to kill Saul Delmano, nobody else. If anyone comes at me, I'll kill them in self-defense. But I have no reason to kill Ramon or Lewis Delmano unless they force me into it. I'm not a cold-blooded murderer, regardless of what they've told you about me." Danielle turned her loose.

Greta slumped on the edge of the bed, rubbing her wrist where Danielle had held her tightly. "If only I could believe that," she said.

"You're free to believe what you will," said Danielle. "But I came for Saul Delmano, and nobody's going to stop me."

"Well, he's not here as you can see," said Greta. "None of them are here."

"I didn't really expect them to be," said Danielle. "I stopped by here only to make sure for myself. I know about the hideout up in the hills. Is that where I'll find Saul?"

Greta hesitated for a second, then answered reluctantly, "Yes, Saul is up there . . . but so is Ramon. There might be others. But listen to me, please. Ramon is trying to break away from Saul. He told me he would slip away the first chance he got and come back for me. You must promise not to kill him if you meet him along the trail!"

"I can only promise you that I won't kill Ramon unless he tries to kill me, ma'am," said Danielle.

"But if he runs into you on the trail, he'll think you *are* out to kill him," Greta exclaimed.

"Then I suppose he and I will have to settle that between us," said Danielle.

Greta straightened up from the edge of the bed, saying in a determined voice, "I'm going with you, Mr. Duggin."

"No, ma'am," said Danielle, shaking her head, "you're not going anywhere with me."

"But I was there once. I remember the way. You could wander around in the rock lands for days if you don't know where you're going."

"I'll follow their tracks," said Danielle.

"But don't you see?" said Greta, pleading. "I must go along to warn Ramon!"

"That's exactly what I'm *afraid* you would do, ma'am," Danielle responded.

"But you don't understand, Mr. Duggin," Greta pleaded, her eyes turning moist and full. "Ramon is a good man. . . . He's not like his brother or his father."

"If he's a good man, than he'll do the right thing, ma'am," said Danielle.

As she spoke, she stepped back toward the window, not knowing that outside the three men she'd seen go into the bunkhouse earlier had returned. They had caught sight of the chestnut mare standing in the shadows. Now two of the men lay in wait, while the third man slipped around into the hacienda and was headed for the bedroom with his pistol drawn and cocked.

Seeing Danielle's shadow at the bedroom window, Gus Latimer and Buck Benton braced themselves with their pistols in their hands and waited.

"All right, Mr. Danny Duggin," Gus whispered to Buck Benton, "it looks like it'll be up to us to take you down."

"Hush," said Buck Benton in a nervous whisper. "He might hear you. This is no saddle tramp we're dealing with here. From what I've heard, Duggin is as tough as they come."

"Is that a fact?" Gus Latimer grinned. "Hell, I wouldn't have it no other way. I just hope Lon is in there where he's supposed to be right now."

"Lon Capps ain't never let me down," Buck Benton whispered, his hand tightening as the two of them watched the dark shadow step out through the bedroom window and onto the ground.

"All right, Mr. Danny Duggin!" Gus Latimer yelled out, his hand already coming up with his pistol. "This is as far as you get!"

His shot exploded in a flash of blue-white fire, the bullet whistling past Danielle's head as her Colt streaked upward from her side. For some reason Buck Benton hadn't expected Gus Latimer to just open fire that way. But he caught on quickly and managed to get a shot off at Danielle as Gus Latimer fell backward with a bullet through his chest.

Buck Benton moved to cover as he fired, feeling Danielle's next shot missing him by only an inch. He ducked back behind an old freight wagon that sat empty in the dirt. He threw two quick shots around the corner of the wagon, then ducked farther back as three shots from Danielle's pistols tore chunks of wood from the wagon and sprayed splinters high in the air.

"Damn you, Duggin!" Buck Benton shouted. "You just kilt ole Gus! Me and him was partners before you was even born!"

"It was his call," Danielle replied, coming forward a few feet from the window and down onto one knee, a Colt in either hand, fanning back and forth in the darkness, lest there be more men hiding there. "Now you've got to make the same decision," she called out. "I came here only to kill Saul Delmano. If you want to die for him, that's your business."

As Danielle spoke, inside the bedroom, Lon Capps slipped across the floor with his pistol drawn and cocked. He looked over at Greta in the dim light and raised a finger to his lips, instructing her to keep quiet as he crept closer to the open window. Greta had squatted down onto the floor beside the bed. She only nodded in reply. At the window, Lon Capps ventured a glance out into the darkness, seeing Danielle's exposed back in the pale moonlight.

He whispered to himself as he raised his cocked pistol and took careful aim from less then fifteen feet away. "I've got you, Danny Duggin . . . you and two thousand dollars to boot!" As he walked forward, pulling the trigger, his next step hit a creaky floorboard.

Danielle's back stiffened at the sound of the floorboard, and as a shot exploded behind her, she fell forward to the ground and spun around to return fire. But at the window all she saw was the body of Lon Capps slump forward and hang down from the window ledge, his arms swaying back and forth lifelessly. Danielle had no time to wonder what had happened. From behind the freight wagon, Buck Benton came running forward, shrieking aloud, his pistol blazing in his hand.

Danielle put two shots into his chest, lifting him and pitching him backward in the dirt. Then Danielle rose back up onto her knees, scanning the darkness for others, listening to the deathlike silence around her beneath a drift of burned gunpowder.

At the slightest sound from the window behind her, Danielle spun toward it, both Colts aimed and cocked.

"Don't shoot!" Greta said in a shaky voice. "It's only me! This one is dead. I—I shot him."

"Yes, ma'am, you surely did."

Danielle stood the rest of the way up, still looking back and forth in the darkness. She lowered her left Colt into its holster, then broke open the Colt in her right hand, punched out the spent cartridges, and replaced them.

"Are there more hands around here that I need to know about?"

"I don't know," said Greta. "I don't think so. These men are just the ones who handle Lewis Delmano's cattle . . . men who used to ride with him in the old days."

As Greta spoke, Danielle walked up to the window and looked at the body of Lon Capps hanging down with a bullet hole in his back. Then she looked up at Greta. "Why'd you do this, ma'am? If you had let him kill me, that would have solved all your problems, wouldn't it?"

Greta shook her head, saying, "No, it would only have put your blood on my hands. I couldn't stand by and see him shoot you in the back."

Danielle studied her face in the dim light through the open window, considering everything. Then she asked Greta, "You really believe Ramon is a good man, not a murdering outlaw like Saul and his father?"

"I know that Ramon is a good man," said Greta. Her hand drifted instinctively to her stomach and rested there as she spoke. "I'm in love with him. . . . I carry his child inside me."

Danielle lowered her right Colt into its holster, took out the left, and reloaded it as she said, "That doesn't mean he's not a gunman like his family. It just means that maybe he's pulled the wool over your eyes."

"No! Ramon and I are leaving this place!" Greta said. "We had already planned to before your name was even mentioned. He sees the kind of people his family is. We want to get away and live our lives and raise our baby somewhere far away from all this murder!"

Danielle finished reloading her other Colt and said as she shoved it down into its holster, "I hope you're right, ma'am. Now hurry up and get yourself ready. You're going with me."

CHAPTER 19

Henri LaBourge had turned his head slightly toward the distant sound of pistol fire in the darkness. But he did not say anything about it until a few moments later when he turned his head back to Vesp, who sat atop his horse beside him near the edge of a cliff.

"Did you hear anything a while ago?" LaBourge asked.

"I have heard nothing out there but the rifle fire of our own men," Vesp responded, nodding out toward the flatlands.

"Not out there," said LaBourge. "Back that way." He jerked a thumb in the direction of the Delmano hacienda.

"No, I heard nothing from that direction," said Vesp. "What was it?"

"It was pistol fire," said LaBourge, a slice of a thin smile coming to his lips as he studied the dark flatlands below them. Sporadic rifle fire blossomed in a wide circle. "If I were to guess, I would say it was coming from Danny Duggin's guns." He nodded down toward the flatland. "Whoever is down there is only acting on Duggin's behalf. Duggin is back behind us, preparing to do what he came here to do."

Vesp gave LaBourge a puzzled look. "You believe this, and yet we sit here and do nothing?"

"We do exactly what our orders tell us to do," said Henri LaBourge.

"I think I must take some men and go pursue—"

Vesp's words were cut short as Henri LaBourge grabbed his horse's bridle to keep Vesp from turning away toward the narrow path.

"When the time comes for us to strike our target, we will do so quickly and without mercy," said LaBourge. "Until that time, we will do what all good soldiers do—we will wait. You were not present when I received our orders, Vesp. But you are my second-in-command, so you must pay attention and do as I tell you."

Vesp let out a tense breath and eased down in his saddle. "But of course," he said. "Forgive my exuberance."

On the floor of the flatlands, C. F. McCord stayed close to the ground even though the rifle fire was coming nowhere near him. He knew that the well-spaced shots were now only meant to harass him into returning fire and revealing his position. But now that he had given Danielle all the time she needed to get through the pass, McCord wasn't interested in keeping this gunfight going. All he wanted to do now was get back across the flatland to where Tim and Jed were waiting, without catching a stray bullet in the dark.

McCord judged the rifle fire coming from the wide half circle surrounding him, and decided there were no more than three or four men left out there now. Where had the others gone? he asked himself. While he had spent the past hour and a half firing, then hurrying to a new position to make them think there was still more than one down here, it suddenly dawned on him that these gun-men must have been doing the same thing. Had they caught on to what he was doing and gone on ahead after Danielle? He hoped not. But whatever the case, it was time for him to move out. A silver-gray line was beginning to form on the eastern horizon. He wasn't about to get caught out on this flat, desolate land in broad daylight.

Moving back silently to where he'd left his horse hitched to a scrub juniper, McCord slipped atop the animal and heeled it into a quiet trot, hoping the sound of its hooves could not be heard by the riflemen. *So far, so good,* McCord thought to himself, moving away across the flatland toward the far end of the basin where the twins would be waiting to cover his back. He'd told them to be ready to provide some long rifle fire for him if these men were close behind him. But as it now looked, McCord was going to be able to slip out of the flatlands unnoticed.

Two miles ahead, under the cover of dirty gray darkness, Tim and Jed Strange lay waiting in a low rise of rocks, seeing the distant flash of occasional rifle fire blink along the ridgelines.

"Think Marshal McCord's managed to keep himself from getting shot?" asked Jed.

"I sure hope so," Tim replied. "I have a lot of respect for that lawman, not to mention the fact that Danielle thinks the world of him. I'd hate to see something happen to him."

"Me, too," said Jed with great concern. "He'd best be getting himself headed this way if he doesn't want to get caught out there in the morning light."

Out on the flatland, C. F. McCord rode with care, wanting to hurry and push the horse forward into a run, seeing the widening glow of sunlight rise up in the east. But he knew better than to press the horse too hard across this rocky land in the darkness. There were too many ways a horse could snap a leg in this rough terrain. Yet, even as McCord thought about the many things that could happen, he felt the horse veer beneath him and let out a long neigh as the sound of a rattlesnake rose up from the ground.

"Easy, boy!" McCord called out in a hushed tone, sawing the reins, keeping the horse from bolting out of control.

The horse settled and sidestepped away from the sound of the rattler, but not before letting out another nervous whinny that echoed across the placid darkness. McCord knew what was coming and he booted the horse forward into a hard run just as a half dozen rifles homed in and fired from what seemed like every direction at once.

At the sound of the horse, followed by the blasts of rifle fire, Tim straightened up from his position on the ground and hurried a few yards forward, staring out into the darkness. He whispered to his brother, Jed, who ran forward beside him, "That had to be McCord's horse! He's in trouble out there!"

Another volley of rifle fire resounded, causing both Tim and Jed to wince at what dire consequences might have befallen the young marshal.

"Get ready to take cover, Jed," said Tim. "I'm going to call out to him, see what we can do to help him."

"Do it," said Jed, taking a step back, getting ready to run back to their position on the ground.

"McCord," Tim shouted into the darkness, "what's wrong out there?"

Rifle fire homed in and fired on the sound of Tim's voice as he immediately ran back and joined his brother.

When the rifle fire ceased, Tim and Jed listened intently for any reply from McCord, but they heard none. All they heard was the low whimpering of a wounded horse somewhere out on the flatland.

"Do you think he's dead?" asked Jed.

"He could be," Tim replied, "or it could be that he's not going to answer and bring more fire upon himself."

From the flatland came the echoing of the wounded horse's voice.

On the ground, three hundred yards out on the flatland, McCord struggled to free his leg from beneath his mortally wounded horse, who had caught a bullet high in its chest. But the weight of the horse held him pinned as another volley of rifle fire resounded. When the horse ceased its pitiful whinnying, McCord felt the animal go limp, pressing his leg even tighter to the ground. He had heard Tim Strange call out to him, but he dared not answer. Instead, he continued struggling, raising his other leg until he could reach the handle of the knife in his boot well.

McCord drew the knife and reached out with it across the dead horse's side as far as he could until he managed to slash through the cinch strap holding the saddle in place. Now that the horse had fallen silent, so had the rifles. But McCord knew he was in a bad spot. Come daylight, if he wasn't able to free himself, all the gunmen would have to do would be to walk down and shoot him to pieces. He pulled at the saddle, bracing his free knee to the dead horse's back and pushing with all his might, but to no avail. After a while he lay spent and panting in the dirt, seeing the sunrise broaden on the far horizon.

"Well, Fox," he whispered aloud to himself, drawing his pistol and laying it atop the dead horse's side for easy access when the time came, "you've managed to get yourself into a real tight spot this time." He lay still long enough to catch his breath and listen to the sound of horses moving down from the rocks. "Was she worth it?" he asked himself. Then he smiled as if in reflection and answered himself in a quiet voice, "You bet she was. . . ." He lay scanning the darkness surrounding him, preparing himself for whatever was to come.

Three hundred yards away, Tim said to Jed, "We've got to go get him, brother." Taking note of the sunlight creeping up over the ridgeline, he added, "I've got a feeling he'd do the same for us if it was the other way around."

"So do I," Jed agreed, standing up in a crouch and taking a step back to where they'd tied their horses. "I just hope he ain't dead already."

"Either way, at least we'll have done our best to help him," Tim said, studying the horizon as he cradled his rifle in his arms.

"I know," said Jed. "I'll go get the horses."

Tim listened to the silence of dawn as Jed moved back to the horses. After a moment, when Jed didn't return, Tim turned and said in a lowered voice, "Jed? What's taking you so long?"

When Jed didn't answer, Tim felt the skin on his neck grow prickly. He drew his pistol, cocked it, and ventured toward the horses, feeling for his steps carefully and quietly across the rocky ground. In a small clearing amid waist-high juniper and cactus, Tim froze at the sight of his brother, Jed, lying facedown on the dirt. As soon as his senses realized what he was looking at, he instinctively fanned the pistol back and forth, searching the gray shadows as he moved forward and bent down to his brother.

"Jed! Speak to me! Are you all right?" Tim asked, shaking Jed by his arm.

He heard Jed utter a faint groan and would have breathed a sigh of relief, had it not been for the solid thud of a rifle butt reaching in and slamming against the back of his head. Tim spun half around as his legs buckled beneath him. He tried to squeeze off a shot from his pistol into the grinning face that swam before him as if in a fog. But his pistol would not rise. His finger would not work on the trigger. He felt blackness draw in close around him as he fell.

"Get them both up and on their horses," said the voice of the man who had just knocked Tim cold. "We'll collect the other one on the way in."

"Why not kill them right here, Preston?" asked one of the other riflemen who had closed into a circle surrounding Tim and Jed Strange.

"Because Henri said bring them in alive if we could," said Preston Bendele with a slight trace of a French accent. "I follow his orders. When Henri wants them killed, he'll say so."

"What about the one out there on the flatland?" asked the other rifleman. "Do you think he is dead?"

"We'll see when we get there." Preston Bendele shrugged.

With Tim and Jed Strange lying slumped in their saddles, their pistols stripped from their holsters, the band of riflemen rode forward three hundred yards. In the thin morning light, they saw the other men who had moved down from the ridgeline and now formed a wide circle around C. F. McCord, who lay with his leg still pinned beneath the dead horse. McCord raised his pistol and fanned it back and forth slowly from one man to the next. Seeing there was little he could do against such odds, he called out all the same, warning them, "Stay back, all of you! That's close enough!"

Rifles rose and cocked in unison as the men moved in, steadily closer. But before anyone fired, Henri LaBourge called out as he and Vesp rode in from the north, "You heard him, men! That's close enough! Now stand fast! I think I would like to talk to this man. I'm curious as to why a man would do something this foolish." Henri LaBourge stopped his horse and stepped down from his saddle.

"I've got nothing to say to you," Marshal C. F. McCord called out to him. "If you've got killing to do here, get it done." He aimed his pistol at Henri LaBourge, causing LaBourge to stop in his tracks and raise his hands chest high.

"*Attends!*" Henri LaBourge chuckled under his breath at McCord's brazenness. "Wait—surely we can take a moment to talk like reasonable men before we shoot holes in each other, eh?"

"Talk, then," said McCord. "I've got no plans made for this morning." Seeing Jed and Tim slumped forward on their horses, McCord asked, "Are those boys all right?"

"They have been better, I'm sure," Henri LaBourge said with a trace of a smile. "But so much for them. Where is this Danny Duggin I have heard so much about?"

"I don't know who you're talking about," said McCord, letting his pistol slump a bit, but still keeping it cocked and pointed. "Me and my friends there came all this way on our own."

"Oh, I see," said Henri LaBourge, "and for no reason at all, you decided to shoot at me and my men? Why? Just to see if we would shoot back at you?" His smile widened as he spread his arms, taking in all of the flatland. "As you see, we most certainly will."

A ripple of low laughter stirred and then settled among the gunmen.

McCord struggled with his pinned leg, then said in a firm tone, "All right, I'll level with you. I'm a U.S. federal marshal who's been on the Delmanos' trail for a long time. I heard about this gunman Danny Duggin headed this way to clean up the Delmanos, and I couldn't stand the thought of him getting here first. So I took off my badge and crossed the border."

"I see." Henri LaBourge nodded as if trying to believe McCord's story. "Let's you and me call a truce for a moment, eh?"

McCord didn't answer, but he did lower his pistol barrel farther.

LaBourge ventured closer with his hands still chest high, moving slowly, one step, then another, until finally he stood three feet from McCord and looked down at him, shaking his head. "It is a most tragic thing to lose a good horse."

"Yeah," said McCord, looking at the body of the horse lying heavily on his leg. "He was one of the best I ever owned."

"And yet you risk your life, the life of a good horse, and the life of your two friends to come all this way in order to kill Saul Delmano?" LaBourge shook his head more vigorously. "That seems too foolish," he said solemnly.

"Well, that happens to be the whole of it." McCord sighed. "Take it or leave it."

Henri LaBourge shrugged it off and said, "The Delmanos must be considered very dangerous men in America, eh?"

"No. Not for my money anyway," said McCord. "I've never thought of them as anything but two-bit thugs and killers. Why do you ask? Don't tell me you have scruples when it comes to who you do your paid killing for."

"No, of course not," said Henri LaBourge, stooping down beside McCord as he spoke. "I work only for *Generalissimo* Ortega. He gives me his orders and I follow them. It makes life simple for me." He smiled, then raised a finger for emphasis. "But still, I can't help but sometimes ask myself why I am ordered to kill a particular person."

McCord looked at him closely and said, "Don't ask me to justify what you do, mister. I came here hunting for Saul Delmano. It didn't work out the way I wanted it to . . . so that's too bad for me. I take what's coming to me with no complaints. Will you be able to do the same when your time comes?"

Henri LaBourge stared into his eyes as he seemed to work something out in his mind. Then he stood up and said, "That's an interesting question, lawman. I don't think I can say what I will do when my time comes." He turned his back on McCord and called out to the men who sat atop their horses beside Tim and Jed, "Take them down from their horses and bring them over here."

McCord raised his pistol back toward Henri LaBourge, saying, "If you think I'll lie here and watch my friends die without trying to help them, you're badly mistaken."

Henri LaBourge seemed not to hear McCord. He gazed off

toward four of his men who came riding in from the south, surrounding Lewis Delmano's open-topped buggy. "Well, well, here
comes the leader of the Delmano family right now," said Henri
LaBourge in a detached manner.

"Do you hear me, mister?" said McCord. "Don't expect me to
keep our truce if you try killing my friends."

"What?" Henri LaBourge looked down at McCord as if he had
forgotten he was lying there. Then he smiled and said, "Tell me,
lawman, how many shots do you have in that pistol?"

"It's fully loaded," said McCord. "Six shots." He looked over to
where three men had pulled Tim and Jed Strange down from their
horses and were now dragging them toward him, the twins still
half conscious and barely able to stand. "What are you getting ready
to do?" asked McCord.

Henri LaBourge smiled. "I'm getting ready to carry out my task,
of course." He gestured a hand toward the horse lying on McCord's
leg. "If we removed this animal, would you be able to stand on your
own?"

"I'd sure give it a try," said McCord. "I don't think my leg is
broken beneath it."

Henri LaBourge motioned for two men to step in and help
McCord as Lewis Delmano's buggy drew closer at a fast clip across
the sand. The men struggled with the dead horse while LaBourge
turned away to acknowledge Lewis Delmano.

"Is that the gunman? Is that Danny Duggin?" Lewis Delmano
asked in an excited voice, sliding the buggy to a halt and jumping
down from it as he spoke. One of the riders had to catch the skittish buggy horse by its bridle to keep it from bolting forward.

Henri LaBourge looked Lewis Delmano up and down before
answering, not liking the way Delmano had barged in without so
much as a nod or a greeting.

"Well," Lewis Delmano insisted, "is it him?"

Henri LaBourge shook his head, watching McCord stand up
with the help of the two men beside him. "No, this is not Danny
Duggin."

"What about either one of those two?" Lewis Delmano asked, cutting his glance to the twins.

"No," said Henri LaBourge. "Danny Duggin is not here. These men only ride with him. We surrounded them overnight."

"Oh, really?" Lewis Delmano's gloved hand clenched around the butt of the pistol on his hip. "Then what is this one doing wearing a gun?" He stared hard at C. F. McCord. "Why haven't all three of them been shot?"

"Because shooting these men is not the reason my soldiers and I came here," Henri LaBourge snapped in response.

"Soldiers, ha!" Lewis Delmano said in a gruff voice, turning a sarcastic expression from man to man, then back to LaBourge. "You and your men are supposed to do as you're told, nothing more, nothing less. Now whatever killing you're paid to do, I demand that you get to doing it"

"I am glad that you feel this way," said LaBourge, raising his cocked pistol. "It makes my task so much easier."

Three shots fired in rapid succession from LaBourge's pistol, each shot slamming into Lewis Delmano's chest, knocking him a step backward. Delmano hit the ground with a stunned look on his dead face.

"There," said Henri LaBourge, "it is done, just as the *generalissimo* ordered. Now we can all go back to Mexico City."

He stood with the barrel of his smoking pistol tipped slightly toward C. F. McCord. Tim and Jed Strange stood addled and speechless as did the rest of LaBourge's men.

McCord found his words, saying in a halting voice, "You—you mean . . . you never were out to kill Danny Duggin? It was Lewis Delmano you wanted to kill all along?" Even as McCord asked, he managed to keep his hand close to the butt of his pistol, unsure of what might come next.

"*Wanted* to kill?" LaBourge asked, lowering his pistol from McCord's direction. "I have never *wanted* to kill anyone." He nodded at Lewis Delmano's body. "But this one had become too demanding over the years. He thought he could tell the government what

he wanted done and they would have to do it for him." Henri La-
Bourge grinned, adding, "You know how overbearing you *Améri-
cains* can get left unchecked."

McCord let it sink in, then asked, "What about the sheriff,
Deweese?" McCord jerked his head toward the twins. "They saw
you kill him. What was his part in all this?"

"He might have been a lawman on your side of the border," said
LaBourge, "but over here he was nothing more than a paid infor-
mant for Lewis Delmano. When Raul Hernandez told the *generalissimo* of how things were going out here, it was easily decided to
do away with all these fools and start anew." Henri Labourge looked
at Lewis Delmano's body and shook his head. "This one never had
the power or the connections he thought he had. He always
thought Raul Hernandez was sent here to do his bidding. In truth,
Hernandez was only keeping an eye on things out here. Lewis
Delmano was nothing more than a well-paid hired hand. Too bad
he never realized it—he could have lived longer." LaBourge lowered the pistol into his holster and let out a breath.

"What about us now?" asked McCord, passing a glance across
the twins, across the other men, then back to Henri LaBourge.

"For all the trouble you've caused, I should kill all three of you,"
said LaBourge, his tone of voice not carrying the conviction of his
words. "But I was not told to do so."

McCord asked in a cautious voice, "Then we can just leave?
Nobody will try to stop us?"

"Makes you feel foolish, doesn't it," said Labourge, "knowing
that all this could have been avoided?"

"I didn't know it at the time," McCord offered. "All I knew was
that I didn't want you shooting my friend Danny."

"I understand," said Henri LaBourge. "If I let all three of you
go, does it mean I will have no more trouble from any of those
troublesome Delmanos?"

McCord let out a tense breath. "Just let me round myself up a
horse and you have my word on it," he said.

CHAPTER 20

In a weathered plank shack on a narrow clearing between two craggy rock peaks, Saul Delmano reached across the small table and took a bottle of rye whiskey from an outstretched hand. In the circling glow of lantern light, he threw back a drink from the bottle and set it down on the tabletop as he wiped the back of his hand across his mouth. He stood glaring down at the outlaws seated at the table. They sat staring, waiting to hear what Saul had to say next.

On a blanket on the floor beneath the front window, Ramon Delmano waited as well. He had been watching his brother drink and talk for the past hour. Ramon marveled at how the whiskey had not seemed to dull Saul's thinking or slur his speech. There appeared to be no drunkenness to Saul Delmano, only a white-hot rage that grew and swelled in intensity from somewhere inside him. With each turn of the bottle to his lips, Saul Delmano became more and more a monster, less and less a man. The others saw it, too, Ramon thought, for how could they have missed it? But then, how could he have missed seeing it himself all these years? His half brother, Saul, was a raving madman, a desperate beast who must soon be put down for good, perhaps for his own sake as well as for that of those around him.

"There is not a stage or bank in the country that can't be robbed," Saul Delmano declared, jamming his fingertip down on the tabletop for emphasis. "Any fool can do it, provided he ain't squeamish about getting somebody's brains splattered all over his shirt." Saul tossed a glance at Ramon. "I even managed to teach my kid brother a little about the business." He spread a flat mirthless grin that turned his face into a death mask in the lantern's glow. "For years our pa was afraid Ramon here was never going to amount to nothing. Now look at him, out here hiding out, just like the rest of us."

One of the outlaws, named Ruppert Terry, turned a half-hearted glance toward Ramon, saying, "Bet it makes you real proud, eh, Ramon?" Then he turned his attention back to Saul. "Bank robbing is fine, so's stage robbing. But let's get back to that reward you was talking about . . . you know, for killing this Danny Duggin." As he spoke, his hand instinctively rubbed back and forth on the butt of his holstered Colt. "That seems like a powerful lot of money to me for just shooting one gunslinging saddle tramp."

"Forget the reward," said Saul Delmano, not wanting to talk about it. "I told you that's all over and done with. Those men Pa hired will kill him at Bloody Horse Pass—if they ain't already." Saul Delmano looked around the table at the four rough faces. "I'm ready to go on to bigger and better things. Think you four boys can keep up with me and little brother here? Wouldn't want none of you choking on our dust."

Ruppert Terry passed the question on to the others with a toss of his head. "What do you think, Wiley? Can you and Tubbs keep up with Saul and his brother?"

Wiley Thornton sneered, giving a glance at Dick Tubbs, who sat beside him. "I expect me and Dick can hold our own." He turned his glance to the other outlaw, Hain Carnes. "What do you think, Hain? Do you see anything here that gives you pause to doubt your abilities?"

Hain Carnes spat on the dirt floor and let his eyes move up and down Saul Delmano. "Not yet I ain't." Carnes looked at Dick Tubbs and Wiley Thornton, then back at Saul Delmano, saying, "You haven't seen anything I wouldn't do, provided the money's right."

"Good!" Saul Delmano nodded, the whiskey boiling in his

brain making him restless, on the verge of spinning out of control. "Come daylight, I say we saddle up, ride across the border, and commence a killing spree that'll keep the locals trembling in their boots for a long time to come." He snatched the bottle and threw back a drink.

Ramon watched for a moment in disbelief. There was no way he'd go any farther with his brother. He'd hoped Saul would have passed out by now, giving him an opportunity to gather his horse and slip away in the darkness. But now that he saw that wasn't going to happen, Ramon was ready to get out of there the best way he could.

He stood up and walked over to the table. "Give me a drink," he said, sweeping the bottle from Saul's hand and taking a short swig. When he lowered the bottle from his lips, he let out a whiskey hiss and headed for the door, his rifle draped over his forearm.

"Where the hell are you going?" Saul Delmano asked, picking the bottle up from the table where Ramon had set it. "We're getting ready to make some plans here."

Ramon gave him a flat stare, reaching for the door. "I'm going to the jake. You don't need me to make plans. It looks like you have everything worked out in your mind."

"Damn right I do," said Saul Delmano. He grinned, tapping a finger to the side of his head as he turned back to the others.

Ramon slipped outside and closed the door behind himself while Saul continued speaking to the men, waving the whiskey bottle about in his hand. Ramon moved quickly across the narrow clearing to the small corral, where they had left their horses for the night. In a moment he had bridled and saddled his horse and swung atop it. He rode the animal through the corral, closing the gate behind him without leaving his saddle. Then he heeled his horse out toward the path leading east down the craggy hillside. A thin sliver of sunlight mantled the far horizon.

Inside the shack, Wiley Thornton and the other three men rose halfway from their chairs at the sound of hooves along the hard rocky path.

But Saul Delmano motioned them back down with a raised hand, saying, "Don't worry, boys. That's only little brother, Ramon, cutting out on me. I've been expecting it."

The four outlaws looked at one another curiously. "You mean, you ain't going to stop him?" Ruppert Terry asked.

"Naw, there's no point in it," said Saul Delmano. "I tried to wise him up to this kind of life, see if he might have a knack for it. But it did no good at all." Saul Delmano shook his lowered head. "He just ain't got the makings."

"Do you trust him enough to think he won't bring somebody back here on us?" asked Wiley Thornton.

"If I didn't, Wiley, he'd be lying dead in the dirt right now, brother or no brother," said Saul Delmano. He shrugged. "Besides, who can he bring down on us? I told you, Danny Duggin is buzzard bait the minute he tries coming through Bloody Horse Pass."

Saul walked to the door, threw it open, and gazed out through the darkness in the direction of the path his brother had taken. "Ramon won't do anything to hurt me. The fact is, he's in love with a servant gal back at the spread. I expect he'll take her and make a run for it, probably play it straight for the rest of his life." Saul spread a tired smile at the dark sky. "Hell, I wish him luck."

"Whoa, that don't sound like the Saul Delmano I know," said Ruppert Terry with a dark chuckle in his voice. "I never saw you give anybody a break or wish anybody luck in your life."

"Well, you're seeing it now, Ruppert," said Saul, gazing away into the darkness. "Ramon leaving doesn't change a thing, though. We're clearing out of here at sunup, boys, as soon as there's enough light on the trail."

"Oh, I get it now," said Ruppert Terry, standing up from the table with the bottle in his hand. "You almost had me fooled, Saul, but now I see what you're doing."

"What are you talking about, Ruppert?" asked Wiley Thornton when Saul Delmano didn't respond.

Ruppert grinned. "I'm talking about why Saul really doesn't mind that Ramon took off and left us. He knows if there's anybody on that trail, we'll hear about it sure enough. But Ramon will be the one to run headlong into them. Right, Saul?"

Saul Delmano seemed to consider it for a second, then said without facing the men, "Now you're starting to get the picture, Ruppert. All my wild talking and drinking was just to rattle ole Ramon into leaving."

"Bull. I don't believe that," said Wiley Thornton. "Nobody would set their own brother up that way. You might have wanted him to leave, but just so's he'd get himself killed and we'd be warned by it? I don't believe I could ride with a man who'd do a thing like that. Tell me it ain't true, Saul."

Saul Delmano turned and looked at the four men in turn, then said to Wiley Thornton, "All right, then, Wiley, it ain't true. Does that make you happy?"

Wiley Thornton nodded and looked down at the dirt floor.

"Why I done what I done ain't important," said Saul, raising his voice to the other men. "Let's get ready to move out. It'll soon be daylight."

Turning to shut the door, Saul Delmano gazed off toward the path one last time as if still listening for any lingering sound of his brother riding away.

T he sound of distant gunfire resounded behind Danielle and Greta when they had left the hacienda and followed the hoofprints toward the hills. But before they had traveled a thousand yards, the guns had fallen silent, leaving Danielle to wonder if McCord and her brothers were all right. When Danielle stopped for a moment and looked back across the dark sky, Greta saw the look of concern and dread on her face.

"If we hurry on, we will be at the hideout before first light," Greta said as if anticipating Danielle's thoughts.

"Good," said Danielle. "The sooner I get this over with, the better." She nudged her horse, quickening the pace. "You said there might be others there. . . . How many do you suppose?"

"I can't say for sure," said Greta, "but Ramon told me there are always outlaws passing through, looking for a place to lie low. Lewis Delmano still provides the hideout for them. Most of them are men he rode with in the past."

They continued steadily and quietly for the next twenty minutes as the sky in the east grew wider in silver light. At an upward turn in the trail, Danielle was the first to hear the sound of a horse's hooves descending toward them. She reached out and grabbed Greta's horse by its bridle, stopping it.

"Listen," she hissed under her breath. "There's a rider coming."

Greta whispered in reply, "Perhaps it is Ramon! He said he would return as soon as he could get away!"

"Keep quiet," Danielle whispered, pulling both horses to one side of the narrow trail and into the dark cover of a rock crevice. "If it is Ramon, we'll know soon enough."

"You—you told me you would try not to shoot him!" Greta said in a shaky voice.

"I know what I said I'd do," Danielle responded, "but if this is Ramon coming, it's all up to him now."

Danielle slid down from her saddle and helped Greta step down as the sound of the hooves drew nearer. She ushered Greta back into the dark crevice and handed her both sets of reins.

"Keep the horses quiet," Danielle said. "If you give up our position, it'll only make matters worse. Don't speak until we know for sure it's Ramon."

"I understand," Greta said in a grave tone of voice. "I'll be quiet . . . but if it is my Ramon, please do not kill him, Mr. Duggin, if not for his sake, then for mine . . . and the baby's!"

Danielle didn't answer. Instead she stepped out into the center of the narrow trail as the hoofbeats came closer.

"Ramon Delmano," she called out into the darkness, "if that's you, raise your hands and come forward slowly. This is Danny Duggin. I have Greta with me."

The sound of the horse's hooves stopped short. Danielle heard the scraping of horseshoes on rock. She saw only the faintest outline of Ramon Delmano as his voice called out, "Yes, it is me, Ramon! Where is Greta? What have you done to her?"

Before Danielle could answer, Greta called out from the rock crevice, "I'm right here, Ramon! I'm all right! Don't do anything foolish. Mr. Duggin has promised to let us go! He wants only Saul!"

"Is that right, Duggin?" Ramon called out, slipping down from his saddle as he spoke and snatching his rifle from its boot. "You want only Saul?"

Ramon pushed his horse to one side and tried focusing in the darkness toward the sound of Danielle's voice. He wasn't about to venture a shot in the direction of Greta's voice, having no idea if she was behind cover or standing in the open.

"That's right, Ramon," Danielle replied, knowing that Ramon was only stalling. She prepared herself for whatever move he might make. "Point me toward Saul and you and the young lady can go your own way. I have no fight with you."

Ramon levered a round into the rifle chamber. Danielle heard the metal on metal ratchet at a distance of twenty yards. "I don't believe you, Duggin!" Ramon shouted. He fired two shots straight up in the air, levering the rifle quickly and sidestepping to his right in the darkness.

Danielle's hands acted on pure instincts. Both Colts streaked up from her holster and fired on the muzzle flash of Ramon's rifle even as she noted that Ramon's shots flew upward instead of blossoming toward her. But there was no stopping her shots now. She heard Ramon Delmano's short cry of pain as her bullets found their target. Ramon's horse also cried out, startled by the gunfire.

From the rock crevice on Danielle's left, she heard Greta scream, "Ramon!" and run forward, sobbing aloud. "No, Ramon! He wants only Saul! Not you!"

Danielle watched Greta run past her in the darkness. Knowing that at least one bullet had hit Ramon, and knowing that whatever the young woman found in the trail would not be a pretty sight, Danielle hurried forward with caution. A few feet back from the body lying on the ground, Danielle caught up to Greta and grabbed her by her arm, holding her back.

"Stay back, ma'am. You don't want to see—"

"No!" Greta screamed hysterically, cutting Danielle off. She slung her arm free and raced forward, sliding down beside Ramon, cradling his head in her lap and clutching his face to her bosom as she sobbed. "Why, Ramon, why?" she pleaded.

Danielle kneeled down beside Greta, noting the long bloody crease above Ramon Delmano's left ear. As Greta sobbed and rocked back and forth on the ground, Danielle looked Ramon over and saw no other wound.

"I think he's alive," she said, opening Greta's arms from around Ramon's head. "Give him room to breathe!"

As Greta unwrapped her arms from his bloody head, Ramon let out a low groan and turned his face back and forth in Greta's lap. He tried to speak but the words came out broken and meaningless.

Danielle reached down in the dirt, picked up Ramon's rifle, and cradled it across her forearm. Taking Ramon's pistol from his holster, Danielle stood up, saying to Greta, "Keep his head up and keep talking to him. I'll go get some water."

CHAPTER 21

At the sound of the gunshots, Saul Delmano and the four other outlaws veered slightly on the trail and came to a halt. When no other shots resounded in the gray morning darkness, Saul Delmano said in hushed tone, "Boys, there ain't a doubt in my mind that was Ramon's rifle."

"Well, as quiet as it's gotten, I'd say somebody has bit the dust," said Wiley Thornton.

Ruppert Terry stepped his horse closer to Saul Delmano and said as he slipped his rifle from its boot, "Looks like Ramon *did* warn us whether you intended for him to or not."

"Yeah, he warned us all right," said Saul Delmano, staring ahead into the grayness. "Now let's ease on down there and see what's waiting for us."

"Damn, Saul!" Ruppert said in surprise. "We've been warned. Shouldn't we swing around a different direction and get out of here?"

"Ordinarily that's exactly what I would do, Rupe," said Saul Delmano, "but not this morning." He pulled the glove from his right hand and stuffed it down into his belt. "I figure out of respect for Ramon, I'll just mosey on down there and check it out." He grinned. "I always was a nosy sort."

"But you already know it *has* to be this Danny Duggin fellow!" said Wiley Thornton. "Let's pull away from here!"

"And what," asked Saul Delmano, "have him on our trail at every turn in the road?" He pulled his pistol from his holster. "No, thanks, boys. That ain't my style of travel. I figured somebody would have killed Duggin by now. Since they ain't, I'd best do it myself."

He raised the pistol and fired three shots in the air, taking his time, pausing a second between each shot. Then he lowered the pistol, replaced the spent cartridges, spun it, and put it back loosely into his holster.

"This ain't like you, Saul," Ruppert Terry murmured, shaking his head.

"I know it," said Saul. "If any of you wants to pull off to the side, I'll not hold it against yas. But I'm gonna ride down and face this Duggin fellow straight up once and for all." He nudged his horse forward on the trail. "I've just got to see if he's as fast and tough as they all say he is."

Ruppert Terry looked at the others as Saul Delmano rode slowly into the grayness. "Well, hell, boys, I'd kinda like to see that myself."

He grinned and turned his horse forward, the others following suit and forming a quiet single line down the narrow trail.

Upon hearing the three shots fired by Saul Delmano, Danielle checked her pistols and waited. Moments passed slowly until she heard the first faint click of hoof on rock. Danielle turned to Greta and Ramon.

"Here they come," she said to Greta. "As soon as he's able, you get him up in a saddle and clear out of here. If my friends run into him on the trail between here and Bloody Horse Pass, there's no telling what will happen."

Before Greta could respond, Ramon looked up at Danielle through blurry eyes. "Duggin . . . I don't know what to say."

"No need in saying anything," said Danielle. "I told this woman I was only after Saul, and I meant it. From here on the two of you get a new start in life. As far as I'm concerned, I wish you both all the luck in the world. Now do like I asked you to. I've got business to settle."

"Duggin," said Ramon, his words still a bit thick and coming slow, "I—I want you to know that I wasn't shooting at you a while ago. It was for Saul. . . . I had to let him know."

"I know how it goes," said Danielle. "I have a couple of brothers of my own."

"What he does now is all up to him," Ramon went on. "I gave him all I owe him . . . didn't I?"

"Yep," said Danielle. "He can't ask for more than that. Now get on out of here."

She stepped out into the trail and started walking forward slowly, a silver morning mist wafting at her shoulders. Behind her, she could hear Greta help Ramon up onto a horse. Then she heard them move away down the trail until only silence lay in their wake. She stopped and waited at a point where the trail turned upward at a steeper angle.

When a few more minutes had passed, Saul Delmano called out from higher up in the gray morning swirl. "Danny Duggin, I'm Saul Delmano. Where's my brother, Ramon? Did you kill him?"

"No, I didn't kill him," Danielle called back. "Ramon left here a few minutes ago with a young woman named Greta. . . . They're well on their way now. It's just you and me."

"On their way, huh?" Saul said. Then he added with a bitter snap to his voice, "Well, God love 'em. Ain't that just fine and dandy? I expect the two of them will be just as happy as two crit-ters in a corncrib . . . probably live the rest of their lives watching the sun rise and set together."

"There's worse things," said Danielle. "Are you ready to come down and finish this?"

Saul Delmano stepped down from his saddle and shooed his horse away. "Yep, as ready as you are, I reckon. Is there anything we need to talk about first?"

"Not that I can think of," said Danielle. "You killed my pa, you and the others that were riding with you that day in the Territory. I've killed them all but you. There's no more to say about it."

Saul stepped forward slowly, seeing the outline of Danielle's head and shoulders take form out of the morning mist. "Hell, you don't even sound mad about it, Duggin."

"I'm past mad, Delmano," she said coldly. "I'm past a lot of things since I started out looking for all of you killers. All I want now is to be done with it."

Saul Delmano chuckled under his breath, stopping forty feet away and planting his feet shoulder width apart.

Danielle saw him through the gray morning light.

"Who are you trying to kid, Danny Duggin? You don't want to be done with killing. Killing ain't an easy thing to get rid of."

"I'll manage," said Danielle, reaching out slowly with both hands and drawing both sides of her duster back behind her holsters.

"You'll manage?" Saul Delmano asked. "After killing Rufe Gaddis, Byler, Grago, Chancy Burke, and all the others—no telling how many more along the way—you think you can just put it down and let it lie?"

Danielle remained silent.

Saul Delmano shook his head. "You poor fool, I reckon killing you is the best thing I can do for you, then."

He raised his left hand slowly and scratched his cheek, taking his time, considering things, it seemed. But Danielle had seen this kind of diversion before, and she was ready for his move when he made it.

"You know something, Duggin? When I first heard you was looking for me, I told a couple of pals of mine that I was going to—"

His voice stopped abruptly as his hand went for the pistol at his hip. But two rounds exploded from Danielle's Colts before Saul Delmano raised his pistol high enough to fire a shot.

"Lord God!" said Ruppert Terry in a whisper, watching with the others from ten feet back behind the cover of rocks.

Saul Delmano rocked backward with the impact of the first bullet, then fell to the ground as the second bullet slammed into his chest. Ruppert Terry took careful aim with his rifle as Danielle stepped forward and stopped, looking down at Saul Delmano with her right pistol pointed at his head.

Saul Delmano groaned and struggled, rising onto his elbow, his left hand clutched to his bleeding chest, the fingers of his right hand less than an inch from his pistol, where he'd dropped it in the dirt. "I reckon . . . that does it for me," Saul said in a strained voice. He managed to shake his head slowly, asking, "All this damn killing . . . just for your pa? Ain't nobody's pa . . . worth all this."

Danielle cocked her Colt, the barrel aimed steady and level at Saul Delmano's forehead. "Mine was," she said softly; and she let the hammer fall.

Before the echo of the final shot had faded off into the hill land, Danielle turned to the silver morning mist lying upward along the trail, and said, "Anybody there wants to be a part of it, come on down and face me like men. . . . Otherwise, lower your sights and ride out of here. I'm finished. Do you hear me? I'm through with it!" There was almost pleading, perhaps even a trace of desperation in her voice.

"Don't shoot him, Ruppert, damn it," said Wiley Thornton in a whisper. "He ain't done no more than anybody else would if somebody kilt their pa."

"I'm not going to shoot him," Ruppert Terry whispered in reply, lowering his rifle. He looked around at the others, then called down to Danielle, "All right, Duggin . . . we're leaving here. We've got no fight with you unless you bring it on."

"Fair enough," said Danielle, replacing her spent cartridges and closing her pistol. She stood in silence and watched the dim figures move back into the silver mist.

Farther down along the trail, riding ahead of Ramon and leading his horse behind her, Greta whispered a silent prayer under her breath and looked back at Ramon as he raised the bandanna from the side of his head and cast a glance back over his shoulder.

"Don't look back, Ramon. . . . We must never look back, neither of us. No matter which one died, we cannot let ourselves think about it."

Ramon started to say something, but then stopped himself and only nodded as he nudged his horse forward and rode closer to

Greta's side. They rode on for another mile until the first long rays of sunlight found their way through the stands of rock and spread golden on the gannet before them. Once they reached the base of the hills, they turned onto the flatland and rode on, leaving a low rise of dust behind them.

In the distance, C. F. McCord watched the two riders through his field lens.

"Who do you suppose it is?" Tim Strange asked.

"I have no idea," said McCord. "But whoever they are, they're coming off the hill trail, just below where we heard the shooting." He lowered the lens and closed it.

"Reckon Jed and I ought to catch up to them, see what's been going on up there?" asked Tim Strange.

"No, I don't think so," said McCord. "I think we'd best keep on your sister's tracks. Something's happened up there. We need to see what the outcome was, one way or the other. I'd hoped we might catch up to her in time to be some help once LaBourge turned us loose. Looks like we missed our chance."

Tim caught the concern in McCord's voice and said, to reassure him, "Look, Marshal, we're just as concerned about her as you are. . . . You know that. But if there's one thing Jed and I have learned about our sister, it's that she's a good hand at taking care of herself."

"I know that, boys," said McCord. "There's not a doubt in my mind that she's taken care of Saul Delmano by now if he was up there. I just want to at least be there when she comes down off the trail."

Tim and Jed Strange gave each other a knowing glance as McCord gigged his horse ahead of them on the trail.

"Looks like we're apt to wind up with a lawman in the family, Jed," Tim said in a guarded tone.

"It wouldn't surprise me a bit," Jed replied, the two of them falling in behind McCord on their horses, letting him lead them.

They rode on for another mile and a half; and as they neared the base of the long line of hills, the sight of Danielle rounding a turn down onto the stretch of flatland caused them to stop cold in their tracks until McCord said in a breathless whisper, "Thank God! It's her! She's all right!"

He heeled his horse forward and raced across the land, raising a high stir of dust. Jed started to heel his horse forward into a run as well, but Tim reached out and clasped his horse's bridle.

"Not so fast, brother Jed. . . . Give the two of them a few minutes alone."

"Yeah, I reckon that's a good idea." Jed Strange settled his horse and sat watching McCord close the distance between himself and Danielle.

At thirty yards McCord began checking his horse down, the big animal turning quarter-wise into a high-hoofed canter that bounced to a halt ten feet from Danielle. Then the horse sidestepped in a half circle as McCord looked Danielle up and down.

"He's dead," Danielle said bluntly.

"I figured as much," said McCord, jerking his horse to a standstill. "But what about you? Are you . . . ?" His words trailed as if he dreaded what he might hear.

"No, I'm not wounded," Danielle said, finishing his question for him. "I came out all right. That was his brother, Ramon, riding off over there." Danielle nodded at the rise of distant dust. "In the end it was only Saul and me face-to-face, the way I'd hoped for it."

As Danielle spoke, she swung her leg over her saddle and stepped down, taking off her hat and letting the cool morning wind blow through her hair. "How did it go for you and the twins?" she asked, glancing off to where Tim and Jed sat atop their horses.

"It was peculiar," said McCord, offering a relieved smile. "I'll tell you all about it sometime . . . but not now." He also stepped down from his saddle and swept his dusty Stetson from atop his head. "What I'd really like to know right now is your real name, Danny Duggin," he said with a sly grin.

"It's Danielle, McCord. I reckon you can call me that from now on." She reached down, unfastened her gun belt, and swung it up over her shoulder.

McCord moved in closer, his reins in his gloved hands, the wind nipping at the bandanna around his neck. "Well, Danielle, you look no worse for the wear," he said gently, standing only a foot from her, waiting for any sign or any hint of what she might want him to do next.

Danielle tried to return his smile, but it didn't work for her. Her expression turned tired, solemn all of a sudden. "But I *am* worse for the wear, C. F. I'm worse for the wear more than I ever thought I would be."

She seemed to sway forward slightly. Then she steadied herself and gazed away into the distance for a second as if trying to accept something in her mind.

"It's over, Danielle," McCord whispered.

"I know," she said, "but I can't feel it yet. It's still in me." Her eyes moved along the far horizon as if in search of something.

"Then let me help you. Tell me what you want, Danielle," Mc-Cord whispered. "I'll do whatever it takes to put this to rest. I'll go if that's what it takes . . . or I'll stay. Just tell me what you—"

"How about if you just hold me, C. F.?" Danielle's eyes glistened wet as she turned them to McCord and stepped forward into his arms.

"Well, I can do that easy enough, I reckon," McCord said, drawing her to his chest. "The hard part might be turning you loose," he said close to her ear.

"Then don't turn me loose, C. F.," she whispered.

Danielle pressed her face to his chest, feeling the warmth of his arms around her, and she stood for a moment, liking the slow, steady beat of his heart through the dusty breast of his riding duster.

"It's over, Pa," she said in a voice too hushed to be heard beneath the breath of the desert wind. And she closed her eyes and let the gun belt slip from her shoulder and fall to the ground at their feet.

DEATH ALONG THE CIMARRON

CHAPTER 1

HALEY SPRINGS, TEXAS

When the first pistol shot rang out from the dirt street, Danielle Strange didn't flinch. As she stood at the counter of McCreary's General Mercantile Store, her hand dropped instinctively to her hip even though she knew she wasn't wearing a gun. In fact she wasn't even wearing her customary riding clothes—her doeskin skirt, her bell-sleeved women's blouse, or her long brush-scarred riding vest. But old habits died hard, she reminded herself, easing her gun hand away from where her holster would ordinarily have been. She smoothed out her gingham dress as if doing so had been her intention in the first place.

Martin McCreary didn't see her gesture. He had ducked down too quickly behind the counter to have seen much of anything. Then, just as quickly, he rose up, embarrassed and shaken, feeling he needed to explain his fearful response.

"I'm—I'm sorry, Miss Danielle," McCreary stammered. "I shouldn't have ducked down and left you standing there all alone. My nerves just ain't what they should be these days." He wiped a trembling hand across his forehead. "Ever since Sheriff Casey got himself killed, I just can't stand the sound of—"

His words were cut short as another pistol shot exploded. "Lord God!" he shrieked, ducking down again.

"I'm going to see what this is all about," said Danielle, turning and walking toward the door.

"Don't go out there, Miss Danielle!" McCreary warned her. "There's a wild bunch in town. It won't make a bit of difference to them that you're a lady."

"I hope it doesn't," Danielle said, swinging the door open, then closing it soundly behind herself, leaving the bell atop the door jingling on its tin spring.

Outside, a third shot exploded. Martin McCreary only flinched this time. He stood for a second, staring at the closed door, then looked around the empty store and said aloud to himself, "Well, shoot . . . I might just as well get myself a little look-see. "Almost on tiptoe, he crossed the floor to the front window and peeped out guardedly from one corner.

At the far end of the dirt street, forty yards away, Danielle saw three men standing wobbly drunk, their smoking Colts in their hands. In the street a few feet from them lay the shattered glass remnants of the whiskey bottles they'd been shooting. These were young men around the same age as her brothers, Tim and Jed, she noted to herself. Yet there was an aura of trouble as thick as smoke surrounding these men, and sensing it caused her steps to sway over to her buckboard at the hitch rail.

"Easy, Sam," Danielle said to the nervous horse hitched to her wagon. She ran a soothing hand down its white muzzle. "Nothing to get yourself spooked about," she whispered. "They're just drunk and loud."

The anxious horse settled, blowing out a tense breath. Danielle reached a hand into the buckboard and, with no wasted motion, slid the Winchester repeater rifle from its boot beneath the wooden seat. She levered a round up into the chamber and carried the rifle loosely. In the street out front of Waldrip's Saloon, one of the drunken young men nudged the other two.

"Ronald, Frisco, look what's coming here," he said, directing his companions' attention toward Danielle as she approached. "It's about time this little pig-apple town sent somebody to welcome us."

"Hush up, Billy Boy," said Frisco Bonham, laughing in a lowered voice, "before you scare her away." He ran a tightly gloved finger along his thin mustache.

"She ain't looking too scared to me," said Ronald Muir, his drunken grin fading as Danielle came closer.

"To me neither," said Frisco Bonham, his leer growing more wary.

From between Frisco and Ronald, Billy Boy Harper took a firm step forward, hoping this action would bring this brash young lady to a halt. It didn't.

"Excuse me, little miss," Billy Boy called out to Danielle, his pistol still dangling in his hand, curling smoke. "Can we help you in some way?"

"Fun's over, boys," Danielle called out, finally stopping fifteen feet away, her rifle coming up from her side into the cradle of her left arm. All three men noticed that her right thumb lay across the hammer, her finger on the trigger. "Holster those shooters and get off the street."

"Well, now, what have we here, boys?" Frisco Bonham whispered.

He took a step forward and stood beside Billy Boy. Ronald Muir did the same. Not one of the three made an effort to holster their Colts. Noting it, Danielle cocked the rifle hammer and prepared herself for whatever was to come.

"You sure are a pretty little thing to be talking so bold at this hour of the day," said Frisco, his smile returning, this time appearing more sober and with no humor to it.

"Yeah," said Ronald Muir, "and we don't see no badge on your chest."

"Not that badges mean a whole lot to us one way or the other," Billy Boy piped in.

"We're without a sheriff right now," said Danielle in a resolved tone. "My name is Danielle Strange. I'm a citizen here, and I'm speaking on behalf of the town. You'd do well to holster up and get off the street. I won't tell you again."

"Oh, I see, Miss Danielle Strange, citizen of the town," said Frisco Bonham with a sarcastic twist to his voice as the other two snickered drunkenly. "And what if we don't?"

"Then somebody will have to scrape you up and carry you off," Danielle replied quickly, her voice steady and low.

The snickering stopped short as silence set in for a moment before Frisco Bonham spoke. "Then I reckon we'd better do as we're told, hadn't we, boys? We surely don't want to get scraped up and carried off this dirt street."

"Sounds right to me," Ronald Muir said.

"To me, too," replied Billy Boy Harper.

But Danielle wasn't buying their act. She knew what was about to happen. "Good, then," she said firmly, going along with their charade. "Holster those shooters and let's all go our own way."

"Whatever you say, ma'am," said Frisco Bonham. The three men looked back and forth at one another slowly, expressionlessly. "You two heard the little lady," Frisco said. "Now holster up before she has to sternly raise a hand to us."

Lifting their pistols slowly and dropping them into their holsters, the three stared long and hard at Danielle.

"I might enjoy a hand raised to me," said Ronald Muir, "depending on where it's raised to."

They were toying with her like three big cats teasing a helpless mouse. Danielle knew that had she been a man, the fight would have already commenced. They were counting her short because she was a woman. Well, that was all right with her. She'd been treated that way before. She knew how to use her being a woman to her advantage. These men standing before her didn't realize whom they were about to face off with.

For well over a year, Danielle Strange had passed herself off as a man in order to hunt down the outlaws who had killed her father and left his body hanging from the bough of a tree. Going under the name Danny Duggin, Danielle had acquired a reputation as a cold-blooded gunman across Indian Territory, Texas, and the Mexican hill country. But that was then and this was now, she reminded herself. A gunslinger was only as good as his or her last fight. Danielle hadn't raised a gun toward a man for over a year now. She hoped he hadn't lost her edge.

She felt the tension in her trigger finger. There was no question she was as fast as ever. And she had no doubt that her aim was still as deadly as the strike of a rattlesnake. But she knew that a year was a long time for a gun handler to go untested. But there was nobody else in Haley Springs to keep the peace. She had to do it. She hoped this could be settled without serious bloodshed.

With their pistols back in their holsters, the three men just stared at her. Frisco Bonham hooked both thumbs into his belt and rested his weight on one side, standing with belligerent bearing.

"Now what?" he said flatly.

Here it came, Danielle thought to herself. "Now all three of you get off the street," she said.

"Huh-uh." Frisco Bonham shook his head. "We ain't making no noise. We ain't disturbing no peace. We'll stand where we damn well please. You run along now before we lose our tempers."

"Yeah," Billy Boy sneered. "What do you think of that?"

"I think you've all three had your chance," said Danielle. She knew they believed they could draw their Colts whenever they felt like it. She knew they felt like they had all the time in the world. "I'm through talking," Danielle added. The rifle barrel swung down from her cradling arm and exploded.

Billy Boy's pistol stopped on its upswing from his holster and flew from his hand as the impact of Danielle's rifle slug hammered his foot to the ground, then slung him backward onto the hard dirt.

For just a split second, the other two gunmen stood stunned at the suddenness of her attack. She hadn't hesitated. She hadn't offered any further warning. She'd simply said she was through talking, and then she'd shot Billy Boy down without a blink of her eye.

"Damn you, woman! Kill her, Frisco!" shouted Ronald Muir, his hand streaking up with his pistol in it.

But Frisco Bonham, staring at Billy Boy as the wounded man

lay wallowing in the dirt holding his foot, didn't move as quickly as Ronald Muir.

Danielle swung her rifle toward Ronald Muir, cocking it on the way. But before she got the shot off, another pistol shot resounded, this one from the boardwalk behind her. She saw Ronald Muir fall backward as a ribbon of blood streamed from his chest. She had no idea who had fired the shot, but she was grateful for the help. It gave her time to swing the rifle toward Frisco Bonham just in time to see his pistol rise halfway from his holster. Seeing that the rifle had him cold, Frisco froze for a second, considering his chances.

Behind Danielle a gravelly voice said to the stunned gunman, "Be real careful what you decide. This ground is full of bad decisions."

"You killed him," said Frisco, glancing at Ronald Muir's body. Blood spewed from the large hole in the dead man's chest.

"Deader than hell," said the gravelly voice. "And you'll be, too, if you don't flip that gun over onto the ground real easy-like."

Danielle only stared at Frisco Bonham. She had no idea who was standing behind her, but she'd seen whose side he was on. For now that was good enough.

Frisco's gloved hand rose slowly, then dropped the pistol on the ground at his feet. "You both just made one bad mistake," he hissed. "That boy happens to be the brother of my boss—Cherokee Earl Muir!"

Billy Boy Harper had struggled to his feet, blood pouring from his left boot. "Earl's going to go wild ape crazy when he hears about this!" Billy Boy said in a strained voice. "He won't abide his brother getting took down by a woman and an old bar swamper."

"He'll have to work it out the best he can," said Danielle. "Get his body across a saddle and get out of town."

"Come on, Billy Boy, give me a hand," Frisco demanded.

"Damn it, Frisco, I'm shot all to hell here," Billy Boy whined, limping over toward the hitch rail where their horses stood.

"You'll be worse than shot when Earl hears you didn't help me bring back poor Ronald's body," shouted Frisco.

Danielle stepped back and to the side as the pair struggled with the dead body and dragged it to the horses.

"Hope you're all right, ma'am," said the rough voice from the boardwalk behind her.

"I'm fine," Danielle reassured her benefactor. She looked away from the two gunmen long enough to get a look at the man who had helped her. It took a moment for her to recognize him. When she did, she smiled to herself, knowing that he wasn't going to recognize her in return.

"How about yourself?" she asked.

"I'll do," said the old man. "I ain't no saloon swamper like that fool said, though."

Danielle recognized the man as an old cattle drover known only as Stick, whom she hadn't seen in over a year. The last time she'd seen Stick, he was working as cook and cowhand for Tuck Carlyle, the young man who had stolen her heart back when she was on the trail of her father's killers. Danielle was eager to ask about Tuck, but she knew she had to bide her time and first explain to Stick who she was and how the last time he'd seen her she was the feared gunman Danny Duggin.

"I knew better than that, Stick," Danielle said. She turned to face the old man as, squinting warily in the direction of Frisco and Billy Boy while they rode out of town, he stepped down off the boardwalk. "I know you're a top hand and a better-than-most trail cook."

"Huh? What's that?" Stick turned to face her, taken aback by the fact that she knew his name. "Where do you know me from, young lady?"

As he spoke, he eyed her closely. Danielle only smiled, cradling the rifle in her arm once again, this time taking her hand down from the trigger guard.

Stick stepped closer, looking her up and down curiously, then studying her face. "You do look familiar . . . but for the life of me, I swear I can't place you."

"It'll come to you, Stick," said Danielle. "Meanwhile, I'm much obliged to you for backing my play."

"Backing your play?" Stick chuckled and spat a stream of tobacco juice. "You're talking like a gunman yourself, young lady." He nodded toward the bloody footprint Billy Boy had left behind. "Looked to me like you would've done all right anyways."

Danielle smiled again. "It never hurts to have an extra gun backing you up with three men like that. They struck me as some real hard cases."

"You're a good judge of character, then," said Stick. He stared off toward the disappearing figures on horseback. "I was listening to them talk in the saloon a while ago. There was eight of them here this morning. Then the other five rode out of here earlier. Lucky for us or we'd have been facing all of them. I heard one mention some cattle they sold to a rancher out near Buckston Crossing. Sounded to me like they might've rustled a herd and sold most of it to him. Of course, it ain't nothing I could swear to, just a powerfully strong hunch."

"Well, it wouldn't surprise me one bit," said Danielle.

Stick scratched his bristly beard stubble and eyed her closely again. "Now, how come you to know my name?"

"I know you, Stick," said Danielle. "And I know the man you used to work for."

"Oh?" Stick looked even more curious. "Now, how would you know that?"

"I just do," said Danielle. "Tell me, how is Tuck Carlyle doing these days?"

"Well, he's not doing so—" Stick caught himself and stopped in surprise. "I'll be dunked straight up!" said Stick. "You sure nailed it on the head. I worked for Tuck Carlyle for the longest time." He stepped back, staring even more closely at her, trying to place who she was, where he might know her from. "So I reckon I must know you from somewhere or other."

"You sure do," said Danielle. She looked around at the townsfolk starting to venture out now that the shooting was over. "But this isn't the best place to talk about it. Have you et anything today, Stick?"

"No," Stick replied, "but I've drunk extra whiskey to make up for it."

As he spoke, Danielle noticed a broom sitting against the front of the saloon. It looked as though the old man had come out to sweep the boardwalk before seeing the trouble between her and the three men. "Then you wouldn't turn down some beans, steak, and biscuits, I don't suppose," Danielle said.

"No, ma'am, not even with a gun to my head," Stick said. Then he hesitated. "That is, if it ain't no bother to you. . . . I never impose."

"No bother, Stick. After you backing me up, it would be my pleasure to fix us up some grub."

"Well, then, all right. Long was as you're sure I ain't putting you out any," said Stick, being polite.

"Go get your horse and ride out with me." Danielle nodded toward the west, out across the rise and fall of rocky ground to where the land reached upward into a stretch of low hills. "My place is nearby. We'll bend a couple of forks together. Then I'll tell you where I know you from."

"I'd sure love to, ma'am," said Stick. "But could you give me just a minute or two?" He jerked a thumb toward the broom on the boardwalk out front of the saloon. "I need to finish up a little job I started."

"Take your time, Stick," Danielle said. "I'm in no hurry."

Stick grinned and touched the brim of his hat as she backed away. "Much obliged," he said.

On their way out to Danielle's eighty acres of scrub grass and mesquite, Stick nodded toward a thin rise of dust far to their left and said, "That would be those two snakes we just run out of Haley Springs if I ain't mistaken."

"I'm hoping that's the last we see of them," Danielle commented, riding in the buckboard beside Stick on his aging dun stallion.

"Oh, I sure wouldn't count on that," said Stick. "We ain't heard the last about what happened today. I can feel it in my bones." He gazed off toward the dust with a wary expression. "I don't know Cherokee Earl Muir, but I've heard plenty, and none of it's been good."

Danielle studied Stick's weathered face and, seeing the look of concern, asked, "Are you having second thoughts about what we done?"

"What?" Stick gave her a bemused look. "Why, Lord, no! I've been picking right over wrong my whole life. So far it ain't never failed me. Cherokee Earl or any of his bunch come looking for me, they'll see I'm easier to find than stink on a polecat."

"That's how I thought you'd feel about it." Danielle smiled, then jiggled the reins up and down, quickening the wagon horse's pace. "Hup, Sam," she said as the big horse seemed to snap out of a lull.

They rode quietly, sharing very little conversation for the next three miles until at length Danielle swung the wagon off the dirt trail onto a narrow wagon path leading over a rise of rocky grassland. At a wood-and-stone house built with its back against a bluff of protruding rock, Danielle stopped the wagon and stepped down at a sun-bleached hitch rail.

"Well, here we are, such as it is," she said, putting a hand on the small of her back and stretching.

"Looks mighty fine and inviting to me," said Stick, taking a long look at the house and outstretched land surrounding it. "I always dreamed of someday having me a place of my own like this . . . somewhere a man can throw down a blanket and not have to roll it back up come morning 'less he wants to."

Danielle looked Stick up and down as he gazed out across the land. She could tell he'd been living hand to mouth for a while. His boots were cracked across the tops and down in the heels. His hat looked as if its edge had been gnawed on by barn critters. She noted to herself how thin he'd gotten since last she'd seen him. It saddened her to see a good cowhand like Stick in such a condition.

"It's just me here running this place. I could use an extra hand if you're in no big hurry to be someplace else," Danielle said, hoping

Stick wouldn't look too closely and notice that there wasn't enough going on here to keep one person busy, let alone two.

"I've no place else to be and all the time in the world to get there," said Stick, his eyes gliding across a small corral, where six horses milled out of the heat on the shaded side of a small open-front barn.

Danielle was certain he saw there was no extra hand needed here. But the fact that he didn't comment on it made her realize what dire straits the old drover was in.

"I'd be pleased to stay here and help you run this place, ma'am," said Stick, "long as you're sure you can use a hand."

"Oh, yes, believe me, Stick," said Danielle, directing him toward the house as she spoke. "I need help. I'm not running any cattle right now, but I might as soon as I get things fixed up around here. Right now I'm mostly dealing in horses when I can."

At the door to the house, Stick stopped and looked back again across the rough, hardscrabble land as if it were a glimpse of paradise. Off to their right, a lone buzzard swung up off its perch in a spindly cottonwood tree beside a dry creek bed. Stick smiled and took in a long, deep breath, his eyes growing a bit moist for just a second.

"Ma'am, I'm glad I happened onto you." The old drover's voice cracked as he spoke. "I swear, this has turned out to be my best day in a long time."

Danielle patted Stick's thin shoulder and said, "You take your time out here, enjoy the view."

Seeing that he might need a minute or two to himself, she stepped inside and left Stick standing on the dusty front porch in a passing hot breeze.

CHAPTER 2

Cherokee Earl Muir stood with a boot planted on the bottom rail of the corral, a half-empty bottle of whiskey hanging from his hand, a short black cigar stuck between his teeth. In the corral, Jorge stuck to the saddle of the bucking dapple gray as if the horse were a part of him. Along the fence, whiskey-fueled voices laughed and cursed and cheered beneath sporadic pistol shots exploding into the air.

"That one-eyed Mexican can stick a horse 'bout as good as any man I ever saw," Cherokee Earl commented.

"Damn his hide," Dave Waddell growled, handing Cherokee Earl a twenty-dollar gold piece.

With each rise and fall of the dapple gray, Jorge's black eye patch flapped up and down, revealing both the clouded white eye and the deep scar running through it.

"What's wrong, Dave? Is that pretty little wife of yours going to throw a fit over you losing money to your bad ole pal Earl?" Earl chuckled to himself, then added, "I bet she's a real squalling wildcat when she's flared up. . . . Most redheads are, they say."

Waddell felt his face redden over the comment about his wife, but he acted as if he hadn't heard it, and nodded toward Jorge. "How do I get the show-off sumbitch off there, shoot him?"

"You could do that," said Earl, inspecting the gold piece before shoving it down into his vest pocket. "Of course if you missed, there'd be one wild Mexican up your shirt." He grinned. "Then even I couldn't help you."

"Well, hell, Earl, I figured you could tell I was only joking," said Waddell, shying back at the thought of what he knew Jorge was capable of doing if Cherokee Earl ever sicced him on a person.

"I bet you were," said Earl, looking away from Waddell with a slight smile, dismissing the matter.

The dapple gray wound down and circled the corral in a show of grudging submission. Jorge slipped down from the saddle at a trot, quickly mounted the corral fence, and grasped the first bottle of rye held out to him. He spread a broad grin, smoothed his eye patch back into place, and tipped the bottle toward Cherokee Earl before taking a long swig.

Earl nodded his approval to Jorge, then said to Dave Waddell as he looked all around the rocky land, "This is a handy piece of ground you've got here, Dave. I could use a place like this."

"It's not for sale," said Waddell. "I'll tell you that before you go any further."

"I never said I wanted to buy it." Earl chuckled under his breath. "I'd just like to have access to it from time to time . . . rent a piece of it, so to speak." He took the cigar from his teeth and blew a stream of smoke onto a passing hot breeze. "You could be my land-lord. How does that strike you?"

"Sounds like more trouble than it'd be worth if you don't mind my saying so," Waddell offered, making sure he didn't say something to Cherokee Earl Muir that he might regret.

Earl was known for his hair-trigger temper. The slightest comment could rub him the wrong way and send him into a blind killing rage. Waddell had seen it happen more than once over the course of their dealings.

Cherokee Earl studied the wet end of his cigar for a quiet second, then said, "You mean, for instance, if I didn't pay my rent, and you had to come throw me off the place? Or if me and the boys got too rowdy of a night whilst you tried to sleep . . . something like that?"

"Well, no . . ." Waddell scratched his forehead up under his hat brim. "I just meant, the way you often get the law on your tail . . . maybe have to shoot it out with a posse or something. Being your landlord could get risky, Earl. I can't say it sounds like something I want to get involved in."

"Good, then, it's all settled," said Earl as if they had just reached an understanding. "Me and the boys will hole up in that little rock canyon down along the high trail. Hell, you'll hardly ever know we're there unless we need to run down here, maybe borrow some grub or whiskey or something."

"Whoa. Now, wait a minute, Earl," said Waddell. "I never agreed to anything here."

Cherokee Earl shrugged. "You didn't disagree either when you had a chance."

"But I—" Waddell tried to protest, but Earl cut him off.

"Don't worry, Dave," said Earl. "You're going to make out good on this. Instead of my boys pushing leftover cattle here after offering them to half the ranchers we deal with, you'll get first pickin's. We'll bring them here, cross-brand them, fatten them up on the high grazes for a few weeks, then drive them to the railhead brokers in Kansas just like they was ours all along."

"I don't know, Earl. It sounds shaky to me." Waddell began to sweat. "I'm glad to buy a few stolen head from you now and then. I mix them in with my own, keep them till the next spring; nobody has ever questioned it. But what you're talking about is more like going into the rustling business with you as my partner!"

"Partners? Well, if you insist." Earl grinned. "I suppose we could do it that way. But it won't be a fifty-fifty split, not unless you're going down south with us, take your chances getting shot or hung like the rest of us. It wouldn't be fair to the boys."

"Hold it, Earl, please!" said Waddell. He held up a hand as if to stop something advancing on him. "I'm not going to go out rustling cattle, not for anybody! Now, I might not mind you boys holing up temporarily in the high canyon while—"

"Then forget about riding out with us, Dave," said Earl, cutting him off. "You just keep things quiet around here so me and the boys don't have to worry about getting woke up some night to the sound of a rope slapping over a tree limb. You'll get thirty percent of our take, rain or shine." He grinned and drew on his cigar. "It ain't that you think your wife might not approve, is it?"

"Ellen doesn't tell me what to do," Waddell said, dismissing such a notion with a snap in his voice. The picture in his mind of a hangman's noose slung over a tree limb had turned him a little queasy. But the thought of what Earl had just said about his cut began to sink in. "Thirty percent, huh?" said Dave.

"Yep, thirty percent," Earl repeated. "And I promise the boys will be on their best behavior, should they be around your missus whilst you're away on business somewhere."

"That isn't even an issue," said Waddell. "Believe me, my wife would tell me right away if someone ever acted in an untoward manner."

"Oh?" said Earl. "Well, I always admired a man who rules his own roost." He looked Dave Waddell up and down with a grin.

Dave Waddell felt uncomfortable talking about his personal life with the likes of Cherokee Earl Muir. He couldn't imagine what had taken the conversation in this direction in the first place, but he was glad when the topic changed.

"Then thirty percent it is?" Earl asked.

"Ordinarily, how much do you make on one of your trips south?" Dave Waddell asked.

Earl saw that Waddell was getting more interested. "Oh, anywhere from a few hundred on slow trip to, say, eight, nine, even ten thousand dollars for a good fat haul along the border."

"Ten thousand dollars?" Dave Waddell looked amazed. "My God! Every steer standing on all fours in Texas ain't worth ten thousand dollars!"

Cherokee Earl cut in quickly, seeing he had overbid his hand. "We're not talking about rustling cattle, Dave. Me and the boys do other stuff besides just handle cattle. But no matter what we do, we still need a place to lie low for a while. . . . You still get the same thirty percent cut."

"What kind of other stuff?" Waddell gave him a dubious look.

"It don't matter what other stuff," said Earl. "As a partner you still get taken care of . . . for doing nothing but keeping us a hiding place ready here."

"Keep a hiding place ready?" Waddell saw the venture getting more and more involved, more and more dangerous as they talked about it. "I don't know nothing about that kind of thing. I think I'd better pass on it—"

"Come on, Dave, damn it," said Earl. "You're making it a bigger thing than it is. Just give it a chance. If it ain't working out in a few weeks, just say so, and we'll split up . . . no hard feelings." He offered Dave Waddell his gloved hand. "What do you say, partners? I mean, unless you later decide otherwise?"

"Well . . ." Waddell hesitated for a moment longer, then gave in, seeing the cold-steel look in Cherokee Earl's eyes. "All right, what the heck? We only live once, I reckon. . . . Might as well make life a little interesting, eh?"

"That's what I always say." Earl grinned and shook his hand firmly. "Live fast, die hard . . . spit in the devil's eye, eh, partner?"

Dave Waddell turned pale at Earl's words. "I don't know about that. . . . I mean the 'die hard' part. That ain't exactly what I—"

Earl slapped him on his broad back, cutting him off. "Just a figure of speech, Dave. Come on. Learn not to take everything I say so serious. Let's drink on it."

Earl hooked his arm around Waddell's neck and pulled him in close, almost in a headlock. Waddell grabbed the whiskey bottle as Earl shoved it hard against his chest.

"Riders coming," called a voice among the men gathered farther down the corral fence. "Looks like something's wrong, boss. Somebody's riding upside down."

"What the—" Cherokee Earl turned from Dave Waddell and gazed out across the scorched, rocky land at the wavering figures advancing through a veil of heat. "Sherman, Jorge! Get out there and hurry them in here! Damned if that don't look like Ronald's horse."

Jorge Sentores and Sherman Fentress gave each other a look, both knowing beyond any doubt that it was Ronald Muir's horse coming toward them with a body facedown across the saddle.

"This is not so good," Jorge whispered. He made a quick sign of the cross on his chest as he jerked his broad sombrero down onto his forehead.

The other two men, Avery McRoy and Dirty Joe Turley, stared at Jorge and Sherman.

"Go on out there—do like he said," whispered McRoy in a guarded tone. "If that idiot Ronald has gone and got himself shot dead, there's going to be hell to pay, sure enough."

"Why you say if he has got himself shot dead?" asked Jorge under his breath as the pair stepped up into their saddles. "Perhaps he fell from his horse or died of a snakebite."

"Yeah, right," said Sherman. "He might've got run over whilst saving an old woman from a runaway freight wagon, but I like the odds on him getting shot dead a lot better. Either way, Earl's going to be wild-eyed loco for a month. You know how brothers are."

Together Sherman and Jorge heeled their horses off toward the approaching riders.

"I'm starting to wish I was anywhere but here," Sherman grumbled.

They rode out and met Frisco and Billy Boy two hundred yards from the ranch. One look at the body of Ronald Muir lying across the saddle caused Jorge to cross himself again.

Sherman winced and said, "Damn, it's just like we figured." He looked at Frisco and Billy Boy. "How'd it happen? Over a poker game? A whore? What?"

"Just wait until we get to Earl," said Frisco. "I don't want to have to tell this story but once." He shook his head and let out a tense breath. "What kind of a mood is Earl in anyway?"

"Well, not bad," said Frisco, "but I expect that'll change right quick once he gets a look at ole Ronald deader than a chunk of rail iron. Don't you think?"

"Yeah, I expect it will," said Frisco, lowering his head as they rode on.

When the riders entered the front yard, all four stepped down from their saddles and eased Ronald Muir's lifeless body to the dirt. Dave Waddell and the rest of the men gathered in a close group, circling Cherokee Earl, who had fallen to his knees over his brother.

"Who did this?" Earl demanded in a hoarse rasp. His gloves grew tight across his clenched fists.

"It was some old man," Frisco Bonham offered in a lowered sympathetic tone.

"Some old man?" Earl whispered, keeping his voice even and in check.

"Yeah, boss." Frisco went on with a slight shrug. "Who knows why these things happen? It just seems like sometimes it's the Lord's will, and all we can do is stand and wonder—"

"The Lord's will?" Earl stood up, dusting his trouser legs. His eyes had taken on dark circles of grief and rage. "Don't 'Lord's will' me! I want to know what happened and what you two did about it." He pointed a long daggerlike finger into Frisco Bonham's chest.

Frisco and Billy Boy Harper fell back a step, Billy limping on his wounded foot. His boot was missing, and a bloody bandanna was wrapped around his toes.

"It's—it's just like I told you, boss!" Frisco said quickly. "Some old man shot him dead in the street! An old bar swamper at the saloon!"

"An old bar swamper killed Ronald?" Earl asked, his rage building with each word. "My brother, slicker than a snake with a pistol, got smoked down by some drunken old bum?"

"Sorry, boss, but yes, that's who did it," Frisco said gently.

"All right." Earl nodded his head as if forcing himself to accept the bitter news. "An old swamper killed him. . . . Then you two killed the swamper? Was that it?"

Frisco and Billy Boy gave each other a worried look. "We couldn't kill him, boss," said Billy Boy. "God knows I would have loved to! Look at my foot."

Earl looked him up and down. "This swamper shot you, too?"

"Well, not exactly," said Billy. "The woman with him did this to me. She shot me. Then Ronald drew on her, and the old man shot him dead."

Earl stopped him with a raised hand. "Maybe I'm hearing this wrong," Earl said. "An old man and a *woman* did this to you and Ronald?"

As Billy Boy nodded his bowed head in shame, Earl turned a cold gaze to Frisco Bonham. "What about you, Frisco? Any holes in your foot? Any wounds you want to show us?"

Frisco's jaw twitched nervously. "Uh, boss, you had to be there to understand how this all come about. She—the woman, that is—shot poor Billy Boy. Then Ronald went crazy all at once, didn't give me a chance to back his play or nothing else! Once he was dead, there was two guns pointed at me. . . . Damn it, I was in a tight spot, had nobody siding with me."

"Yeah, I can see how that could unnerve a man all right," said Earl, "caught between a woman and a drunken old bar swamper."

"Boss, he didn't handle that Colt like a bar swamper." Frisco tried to come up with something to help himself. "Fact is, I believe he might have been some kind of gunslinger. You know, one of them hard-core killers from the old days, back before our time?"

"Shut your mouth right now, Frisco," Earl hissed, "and you might keep me from killing you." He turned his gaze to Billy Boy Harper. "You and Ronald was good friends, Billy Boy. Is there any truth at all to what Frisco's telling me?"

"Yep, it's the truth, Earl," said Billy Boy, "bad as I hate admitting it. A woman in a gingham dress and an old man who was sweeping out the saloon did all this."

"A woman in a gingham dress," Earl growled to himself. "And that's all I get to go on for who killed my poor brother?"

"I heard her say her name is Strange," Billy Boy offered meekly.

"Strange how?" asked Earl. "Strange sounding? Strange for a woman? What?"

"No, boss," said Frisco. "He means that is her name. S-t-r-a—"

"I can spell! Damn it!" Earl shouted. He swung his hard gaze toward Dave Waddell.

"Danielle Strange is who they're talking about, Earl," said Waddell. "I know her, or I should say I *know of* her. She keeps a one-hand spread over somewhere past the mesa." He nodded off toward a distant upthrust of dark rocky land. Behind it stood a long stretch of hills. "But you'd play hell finding it unless you knew where to start looking."

"She's got perfect ambush country protecting her," said Cherokee Earl. "Reckon she was smart enough to know that when she picked the place?"

"I wouldn't be surprised," Dave replied.

"Figures," Cherokee Earl grumbled. He seemed to dismiss the idea of searching the hills. "Do any of the townsfolk know the way to her place?"

"I'm sure they would," said Dave Waddell. "She deals horses. There's plenty of folks from town probably been out there."

"Then they'll tell me how to get there," said Earl with a slight shrug. "Now, who's this old man they're talking about?"

"Beats me," said Waddell. "Probably just some drifter passing through, swamping the bar for a meal and a cot in the back."

"These don't sound like hardened gunslingers to me," Earl said, narrowing his gaze back coldly in Frisco Bonham's eyes.

"Well . . . the fact is, this Danielle Strange is known to be pretty good with a gun," said Waddell.

"Yeah, I bet she is," said Earl skeptically.

Dave Waddell shrugged. "I'm just telling you what I've heard, Earl. I ain't saying it's true."

"She never hesitated a second before putting a bullet through Billy Boy's foot," said Frisco Bonham. "I reckon that's what took us all by surprise. You don't expect a woman to just up and start shooting hell out of you."

"Is she one of those women goes around wishing she was born a man?" Earl asked Dave Waddell.

"Far as I know she's not," Waddell responded, shaking his head.

Earl looked down at his dead brother. "Jesus, what a mess," he whispered in regret.

Jorge cut in. "Wants us to go kill them pretty good right now, boss?"

"Yeah, Jorge," said Earl. "Get on your horse and go kill them both pretty good. They'll be standing right there in the street where these two idiots left them, just waiting for somebody to come riding in to kill them."

"*Sí*, then I go kill them right now!" Jorge sounded excited.

But when he turned, Sherman Fentress grabbed his arm and whispered close to his ear, "Jorge, he don't mean it. Just stand still here and keep your mouth shut. Give him a minute or two to let things settle."

Hearing Fentress, Earl swung around toward him, saying, "Settle? There ain't a damn thing going to settle! Not until my brother's killers are both lying dead in the dirt!"

"I know, boss! I agree with you!" Sherman raised his hands chest high as if Earl might attack him. "I'm ready to ride into hell with you if that's what it takes. We all are! Right, boys?" He stepped away from Earl and looked to the others for support.

Earl turned to Dave Waddell. "You're going to ride into town with us . . . point out the best person to take us to this woman's spread."

"Me?" Waddell looked stunned. "Earl, I can't ride into town with you and these men."

"The hell you can't," Earl barked. "You're going with me! Don't think you get a free ride around here, Dave! Everybody does their part!"

Waddell stared wide-eyed and speechless. They'd just gone over all this. He wasn't supposed to have to ride with this gang of rustlers. Where had Earl suddenly gotten that idea?

"Earl, I can't go. My wife's expecting me back at the house for supper!"

"Not tonight, Dave. If you're going to be part of this bunch, you might just as well get started."

"This makes no sense, Earl," Waddell coaxed, "me riding into town with you. How are you going to lie low here after letting everybody see that we ride together? That'll ruin any chance of you using this place for a hideout."

"He's right, boss," Dirty Joe Turley offered in a quiet tone.

Earl simmered down and took a deep breath, giving some thought to Waddell's words. "All right, Dave, you get on back to your house. Enjoy your supper," he added with a sneer. "Me and the boys will go take care of this matter and ride by your place afterward."

"Why?" Dave Waddell asked. "There's no reason for you to come by where I—"

"Just to let you know how we did," said Earl, cutting him off. "Don't worry. We won't be staying for tea." He slid a knowing glance across the faces of the gathered men and added, "Or nothing else we ain't welcome to."

Waddell felt his face tighten with embarrassment. "I was only trying to keep your being here as quiet as I can. What good's a hideout if everybody knows you're there? That's all I'm getting at." He shrugged.

"Well, thanks for looking out for us, Davey," Earl said, a sarcastic grin coming to his face. "I believe we'll be all right."

The men let out a nervous laugh, then cut it short as Earl looked at each of them in turn. "Get some shovels and get Ronald in the ground good and deep. I'd better not come by here in a day or two and find him strung all over the ground with some varmint chewing on his innards."

"*Sí*, boss, we take good care of him right now," said Jorge.

"Then get to it," said Earl. "Soon as Ronald's planted properlike, be ready to ride into Haley Springs. We'll snatch us up a trail guide, then head out to those hills. We've got killing to do!"

CHAPTER 3

By the time Danielle and Stick had finished eating, the sun had moved over to the western sky, beginning its fiery descent toward the flat horizon. Owing to his powerful hunger, Stick had spoken very little throughout the meal. Now he finished his cup of coffee and stifled a belch.

"Ma'am," he said, "I can't remember the last sit-down meal I et . . . but I swear it seems like forever."

Danielle looked down at the small portion of leftover biscuits, beans, and beef. "You're welcome to finish them up, Stick," she offered.

"Much obliged, but thank you, ma'am," Stick replied. "I'm full enough to falter as it is."

"Yet you didn't eat that much," Danielle commented.

"I always thought it an odd thing," said Stick, "that the more hungry a man goes over a period of time, the less he can eat when he sits down to big meal."

Danielle nodded her understanding. "I've got a mason jar of apricots if you'd like a helping."

"No, please," said Stick, raising a hand. "Don't tempt me. I got some wood to split twixt now and sundown."

"Not here you don't," said Danielle, reaching out, picking up the coffeepot, and refilling Stick's tin cup. "I've got plenty of firewood for the cookstove, enough to last the next month."

Stick looked at her firmly. "Then I've got a fence to mend or stalls to clean or something, ma'am. Where I come from, no man eats 'less he earns his keep some way or another. I can't stay around someplace without plenty to do. It wouldn't be right."

Danielle smiled. "Ordinarily I'd agree with you, but by siding with me in town, let's consider this meal as earned in advance."

"Just this once." Stick smiled brokenly and raised a finger for emphasis. "And just because you're twisting my arm. I'll not allow myself to be kept and pampered in my old age."

"I wouldn't dream of it," said Danielle. "Believe me, I'll find plenty for you to do." She stood up and collected the empty tin plates and set them aside as she continued to speak. "Now, I know you're too polite to ask me again where I come from, so I'll go ahead and tell you."

"Much obliged, ma'am. I hoped you would," said Stick.

Danielle stepped back from the table into the middle of the small room with both hands on her hips. "Do you recall a year back, you were riding with Tuck Carlyle and some others, pushing a small herd of cattle across Indian Territory?"

"Well, yeah, was as best I recollect," said Stick. "Fact is, I've left lots of hoofprints back and forth across the Territory."

"But on this drive, a friend of Tuck's showed up and took the evening meal with you. Remember that?"

"Why, sure I do," said Stick. "That was Danny Duggin who showed up. Danny was as fine a young man as I ever met. . . . Had a little trouble with the law if I remember correct, not that I fault him for that. It happens to the best of us when we're young and full of vinegar." Stick stopped and contemplated for a second. "There was a real troublemaker with Danny, though, a fella called Dunc."

"Yep, that was Duncan Grago," said Danielle.

"Yes, so it was," said Stick, eyeing her with curiosity. "Dunc picked a gunfight with one of our drovers and shot him dead." Stick took another second as if to go over the picture of the gunfight in his mind. Then he asked, "But what's all that to do with where you know me from?"

"I'm getting to it." Danielle nodded. "First, answer this one question for me. Tuck Carlyle had fallen in love with a young woman named Ilene Brennet." Danielle stepped closer, deeply interested in what his answer would be. "Did he ever go back to the Flagg Ranch and marry her?"

"Yep, he sure enough did," said Stick.

With Stick's answer, Danielle felt her heart sink. For one hopeful moment, she had imagined there might still be a chance for her and Tuck Carlyle. Meeting Stick in town had brought it on. But now she knew better.

"Oh, I see," she said, trying to keep her voice from sounding like her breath had just been stolen from her.

"Now, then," said Stick, his curiosity having gotten the better of him, "are you going to tell me or not?"

"They say a picture is worth a thousand words." Danielle's voice softened, the eagerness in it not as sharp as a moment before. She stepped back toward a narrow doorway and pushed aside a worn blanket. "Drink your coffee. . . . I'll be back right back."

In the small bedroom, Danielle stepped out of her dress and into her road clothes: her faded denim trousers, and her boots. Then she opened a drawer in the stand beside her bed and took out the wound-up cloth binder she had used to conceal her womanly proportions. She unrolled it and wrapped it around her chest. As she watched herself in a dusty mirror, her firm young breasts seemed to vanish before her eyes. She sighed at the memories both good and bad that posing as a man had left with her. Then she strapped her gun belt around her waist, slipped into her long riding duster, and took her battered Stetson from a peg on the wall.

At the sight of her stepping back into the room, Stick gasped and half rose from his chair, his right hand going instinctively to his pistol butt before she caught herself.

"Take it easy, Stick," Danielle said, holding her voice lower, her broad Stetson brim blacking out most of her face. "You wanted an answer, and I figured I could tell you all day . . . but it wouldn't do no good unless you saw for yourself."

As she spoke, her pistol streaked up from her holster and twirled expertly on her finger, first forward, then backward. Then it slid quietly back into her holster.

Stick's jaw had dropped. He shook his head as if trying to clear it.

"Miss—Miss Danielle?" The old drover couldn't hide the surprise and bewilderment in his voice. "Is that you?" But before she could answer, he added, "What am I saying? Of course it's you! But danged if you don't look and sound more like Danny Duggin than—" He stopped short, the truth sinking in. Then he dropped back into his chair with a low chuckle. "You mean to tell me all that time the young gunslinger Danny Duggin was really you?"

Danielle reached up, peeled her Stetson back off her head, and shook out her long hair. "If I'd had no other reason for telling you, Stick, believe me, it would have been worth it just to see the look on your face." Danielle smiled and leaned one hand on the tabletop. "That was my secret those days when I rode with Tuck, you, and the rest of the drovers. I would have given anything to tell Tuck who I really was . . . but I couldn't. I was riding the vengeance trail, and I couldn't let anything come between me and catching my pa's murderers."

"My, my," Stick murmured, shaking his head slowly, sinking back into his chair. "Tuck always said there was something peculiar about you. I reckon he was right."

"Peculiar?" Hurt flashed in Danielle's eyes.

Stick saw it. "Oh, not in any bad way," he said quickly. "Tuck said he couldn't quite put his finger on it, but that there was something odd about you, something different. He wouldn't admit it, and I know how it sounds, but I swear there were times I thought he was overly fond of you."

Danielle smiled. "Stick, you don't know how much that means to me, hearing that." Her eyes grew misty for just a second until she checked herself. "No matter how strange it might have sounded, I would given anything to know it. You see—" She stopped for a moment as if wondering whether or not to finish her words. Then she let them spill. "I love Tuck. . . . I've loved him since I first laid eyes on him. There, I've said it."

"Why, that's plumb unnatural." Stick stared wide-eyed in shock. Then, realizing his error, he said softly, "I'm sorry. That ain't what I meant. For a minute there, I was believing that Danny Duggin actually was a man."

"I know," said Danielle. "I played my part to the hilt. There were times I came near fooling myself. Being a woman posing as a man has done things to me that'll take a lifetime for me to sort out, let alone understand." She paused in reflection, then added, "But I did what I set out to do. I've got no regrets. . . . Well, only one. I've always wished Tuck and I had met under ordinary circumstances. I believe there would have been a place for us in each other's lives."

"Oh, I see." Stick gave her a questioning look. "You loved Tuck that much, and you still do?"

"Yes, I did. . . . I mean, yes, I still do. For a while I tried to forget about my feelings for Tuck . . . even thought I'd fallen in love with another man, Federal Marshal C. F. McCord. But it didn't work out between us. He's been gone the past year. Said it was easier getting along with wanted outlaws than it was for us to get along with each other. He was right. . . . We needed to break it off clean and start over."

"C. F. McCord?" said Stick. "You mean, the man the outlaws along the strip call the Fox?"

"Yep, that was who I took up with," Danielle said wistfully. "And I can't fault him a bit. He tried. We both did. But in the end we both decided we was just too much for each other."

"Too much for each other, eh?" Stick repeated. "I like hearing it put that way. I reckon any man and woman who tried and failed could say the same thing."

"I suppose so," said Danielle. She shrugged. "Anyway, C. F. is gone. Tuck's gone. Now it's just me, and I don't reckon I have whatever heart it takes to ever fall in love again. I wouldn't want to if I could."

"Careful what you say, ma'am," said Stick. "I'm fixing to tell you something that might just turn your world upside down."

"What is it, Stick?" Danielle asked.

"First, tell me this, Miss Danielle. If you love a man the way you claim you love Tuck Carlyle, would you do just about anything you could to see that he never faltered or fell or got so low-down that he could never get back on his feet again?"

"What are you talking about, Stick?" Danielle asked, not getting a hint of what he could be leading up to. "Of course I would. What woman wouldn't if she truly loved a man? What makes you ask something like that?"

"Well, I just wanted to make sure that once I tell you this, we'll both remember what you just said. You see, I believe Tuck Carlyle could use your help right now. Fact is, if you love the man, that might be exactly what it'll take to save his ornery life."

"What is it, Stick?" Danielle demanded. "Is Tuck in trouble? How can I help him?"

"I told you he married Ilene Brennet, but I never told you what happened." A sad expression came to Stick's weathered face as he continued. "Ilene up and died last fall."

"Oh, no, that's terrible," said Danielle. "No matter how much I love Tuck, I would never want something like that to happen to his wife."

"I know you wouldn't," said Stick. "If I thought otherwise I'd never tell you what I'm about to." He paused long enough to sip his coffee as if it would give him the strength he needed to continue. "Losing Ilene has just about destroyed poor Tuck. He rode off plumb wild and heartbroken no sooner than she was in the ground. I'm afraid he's turned to rotgut rye and tar opium to heal himself."

"Couldn't you stop him, Stick? Wasn't there something you could have done?" Danielle sank down slowly into her chair, listening intently.

Stick shook his head. "Don't you know if there was something I could have done, I would have?"

"Yes. I'm sorry," said Danielle, reaching out and cupping her hand down over the old drover's hard, bony knuckles. "I know you would have done something if you could. Where is he, Stick? What's become of him?"

"Last we heard he was up in Greely, staying drunker than a skunk, living on black-tar opium when he can get it and swigging laudanum when he can't. He's lost everything, Danny—I mean, Miss Danielle. His cattle's all gone up in drink, along with his horses and his land. He's down to what's hanging on his back, I reckon." Stick winced, thinking about it. "God, it just tears me up inside, seeing it happen to him."

"Stick, there's got to be something I can do," said Danielle. "There just has to be."

"I swear, Miss Danielle," said Stick, "if I thought you could help him in any way at all, I'd give anything to see you do it. Tuck has been just like a son to me. I'm hoping maybe there was some deeper purpose for you and me meeting in Haley. . . . Maybe it was meant to be. I'm afraid if somebody doesn't reach Tuck afore long, he'll soon be dead in some back alley or muddy street somewhere."

"Not if I can help it," Danielle said firmly. "I'll go to Greely if that's where he is. I'll find him, and I'll—" She stopped short as if uncertain what to say next.

"You'll do what, Miss Danielle?" Stick asked quietly. He paused for a second, letting Danielle consider his words. Then he continued. "You see, it ain't easy stopping a man bent on drinking himself to death."

"I know," said Danielle. "I've seen it happen to men in every board-front town and cow camp I've been through." She stood up and paced back and forth restlessly. Finally she said, "Well, I'll figure out what to do when I get to him. Right now I'll have to take it one step at a time. Are you game for a ride up to Greely?"

"I'm always game for a ride anywhere," said Stick, "especially if it might straighten out Tuck and get him thinking right again."

"Good. We'll get ourselves a good night's sleep, be in Haley before sunup, sell off my string of horses, get us some traveling money, then strike out for Greely. Does that sound right to you?"

"Sounds right to me," Stick agreed. Then he looked at her a bit dubiously. "You won't be wearing those men's clothes, will you?"

"No," said Danielle. "I'll be wearing what I usually wear these days on the trail. My doeskin skirt, my riding blouse, and my vest."

"Not that I mind what you wear." Stick smiled. "I'm just pleased to have something to do. I've been wandering about like a homeless dog."

"I'll keep you busy, Stick," said Danielle. "I think I can promise you that."

D arkness had fallen by the time Cherokee Earl Muir and his men rode into Haley Springs. The street lay empty except for a skinny hound who came scooting his way from beneath the boardwalk and began barking loudly.

"Shoot that loudmouthed sumbitch!" Earl demanded of his men.

A shot rang out, and the dog let out a short yelp as a bullet hit the ground and dirt kicked up against his bony legs. The mutt turned and disappeared, barking as he fled.

"I said, *shoot* him," said Earl over his shoulder, "not shoot *at* him."

Dirty Joe slipped his pistol back into his holster and whispered sidelong to Avery McRoy, "Ain't nothing going please him till we catch Ronald's killers."

"I know," Avery whispered in reply. "And like as not, Ronald was asking for what he got."

"I wouldn't let anybody hear me say that if I was you," said Turley, his whisper growing even softer.

"I already let you hear it," said Avery. "Do I have to kill you now to keep you quiet?" He chuckled under his breath.

"Don't be kidding around about this," Turley warned.

"All right, I'll stop," said Avery McRoy, chuckling even louder.

"What's so funny back there?" Earl asked, sounding none too friendly.

Faces turned to Turley and McRoy in the darkness.

"Nothing, boss," said Turley. "Just laughing at the hound."

Behind dusty windows along the dark boardwalk, a small number of kerosene lamps came to life. From the saloon a half block away,
three heads stuck out above the batwing doors, staring toward the
sound of the gunshot.

"Get ready, boys. Here comes our welcoming committee," said
Earl Muir.

The three men from the saloon stepped down from the boardwalk and hurried along the dirt street. Two more men appeared
out of the darkness, one from behind a door where a woman stood
watching with her sleeping gown held tight at her throat.

"What's the shooting about out here?" asked one of the townsmen, sounding cross and hooking his suspenders up over his shoulders. "It's the middle of the night for God sakes!"

Stepping down from his saddle with his rifle in his hands, Earl
slammed the rifle butt into the townsman's stomach. The townsman hit the ground and rolled into a ball, both arms wrapped across
his middle.

From the doorway the woman came screaming, her gown and
robe fluttering in the darkness. "Robert! Robert!"

Earl grabbed her and threw her to the ground. "Shut up, woman,
or you'll get the same thing!"

She crawled sobbing to her fallen husband and tried to lift him
to his feet. But with his breath still knocked out of him, all he could
do was make tight gurgling sounds as he squirmed in the dirt.

Seeing what had happened, the three men from the saloon came
to a sharp halt and turned around, ready to slip away into the night.

But Earl saw them and called out in a threatening voice, "Get
over here, you cowardly peckerwoods, before I kill the lot of you!"

As more townsfolk appeared from behind doors, Earl's men
jumped down from their saddles and hurriedly rounded them up in
the middle of the street. The frightened faces looked down at Robert
Blanchard lying in the dust and at his wife, Annabelle, who knelt
sobbing beside him. One townsman stepped forward to help the
Blanchards, but Earl shoved him back.

"You stay put. He's doing fine on his own!"

"He's hurt, and I'm the town doctor!" the man said, pointing a finger down at Robert Blanchard.

"You'll be treating yourself if you don't stand back and shut the hell up," Earl growled. He shoved the old doctor back, then called out, "Everybody, listen close to what I'm saying. I ain't about to repeat myself." As he spoke, he drew his pistol and flashed it back and forth. "This morning an old man and a young woman killed my brother right here on the street in this hog wallow of a town! I'm holding everybody here responsible! I know the woman has a spread out in the hills beyond the mesa. Who wants to be the first to tell me how to get there?"

A grizzly old teamster stepped forward and spat in the dirt at Cherokee Earl's feet. "Your brother got what he deserved. He started the whole thing. So you and him both can go straight to—"

A shot exploded from Earl's pistol barrel. The man flew backward with the blast and fell dead on the ground, a gout of blood rising from his chest. A woman screamed. The rest of the townsfolk looked on, horrified.

"Now, then, who among you good folks wants to be next?" Earl called out. "I got all night and a saddlebag full of bullets. I'll kill everybody here if I have to."

CHAPTER 4

In the predawn light, a thick layer of smoke loomed above the smoldering remains of Haley Springs. From atop her favorite mount, a chestnut mare named Sundown, Danielle led her eight-horse string cautiously as she and Stick rode into town from the outer darkness of a sandy stretch of flatland. At the far end of the street, short flames licked at the remaining framework of the livery barn. Danielle and Stick had hurried from the moment they'd first spotted the fiery glow from a distance across the rolling land. But even though they'd pushed their horses as hard as they dared to, it had still taken them over an hour to get here. By now the raging inferno had run its course. Except for a few charred hulls, the plank buildings that had made up the main street of Haley Springs were gone.

"Lord have mercy," Stick murmured, looking around at the devastation.

Embers crackled peacefully like some large animal whose hunger had been satisfied. The empty street lay as silent as stone.

Danielle brought her mare to a halt and sat studying the scene in stunned disbelief as her string of horses bunched up and stopped beside her. She shot Stick a glance, their eyes meeting for only a second, but long enough for Stick to get an idea what she was thinking.

"We don't know for sure it was Cherokee Earl and his bunch," Stick said, "and even if it was, there was no way you could have known he was coming back here." As Stick spoke, he sidestepped his horse a few feet away from Danielle as he looked around and shook his head. "But I got to say, given what happened earlier, things sure point in his direction."

"Oh, it was him all right," said Danielle. "And I should have seen it coming. When we left here after the shooting, I should have expected the unexpected."

"But all the same," said Stick, "there was no reason to—"

His words were cut short beneath a blast of rifle fire coming from the direction of the fallen livery barn.

Danielle spun the lead rope around her saddle horn quickly and jumped down from the saddle. "Move 'em out, Sundown!" she shouted, slapping a gloved hand on her chestnut mare's rump, shooing the animal out of the street.

The big mare knew what was expected of her. She bolted away to the right, pulling the frightened string of horses into the shadows.

"Take cover, Stick!" Danielle shouted instinctively, already realizing she needn't worry about the old drover. Stick knew how to take care of himself. She saw that he had jumped down from his saddle almost in unison with her.

The rifle shot had kicked up dirt ten yards short. Danielle dropped into a crouch and hurried toward the shelter of a water trough, snatching up her Colt and firing a quick shot just to draw any incoming rifle fire away from the fleeing horses. The horses bunched up around Sundown when the mare slid to a halt twenty yards away. They nickered in fright and jerked against the lead rope. But Sundown stood firmly, keeping the animals under control.

Danielle reached the water trough as another shot whistled through the air. Stick had pulled down a well-worn Spencer rifle from its boot before his horse bolted away with Sundown and the others. Danielle heard the big rifle cock from across the street. Something didn't feel right about all this, she told herself. A third shot flashed from the dark alley. The bullet hit the ground a full five yards short and three yards to the left. A wild shot. *Too wild*, she thought to herself.

Knowing that any second Stick would draw a bead on the muzzle flash, she called out, "Stick, hold your fire!"

Another rifle shot rang out, but then a woman's voice called out from farther away in the smoky darkness, "Is that you, Danielle Strange?"

"Yes, it's me, Mrs. Blanchard," said Danielle, recognizing the voice. "Don't shoot."

"Oh, dear, Miss Danielle! I'm so sorry," Annabelle Blanchard cried in a shaky voice. "Are you all right, child?"

"I'm all right, Mrs. Blanchard," Danielle replied. "Aim your rifle at the ground and come on out where I can see you." Danielle wasn't about to be the first to step out from behind her cover. Instead, she scanned the smoky shadows and the glittering embers and saw no one else. "What's gone on here? Is there anybody else around?" she called out, wanting to make sure that anyone who might be listening would hear her voice and recognize it.

Across the street, Stick kept his Spencer rifle aimed into the darkness as Annabelle Blanchard stepped out cautiously, wearing a long sleeping gown with a long wool coat over it. Annabelle began to hurry forward when Danielle showed herself and kept her Colt down by her side in her gloved hand.

"Here I am, Mrs. Blanchard," said Danielle.

"Oh, Miss Danielle!" Annabelle sobbed, letting her rifle slump down to her side. "It's been just awful here! They killed poor Klute Kinsky, the ole teamster . . . and Milton Shirley, our telegraph clerk!" She let out a tortured sigh and shuddered. "They just killed everybody."

Her eyes were large and shiny with fear. *Touched with madness,* Danielle thought to herself, looking Annabelle up and down.

"They would have killed my Robert, too," Annabelle continued, "but I dragged him out of the street and hid him from them."

Danielle saw the woman was nearly delirious. She stepped beside her, giving Stick a look, and said, "Come on, Annabelle, take me to Robert. Then we'll get you something warm to drink and get you out of the morning chill."

Annabelle shivered slightly. "Yes . . . I'll take you to Robert, but I must warn you he isn't himself this morning." She looked around at the burned shamble of a town. "Not that I can blame him, though, with all this going on."

With Danielle guiding her along the empty dirt street, Annabelle murmured to herself about the condition of the destroyed town. A few yards down the street, they came upon the bodies of the two men who had been the first ones Earl Muir had asked for directions to Danielle's spread. When they had refused to tell him what he wanted to know, Earl and Frisco Bonham had shot them dead.

"Excuse us, gentlemen," Annabelle said to the bloody corpses as if they were still alive.

Danielle continued helping her along, casting a glance over her shoulder long enough to see that Stick was gathering their horses.

"I'm afraid it will take some time for this town to recover from a mess such as this," Annabelle said, stepping daintily around the bodies.

Danielle was not surprised when they approached the blank dead face of Robert Blanchard staring off toward the sky as he lay slumped against the side of a small plank shack, the only building Earl Muir and his men had overlooked in their rampage. "I was concerned about Robert at first," said Annabelle. "But now I think he's going to be all right. Don't you, Miss Danielle?"

Seeing the two ragged bullet holes in Robert's chest, Danielle took a deep breath and placed a consoling arm across Annabelle's shoulders. "Listen to me, Annabelle," she said as gently as she could. "Robert is dead. . . . So are those two men in the street."

"Oh, dear," said Annabelle, raising a hand to her lips.

Danielle saw the woman's eyes begin to well up with tears as reality tried to sink in.

"Yes, I'm afraid so," Danielle said, firming her arm around the trembling woman's shoulders. "And I'm going to have to ask you to be strong, Annabelle, and accept the fact that Robert and all these people are dead. Can you do that for me?"

"I-I'll try," Annabelle replied softly, but with resolve.

"Good," said Danielle. She bent down long enough to close Robert Blanchard's eyes, then stood silently with Annabelle for a moment until Stick walked up leading the horses.

"It's pretty bad over past where the saloon stood," Stick said, lowering his voice to shield Annabelle from his words.

"How bad?" Danielle asked. "You can talk in front of Annabelle. She's promised me she's going to be real strong and help us out."

"I see," said Stick. He looked Annabelle up and down, then said to Danielle, his voice still lowered, "I believe the bastards have killed everybody in town."

Danielle felt Annabelle shudder and begin to sob quietly beside her. "We're going to need your help to get these folks gathered and buried proper. Are you up to it, Annabelle?" she asked.

The heartbroken woman summoned up her courage and stepped from beneath Danielle's consoling arm. "I will be as strong as I need to be."

She took a deep breath and let it out in a sigh, looking down at her dead husband's face. In the east, the first thin wreath of sunlight crept upward from the horizon, casting a ghostly silver glow over Haley Springs and its dead.

"But let's get started, Miss Danielle," Annabelle added. "I can't bear to see Robert lying here this way."

"I understand, Annabelle."

Danielle led the shivering woman into the small shack. Stick hitched the horses to a single hitch pole and followed. Inside the cluttered shack, Danielle took a small kerosene lantern from a wall peg, dusted it off, and lit it. Stick began to search through a line of long-handled tools leaning against the wall, quickly choosing two shovels and a pick. Danielle prepared a place for Annabelle to sit down on a nail keg near a small woodstove. With some kindling and newspaper, Danielle soon had a small fire dancing in the round belly of the stove.

"I'll get some coffee from my saddlebags," she said, patting Annabelle on her shoulder. "You sit here and rest."

After a hot cup of coffee, Danielle and Stick went to work, digging graves while the sun rose higher from the eastern rim of the sky. Annabelle stayed close by them as they worked, telling them what had happened, her eyes darting around at the least little sound among the smoldering ashes of what had been the town. Yet when it came time to bury the dead, Annabelle pulled herself together. Corpse after corpse, she washed their faces and their hands, made certain their eyes were closed and that their hair was properly parted and combed. Danielle and Stick watched in silence as the woman prepared the bodies of her husband, her neighbors, and her fellow townsfolk. Then, with their hats in hand, they joined Annabelle in a short prayer over each of the dead. Once done, Danielle and Stick put their hats back on and resumed their work.

Shortly after sunup, the northbound stage arrived in a cloud of dust. Hap Smith, the driver, and his young shotgun rider, Paul Sutterhill, immediately lent a hand with the burying, using two spades they took from the small shack. It was almost noon before the tired burial group patted their shovels on the last mound of freshly turned earth. Eleven new graves now lay inside the short wall of loose stones surrounding the town cemetery. Her hands folded in her lap, Annabelle sat quietly beside her husband's grave as the others looked on.

As they had worked together, Danielle and Stick had filled in Smith and Sutterhill on what had happened. With each rise and fall of the pick into the hard ground, Stick had told them about Cherokee Earl and his band of rustlers and about the shooting in town. But it was only as they finished up the last grave that Hap Smith scratched his scruffy white beard and commented on the matter.

"Who in the world would have ever dreamed a band of cattle rustlers would come back and do something like this?"

"It's simple. They came back to town looking for someone to point them toward my house," Danielle said in a bitter tone. "Annabelle told me no one in this town would tell them where I live . . . so Earl and his men took turns shooting everybody."

"Lord God," Hap Smith murmured. "I reckon that leaves you only one way to go, young lady. You'll have to go find a marshal and put him onto these murders."

"That's one way," said Danielle. "But I have another idea." She turned, rolling down her shirtsleeves, and walked away.

Hap and Sutterhill both looked at Stick. "Did I say the wrong thing?" Hap asked.

"Nope," Stick replied. "But I believe she's already decided to go after them herself."

Hap Smith almost scoffed, but then he caught himself, seeing the serious look on Stick's face. "Herself? What chance would a woman have against a bunch that would do something like this?"

"I don't know," said Stick, "but I sure plan on being there to find out."

E llen Waddell had noticed how tense and worried her husband had been the night before. He'd barely touched his food. After supper he'd spent the remainder of the evening pacing back and forth on the front porch. She noticed that he had laced his coffee with whiskey, slipping the thin flask from inside his vest and pouring it when he thought she wasn't looking. Something was wrong, but she had no idea what it could be. Late in the evening, when gunfire resounded on the distant horizon, she had craned her neck slightly and looked off in that direction.

"Pistol shots," Ellen said attentively.

"Yes, so what?" Dave Waddell snapped, only increasing the intensity of his monotonous pacing.

"Well, nothing, I suppose," Ellen replied. But then, when the shots came again, this time in greater number, she said, "Doesn't that sound like it's coming from town?"

"Yes, damn it, it does!" Dave Waddell barked at her.

Ellen was taken aback that her simple comment had prompted such a harsh response. "Watch your language, if you please. . . . And you needn't raise your voice." She nodded toward his coffee cup sitting on the sun-bleached porch railing. "Perhaps if the coffee is too strong. I'll need to—"

"No!" Dave cut her off. "There's nothing wrong with the coffee. Can't you see I'm trying to think here? There's a time when a man has more on his mind than figuring out whether or not gunfire is coming from town." He took a quick swallow of the laced coffee and muttered, "Good Lord, woman!" Then he fluttered a nervous hand in the direction of Haley Springs. "Probably just some hunter shooting at jackrabbits," he said. "Why does everything have to be such a big event to you?"

"A big event?" Ellen sat stunned for a second. "I was only making conversation."

"Then make it to yourself," Dave snapped. Then he had turned, snatched up his cup of coffee, and stomped off the porch and toward the barn.

"My goodness," Ellen whispered to herself.

That wasn't the first time she'd seen her husband upset about something. But the next morning, when she awakened just before dawn, she noticed that his side of the bed hadn't been slept in. She arose and lit the lamp beside the bed and carried it with her through the predawn gloom. Padding barefoot out onto the front porch, wearing only her loose-fitting cotton gown, she saw Dave Waddell sitting slumped in the wooden porch rocker. She also saw the almost empty whiskey bottle between his legs, the cork lying discarded at his feet. He stared blankly off toward Haley Springs.

Ellen shook her head and walked closer. "Dear?" she said gently, stepping up behind her husband and laying a hand on his shoulder.

Waddell stiffened, making a slight gasp of surprise. Then he turned in the rocker and looked up at her through hollow red-rimmed eyes. "For God sakes, don't sneak up on me like that! You could give a man heart failure!"

"I'm not sneaking up," said Ellen. "I was concerned about you. You didn't come to bed."

"I have other things on my mind," he snapped at her. "There are other things besides going to bed, you know. Some of us have to figure out what to do next in the world!"

"Well, pardon me," Ellen said, seeing his dark mood and not wanting to aggravate matters further. She backed up a step.

But Dave Waddell half rose from the rocker, the whiskey bottle falling to the porch and rolling back and forth. He snatched the bottle up before the last drops could spill from it. He threw back the last drink and let out a whiskey hiss, holding onto the empty bottle as he looked Ellen up and down. In her revealing cotton gown, Dave clearly saw the outline of her breasts. He gave her a look of disgust.

"Don't run around here naked like some harlot!" He shot a frantic glance at the trail as if someone might be watching.

"A harlot, did you call me?" Ellen's voice struggled to keep her anger in check.

"I'm sorry. I didn't mean that," said Dave relenting but only for a second. "But have you no shame? What if somebody happened along here and saw you this way?"

"Don't be ridiculous, David." She managed to swallow her anger and keep her voice settled. "Has anybody ever come along at this time of morning? We live far from town, far from any other ranch."

Dave Waddell slung the wooden rocker aside drunkenly and raged at her. "Don't you dare make light of what I say, woman! I'm the man of this house, and when I tell you something, I don't expect it to be turned into some lighthearted joke!"

Ellen Waddell turned rigid; her words turned cold. "Oh, don't you worry, man of the house. There won't be anything lighthearted going on in this household for a *long* time to come."

She turned in a huff and disappeared inside the house, slamming the front door behind her.

It was an hour later when Dave Waddell walked inside and looked around. The coffeepot sat cold atop the stove, which was itself cold and unfired. The table sat empty. The door to the bedroom was closed. Dave rapped on the door gently, still feeling the effects of swigging whiskey all night.

"I'm—I'm sorry, Ellen," he offered. "I reckon I just lost control of myself. Will you forgive me?"

His words were met by a chilled silence. He turned and left the house and spent the next two hours in the corral beside the barn, attending horses and preparing two of them for the trail. When he returned to the house, the kitchen looked the same. The bedroom door remained closed.

"Honey, I've been thinking," said Waddell, rapping again gently. "Things have been getting the best of me lately around here." He paused, then added, "Remember how you said you'd like to go up to Denver? How you said you'd like to stay a few days in one of them fine hotels where you pull a sash and get food brought up to you?"

After a slight pause, Dave heard the latch fall on the other side of the door. He breathed a sigh of relief.

"Yes, I remember," said Ellen, not giving in all at once.

"Well, I've been thinking," Dave continued. "We've got the money, and we've got the time. . . . Hell, there ain't nothing keeping us here right now. What cattle are out there are in good grazing for now. What say we just up and take off?"

"You mean, soon?" Ellen asked, opening the door a crack, enough for Dave to see that she was still wearing her cotton gown.

This time he was not at all disgusted at the sight of her breasts. In fact, this time the partial sight of her through the narrowly opened door stirred desire within him.

"Soon?" Dave chuckled, putting aside any ideas he might have just had and reminding himself that there was a good reason for what he was proposing. "Honey, I'm not talking about soon! I'm talking about right now . . . this minute. I've already saddled up two riding horses. I'll open the corral and turn the rest out to graze when we leave. Denver, here we come!"

"Oh, Dave, do you really mean it?" The door squeaked open another foot. "I mean, this isn't just the whiskey talking, is it?"

"Oh, yes, I'm sure the whiskey has a hand in it." Dave smiled, putting his arms around her and pulling her against him. "But, little darling, I've never been more serious about anything in my life."

"Oh, my goodness, Denver!" Ellen squealed with delight, then pushed herself away from her husband. "Don't you dare change your mind! I'll throw some things in our grip bag and be ready before you know it!"

"You do that, darling, and hurry yourself up," Dave said, cutting a quick glance across the room and out the window toward the main trail.

He watched Ellen throw back a blanket that covered the dressing trunk where she kept her clothes. As she began pulling out a hatbox and a pair of lady's high-topped dress shoes, Dave said, "I'll grab a couple of clean shirts and some trousers when you're done. Meanwhile, hurry up!" He clapped his hands to speed her along. "I'll make sure all the dry food is topped and stored." Another glance out along the empty trail brought a sense of relief to him. "Who knows?" he said, feeling better by the minute. "We might be gone for the next month or two."

CHAPTER 5

Well, now, look here," Cherokee Earl Muir said, crossing his wrists on his saddle horn and looking down at the Waddell spread from the shelter of a pine thicket lining a cliff behind the house.

Four of his six men drew their horses up quietly around him. Earl had begun to split his men up, sending Frisco Bonham and Billy Boy Harper on head, riding a different trail in case anybody followed their tracks from Haley Springs.

"Don't forget, boss," said Sherman Fentress. "We're down to six men now."

"I ain't worried about it, Sherman," said Earl. "Dave is the only gun on the place." He dismissed the matter and sat watching Dave Waddell lead two horses hurriedly from the barn to the front of the house until the tin roof blocked him from sight. Earl spat a stream of tobacco and said, "Looks like my new partner's in a big hurry to get someplace."

"Yep, it does," said Dirty Joe. "Why don't I punch a couple holes in him for you?" He reached down, slipped his rifle from its saddle boot, and started to raise it to his shoulder.

"Put that damned rifle down, Joe," said Earl. "I don't care where Davey goes." He chuckled under his breath, turning his gaze back to the house, studying it like a hungry wolf. "I just don't want him taking that pretty little redheaded woman with him. I would call that unobliging of him."

"*Sí*, boss," said Jorge Sentores, grinning. "I thinks maybe you gots the plan for that pretty woman, eh?"

"Watch your dirty mind, Jorge," said Earl, his voice turning tight with indignation. "I'm not some pig . . . some animal who would dishonor a man's woman, him standing by whilst I done it."

"No, boss, of course not," said Jorge, shrugging, unable to tell if Earl was serious or not.

He looked at the others for some sort of clue. The men only stared down at the house in silence.

"All right, here's the deal," said Earl without taking his eyes off the house below. "We're going down there. Any of yas says anything out of the way to that little redheaded woman, it'll take you the rest of the day to pull my boot out of your ass."

"Can't we even say howdy?" asked Sherman Fentress, tweaking his thin, well-trimmed mustache.

"No," Earl said bluntly. "You especially can't say howdy to her."

"Not even if she says howdy first?" asked Fentress.

"Keep in mind the size of my boot," Earl Muir warned. He heeled his horse forward at a walk, down onto a thin path.

"Damn," Sherman Fentress objected quietly. "I never seen a person you can't even say howdy to."

Beside him, Dirty Joe said in a whisper, "I wouldn't cross him now if I was you, Sherman. You saw what he did to that town back there."

"Yeah, I saw. I also saw that nobody back there ever told him a damn thing," said Fentress. "We've got no more notion where that woman and the old man is than when we started out."

"I know Earl," said Turley. "He's got a plan. I figure instead of riding into those hills, maybe facing an ambush, Earl figures after killing all them folks, that woman and the old man has got to come looking for us." He nudged his horse forward. "Then we've got them."

"Yeah, or they've got us," Sherman retorted, looking around at Jorge and the others. "I ain't sure which."

"I think this is a bad thing we have done, killing those peoples. I always steal the cattle. I am never been a murderer," Jorge said to Avery McRoy as they stepped their horses onto the trail behind Sherman and Dirty Joe.

"Well, you are now, Jorge," McRoy said, "so tell it to yourself a few times and get used to it. You've killed once, and I expect you'll have to kill some more before this traipse is over."

The five horses moved down the path silently in single file.

Out front of the house, Ellen Waddell sat atop one of the horses, a small black gelding. "Dave, I thought you were in such a hurry to leave?" she called out playfully to the open door.

"Just one second," Dave replied.

He jerked open the bottom drawer of the battered oak desk sitting against the back wall and pulled out the extra pistol he kept there. He hefted the small .36-caliber Navy Whitney in his hand, made sure it was loaded, and shoved it down into his belt. Then closed and buttoned his suit coat over it.

"I want to make sure we don't leave here forgetting something we might need down the road." Before shutting the desk drawer, he caught sight of a dusty bottle of whiskey. "One to grow on," he said to himself.

He pulled the cork, raised the bottle to his lips, and drained it. Letting out a breath, he corked the empty bottle, put it back in the drawer, and locked the desk with a small key.

"Dave . . . ?" Ellen's voice trailed off with an edge of apprehension that Dave didn't notice in his rush to get under way.

"Shhh," said Cherokee Earl, sitting on his horse beside Ellen, lifting the reins from her hands. He leaned in close to Ellen's ear and said softly in his raspy voice, "Let's surprise ole Davey. What do you say?"

"I'm coming, I'm coming," Dave replied, hurrying through the house and out onto the porch. He closed the door behind him without even looking out at the five horsemen surrounding his wife. "You know, darling," he said, looking down at the door key in his hand for a second as he spoke, "if we like Denver, we might just arrange to have this place sold and never even have to come back—"

Dave's voice stopped as he looked up, stunned at the sight of Cherokee Earl sitting on his horse, too close to Ellen, holding her horse's reins in his gloved hand.

"Never come back." Earl chuckled flatly. "My, my, this must be some outing you've got planned, *partner.*"

Ellen looked back and forth between her husband and the stranger with a puzzled, frightened expression. "David, what does he mean calling you partner? I think you'd better explain."

The surrounding horsemen stifled a short laugh under Cherokee Earl's cold gaze as he looked from one to the other, then back at Dave Waddell. "Yeah, Davey, I agree with the little lady. Maybe you'd better explain some things. I get the feeling you haven't mentioned any of us pals here to your missus."

"Earl, I haven't had the chance, and that's God's truth," Waddell said in a shaky voice. He spread his hands. "I didn't know what became of you. We heard shooting last night coming from town. I was just on the verge of clearing out of here. I was worried something had happened to you."

"No fooling?" said Earl, turning his gaze to Ellen Waddell, seeing the look of total bewilderment on her face. "And what about you, ma'am? Was you worried something might have happened to us?" He offered a sly grin, pulling on her horse's reins, drawing the animal closer to him.

"I have no idea who you people are!" Ellen said sharply. She snatched at the reins and stopped her horse, but failed to free the reins from Earl's hand.

"Yeah, but if you did know us, would you have been concerned for my safety last night with all them guns going off?"

"David . . ." said Ellen, her voice still strong but issuing a plea for help.

"Earl, turn her horse loose," Waddell said, the firmness in his voice surprising even himself.

Heavy silence set in. Cherokee Earl gave Dave Waddell an even stare and stepped his horse forward, leading Ellen and her horse beside him. He stopped a foot from where Dave stood frozen in place. With exaggerated politeness, he held the reins down to him and said, "Begging your pardon, Davey, but the little lady's horse spooked a bit when we rode in. I grabbed the reins to keep her from a bad spill. I couldn't bear to see something bad happen to such a lovely woman. . . . Could you?"

Dave's face reddened, yet there was nothing he could do but stand there powerless. He knew that Earl Muir wasn't going to allow him much more slack after talking the way he just had to Earl in front of his own men. "Of course not, Earl," Dave said, giving Ellen a glance to see if Earl had spoken the truth. The look on her face told him that it had been a lie. But again, what could he do about it? The bemused gleam in Earl's eyes told him the same thing. Earl could do what he pleased here. . . . No one could stop him. "Thanks for stepping in when you did."

"Think nothing of it, partner," Earl said, a dark smile on his face. "You'd have done the same for me, had it been the other way around. . . . If I had myself a lovely wife and something bad was about to befall her, I bet you'd be in there like a shot. I hope so anyway. Partners ought to always be prepared to look out for one another . . . become like family, so to speak." As he spoke, he stepped his horse aside and looked Ellen up and down, not even trying to hide his lewd appreciation. "I've always said partnerships should be one big happy family."

"Why does he keep saying you're partners, David?" Ellen asked, avoiding Earl's eyes, ignoring his overtures.

"Ellen, it's a long story," Dave replied promptly. "I'll tell you everything about it as soon as—"

"Come on now, Davey," Earl cut in. "We can't be having secrets in this happy family of ours, now, can we?" He gave Waddell a wink, then said to Ellen, "You see, Davey and me has had ourselves an arrangement for some time now. I bring up border cattle—what you might say is beef of questionable origins. I give Davey here part of the herd just to let me hide them out here awhile in the upper grasslands. Then I cross-brand them, take them back down, and push them to the makeup herds heading for Abilene or Dodge City. We all make a little—Davey, the rest of the boys, and me—and nobody gets hurt." He grinned and crossed his wrists on his saddle horn.

"Cattle thieves? Rustlers?" Ellen looked back and forth between her husband and Earl Muir in disbelief. Then she said to Dave Waddell, "You've been involved with a cattle-rustling operation? All those cattle that have shown up here and you told me they were strays that wandered onto the grazing range . . . all the while they were stolen?"

Before Dave could answer, Earl stifled a laugh and said, "Oops, I sure hope I haven't spilled the beans on you, Davey. That was not my intention."

"Ellen," Dave said, fighting to keep control of his voice and to keep his wits about him, "you'll have to let me explain everything to you. . . . And I will—I swear I will—only not right now, not right here. This isn't the time or place!"

Ellen Waddell saw beads of perspiration form on her husband's forehead.

"Yeah, you'd best go along with your husband, Missus Ellen," Earl said, including himself in their conversation. "There ain't time for explaining things now. We've got to get our horses changed and get moving."

"Get moving?" Ellen stepped hurriedly down from her saddle and stood by her husband's side. "Dave, tell them to leave," she whispered close to his ear.

"Yep, you heard me right," said Earl. "We've got to cut out of here fast. You heard the shooting last night—you said so yourself. We killed everybody in that town and left it burned to a cinder. I reckon we'll soon have somebody dogging our trail. I don't want them coming out here sniffing around, maybe getting you to tell them where we might be headed. I like you, partner, but I've got to tell you: I'd kill a man before I'd leave him to jackpot me to the law." Earl gave Dave a hard stare.

"Earl, we can't go with you," said Dave with a sinking feeling in the pit of his stomach. "We're heading north, going to take a few days of holiday in Denver."

"Well, that's just fine. We'll head right along with you," said Earl. "Never let it be said that I'd spoil a holiday for anybody."

"Our plans are already made, Earl," said Dave, slipping an arm around his wife's waist as if to protect her. "We prefer traveling just the two of us. You don't have to worry about either of us telling the law about you. I stand to lose as much as you do if I did something like that. I don't want to get arrested for harboring stolen cattle."

"I beg to differ with you, Davey," said Earl, "but you don't stand to lose as much as I do." Pointing a gloved finger at him, Earl stepped his horse closer as he continued. "They'll drop the charges on you just to get to me." He turned his horse sideways to them and leaned slightly down. "I can't afford that, partner, now, can I?"

Before either Dave or Ellen could say another word, Earl leaned farther down, snatched Ellen under her arm, and swung her upward. Ellen let out a short scream and batted her fists against Earl's shoulders as he held her against his chest. He stepped his horse back as Dave Waddell lunged at him.

"Let her go, Earl! Let her go!" Dave shouted. He grabbed at Earl's stirrup, but Earl cocked his boot and kicked him back a step.

"Now you've gone and done it, partner," Earl said, seeing Dave stagger backward, his hand going for his pistol. Earl drew his first, aimed it, and cocked it, keeping Ellen against him, giving Dave nothing to shoot at but his wife.

"You was going to shoot me, I do believe!" Earl said in mock surprise.

Dave stopped cold and spread his hands away from his gun belt.

"Earl, I'm sorry! I didn't mean it!" said Dave. "Just let her go!"

Earl shook his head. "No, no, partner. I just can't overlook something like that. I suppose I'm going to have to go on and kill you." He leveled his pistol out at arm's length.

"No, wait!" Ellen shouted, squirming against Earl's arm. "Don't kill him, please!" She spoke quickly. "It's me you want, but don't kill him! If you kill him, you'll have to kill me, too—I swear it! Leave him alone, and I'll go with you. I'll do anything you say! You have my word! Just let him live."

"Well, listen to this." Earl chuckled, letting his pistol slump, not as intent now on shooting Dave Waddell. "This little honey of yours ain't no fool, Davey. She knows this ain't really about you saying anything to the law." He lowered his pistol and hugged Ellen up closer, pressing his beard-stubbled cheek to hers. "We're going to get along fine, you and me," he said, half whispering his words to Ellen as he watched the sickened expression on Dave's face.

Backing his horse without taking his eyes off Dave Waddell, Earl called out over his shoulder, "Sherman, get over here and give me a hand."

Sherman Fentress kicked his horse forward, snatching Ellen Waddell from Earl's arm as Earl held her out to him. "Keep an eye on his little filly while I step down and talk some sense to my partner here."

"Earl, let her go, please!" said Dave Waddell. "I'm begging you."

Almost sobbing, Dave stepped forward, still carefully keeping his hands away from his guns as Earl slipped down from his saddle and swaggered up to him, pulling off his right glove one finger at a time.

"Davey, get a grip on yourself." Earl threw his arm across Waddell's shoulders, drawing him close, almost in a headlock, the same way he had earlier. "Listen to me, partner. We can kick this subject back and forth and call it anything we want to." He slipped Dave's Colt .45 from its holster and shoved it down behind his belt as he continued speaking. "But the fact is, I'm taking that woman with me. . . . I'm doing as I please with her, and I'm keeping her as long as it suits me. You might as well understand and get used to it." He spread Dave's suit coat open, eased the small .36-caliber pistol from his waist, and held it barrel first in his hand, hefting it, judging its weight. "When I'm through with her, you can have her back."

"No, Earl, please, for God sakes!" Dave begged, his eyes filled with tears. "Don't do this. . . . That's my wife."

"Wives, cattle, horses, what have you." Earl shrugged. "It makes no difference to me. . . . I take what I want. You ought to have seen this coming from a mile down the road. Hell, man, I'm a thief and a killer. You think her being your wife means a damn thing to me? You ought to have had better sense, dangling something as sweet and pretty as that little redheaded woman before my eyes. I'd be a fool not to take a taste. What made you think you could deal with the likes of me and ever come out ahead?"

"Earl, please—"

Dave Waddell's voice fell silent as Earl bowed him forward at the waist and crashed the butt of the Navy Whitney against the back of his head. Seeing her husband fall face forward into the dirt, Ellen screamed long and loud, scratching the outlaw and jerking free from Sherman Fentress's grip. She hit the ground at a run toward her husband and didn't stop until Earl's strong hand caught her by her arm and slung her away. She landed in the dirt and came crawling toward Dave Waddell. Earl swooped an arm down, caught her around the waist, and held her hanging down his side, kicking and screaming.

"He'll be okay . . . just wake up with a headache, is all. You gave your word you'd come with me, no trouble. You ain't backing out on it, are you?" He flipped the Whitney around and cocked it in Dave Waddell's direction.

Ellen caught hold of herself, seeing the gun pointed at her unconscious husband's head. "No, wait!" She settled down immediately. "I won't cause any trouble, I promise. I'll keep my word."

"All right, then, that's more like it." Earl eased his grip and let her stand on her feet. He slipped an arm around her thin waist and hugged her up close. "I swear, woman, since the first time I laid eyes on you from a distance, it's been all I could do to keep my hands off you." He nuzzled his face into her long, flowing red hair, the scent of her seeming to overpower him for a second as he closed his eyes.

"I won't be any problem from now on," Ellen said in a soft, relenting voice. "Whatever you want, I'll do it."

Earl's breath quickened at the sound of her voice. "Lord, what a waste, something like you hooked to the likes of something like him." He shook his head as if to clear it. "But that's over now." Then he turned, pulling her back to the horses. "Come on, let's get these horses swapped out and put some miles between us and Haley Springs. I've got to get an ambush set up for a couple of real tough gunslingers who're going to be on our trail." He grinned and spoke to Ellen as he dragged her along. "The more you get to know me, the more you'll come to realize that I'm a man who likes staying one step ahead of the game."

Ellen looked back once more at where her husband lay crumpled in the dirt, a trickle of blood oozing down the back of his head. Then she forced herself to swallow the bitter taste in her mouth and follow Cherokee Earl at a quicker pace, trying her best to keep up with him.

"Where we headed from here, boss?" asked Sherman Fentress, hoping nothing would be said about the way the woman had broken free from him. But Earl was letting nothing past him.

"I reckon the first place ought to be a doctor so's you can have your face looked at. You've let this little girl scratch you like a wildcat."

He walked steadily on, pulling the woman behind him. The men laughed as they stepped down and led their horses toward the corral.

Sherman turned red and touched his fingers to the stripe of blood along his cheek. "Aw, this ain't nothing. She just wiggled loose, is all." He hurried to catch up with Earl.

"Yeah, wiggled loose," Earl said wryly. "Go help swap out some horses. We've been here long enough."

"But where are we headed from here, boss?" Sherman persisted. "We told Billy and Frisco we'd meet them along the south trail."

"I lied, Sherman. . . . Those two are on their own. I used them as bait for the woman gunslinger and the old man. We're going to throw a little raid on the next town up the line, get ourselves some real money. Then we're heading north of here, where there's good ambush country. By the time Billy and Frisco tangle with the woman and the old man, we'll be higher up, able to look down at anything on our trail. This is how I'm going to play it—instead of looking all over for them, I'll keep them looking for me right up until I'm ready to kill them."

CHAPTER 6

Within moments, Cherokee Earl and his men had swapped their tired horses for fresh ones from the corral. As the group gathered at the corral gate, Earl looked over at where Dave Waddell stirred slightly in the dirt.

"Hold these for me, Turley," he said, handing Dirty Joe the reins to Ellen's horse. "I've got one last thing to do before I leave."

Ellen gasped as Earl turned his horse toward Dave Waddell.

Hearing her, Earl looked back over his shoulder. "Don't worry. I ain't going to kill him. Bullets cost money."

As he rode his horse across the yard, Sherman Fentress said to Dirty Joe in a hurt tone, "I don't know why he didn't ask me to hold the reins. I'm the one he was always asking to do stuff like that."

"Because you messed up, you idiot." Dirty Joe laughed. "You let this woman scratch your face and make a fool of you." He jiggled the reins to Ellen's horse, grinned, and winked at her. "Ain't that right, sugar?"

Ellen looked away from Turley's leering face.

"Don't talk to her that way, Turley," Sherman warned.

Turley laughed; so did Jorge and Avery McRoy. "Boys, I believe Sherman's gone love stricken on us."

"*Sí*," said Jorge, "and I think it is not such a wise thing to fall for the boss's woman."

Dirty Joe's voice fell quieter, just audible to those near him. "The boss's woman today maybe. But who can say about tomorrow? He might decide what's good enough for himself is good enough for all of us. I don't reckon ole Sherman here would object to that. Would you, pal?" He gave Sherman a sly look.

"You'd best watch your dirty mouth, Joe, I'm warning you!" said Sherman Fentress, his hand dropping to the pistol handle on his hip.

Ellen listened closely to every whispered word, knowing that her only chance out of this was to keep her wits and weigh every possibility. Halfway across the dirt yard, she saw Cherokee Earl turn in his saddle upon hearing Sherman's angry voice.

"Can't you men be this close to a woman without it turning you into lunatics?"

The men fell silent. Earl shook his head and rode the last few steps over to Dave Waddell, who tried to struggle to his feet. "You lay right there, Davey," said Earl, bumping his horse into Waddell, sending him back facedown in the dirt. "I like looking down at you."

"Don't—don't take her . . . please," Dave gasped, dirt-streaked tears streaming down his face, a string of spittle dangling from his lips.

"Oh, I'm taking her, Dave. That's already been settled." Earl grinned, drawing the Whitney from his waist. As he continued to speak, he opened the percussion gun's cylinder and dropped out all of the loads but one. "But I want it to be said that I was a good sport about this." Then he closed the gun and pitched it to the ground a few feet from Waddell's dirt-crusted hands.

"Please . . . !" Dave glanced at the pistol but made no move for it. Then he dropped his cheek back to the dirt.

"There you are, partner," said Earl, stepping his horse to the side, hoping for Ellen to get a look at what was going on. "You've got one shot in there. Either take it at me whilst I turn and ride away with her or else after I leave . . ." He let his words trail, then added, "Well, I reckon you can use your imagination what to do with it then. One bullet can mean a lot to a man, depending how he uses it."

He turned his horse and heeled it away, unconcerned about Dave Waddell going for the pistol. If Earl heard the sound of the pistol cock behind him, he knew he was fast enough to turn and kill Dave Waddell without batting an eye.

At the corral, Earl took the reins to Ellen's horse from Dirty Joe Turley and said to the men, "Let's ride, boys."

Then, as his men heeled their horses up and rode off in a rise of dust, Earl turned to Ellen, who sat staring across the yard at her sobbing husband in the dirt. "That's it. Take one good long look at him. Did you see? I threw him a gun . . . gave him a chance to claim you or let you ride off with me. He was too scared to make a move. He'd rather wallow in the dirt to save his own hide. That ought to show you clear enough which one of us can protect a woman when it comes down to it."

Ellen summoned her courage and said with an air of defiance, "I didn't marry to have a man protect me."

Earl stared at her for a second, grinned, and said, "Then maybe you should have."

Dave Waddell lost track of how long he'd lain sobbing in the dirt, his head still pounding where Cherokee Earl had knocked him cold. The sun had moved lower in the western sky by the time he collected his senses enough to drag himself to his feet and stagger to the front porch. On his way, he managed to stoop down and pick up the Navy Whitney. After collapsing onto a porch chair, he wiped his blurry eyes and checked the pistol, seeing that only one round of ammunition remained in the cylinder. For a moment he was lost, but then the whole terrible, hopeless scene came back to him. He gazed out and along the trail leading up over a rocky rise to the north.

"God, what have I done?" he whispered aloud to himself.

Then he hung his head and stared long and hard at the pistol in his trembling hands. He had no idea how long he sat there, cocking and uncocking the Whitney. But evening shadows had grown tall and thin across the dusty, rocky land when he finally left the gun cocked and raised it slowly until he felt the hard steel tip of the barrel against the side of his throbbing head. He took a deep, tortured breath and held it, struggling to keep his hand from shaking uncontrollably. He pressed back on the trigger slowly.

When the sound of a pistol shot exploded, he flung the cocked pistol away in horror. His first thought was that he'd done it; he'd actually shot himself through the head. Yet, if that was the case, how was he still there, alive and able to wonder about it? He sat frozen, stunned, his mouth hanging open. On the front of the house, he saw the bullet hole, right where he had heard it thump into the plank siding. He rose woodenly halfway from his chair, leaning toward the fallen pistol as he looked out at the two riders coming across the front yard.

"Stand real still, Mr. Waddell," said Danielle Strange. "That shot wasn't meant to kill you. It was meant to keep you from killing yourself."

"I—I understand," Dave managed to say, his mind becoming clearer.

He'd seen Danielle Strange in town enough times to recognize her. He'd never seen the old man before, but there was no doubt the two were on Cherokee Earl's trail. He had to think up something to keep anyone from knowing he'd been a part of Earl's stolen-cattle operation.

"Thank God you've come along!" He straightened up and wiped his shirtsleeve across his face.

Danielle and Stick swung down from their saddles, keeping an eye on Dave and taking a quick, steely look around the place. Danielle nodded at the Navy Whitney lying on the porch, cocked and ready to fire.

"What's going on here, mister?" she asked, stepping up onto the porch, then reaching down and picking up the gun. She looked the gun over, noting the single round of ammunition in the cylinder. Then she let the hammer down gently but didn't hand the gun to Dave Waddell when he reached out for it.

Dave dropped his hand and rubbed it on his trousers. "It's not what you think, ma'am," he said.

"Oh? And what do I think?" Danielle responded.

"Well, I know it looked like I was getting ready to shoot myself. But I wasn't—that is, I wouldn't have . . . I don't think."

Dave struggled with his words while Danielle and Stick only stared at him. Finally he gave up and collapsed into the chair.

"What's the difference? Maybe I should have pulled that trigger." He hung his head and continued. "I know why you're riding this way—you're hunting for Cherokee Earl and his bunch. And yes, they were here. They took my horses and my wife, Ellen. Then they rode on."

Stick and Danielle looked at each other, then back at Dave Waddell.

"They took Miss Ellen?" Danielle asked.

"Yes," said Dave. Then he asked a bit surprised, "You . . . knew my Ellen?"

"We met only once," said Danielle, "at the mercantile in Haley Springs. How long have they been gone? We'll have to catch them quick before . . ."

She cut herself off, letting her words trail, but Dave caught what she'd kept from saying.

"I'm not sure," he said, rubbing the back of his head. "Cherokee Earl knocked me out. Then they took her and rode off. It's been a while—I know that."

Stick butted in. "Damn it, man, weren't you going after them?"

"Easy, Stick," said Danielle although she had been wondering the same thing.

"I wanted to," Dave said, a slight whine to his voice. He gestured a hand toward the empty corral. "But as you can see, they took all the fresh horses."

Fifty yards away, three of the spent mounts left by Earl Muir's men grazed on scattered clumps of wild grass.

Stick said, "So instead of cooling out one of them horses and going to save your wife, you decided to blow your brains out." He shook his head.

Danielle cut Stick off with a firm gaze. She looked back at

Dave, studying his eyes as she spoke. "I've got a string of horses waiting just beyond the rise in the road. Are you up to going with us to get your wife back?"

"Yes, of course!" Dave sprang to his feet. "I didn't mean to give you the notion that I wasn't interested in saving her. You just have to excuse me. . . . That lick on the head has left me addled."

"Then go throw some water on your face," said Stick. "Be ready to go when I bring the horses in here." He turned, climbed into his saddle, and looked down at Danielle as Dave Waddell staggered into the house. "Don't turn your back on that peckerwood," he cautioned her in a low, guarded tone. "Something ain't right about him."

"Don't worry about me," said Danielle, her hand resting on her pistol butt. "But let's give the man the benefit of the doubt. A hard lick on the head can take a spell to get over."

"Yeah," said Stick, backing his horse. "The question is, why'd he let a bunch like Earl Muir's boys ever get close enough to do it in the first place?"

"I wondered that myself," said Danielle under her breath, watching Stick tug his hat brim down and ride off toward the rise in the trail.

"There, all ready to go," said Dave Waddell, coming back through the open door, drying his head on a wadded-up towel.

Danielle looked off along the trail as Stick disappeared over the rise. "He'll be a couple of minutes," she said. She looked at the empty holster on Dave's hip, much too big for the smaller, slimmer Navy Whitney, she noted to herself. Then she leveled her gaze onto Dave Waddell's eyes and said, "This Cherokee Earl is known as a cattle rustler. How many head of cattle are you running now, Mr. Waddell?"

Dave Waddell made the mistake of not holding her gaze as he answered. Instead, he ducked his eyes for a second and said, "It's been a while since I pulled a head count. Must have upward of three, four hundred head maybe."

"The cattle business has gotten so good a man don't need to keep track of his holdings anymore?" Danielle asked, not even hiding her skepticism.

"Well, Miss Danielle, you know how it is," said Dave, holding the wet towel to the back of his head. "Cattle come and go on the breaks and high grasslands. But if I was held to it, I'd say I've got three hundred head easy enough."

"You've had quite a run of luck, then," said Danielle. On a bluff, she added, "Last year when I talked to Ellen in town, she said you had only about half that many."

"She did, huh?" said Dave, looking as if he couldn't understand why. He offered a weak, patient smile that Danielle saw through right away. "My Ellen's a fine wife, but she never knew beans about my cattle business. My fault, I suppose. . . . I should have told her more, I reckon. But the only gains I made this year are a couple of range strays wandering in, plus my calves, of course."

"I see," said Danielle.

Noticing Stick top the rise with the string of horses in tow, Danielle decided not to pursue any more questions right then. Instead, she flipped the Whitney around in her hand and handed it to Dave Waddell, butt first.

"If this is what you carry, you'd best load it up. If you want to borrow a big Colt Forty-five, I've got an extra in my saddlebags."

"Much obliged. I'll take you up on the offer," said Dave, shoving the small Navy Whitney into his belt. "I normally carry a Colt, but Cherokee Earl took it after he knocked me out."

Danielle only nodded, but Dave could tell she had just asked herself how a man with two loaded guns could have allowed himself to be so easily caught off guard. "Look, Miss Danielle, I know how bad this looks on my part. But all I can say is that it happened so fast, I never got a chance to act. There's nothing in this world I want more than to get my wife back safe and sound. After that, I don't care what anybody thinks of me."

"Take it easy, Mr. Waddell," said Danielle. "We're both on the same side here. I want Earl Muir for the killings in town, but saving your wife is all the more important." Her gaze narrowed as she added, "Anything we need to talk about can wait. Fair enough?"

"Fair enough for me, Miss Danielle," said Dave.

"All right, then." Danielle stepped down and opened the saddlebags behind Sundown's saddle.

She pulled out a thick cloth, unfolded it, and took out a large Colt. She checked the gun, made sure it was loaded, then passed it to Dave.

"Here you go. And now that we're going to be working together for a while, I want you to drop the 'Miss.' . . . Just call me Danielle." She looked up at Stick and said, "That goes for you, too, Stick, all right?"

Stick blushed at such informality but nodded in agreement. "All right, then, Miss—" He caught his error and quickly said, "I mean, Danielle."

BRADEN FLATS, INDIAN TERRITORY

Outside the New Royal Saloon, Sheriff Oscar Matheson stepped down from the boardwalk and moved out into the dirt street, getting a better look at the five men and one woman who had just ridden in from the glittering stretch of sand. It took a second for him to see that one of the men held a short lead rope to the woman's horse. What was this about? he wondered. The riders had now stopped in a low cloud of dust. They sat abreast at the edge of town, staring along the darkened shade of boardwalk overhangs and recessed doorways.

Matheson didn't like the looks of this. Keeping a wary eye on the group, he said to his part-time deputy, young Gerald Noel, "Boy, I believe you'd best go round up the blacksmith and some others. Tell them to bring their guns."

But Gerald didn't look up right away. He stood on the boardwalk, whittling intently with his pocketknife, shaving long, fresh-curled strips of pine from a stick.

"Did you hear me, boy?" said Matheson, raising his voice a bit, still staring at the riders fifty yards away. "We might have trouble coming."

"Huh?" Gerald raised his eyes grudgingly from his pastime, a long, curled pine sliver falling from behind his short knife blade. He managed to catch the word "trouble." His eyes shifted in the same direction as the sheriff's. "Holy!" he exclaimed in a hushed tone. The blade of his pocketknife snapped shut. He bounded down from the boardwalk in a run, his low-topped shoes batting up dust as he cut straight across the street toward the blacksmith's shop.

At the end of the street, Cherokee Earl said, "Joe, you got him?"

"Sure do, boss," Dirty Joe replied, raising his rifle from across his lap and cocking it on the upswing.

"Oh, Lord, it's commenced," Sheriff Matheson whispered, seeing what was about to happen. As he stepped sideways, drawing his pistol, he shouted, "Look out, Gerald!"

But instead of the sheriff's words causing the young deputy to duck behind cover somewhere, Gerald skidded to a halt on the other side of the street. He turned and looked back at Matheson, spreading his arms.

"What?" he asked, having no idea that a rifle was homing in on him.

"For God sakes, Gerald, run!" Matheson screamed.

He raised his pistol as he spoke and fired repeatedly toward the horsemen, hoping his shots would throw off the rifleman's aim. But it didn't work.

"Got him, boss!" said Dirty Joe in the wake of the rifle shot resounding along the street.

The shot struck Gerald Noel in the chest like the blow of a sledgehammer. He flew backward a step, bowing at the waist, his left shoe leaving his foot, exposing his big toe through a hole in his worn-out sock. His shirt puffed out in the back. A wide spray of blood rose and fell. Gerald managed to straighten up for a second. Then he sank to his knees, his arms falling limp at his sides, and pitched face forward in the dirt.

Even as the sheriff's pistol shots whistled past them, Avery McRoy gigged his spurs to his horse's sides, drew his pistol, and shouted, "He nailed that sucker right through the heart, good as ever I've seen."

Hearing the gunfire from his shop, the blacksmith dropped his hammer. "What the hell?" he said, and hurried out the front door in time to see the horsemen descend upon the town like a pack of ravaging wolves.

Three shots thumped into the front of his shop, forcing him back inside. But not for long. Grabbing a double-barreled shotgun from against the wall, he ran outside again. This time he stood his ground long enough to fire both barrels into the oncoming flurry of men, guns, and horses.

Sherman Fentress's horse took most of the double blast of buckshot in its side. Fentress felt his left leg ripped to shreds as the horse whinnied painfully and slammed into the horse beside it, the horse Ellen Waddell was riding, being led at a full run by Cherokee Earl.

All Ellen could do was hold on to the saddle horn with all her strength. Sherman Fentress's horse tried to right itself but couldn't. With Fentress himself badly wounded and barely able to stay in his saddle, the poor horse veered away blindly, still at a run, until it hit the edge of the boardwalk and rolled up onto it. Fentress left the saddle and crashed through the front plank wall of the telegraph office, landing spread-eagle on the operator's desk, sending the telegraph machine across the room.

The telegraph clerk had heard the shooting and luckily had just pushed his chair back from his desk to go see what was happening in the street. Seeing the bloody man land on his desk in a spray of broken boards, the clerk gasped and sat frozen, his hands held chest high as if he were being robbed.

Fentress groaned and lay staring at the clerk, his leg chewed to the bone by buckshot, bloody face and chest filled with splinters. "God . . . I'm hurt," he managed to say.

The sound of Fentress's voice caused the telegraph clerk to snap out of his dazed state. He sprang from his chair and ran shrieking from his office out into the roaring gunfire. Six bullets pounded into him no sooner than he'd leaped out into the street. He had time only to see the bodies of the sheriff, the deputy, the blacksmith, and two other townsmen before he crumpled to the ground and joined them in death.

Cherokee Earl had stepped down from his horse and forced Ellen Waddell to step down and stand beside him, his left arm wrapped firmly around her thin waist.

Inside the town's bank, Arnold Flekner, the bank president, hurriedly locked the front door.

Seeing him through the glass, Cherokee Earl chuckled and said to Jorge Sentores, "Get around there, Jorge, and take care of him." Then Earl pressed his face to Ellen's hair, took a deep breath, and said to her, "Watch this. . . . He'll try running out the back door any minute now. But Jorge will smoke him."

Ellen shuddered, filled with horror by all that had just gone on around her. Yet she stood in wide-eyed silence, unable to turn her eyes from the carnage.

Jorge raced his horse alongside the brick-and-wood bank building, sliding the animal to a halt just in time to catch the bank president as he ran away from the back door, a ring of keys in his hand.

"No! No! Please!" the hapless banker pleaded. "Here, take the keys!" He flung them up to Jorge, but Jorge let them fall to the ground. "The money's all yours! But please don't kill me!"

Jorge shrugged. "Okay, I won't kill you. Now you go, take off, get out of here pronto!"

"Oh, God, thank you! Thank you!" the poor man sobbed, turning as he moved away, his legs visibly shaking through his black trousers.

"Here comes the fun part," Earl whispered into Ellen's hair, his breath hot against her skin.

Ellen managed to squeeze her eyes shut as Jorge extended his pistol down at the fleeing banker's head. Three shots resounded, followed by Earl's low laughter near her ringing ear.

"See? Jorge was just funning with him. . . . I knew he'd kill him."

Ellen felt a bitter sickness well up at the back of her throat. She

fought to hold it down and did, taking a deep breath and reminding herself that the only way she could survive the lot that had been
cast upon her was to refuse to let this or anything else get to her. She
knew this was only the beginning. There were worse things ahead
of her, and if she wanted to live through this, she had to prepare
herself mentally. *You can do it! You can do it!* she repeated to herself.
By sheer determination, she forced herself to block out Earl's words
as his raspy voice whispered to her. She forced herself to no longer
smell his hot breath or feel his hot smothering arm around her.

"Hey! Hey! Wake up now! You're missing everything!" Earl
chuckled, shaking her back and forth against him.

Her eyes had closed slightly. But now she stared silently up at
the grinning, beard-stubbled face held so close to hers.

"You're riding with a rough bunch, darling. It ain't going to get
no better, so you might as well learn to take it."

As he shook her, she felt the edge of a pistol butt dig into her
side. It was the pistol that he'd taken from her husband and shoved
down into his belt. She had a sudden urge to grab the pistol and
use it on herself before he could stop her. But something kept her
from doing it. *You don't deserve this,* she told herself. *You're not the
one who should die.*

She put the notion of grabbing the pistol out of her mind for
now and said in a meek voice, "I'll be all right."

Then, biting her tongue to keep from shouting aloud, she said
to herself as she imagined her hand closing around the pistol butt
the first chance she had when he wasn't looking, *I'll take anything
a worthless pig like you can dish out.*

CHAPTER 7

For more than two hours, Cherokee Earl's men pillaged and terrorized the helpless town. With a bullet through his right shoulder and another through his left hip, Sheriff Oscar Matheson could do no more than get out of the gunmen's way and stay out of their sight. Avery McRoy and Dirty Joe forced the town doctor, Latimar Callaway, to clean and dress Sherman Fentress's leg wound and the many cuts, scraps, and broken ribs Fentress had received when he'd blasted headlong through the front wall of the telegraph office. Once the doctor had finished, he left Fentress lying on the billiard table and nursing a bottle of red rye in the New Royal Saloon. Making sure no one was watching, the old doctor hurried from the saloon to the livery barn, where he'd left Sheriff Matheson resting on a pile of fresh straw.

"Who goes there?" Sheriff Matheson asked, hearing the barn door creak open as a sliver of sunlight striped across the dirt floor.

Dr. Callaway whispered as he closed the door and heard the sound of a pistol cocking in the grainy darkness, "It's me, Oscar, dang it! Don't cock that hammer at me. The shape you're in, that thing could go off. Then who'd be left here to look after you?"

"Sorry, Doc," Sheriff Matheson said in a weak voice.

Lying with his back propped against a stall post, he let the cocked pistol drop across his lap. The doctor stepped into the stall and frowned, seeing the pistol in the faint striped sunlight through the cracks in the barn wall.

"Give me that," Dr. Callaway said, stooping and taking the gun from Matheson's hand. He let the hammer down and shoved the pistol into the holster lying by Matheson's side. "Confounded guns!" he growled. "They're the cause of all the trouble in this world."

"Don't start on guns, Doc," Sheriff Matheson said in a voice labored with pain. "If I hadn't had this with me a while ago, I reckon I'd be dead right now."

"I suppose," the doctor grumbled, already opening the dressing on the sheriff's upper-right chest. "Of course, if those jackasses didn't have guns, they couldn't have shot you in the first place. That's how a more civilized man would reason with it."

"I'm all for civilization, Doc," Matheson said, offering a tired, painful smile.

He nodded toward the street beyond the dark, quiet shelter of the barn. Distant laughter rose above the sound of breaking glass.

"How bad is it out there?"

Two pistol shots roared from the direction of the saloon.

"It's bad enough," the doctor said, shaking his head as he examined the sheriff's wounds. "The blacksmith buckshot one of them, sending him sailing. The ringleader laid up at the Crown Hotel with some woman under his arm before the smoke cleared. Poor Gerald's dead, so's our telegraph clerk . . . our banker, the blacksmith, too. We didn't have many folks here to begin with. This will just about do us in."

"The Crown Hotel, huh?" said Matheson.

"I saw him go there," the doctor replied. "Can't say the woman looked real happy. They might've just had a lovers' spat or something."

Thinking about it for a moment, Sheriff Matheson said, "I sure did let this town down, didn't I?"

"Hush, Sheriff," said the doctor. "You know better than that. You did the best you could. Nobody will ever fault you for what's happened here."

"I fault myself," said Matheson.

"Then I reckon that's your own stubborn lawman's prerogative," said the doctor, looking closely at the wound before closing the sheriff's shirt over the bloodstained bandage, "so I won't waste my breath arguing with you. I won't change this dressing until it clots up some more." He turned his attention to the dressing beneath the sheriff's split trouser leg. "Lucky this one didn't hit the bone. A feller your age gets a shattered hip bone, he's ready for the pasture if he can even walk out to it."

"Yeah, a feller my age . . ." Matheson let his words trail in contemplation.

"No offense, Sheriff," said Doc Callaway. "But like myself, you've grown long in the tooth."

"I reckon I have, Doc."

A silence passed as the doctor spread the split on the sheriff's trouser leg, pulled back the corner of the bloody bandage, and looked at the wound.

Sheriff Matheson let out a long breath. "I was getting ready to retire, hand in my badge, you know."

The doctor turned his eyes upward, looking at the sheriff above his spectacle rims. "I had no idea."

"Well, it's true," said Matheson. "I've got a daughter I ain't seen since she was nine . . . when her ma up and left me in Abilene. She's married to a rancher out in California. They've got two freckle-faced kids. She wrote me, said, 'Pa, come on out, meet your grandchildren.'" He nodded and gazed off across the darkened barn. "That's where I was retiring to."

"Well . . . you still can, can't you?" the old doctor inquired, closing the bandage, then the split trousers.

Sheriff Matheson continued staring off as he spoke. "She said they've got a room off to the side of the house where I could stay—close the door and be left alone for days if I didn't want to talk to nobody." He grinned. "I reckon folks with grandchildren never get lonesome for talk or for getting their stories listened to."

"I reckon not," said the doctor. "You could go there, say, a week from now, maybe two. Lie low for now. Let this bunch of trash clear out of here. Give these wounds time to heal and then head for California. Nothing's stopping you."

"I know it," said Matheson. His fingertips brushed the tin star on his chest. "My daughter said you can ride less than three miles from her front door and stand on a cliff that looks out over the ocean. Can you imagine that, Doctor?"

"Sounds real fine, Sheriff," said Dr. Callaway. "I envy you."

Another silence passed, and the doctor saw the trace of a tear in the sheriff's tired, distant eyes. "Well, hell, Sheriff," he said with resolve, "I suppose you'll want me to bring you a shotgun."

"Yep. The biggest ten-gauge double-barreled you can find, Doc," said Sheriff Matheson. "I'd hate going out with whimper instead of a bang."

"But can you get on your feet and walk by yourself?" the doctor inquired.

"I'll walk on my own when the time comes. I might need you to help me to my feet." The sheriff managed a thin, tight smile. "I reckon you'll do that much for the only man in town who ever kept his bill paid."

Dr. Callaway returned the thin smile. "Well, I can see you're feeling much better." He patted a hand on the sheriff's good shoulder as he closed his black bag and stood up. "I want you to know I'm not the kind of man who can shoot a person, Sheriff, no matter how justifiable the situation."

"I understand, Doc," said Matheson. "I'd never ask you to. Just get me a shotgun and get me on my feet. Wearing this badge has always meant I'd be the one to take the bullet . . . or give it, however way the chips fall."

The old doctor nodded as he backed away toward the door. "I'll be back as quick as I can."

Sheriff Matheson watched the door open a crack, then close.

Outside, Dr. Callaway slipped unnoticed along the backs of the buildings toward the New Royal Saloon, where he knew the owner kept a spare loaded shotgun stuck beneath a whiskey pallet in the stockroom. On his way to the back door of the saloon, the doctor saw the first steam of smoke rise atop the buildings from the direction of the telegraph office.

"Sonsabitches," he whispered to himself, hearing hoots of drunken laughter from the street.

Finding the rear door to the saloon unlocked, the old doctor slipped inside and held his breath as he passed the open stockroom door and saw Sherman Fentress lying atop the billiard table, drunk and waving a cocked pistol back and forth aimlessly. Dr. Callaway kept an eye on the wounded gunman as he slipped over to a darkened corner where a wooden pallet lay supporting a half dozen whiskey crates. Before his eyes grew accustomed to the darkness, the doctor reached a hand out to the crates. But instead of feeling the rough wood, he felt the familiar round hardness of a knee bone and jerked his hand back, startled, as a deep voice said, "Doc, what're you looking for, slipping around back here?"

"Damn it, Leonard! Scare the bejesus out of a man!" the doctor cursed in a whisper. "Sitting here in the dark like some lunatic!"

He collected himself and took a deep breath, looking at the darkened face of Leonard Whirley, the saloon owner, sitting slumped atop a whiskey crate. Atop Whirley's head, a ruffled-up toupee sat crooked and slanted too far to one side.

"Fix your hair, Leonard. It looks like a rat's got his head stuck in your ear."

The saloon owner reached up, adjusted the toupee, and smoothed it down. "Sorry, Doc. Had I expected company, I would've been better groomed."

The doctor shot a glance out to the billiard table and saw the bartender carry a fresh bottle of rye from behind the bar and hold it out to Sherman Fentress's grasping hands. Then he said, looking back at Whirley, "Sheriff Matheson is still alive and kicking. I reckon you know why I'm here."

Whirley nodded and moved his right foot to one side. The doctor stooped down, pulled out the shotgun, blew dust from it, and broke it open, taking pains to keep his actions quiet.

"There's a couple extra loads down there if you want them," said Whirley.

"Why not?" said the doctor, reaching back under the pallet and bringing out two shotgun loads. He dropped them into his pocket.

Watching the old doctor check the loaded shotgun, the despondent saloon owner said, "Believe it or not, I was just thinking about pulling that out myself. There's only five of them, one already wounded all to hell. I figured I could walk out and blast that bloody buzzard off my pool table, then go to the street and take my chances with the rest of them."

"Only five, huh?" The doctor stared at him for a second, then said, "Five is no small number when there's guns pointed at you."

"I said I was just thinking about it, Doc," said Whirley. "I never said for sure that I was going to do it."

"That's what I figured," the doctor said. "While you've been thinking about it," he said, clicking the shotgun shut, having seen that both barrels were loaded, "our sheriff is getting ready to do it." He looked the saloon owner up and down. "Of course, I don't suspect he'd be opposed to some help if you'd like to join him."

Whirley swallowed a dry lump in his throat. "Who was I kidding, Doc? I ain't going to do nothing but sit here, thinking how bad I want to. I ain't no hero. . . . I never was." His hand went nervously to his hairpiece. "I can always think things out, how to go about doing something like that. I can picture it in my mind clear as day. But I ain't got the sand to kill a person." His shoulders drooped even more. "I reckon all I can do is roll onto my back and show my belly like a beat dog."

"Don't be hard on yourself, Whirley," the doctor relented in a low tone. "I can't shoot a person either." He ran a hand along the glistening black gun barrel. "Oh, I say it's because I'm in the healing arts. Truth is, I'm as big a coward as you. I just plain ain't got the guts."

At the Crown Hotel, Cherokee Earl stepped into his trousers and pulled them up, turning back to face the bed where Ellen Waddell had just sat up and pulled a blanket around herself, clasping it under her arms, holding it closed in front.

"What did you expect?" she said flatly, keeping her eyes from looking directly at him. "I've been dragged here against my will . . . by a total stranger. I've seen my husband left for dead."

"Well, I reckon I just expected a little more fire and thunder, darling," said Earl mockingly as he leaned forward, took her by the chin, and tilted her face up, forcing her to look into his eyes. "I might've thought that just maybe you'd be a little obliging, seeing as how I didn't leave you dead in the dirt. You know I could have had my way with you back there on that three-cow spread, then left . . . no witness, no nothing."

"Then why didn't you?" Ellen said, carefully weighing how much snap to put into her words. "What kind of an animal did you think I was? Did you really think that I would just throw in with you after what you did to my husband?"

Earl found himself stuck for words, looking into her eyes, not fully understanding what he was looking at. There was something puzzling about this woman. She hadn't fought him, hadn't resisted him. She had in fact done everything demanded of her. Yet he felt now as he'd felt before they'd arrived. He felt as if he hadn't touched her. Her eyes seemed to look straight through him. They made him think that whatever he might say, she had already heard it.

"Don't play with me, woman!" he hissed, holding her chin roughly between his finger and thumb and leaning close to her face. She didn't so much as flinch or brace herself. She sat limp, spineless, he thought, but still untouchable. "Do you hear me?"

"I hear you," she said calmly, not trying to avert her eyes now but rather staring into his so steadily that he himself had to look away for a second.

"See . . . I believe there's more than meets the eye with you, little lady. I think maybe ole Dave Waddell didn't know the whole story on you when he hitched you to his wagon."

"I don't know what you're talking about," said Ellen, her eyes still steady, still cool and fixed.

"Yeah, I bet you don't," said Earl. "I get the feeling that you were an old hand at this sort of thing long before you crawled under Dave Waddell's blanket."

"Then you are badly mistaken, sir," said Ellen. "Mr. Waddell is the only man I have ever known."

"Until now, you mean," said Earl, a trace of a triumphant smile coming to his face.

"No . . . including now," she said distantly. "This doesn't count. This is just something that happened that never should have. It is best forgotten."

Earl stood frozen for a moment. Then he said with an almost hurt sound to his voice, "Well, I ain't going to forget. And I still ain't had my fill of you."

"Very well," Ellen said softly. She started to unwrap the blanket from around herself in submission.

"Wait, damn it. Not now." Earl stopped her, tucking the blanket back up under her arms. "That ain't what I meant." He ran his fingers back through his hair in frustration and chuckled. "See? See what I mean about you? You're as cold, spiteful, and deliberate as any whore I ever laid hands on. You don't fool me any longer."

"You think I'm a sporting woman?" Ellen asked flatly.

"I think you have been at some time or other," Earl offered.

"And if I was?" said Ellen. "Would that make any difference?"

Earl shrugged. "I wouldn't waste any more time on you if I was convinced you were. I have no respect for a sporting woman. I never did. I want a woman who is *my* woman—mine alone." He thumbed his bare chest.

"So you kidnap me? You force me to go to bed with you?" said Ellen. "That's the kind of woman you want, a slave?"

Earl looked confused. "Don't put words in my mouth. If I thought you was ever that kind of woman, I reckon I'd just turn you over to the rest of the boys, then ride on."

Ellen looked away now and took a breath, running a hand across her damp forehead. Then she sat quietly until Earl said, "So are you? I mean, was you ever?"

"No, of course not," said Ellen. "I was a schoolteacher, a professional woman, before I met my husband."

Earl reached out and suddenly grasped a handful of her red hair, forcing her eyes back to his. "You're lying, ain't you?"

"If you think I'm lying, do what you just said." She stared back at him unflinchingly. "I'm powerless to stop you, whatever you've got in mind."

"Awww, damn it!" Earl turned loose her hair roughly, shoving her head sideways. "It doesn't have to be this way, woman! All you got to do is get used to being with me instead of Dave. Why is that so hard to do?"

Ellen stared at him. "Not hard at all if I were a bitch dog or if I were the kind of woman you accused me of being. But you just said if I were that kind of woman, you would have no more use for me." She paused and shook her head. "I think you need to do some thinking about—"

Her words were cut short by a knock on the door and the sound of Dirty Joe's voice in the hallway.

"Yeah, Dirty, what is it?" said Earl. Before Joe Turley answered, Earl said to Ellen, "We'll finish this some other time."

Ellen didn't even bother to answer.

"Boss," said Turley from outside the door, "you said to come wake you up, tell you when we've done all we set out to do here."

A silence passed; then just as Dirty Joe started to knock again, Cherokee Earl growled in a sleepy voice, "All right, damn it to hell! I heard you! Hold your horses."

Dirty Joe looked back and forth quickly in the hallway as if to find some horses and do as he was told. But as the door opened a bit, Dirty Joe snatched his hat from his head and stood rapidly smoothing down his hair as Cherokee Earl stood before him wearing only his trousers, his belt and fly both hanging open.

"You sure are getting a case of the propers, ain't you, Dirty?" Earl opened his eyes wider and added, "Did you bring me any flowers?"

Dirty Joe looked embarrassed and wrung his hat brim between his hands, saying quickly in his own defense, "Boss, I just thought it might be the lady opening the door, is all. . . . I didn't figure it would look right, me standing here with my hat on. That's all I meant by it, honest."

"I believe you, Dirty Joe," said Earl in a tired voice, stepping back and flagging him into the room. "If I'd thought otherwise, I'd have cracked your skull."

Inside the room, Joe started to speak, then fell silent when his eyes fixed on Ellen Waddell. She sat on the edge of the bed, shivering in spite of the heat, a blanket wrapped around her. She stared at the wall as if it were a thousand yards away. Her red hair lay damp and curled against her forehead and her bare shoulders.

"Well, Dirty," said Earl, seeing what effect a half-naked woman was having on this dumbstruck cattle rustler, "are you going to tell me what's gone on out there, or did you just stop by for tea?"

"Well, uh—" Dirty Joe stammered. "We, uh, looted all the, uh, cash from the, uh, bank—"

"Hold it, Dirty," said Earl, cutting him off. He reached out with both hands, took Dirty Joe by the shoulders, and turned him away from the woman. "Now try again."

Dirty Joe wiped a trembling hand across his brow and took a deep breath. "Sorry, boss. What I meant was, the bank money came to a little over three thousand dollars." He settled himself and went on. "We got Sherman Fentress patched up and liquored up, and it looks like he might be all right. Jorge set fire to the telegraph office, so ain't nobody going to be telling on us . . . not for a while anyway." His eyes drifted back around toward the woman as he spoke. "We, uh . . ."

"Joe, damn it!" said Earl, a threat rising in his voice. "Look at me when you talk!"

"Yes, boss!" Joe snapped his eyes back to Earl. "We swapped out what fresh horses we could find and loaded a few bottles of rye for the trail . . . and I reckon we're ready to cut out of here most anytime now." He felt his eyes draw toward the woman, but this time he caught himself and pulled them back to Earl. "When you're ready, that is."

"Good work, Dirty," said Earl. He started to say something else, but a shotgun blast coming from the street below caused both men to duck instinctively. "What the . . . ?"

They both hurried to the window and looked down.

"Over there, boss!" shouted Dirty Joe Turley, pointing down at the dirt street out front of the New Royal Saloon. In the open door of the saloon, Sherman Fentress lay flat on his back, his bandaged wounds ripped to shreds by the blast of the ten-gauge shotgun. His bloody right hand grasped the bottom edge of one of the batwing doors as if it were the only thing keeping him from sliding downward to hell.

"That damned old sheriff!" Earl growled.

On the street below, Sheriff Matheson came limping toward the hotel, dragging one foot behind him and using a barn pole as a walking stick. The double-barreled shotgun was propped against his good hip, a curl of smoke still rising from its tip.

"I reckon I'll have to kill that old bastard again—this time it'd better take!"

"Boss, let me go down and—"

"Huh-uh," said Cherokee Earl, turning and snatching his holster from a peg on the wall beside the bed. "I'll take care of this myself personally."

He quickly buttoned his fly, buckled his belt, and slung his gun belt around his waist. As he buckled the gun belt, his eyes went to Ellen Waddell.

"Get dressed!" he commanded, snatching up his boots and throwing them under his arm. But as she rose slowly from the edge of the bed, he glanced impatiently toward the window, then said to Dirty Joe Turley, "Stay here and make sure she gets dressed. . . .

Make sure she doesn't try to sneak away. Don't take your eyes off her for a minute."

Earl slung his shirt over his shoulder. He grabbed his hat.

Joe's eyes widened. "But what if she does try to make a run for it? What do I do about it?"

Cherokee Earl had already made it to the door and swung it open. Stopping for only a second, he said to Dirty Joe as he gazed coldly at Ellen, "What the hell do you think I would want you to do, Dirty Joe? I'd want you to kill her!"

CHAPTER 8

No sooner had Cherokee Earl left the room than Dirty Joe Turley turned red-faced to Ellen Waddell and said, "Ma'am, you heard him. Now get yourself dressed with no funny stuff."

"Funny stuff?" said Ellen quietly. She seemed to consider his words for a moment. "All right, excuse me."

Picking up her dress from the bottom bedpost, she walked halfway across the room toward the door to an adjoining room.

"Wait up now!" said Dirty Joe. "You heard the boss." He took a step forward, stopping less than three feet from her. "He said not to take my eyes off you . . . and I'm not about to."

"I understand."

Ellen seemed to once again ponder what he said. Then she turned loose of the front of the blanket and let it fall to the floor around her feet. At the sight of her standing naked before him, Joe Turley actually jumped back and gasped.

"My God Almighty!" He looked at her, then jerked his head away; his hat fell from his hands. He quickly looked back at her, then ducked his eyes with a hand raised as if to hold the world in place while he gained his bearings. "Ma'am, cover yourself, please! You're going to get me into big trouble!" He shot a frightened glance at the door as if Cherokee Earl might return at any second.

"What's it going to be, then?" Ellen said, her voice taking on a slight authority. "Do I go in there and dress? Or do I dress here while you stand and watch me?"

"Ma'am, please, just stand still and put that dress on! I won't look—only hurry, though!" said Dirty Joe.

"Joe," she said, her voice low and silky, "just between you and me, I don't mind if you look . . . a little, that is."

Dirty Joe felt the hair on his neck tingle. He turned his eyes back to her, the sight of her pearly white skin causing him to have difficulty breathing.

Ellen stood with her dress clasped in one hand and held between her naked breasts. She held her feet shoulder width apart, the dress hanging down the middle of her, leaving little to the imagination. "I always say it costs nothing to look."

"Yes, ma'am. . . . I mean, no, ma'am! I mean, God Almighty, you are the most beautiful woman I ever saw!"

He rocked back and forth on his bootheels, opening and closing his hands. It seemed to take all his self-control to keep from lunging upon her.

She smiled coyly, half turning from him as she gathered the dress and raised it over her head. He caught a glimpse of fiery red hair and pale white thighs.

"Tell me, Joe, why does he call you Dirty? You look as clean as the rest of this bunch."

She waited on dropping the dress down past her head, taking her time, knowing how much she was torturing him.

"Yes, ma'am, I am. Clean, that is. It's just a moniker, you know? Like some men they call Lefty?"

"Oh, I see," she said. She dropped the dress down and smoothed it, the open buttons up the midriff still exposing her breasts. "But isn't that a case where the person is left-handed?" she said softly.

"I—I don't know," Dirty Joe stammered. "Nobody ever called me Lefty."

Dumber than a cellar rat, Ellen thought. *Perfect.* She closed the dress in front and buttoned the lower buttons one at a time slowly. "Does it bother you that he leaves you here alone with me?"

"God, no." Dirty Joe grinned. "This is the best thing happened to me in a long time!"

"Will you get my shoes for me, Joe?"

She nodded at the dust-covered shoes beside the bed. As he scurried past her to get them, she almost felt her hand brush the handle of the pistol on his hip. She fought to keep herself from snatching it up and shooting him, then making a run for it. But run to where? What would that get her—a few minutes of freedom before they caught up to her? She was in this game to stay alive. She had to play it on out. She would know when the time was right.

"Why would it bother me?" Joe asked, coming back and dropping the shoes before her. His breathing was labored. Sweat had beaded on his brow. He stood close to her.

She could feel the heat of him. "Just that maybe he thinks you're not man enough to try anything," she said tauntingly, "the way some of the others would, the two of us alone like this."

"Ha! He knows I'm as much man as the next." Joe looked her up and down. "He just knows he can trust me, is all. I've been with Earl for a long time." He extended a hand slowly toward where her dress remained open in the front.

But she artfully stepped away from his probing hand and said, nodding down at her shoes, "You'll have to help me, Joe."

"Huh?" Dirty Joe seemed to have gone blank for a second.

"My shoes," she said almost in a whisper. "Will you bend down there, put my shoes on me?"

"Well . . ." He glanced at the door but had already begun to sink down onto his knees. "Sure, I reckon I can do that." He picked up her left shoe.

She placed a hand on his bare head for support and entwined her fingers into his thick, damp hair. "There now," she said, almost moaning, raising her foot and propping it onto his knee. "Do it for me."

He fumbled, her foot in one hand, her shoe in the other. She raised her dress above her knee. "Ma'am, I hope this is going to be our little secret, me and you getting this close," he said.

"I'll never tell a soul, Joe," she said, guiding her foot, helping him slip it into the trembling shoe. "You can count on it."

"Lord, I hope so, ma'am," he said, his voice turning thick with passion. "I hope I can count on you. He'd kill us both if he was to ever think—"

"Shhh, hush, Joe," she cut him off, reaching down, taking his hand, and placing it inside her thigh, just above her knee. "Now, if I told him, whose fault would it be? It would be mine, wouldn't it, Joe, getting you to do this?" She pressed his hand there, slicing a breath as if in ecstasy.

"Oh, yes, ma'am, it would be," Joe said, giving in, letting go of his fear of death for the moment. "It would be indeed." He tried to raise his hand farther up, but she stopped him.

"No, Joe, not now," she whispered. "Not now but soon. I promise, soon."

"Ma'am, now I'm this far, I just don't think I can hold off," he said, panting, his hand fevered and trembling.

"But we've got to wait, Joe. Please!" She struggled halfheartedly. "Right now I need a friend, Joe." She entwined her fingers in his hair again and pulled his head up, pressing his chin into her flat lower belly. "Will you be my friend for now, Joe?"

"Oh, yes, ma'am," he gasped, clinging helplessly to her. "I *am* your friend . . . your *best* friend. . . . You can *believe* that!"

Outside the open window, the sound of a shotgun roared, followed by repeated blasts of pistol fire. But Dirty Joe only heard them from a distance, through the pounding of his pulse and the rush of hot blood through his veins and his senses.

On the dirt street, Cherokee Earl stopped long enough to pull his socks from inside his boots. He put them on, then stepped into his dusty boots and stamped them onto his feet. He pulled on his shirt as he walked toward the spot where the old sheriff lay crumpled in the street. Blood spilled from the sheriff's lips as he struggled to speak. From the middle of the street, Avery McRoy and Jorge Sentores closed the open space between them and came forward also, each of them flipping out the spent cartridges from their pistols and replacing them as they walked.

Cherokee Earl looked up at the open hotel window as he reloaded and said, "What the hell's taking Dirty Joe so long?"

"Where is he anyway?" asked Avery McRoy.

"He's getting the woman dressed," said Cherokee Earl.

"Oh?" Avery McRoy and Jorge looked at each other. McRoy raised an eyebrow and said, "I wish I'd heard you ask for volunteers. I'm a good hand at getting women dressed . . . or undressed, either one."

"Shut up, McRoy," said Earl. "I couldn't leave her alone. I left him to watch her, make sure she didn't take off."

"Again," said McRoy, "had I only known you was looking for someone to—"

"Do you think I won't open your belly, McRoy?" Earl spat at him. Having reloaded his Colt, Earl slapped the cylinder shut and cocked it with a snap of his thumb. "Huh? You think I have a sense of humor when it comes to my woman? Do you?"

His woman! "Easy, boss!" said McRoy. "No, I reckon you don't! I was just making man talk, is all! Hell, I take it back."

Cherokee Earl eased the pistol down and turned slowly to the sheriff in the dirt. "Look at this old buzzard. Still trying to set things right for himself." He leveled the pistol down at arm's length. Seeing the sheriff struggle to speak, Earl said, "What's that, old-timer? What're you saying?"

The sheriff summoned all his strength and rasped, "You son of a low, white-livered—"

"Whoa, now!" said Earl with a dark chuckle. "You can't talk about my mama that way!" The pistol jumped once in his hand, and the old sheriff fell silent. "The hell's the matter with you anyway?" he said to the still form. As he looked down, he saw the faintest flicker of the sheriff's wrinkled eyelid. "I'll be switched if this old turd ain't still alive."

"You're kidding," said McRoy, leaning in for a better look. He reached his hand out and cocked his Colt toward the sheriff's head. "I'll fix that."

But Earl stopped him. "Forget it. Hardheaded as he is, it'll just ricochet, hit one of us." He looked up toward the hotel window as he holstered his Colt. Beside him, McRoy and Jorge did the same. "What the hell is taking him so long?"

McRoy and Jorge gave each other a look, but neither offered any comments.

"We got a good take from the bank, boss," said McRoy, changing the subject.

Earl ignored him. "Jorge, get up there and see what's keeping them," he said, growing irritated. "I'd like to set fire to a few buildings before we leave . . . if that doesn't interfere with anybody's plans." There was a sarcastic snap to Earl's voice.

"*Sí*, boss, I'll tell them to hurry up," said Jorge, hurrying off across the street toward the hotel.

Earl and McRoy turned back and looked down at the sheriff, seeing that the man was still alive and had even managed to claw his hand toward the shotgun lying two feet away in the dirt. McRoy chuckled and kicked the shotgun closer to the sheriff's hand.

"There you go, old slick. Grab it and give us hell." He grinned at Earl. "It ain't loaded, of course."

Earl said to the sheriff, "You sure know how to try a man's patience, you old bastard."

He drew back his boot and kicked the sheriff in the face. The sheriff fell limp.

McRoy's grin broadened. "If you ain't careful, you're going to hurt him, boss."

Inside the door of the Crown Hotel, Jorge met Dirty Joe and Ellen Waddell coming down the stairs. He gave Dirty Joe a questioning look and said, "Everything is mostly all right, Dirty?"

"Yeah, why?" asked Joe, a defensive look coming to his eyes.

Jorge shrugged, looking the woman up and down. "Boss, he say why it take you so long. He send me to get you so we can burn some buildings. Now you hurry up, eh?" As Jorge spoke, he reached out and took Ellen by the forearm to hasten her along.

"Take your hands off her, Jorge!" Dirty Joe bellowed, shoving the Mexican back a step. Both men's hands went instinctively to their pistol butts. Then Dirty Joe caught himself and said, letting his hand fall, "He told me to keep an eye on her, not you. I don't like nobody horning in when it's me supposed to be in charge of something, all right? *Comprende?*"

Jorge raised both hands in a show of peace. "*Sí, comprendo, mi amigo!* I mean nothing by it."

"All right, then, let's forget it," said Dirty Joe, getting himself fully collected.

Ellen watched closely, taking in every action, examining every response between the two men.

"I reckon it just took her longer than it should to get dressed," Dirty Joe said.

"*Sí,*" said Jorge. He looked Dirty Joe up and down. When Joe reached for the doorknob, Jorge stopped him. "*Uno momento,*" he said.

Joe stopped with his hand still on the knob. "What do you want, Jorge?" His tone of voice turned a bit testy.

"Do like this before you go out there," said Jorge, rubbing his own chin vigorously.

"What the hell?" Dirty Joe gave him a strange look.

"You have lint on your chin," Ellen cut in, lowering her eyes modestly. She idly smoothed down the wrinkled front of her gingham dress.

Dirty Joe picked at his beard stubble with nervous fingers, his face red and frightened. "Damn . . . I don't know how I got that," he muttered, seeing—and knowing that Jorge saw as well—the small fleck of lint and a short scrap of thread that had undeniably come from Ellen's dress. "Much obliged, Jorge."

Jorge shook his head slowly, giving Joe a warning gaze. "Don't tell me 'much obliged.' I want to know nothing about what is going on. This is not my business. When Earl hears about this, you are on your own."

Opening the door, Dirty Joe allowed Ellen Waddell to step outside. Then he stopped and said to Jorge, "What do you mean by that? You going to tell him?"

Jorge said, "I am not loco. It is a bad thing that I want no part of."

"It ain't what you think it is, Jorge," said Dirty Joe. "Nothing happened between us, I swear."

"It is no business of mine," Jorge said, stepping through the open door after the woman.

"Answer me, Jorge," said Dirty Joe. "Are you going to tell Earl?"

Jorge only shook his head and walked on.

From across the street, Cherokee Earl called out, "It's about damn time! We need to get a move on." He turned from the limp body of Sheriff Matheson and walked toward the hitch rail, where fresh horses stood ready to go.

Matheson opened his eyes thinly and let his hand crawl once again to the stock of the shotgun. With all his waning strength, he forced his free hand inside his coat pocket, found the shotgun load, and brought it out. He saw the woman and the two men coming across the dirt street. *God,* he whispered to himself, *just give me one more round.*

Jorge gave Avery McRoy a telling glance as they all met up near the horses.

"What's going on, Jorge?" McRoy asked, looking at Dirty Joe and the woman.

"He is playing with dynamite, that one," Jorge whispered, nodding toward Dirty Joe.

"You mean, him . . . and her?" McRoy looked stunned. "Dirty Joe and a woman?" The prospect of it seemed ridiculous to him.

"*Sí,*" said Jorge. "It is so. And now that I know about it, I must be a part of their secret. So it is I who is in the big trouble."

Dirty Joe caught a trace of Jorge's words and snapped his head toward him. "What the hell are you saying, Jorge?"

"I said nothing," Jorge responded. "But I am not such a fool that I will put myself on the spot for you."

Five horses away at the other end of the hitch rail, Cherokee Earl busily riffled through the bank bag, taking a loose count, too occupied to pay attention to what was being said.

"Yeah?" Dirty Joe stepped toward Jorge. "You'd best keep your mouth shut about me, Mex!"

"Or what?" said Jorge defiantly. He dropped his hand to the pistol on his hip. Then he called out to Cherokee Earl as he kept his eyes on Dirty Joe, "Hey, boss, I got something to tell you."

"You son of a—"

Dirty Joe's words were cut short by the blast of the shotgun from where the sheriff lay dying on the ground. The shot lifted Jorge a foot off the ground and hurled him sidelong up onto the boardwalk. Ellen jumped back a step but stayed calm, seeing Earl, Dirty Joe, and Avery McRoy turn as one, their pistols coming up cocked from their holsters.

They fired with accuracy, but their shots were powerless against the old sheriff. He lay dead, a slight smile of satisfaction on his weathered face, his eyes staring blankly upward at the wide, clear sky.

Cherokee Earl turned slowly to Avery McRoy, his pistol cocked and still smoking. "You stupid sumbitch! You kicked that shotgun right back into his hands! I ought to blow your empty head off!"

"Boss, it was empty! I never meant for something like this to happen! I swear to God I never. Who the hell would have thought that old man was going to be able to do anything but go on and die?"

"Yeah, he went on and died, but not before he killed Jorge," said Earl, his temper easing down to a simmer as he lowered his pistol and stepped up onto the boardwalk where the Mexican lay dead. "One more mistake out of you, McRoy, I'll drive a barrel spike through your ears and leave you nailed to a tree somewhere." He stooped down beside Jorge Sentores. "This man was not only one hell of a thief and gunman, but he could stick on a horse better than any man I ever saw, white or colored. Now some flea-bitten law dog has gone and sent him straight to hell." He looked around at the pillaged town, sadness in his eyes. "I don't even feel like burning nothing else right now."

Down the street, flames licked out and upward from the telegraph office. Farther down the street, the livery barn boiled in a cloud of black smoke.

McRoy and Dirty Joe looked at each other. "That ain't like you, boss," Joe offered.

Cherokee Earl didn't answer.

Ellen Waddell stood back by the horses, a cold gaze in her eyes as she stared from one face to the next. When Dirty Joe looked at her, she softened her expression enough to offer a trace of a guarded smile just between the two of them. Then, as he turned his eyes back to Jorge's bloody body, Ellen's eyes stabbed at his back like sabers. She knew she had gained some ground for herself by the way that she had resisted Cherokee Earl without putting up a struggle. No matter what she had done, Cherokee Earl would have overpowered her and taken what he wanted anyway. All a struggle would have gotten her was a beating, and that might have been exactly what an animal like Earl would have enjoyed. She had no time to nurse a broken nose, battered ribs, or worse.

No, thanks, she thought.

She could force herself to play this game. She just had to keep her head and bide her time. She had to keep control of her faculties at all times. She had to keep from showing any emotion, no matter what the situation. The main thing was to stay alive. But if that wasn't possible, she promised herself that, like the old sheriff lying dead in the street, she would not go down without a fight.

When Cherokee Earl turned his gaze toward her and saw the way she was staring at them as the gathered around Jorge's body, his face grew tight with anger. "What the hell are you looking at? This man was a good friend of mine! I reckon you think the more of us that dies, the better your chances of getting away—is that it?"

Ellen didn't answer. Instead, she stared down at the ground, letting her helplessness show.

Cherokee Earl took a step toward her, noting her meek demeanor and noting as well the way that Dirty Joe and Avery McRoy were watching him. "You ain't fooling me, woman!" Earl growled. "I see through your way of acting pitiful . . . thinking somebody is going to speak up and come to your rescue!" He stalked closer, tightening a fist at his side. "But it ain't going to happen. Do you hear me? It ain't about to happen!" He stopped short at the sound of Dirty Joe behind him.

"Boss, leave her alone," Dirty Joe said.

A deathlike silence fell around them. Earl turned slowly, his eyes fiery with rage. "What did you say to me, Dirty?"

Avery McRoy cut in before Dirty Joe could speak. "Boss, he means we ain't got time to fool around with that woman. We're down to three of us now till Frisco and Billy meet up with us. We got folks on our trail . . . and more coming once word gets out across the Territory. Let's get moving. You can smack her around anytime."

Earl looked at the body of Jorge Sentores lying on the bloody boardwalk. McRoy was right, and Cherokee Earl knew it. This was no time to go shooting one of his own men, no matter what the situation. He looked the woman up and down. All right, he'd had her, and so far all she'd been was a disappointment. Whatever he decided to do with her would have to wait.

"You're right, McRoy. We got to get moving." His eyes went to Dirty Joe, but only for a second and only long enough to give him an admonishing look. Then he said to McRoy, "Avery, you take the lead rope for a while. . . . I got to do some thinking."

He rubbed his sore shoulder, the one he'd used leading Ellen's horse by its reins before he'd taken the time to stop along the trail and tie the short lead rope to the horse's bridle. He'd never seen a woman have so much trouble keeping a horse moving.

Ellen saw Dirty Joe stiffen a bit at Earl's words. But she knew this was no time for Joe to say anything. She saw jealousy in Joe Turley's eyes as he watched Avery McRoy step forward and say, "Sure thing, boss."

Then Avery stood before her and jerked his thumb toward her

horse and said, "Okay, ma'am, up you go. Let's get you into the saddle."

Ellen shot a quick glance to Dirty Joe as if to say there was nothing she could do about it. Then she stepped over to the horse, hiked her dress slightly, and said to Avery McRoy in a modest tone of voice, "I can't reach it on my own. . . . You'll have to give me a hand."

As she swung up into the saddle, she saw the seething expression on Dirty Joe's face. Looking down at Avery McRoy, she took a second longer than she needed to turn loose of his shoulder. "Thank you," she said softly, giving him a slight squeeze before letting go.

When the rest of them had mounted and headed north along the street out of town, Dirty sat rigid in his saddle, staring straight ahead at Cherokee Earl's back. He said to Avery McRoy out the side of his mouth in a harsh whisper, "I saw how you was making up to her."

Leading Ellen's horse by the short length of rope, McRoy replied in the same tone of voice. "Making up to her? Jesus, Dirty, boss asked me to help her up and lead her horse. What was I supposed to do?"

"Huh-uh," said Joe. "He asked you to lead her horse. He never said nothing about lifting her up that way, taking your time, putting your hands all over her!"

His words grew stronger as he spoke. He actually leaned closer to McRoy, so close that McRoy stepped his horse away from him.

"Take it easy, Joe!" said McRoy. "This ain't nothing to get worked up over."

"I ain't worked up, damn you!" Dirty Joe said, his voice getting loud now.

Five yards ahead of them, Cherokee Earl turned in his saddle and looked back. "What the hell's going on back there? Are you two scuffling about something?"

"Uh—no, boss," McRoy offered, collecting himself and leveling his hat brim. "Just a dispute over which one of us was the best friend to poor Jorge, is all."

"Arguing over the dead," Earl said flatly. He shook his head as he looked forward. "Let the dead bury the dead—that's what the good book says."

"The hell does he know about the good book," Dirty Joe whispered.

"The hell does any of us know?" McRoy chuckled.

The two looked at each other and laughed quietly, the storm between them having passed for now.

Close behind Avery McRoy, Ellen Waddell sat with her eyes lowered, looking down, not missing a word they said. She kept a slight tension on the reins in her hands, causing her horse to drag a bit, just enough to keep McRoy's arm having to constantly stay in a strain, keeping the horse from lagging.

McRoy gave a jerk on the rope and caused Ellen to let the horse come forward, almost beside him. "Lady, you can't ride worth a damn!" McRoy said to her.

"I'm—I'm sorry," Ellen replied meekly. "I'm not used to—"

"Leave her alone, Avery," said Dirty Joe. "She's just a woman. You can't expect her to ride like a man, can you?"

McRoy took a deep breath, not wanting to start arguing with Dirty Joe all over again. "No, I reckon not," he said.

They rode on, Ellen once again letting the horse lag back on the lead rope.

CHAPTER 9

BLACK MESA, INDIAN TERRITORY

Danielle drew Sundown to a halt and looked forward along a saddle of rock above the winding trail. On the other side of the trail stood a short stretch of jagged rock, not as tall, perhaps no more than thirty feet, but just as impenetrable. *A perfect ambush spot,* she told herself. She drew the chestnut mare sidelong and sat waiting for Stick and Dave Waddell to catch up to her from thirty feet back. She looked down at the two sets of horse tracks they had been following. The tracks belonged to Frisco Bonham and Billy Boy Harper.

"What's the matter?" asked Dave Waddell, seeming eager to keep moving. He nodded down at the hoofprints. "They're leading straight ahead."

"I know," said Danielle. "Nothing's the matter. But we're going to swing wide here and take shade beneath the mesa until the sun drops behind us. It'll be for only three or four hours."

"Three or four hours? What for?" asked Dave, looking back and forth between Danielle and Stick as he halted his horse.

"Because she said so," Stick cut in gruffly, having little tolerance for Dave Waddell.

Danielle was more patient. "Because that's a bad stretch of trail." She nodded ahead. "One rifle along that ridgeline can drop one or two of us or our horses pretty easily, and that would just about put this manhunt out of business."

"But what good is waiting going to do us?" Dave asked, still not seeing the point in wasting precious time. "This sounds like you're both afraid to catch up to these people!"

Danielle reminded herself not to let him upset her. She tipped her hat brim back and wiped her gloved hand across her wet forehead. "Because, Mr. Waddell . . . right now, with the sun high, we make a clear target going along that trail from the west. But once the sun drops behind us, anybody looking down along a gun barrel is going to go about half blind from sun glare."

Dave Waddell considered what she'd said, his face growing red because he hadn't realized it in the first place. He saw Stick give a smug grin and spit a stream of tobacco.

"Well," Dave said, still unable to give up his position, "I don't see how that's going to help. If somebody's up there, they can still shoot us, sun glare or not."

Danielle nodded slowly. "That's true, Mr. Waddell. But it's all about who gets the best advantage, them or us. Stick and I are going to take shade, rest the horses, and ride in with the sun to our backs. If you feel like you've got to do it a different way, I understand. . . . We'll pick your body up when we come through."

Turning Sundown, Danielle stepped the mare off the trail, Stick following close behind her.

"Wait, please," said Dave. "I didn't mean to be testy with you. I'm going along with you on this. Hey, I never claimed to know a lot about this sort of thing."

"Leave him behind," Stick said to Danielle. "I don't trust that peckerwood."

Danielle grinned but slowed her mare enough to let Dave Waddell catch up. "Neither do I, Stick. But it is his wife they've taken. I reckon that alone can cause a man to act a little crazy."

Stick slowed a bit beside her. "All right, whatever you say." He looked back as Dave Waddell hurried his horse forward. "I just can't get a good picture of how he says things happened. Maybe I just slept too many nights with my head on a cold saddle."

Danielle grinned. "Maybe you have at that," she said, and heeled her mare forward.

They rode around the base of the tall mesa and into a shaded area. Even though the air was still dry and hot, the heat was not nearly as violent as it was on the open, sun-beaten flatlands. While they rested themselves and their horses, they ate jerked beef and hardtack and chased it down with tepid canteen water. The horses stood picketed, grazing among clumps of wild grass less than twenty feet away. Stick took this rest period as an opportunity to clean and inspect his shooting gear. His pistol lay broken apart on a blanket he'd spread before him on the dirt. Danielle sat watching the animals as she chewed on a long blade of grass.

"I just can't stand waiting here, doing nothing," said Dave Waddell.

He'd turned even more restless after he'd eaten. While Danielle and Stick had rested for an hour and a half, he'd spent much of the time pacing back and forth, raising a small cloud of dust around his feet.

Stick looked through the barrel of his pistol, blew through it, and wiped it with a worn bandanna. "You were given a choice, Waddell, remember?" he said calmly.

"I know, I know," said Dave. "I'm just nervous by nature, I suppose. I just can't stand the thought of my poor wife being with a rotten piece of work like Cherokee Earl!"

"Thought you didn't know the man," said Stick, paying Waddell little interest.

"I don't personally," said Waddell. "But I don't have to personally know a skunk to know how bad it smells."

Stick nodded. "I agree with that." He picked up the cylinder to his pistol and rolled it back and forth slowly between his palms, inspecting it.

Dave Waddell stopped and let out a breath, then said, "Look, I know that neither one of you has much use for me. You don't trust me, and I don't know why. But that doesn't really matter. All I'm after is getting my wife back alive."

"That's what we're interested in also, Mr. Waddell," said Danielle. "So what's eating you?"

"I think you could tell me more about what's going on," said Waddell, "instead of leaving me in the dark until the time comes to decide things." He jerked a thumb back toward the trail they'd been riding. "Like back there a while ago. I had a right to know why you wanted us to pull off out of the sun. Once I knew it, I went along with it, didn't I?"

Stick and Danielle looked him up and down. "Okay," said Danielle, "what is it you want to know?"

It took Dave Waddell a moment to realize she meant it. Then he said, "All right, for starters, when these men's trail split up before you followed the five horses to my place, how did you know which set of tracks to follow? What made you think Cherokee Earl was still with the five horses you followed to my front yard instead of the two horses that went up into the hills?"

Danielle took the length of grass from her mouth and tossed it away. "It's an old Apache trick they're doing, Mr. Waddell," she said. "They'll drop off one and two at a time until you're left looking at an empty trail if you're not careful. In this case, there were only seven of them to begin with. The two that split off had to either draw us off the others' trail or ambush us. They pulled up above us. Then they watched our move. Once they saw we weren't going to split off after them . . . they began to look for a good spot to hit us from." She nodded at the jagged hill line along the trail ahead. "My bet is, that's it."

Dave Waddell swallowed a dry knot in his throat. "And all we can do is ride into it?"

"Any better ideas?" asked Danielle.

"What about one of us riding up, getting around the hills behind them?" Waddell asked.

"No good," said Stick, fitting his cleaned pistol back together and wiping it with the bandanna. "On flatland like this, they'll see us split up long before we get into their trap. All they'll do is light out, make us chase them. While we chase these two, the rest get farther away."

"And so does my wife," Waddell said, sounding helpless.

"Yep, that would be the case," said Stick.

"So all we can do is get the sun to our backs and ride in there like tin ducks at a shooting gallery?" Dave asked.

"Well, maybe not," said Danielle. She looked back and forth between the two men, then said, "I've been giving that some thought while I was sitting here. They'd see us if one of us split off now. But once we get inside the narrow trail between the rocks, it'll be a different story." She considered something, then said, "I'd sure like to take them alive, hear what they've got to say about your wife."

Dave Waddell didn't answer, realizing that those two were most likely Billy Boy Harper and Frisco Bonham and that they had already split off from the rest of the gang before Cherokee Earl came to his spread and took Ellen.

"There's no way a horse can climb off the trail up into that hill line," said Stick; neither he nor Danielle noticed Waddell's silence.

"No, but a person can on foot," said Danielle. "If I can find a blind spot along the trail, I can slip up out of the saddle with a rifle and get up along the high ridges before anybody knows what hit them."

Stick shook his head. "No, Danielle, that's too dangerous. Anybody climbs up there, it'll have to be me or Waddell here."

"Me?" Dave Waddell looked sick all of a sudden.

"No, I'll do it," said Stick.

"It's my idea. I'm the one who's going to do it," Danielle insisted.

Dave Waddell looked relieved.

"No, it's a bad idea," said Stick. "Too risky. Besides, if you climb all the way up and they're not up there, all you've done is worn yourself out for nothing."

"If that's how it turns out, so be it," said Danielle. "But I'm going, and that settles it." She looked back at the sun, gauging it. "It's a half hour ride to the hill line. By the time we get there, the sun ought to be dropped about right." She stood up, dusting her trouser seat, and walked away toward the horses.

Waddell and Stick stood looking at each other for a moment. Then Stick said, "Well, you heard her. What are we waiting for?"

Within minutes the three of them had gathered their horses, bridled and saddled them, and readied them for travel. On their way along the flat, dusty trail, Danielle kept a close eye on the level of the sun lowering behind them.

"Keep it slow and easy," she said to the two men. "We've got to time it just right to the foot of the rocks. And remember, if we can, let's take them alive."

They slowed the pace of their horses and rode loosely abreast until the trail tipped slightly up and narrowed into a jagged rock-lined path barely three horses wide.

"Get ready, Stick. Here I go," Danielle said, easing her mare's reins to him as she rose and posted in her stirrups.

As the mare stepped past a crevice snaking upward into clinging mesquite brush and creosote bushes, Danielle slipped her rifle from its boot and moved sleekly from her saddle into the rocky upthrust

"Be careful," Stick whispered, watching her disappear into the steep hillside as the horse continued without breaking its slow, steady stride.

Hearing Stick whisper, Dave Waddell looked around to see what was going on. But in the blink of an eye, it seemed, Danielle's saddle was empty and Stick was staring straight ahead. Looking up along the crevice ledge, Waddell saw a creosote bush tremble as if stirred by a gust of wind.

Then Stick said to him in a gruff whisper, "Don't look up! Look ahead!"

"Sorry. I—" Waddell stammered. "I just didn't realize when she would make her move."

"All the better," Stick said, his waxen expression giving in a little to a faint smile of pride. "This is one young woman who knows her way around the rough country." He heeled his horse on, keeping the chestnut mare close beside him.

In the narrow crevice, Danielle climbed until she perched for a moment twenty feet up and looked down along the trail at Stick and Waddell riding forward. Knowing that any moment they could draw fire from the ridge above them, she caught her breath and hurriedly climbed upward, moving as quietly as possible. At the crest of the ridge, thirty feet above the trail, she hurried along across loose rock and buried boulders, looking down as she caught up with Stick and Waddell. Seeing their shadows and the shadows of the horses stretched in front of them on the rocky path, she squinted at the sunlight glaring on their backs.

"That's good, Stick," Danielle whispered to herself. "Keep it just like that."

Then she slipped along the ridge in a crouch, rifle in hand, scanning back and forth along both high ridges atop the thin trail.

She moved along the ridge, getting ahead of Stick and Waddell on the trail below as the ridgeline sloped upward. At the peak of a higher cliff, she looked just in time to see two riflemen stretched out on a flat rock and looking down their rifle barrels toward the trail. Their appearance came to her so suddenly, it caused her to duck down for a second. She leaned against the side of a half-buried boulder and silently eased the lever of her rifle back and forth, chambering a round. Then she leaned slightly and looked down at Stick and Waddell. There was no question the riflemen had seen them. They were only waiting now for the two hapless riders to get beneath them before they opened fire.

Even in an ambush situation, Danielle could not abide shooting the two men without first having them face her. Rising from behind the sunken boulder, she cocked the rifle and called out as she took aim, "Up here, you dry gulchers!"

Frisco and Billy Boy Harper knew what was coming as they rolled onto their backs, already taking aim at her. Danielle's first shot nailed Billy Boy in the shoulder and slammed him back down onto the flat rock. He yelped like a kicked dog. His rifle went off as it flew from his hands and out over the edge of the cliff. But Frisco Bonham proved to be quicker than his companion. As Billy Boy rolled back and forth, writhing in pain, Frisco Bonham rolled sidelong over the edge of the cliff onto a dangerously thin ledge. He managed to fire a shot that ricocheted off the boulder in front of Danielle and whined away into the sky.

"You're not taking me back alive!" Frisco shouted.

"That thought never crossed my mind," Danielle called out, ready for her shot when Frisco rose up to take aim at her.

On the trail below, Stick and Waddell had both dropped from their saddles as Billy Boy's discarded rifle thudded to the trail in front of them. Stick was also ready for Frisco's move. He raised his rifle and took aim.

"It's that damned woman again!" Frisco raged aloud as if he couldn't believe his eyes.

He started to squeeze off a shot, but seeing him level his rifle, both Danielle and Stick fired at once, catching the outlaw in a cross fire from above and below. Dave Waddell squatted behind the cover of a rock, holding the reins to the horses. He winced, seeing the two shots hit Frisco Bonham and twirl the outlaw like a top.

"Ayiiii—!" Frisco screamed.

He spun off the slim ledge and bounced and slid and rolled until he spilled onto the path beside the rock where Dave Waddell sat holding the horses. Not knowing if the outlaw was dead or alive and not wanting to take a chance, Stick stepped over and planted a boot firmly on Frisco's back, pinning him to the dirt. Blood flowed from a wound in Frisco's right shoulder and another in his left side.

"Lie still now," said Stick, "or I'll put the next one in the worst place you can think of."

"You've . . . got . . . the wrong . . . man," Frisco managed to gasp into the dirt.

Stick grinned wryly. "You've said them words so often, they've become second nature to you." He jostled his boot against the wounded outlaw. "Now shut up and lie still till we get your partner."

Atop the ridgeline, Danielle worked her way down to Billy Boy Harper. He sat squeezing his bleeding shoulder, his wounded foot swollen to twice its size beneath a dirty bandage.

"Damned if you ain't gone and shot me again," he seethed, staring at Danielle with hate-filled eyes. "If I could draw this pistol, I swear I'd blow you to kingdom come!"

"You already would have if you and that snake you ride with could have gotten the drop on us," said Danielle, stepping down onto the flat rock, lowering her rifle, and drawing her pistol from her holster.

"What?" Billy Boy looked incensed by her suggestion. "Woman, you don't know what you're talking about! We had no idea you was even on this trail. We was just watching, making sure some road agents weren't trailing us. That's the God's honest truth."

Danielle laid the rifle flat as he spoke, keeping him covered with her Colt. Then she reached over and lifted his pistol from his holster and shoved it down behind her gun belt. "Now listen close, because I'm only going to ask one time. Where is Cherokee Earl headed with Dave Waddell's wife?"

Billy looked genuinely bewildered. "Hunh? His *wife?*"

"You heard me," said Danielle. "Earl has Waddell's wife. Where would he be headed with her?"

"Dang . . . !" Billy Boy turned loose of his wounded shoulder long enough to scratch his head with his bloody hand. "I knowed Cherokee had a powerful hankering for that little redheaded woman, but I never thought he'd go so far as to snatch her up." He spread a bemused half smile. "I was wondering what ole Dave was doing, fanning our trail that way."

"Keep your voice down," said Danielle. "I don't want Waddell hearing you."

She craned her neck enough to look down over the edge to where Stick stood with his boot on Frisco's back thirty feet below. Stick stared up toward her, his pistol cocked at arm's length and pointed down at the wounded outlaw.

"Now, what's the story?" she asked. "How do two birds like Waddell and Cherokee Earl come to light on the same limb?"

"What kind of break do I get if I tell you?" Billy Boy cocked his head to one side, looking smug.

Danielle swung her pistol barrel across his forehead, not hard, but hard enough to raise a welt. "You'd better worry about the break you'll get if you don't tell me," she said, drawing the pistol back for another swipe.

"All right! Take it easy!" Billy Boy pleaded. "I'll tell you whatever I can." He ducked his head slightly. "I never seen a woman so prone to acts of violence!"

"And we've only just started." Danielle gave him a cold stare.

"Dave Waddell started out buying stolen cattle from us a year ago," Billy Boy said quickly. "Nowadays most of the cattle we rustle go through him. He's gotten chicken rich off of us. Earl took a liking to his wife the first time he ever laid eyes on her. Can't say as I blame him." Billy shrugged with his good shoulder. "She's a looker, that one."

"I see," said Danielle. "So Cherokee Earl and Dave Waddell were business partners?"

"Well, yes, you might as well say that," said Billy. "Only for some reason, Waddell never seemed to be able to admit it to himself. Used to really tighten Earl's jaw . . . Waddell thinking he was so much better than the likes of us. I'd say that had something to do with Earl wanting to take his wife, wouldn't you?"

"I have no idea," said Danielle.

"Well, I think it must've." Billy noted that the bleeding from his shoulder wound had grown worse. He loosened his bandanna from around his neck and tried to tie it around his shoulder, failing miserably.

"Here, give it to me," said Danielle, stepping over and taking the bandanna. As she tied it around his shoulder, up under his arm, she continued. "But as far as you know, Waddell never stole any cattle himself, just provided a place and bought the ones the rest of you rustled?"

"That was the way of it," said Billy Boy. He looked closely at Danielle as she tended his wound. "Any chance of you letting me go after me telling you and all? That, I mean, and promising never to do anything wrong again in my life?"

"No, there's not a way in the world I'll let you go," said Danielle, "so save your breath. We'll turn you over to the law first chance we get. I'll tell them you were helpful with information. That's all I'll do for you."

"I was afraid of that," said Billy Boy, raising a small hideaway derringer he'd snuck from inside his shirt as she took care of his wound. "You've shot me for the last time, woman!" he shouted.

From below, Stick and the other two heard only the sound of Danielle's Colt, the big pistol drowning out the sound of Billy Boy's derringer.

"Danielle?" said Stick. "Are you all right up there?"

A silence passed, and Stick took on a concerned look. "Danielle, answer me. . . . Are you all right?"

"I'm shot, Stick," Danielle replied in a strained voice. "I'm all right . . . but this little sidewinder shot me."

"I'm coming!" Stick shouted.

"No, Stick!" Danielle shouted. "Stay there!"

"Why?" said Stick. "You're shot—you need help!"

She wasn't going to risk saying any more about what Billy Boy had just told her. Instead, she just said, "Stick, stay down there. I'm all right."

But Stick wouldn't hear of it. He reached down, snatched Frisco's pistol from his holster, and said to Dave Waddell, "Keep an eye on this one! I'm going up to get her!"

"Sure thing," said Dave Waddell, pointing his pistol at Frisco Bonham.

Recognizing Waddell's voice, Frisco turned a surprised look at him as Stick hurried away up the steep, rocky hillside.

"Well, well," Frisco whispered, "look who we've got here."

"Hello, Frisco," said Waddell, keeping his voice low. "Where's my wife, you rotten bastard?"

"Your wife? How in the hell would I know where your wife is, Waddell?" Frisco said.

The two stared at each other for a second. Then the picture of what was going on began to form inside Frisco's head. "You mean to tell me Earl has taken off with your little redheaded wife?" He shook his head. "I always figured he would someday, but damn, you mean right after me and Billy split up with him and the others on the way to your spread? Is that when?"

Waddell sat tight-lipped. His knuckles turned white around his pistol butt. "If you've got nothing for me, then I've got only one thing for you!" he hissed.

"Hold on, Waddell," said Frisco, seeing the serious intent in the man's red-rimmed eyes. He flashed a quick glance at Stick climbing hand over hand, getting closer to the top. "I can't tell you where he'd take her, but I might be able to take you there." He looked up again, then back at Waddell.

"You're not taking me anywhere," said Waddell.

"Oh? Well, then, that's a shame . . . because you see, I know Cherokee Earl a lot better than you do." He lifted an eyebrow as if asking whether Dave was interested in hearing more. When Dave made no response, Frisco continued. "I believe you can get your wife back if you show up and ask real polite. She might be a little worse for the wear, but we can't always have everything our way, can we?"

Dave Waddell fought the urge to put a bullet through his forehead. Frisco seemed to be able to read it in his eyes.

"I know you're all stoked up right now," he said, "but give it time to sink in. See where your best chance lies. As soon as I get these wounds patched up and we can see our way clear, you be ready to help me make a move. Then we'll go get your wife back. Fair enough?"

Dave considered it for a moment. Frisco saw the color begin to come back into his face as his knuckles slacked off around the pistol butt.

"I'll think about it," Dave finally said.

Frisco took a short breath of relief. His eyes gestured upward to where Stick was still climbing the hillside. "You don't want to spend too long thinking about it, Dave," Frisco cautioned. "Seems to me like you made your decision last year which side of the law you stood on. Nobody twisted your arm, getting you to buy our stolen cattle. I don't suppose you happened to mention all that to the old man and woman, did you?"

Dave Waddell's expression answered for him.

"That's what I thought," said Frisco. "It must've slipped your mind."

"I told them no more than I had to." He looked more troubled as he spoke.

"It's a hell of a spot you're in, ain't it?" A trace of a sinister smile came to Frisco's lips. "The devil's knocking at your door, Dave. You've got to figure out real quick whether or not you're going to answer." Again he nodded upward toward Stick's back. "You quit those kinds of folks the day you crossed over to us. You ever want to see your woman again, you'd better prepare yourself to do whatever it takes. I can promise you those two will never make it to where Cherokee Earl's trail will take them."

"I told you I'd think about it," said Dave Waddell. His hand slackened around the pistol.

CHAPTER 10

With a hand pressed against the bullet wound low in her left side, it took much effort for Danielle to make it over to the edge of the cliff. When she did, she looked down at Stick, who was no more than a few feet below her. "Stick, I told you not to come up here! I'm all right!"

"Hunh?" Stick looked baffled, staring up at her as he reached to pull himself over the edge.

Looking down to the trail below, Danielle saw the rifle barrel reach up above the top of a rock. She couldn't see who was behind it, but whether it was Dave Waddell or Frisco Bonham made no difference. The intent was the same. As she saw the rifle barrel, she also saw Stick falter and almost lose his footing. As he rocked back, she was torn between going for her pistol to give him some covering fire or grabbing his hand to keep him from falling.

"Hurry, Stick!" she shouted, hoping to get him up over the edge in time. She threw her right hand down to him, ignoring the pain in her side.

But Stick had no understanding of what was going on below him. He only knew he had lost his balance. He grasped wildly for her hand.

But the rifle shot caused him to stiffen just at the second their fingertips touched. Danielle saw the stunned look come upon his weathered face at the same time the bullet exited his chest. She

made an extra lunge forward, but his hand had already fallen farther away from hers. She could only watch as his face registered a
look of regret.

"I'm . . . sorry," he gasped. Then he fell backward and tumbled
down until he came to a halt in a swirling cloud of dust and rock
on the trail below.

Another shot exploded. This one kicked up flecks of rock only
inches from Danielle. There was nothing she could do for Stick.
She ducked down only slightly, long enough to draw her Colt.
Then she came up quickly, her eyes scanning for a target. But all
she saw was a brief glimpse of the two men and a rise of dust from
the horses' hooves. She heard the long neigh of her chestnut mare
and saw the animal rear above the rocks and come down running
while the sounds of the horse string and the two riders disappeared in the other direction.

Danielle held her pistol at arm's length with both hands, taking
careful aim, preparing for the moment when Frisco Bonham and
Dave Waddell would ride into view farther down the trail, where
the rocky cover parted for a few yards. But when they did streak
along that short stretch of open trail, she lowered her pistol, knowing the shot was too far out of range. Her eyes went down to Stick.
Although badly wounded and injured from the fall, he was trying
to raise his pistol from his holster.

"Lie still, Stick!" Danielle shouted. "I'm coming!"

Even with pain gripping her side, Danielle hurried down the
steep hillside. Reaching Stick on the dirt trail, she sank onto her
knees and turned him over, resting his head in her lap. "Stick, lie
still! You're going to be all right!"

Stick coughed and struggled with his words. "Save that talk . . .
for some tinhorn. I'm done here."

Danielle knew he was right; it just took her a second to accept
it. "Oh, Stick," she said with deep regret. "I told you to stay put.
Why wouldn't you listen to me?"

Her voice was shaken by grief. She hugged his head against her,
seeing the scrapes, cuts, and bruises he'd acquired from the fall.

On her leg she felt warm blood oozing from the wound in his back. The exit wound in his chest looked fierce and hopeless.

"I—I tried, Danielle," Stick gasped. His glazed eyes stared up into hers. "It's hard . . . for a man—"

His words stopped short, but she knew what he meant. "To take orders from a woman," she whispered, finishing his words for him.

He offered a faint smile. "Don't hate us . . . for how we are."

"I don't, Stick," she said, trying hard to keep tears from spilling from her eyes.

"You . . . get out of here," Stick said in a faltering voice. "Go find Tuck Carlyle. . . . Promise me?"

"I will, Stick, I promise," said Danielle. "As soon as I settle up with these rats, I'll go find him."

"No," said Stick, taking all his waning strength to shake his head. He gripped her forearm with his bloody hand. "Go now! Forget . . . these people. This . . . ain't felt right . . . from the start."

"Stick, you know I can't let this go," Danielle said, unable to keep the tears back any longer at the sight of this good old man dying in her arms. "Don't ask me to promise something like that."

Stick patted her arm. "I know, I know." A short silence passed. Then he said, "You and Tuck . . . remember me kindly."

"Of course, Stick. How else could we possibly remember you?" She wept openly now.

"Quit that," Stick said. He offered a weak smile. "I've had the best . . . of lives. Look at me . . . leaving a beautiful woman crying over me." He swallowed, a knot in his throat. "If I'd . . . been a younger man . . ." His words trailed; then he added, "Well, I reckon you . . . know how I feel about you."

His eyes closed softly, with no promise of ever opening again. Danielle felt him turn limp in her lap.

"I know, Stick," she whispered. "I know."

She lowered her cheek to his for a second and sat quietly cradling him in her arms. At length Danielle felt the chestnut mare press her warm muzzle against her neck. She turned her face up to the animal. "Good girl, Sundown," she said, raising one gloved hand and stroking the mare's face. "You did fine, just fine."

She lifted Stick's head from her lap and stood, gazing down the thin path where the dust of the fleeing riders had begun to settle. She thought about Stick's words: *This . . . ain't felt right . . . from the start*, he'd said. He was right, and she knew it. From the beginning, the day she'd met the three drunken rustlers in the street at Haley Springs, no one had taken her seriously. Even after putting a bullet through Billy Boy Harper's foot, they hadn't learned any respect for her.

She was a woman doing a man's job. *Nothing more*, she thought, *than some novelty act in a traveling show.* Through her grief at Stick's death and the dark anger she felt for his killers, Danielle also felt a weariness that ran so deep, it made her ache inside. Some things never changed. She should have realized that coming into this mess. She began to chastise herself. Who did she think she was, that just because she could ride and shoot and handle herself like a man . . . ? *Stop it*, she told herself, forcing the train of thought from her mind. What was done was done, and she couldn't go back and change the past. All she could do was try to influence the future.

With the pain in her side throbbing and sharp, she took down her lariat from her saddle, looped it around Stick's feet, and walked the mare slowly, dragging Stick's body to a wider spot along the trail. With the help of the mare and the rope, she spent the next hour raising rocks from the ground until she'd uncovered a spot the proper size for a shallow grave. Then she rolled Stick over into the grave and as carefully as she could rolled the rocks back over him.

"It ain't the best, Stick," she said quietly, standing bowed slightly at the waist, her hand pressing a bandanna to her side, "but it's the best I can do." With her hat between her hands, she stood with her head slightly bowed and said, "Lord, I'm too hurt to know what to say over this good man right now. I never knew him that long, but he sure fit what I would call an angel . . . if I was you. Amen." She stepped back and wiped an eye and put her hat on.

In moments she had dragged herself up into her saddle and

heeled the mare into a slow walk. Pain radiated in her side and stabbed her with each step. Danielle didn't look back toward Stick's rocky grave, nor did she look back along the trail in the direction his killers had taken. Pursuing them would have to wait. She was shot deep. It was a small wound, but the bullet was lodged inside her, and that gave it the potential to turn bad. She'd have to get somewhere and have it removed before infection set in. Once that was done, she'd need a couple days' rest.

Time to make new plans, she thought to herself, heeling the mare's pace up a bit. Then she'd be back on the trail. She would track down Stick's killers and settle all accounts.

The horses were winded by the time Dave Waddell and Frisco Bonham hit the low stretch of flatlands. They had moved at a fast pace down the narrow trail until finally Frisco sat back on his reins and brought both his horse and the string of horses to a halt.

As the string bunched up beside him and Dave Waddell slid to a stop almost in their midst, Frisco said, "That's about enough running for one day, Davey Boy. You heard her say she'd been shot." He let the horses circle amongst themselves and settle. "I figure Billy Boy must've got to that derringer he carried while she wasn't looking and put a bullet in her."

Dave Waddell sounded worried when he replied, "I don't know. She was sure able to shoot at us."

"Yeah, but she's hit," said Frisco. "No matter how tough she thinks she is, unless she's a complete mumbling fool, she'll have to take care of that wound. She ain't coming after us."

"I hope you're right," said Dave, looking back, already regretting what he'd gotten himself involved in but realizing there was nothing he could do now but see things through.

Frisco studied the frightened look on his face and chuckled under his breath. "Looks like I've got a born worrier on my hands, Davey Boy."

"I don't like that name," Dave Waddell snapped.

His horse spun beneath him in a rise of dust. He still held the Colt Danielle had lent him in his hand. The smaller Navy Whitney pistol was stuck down behind his belt.

"Don't get so riled," said Frisco. "It's only a name."

Dave Waddell glared at him. "I just don't like it," he said.

Frisco shrugged. "There's no harm intended. We all called Billy Harper Billy Boy."

"It ain't the same," said Waddell. "So don't do it."

Taking note of Waddell's firearms, Frisco said, "All right, take it easy. I'll remember that from now on! No cause to get cross about it."

Frisco had Stick's rifle, but it was stuck down in the rifle boot. Ever since they'd made their getaway, Dave Waddell had managed to stay behind him, keeping a close eye on him. Too close for him to make a move, Frisco thought. But that was okay. He needed Dave Waddell for now. Once he got out of this tight spot, he could either kill him or let him live. It meant nothing to him.

"Which way?" Waddell asked in a no-nonsense tone of voice.

"Settle down, Waddell," said Frisco. "I told you I'd take you to Earl and your wife . . . and I will."

"The woman was following their trail north," said Waddell, "but now you and I are headed back the other way."

"Yep, that's right," said Frisco. "That's because I know where they're going, and I know the roundabout way Cherokee Earl will take to get there."

His answer satisfied Dave Waddell. "Okay, then, take me to them."

"I will." Frisco raised a finger for emphasis. "But first things first."

"First things first? What are you talking about?" Dave demanded.

"I'm talking about we need some grub and some traveling money before we can get anywhere. It's a long ways to where Cherokee Earl and the boys go to play," said Frisco.

Dave Waddell didn't like the nasty grin on Frisco's face, knowing what his words were implying. "We'll be all right," said Dave. "Let's get going."

"Be all right?" Frisco cocked his head, giving Dave a sarcastic look. "Waddell, have you got any food in your saddlebags? Any coffee even?"

"No," said Dave. "We had jerked beef, some beans, and coffee with us. But it was in the woman's saddlebags."

"Well . . . it ain't decent," said Frisco, "traveling without coffee, far as I'm concerned. Or money either," he added.

"I'm not robbing anything or anybody, Frisco," Waddell said firmly, "so don't even bring it up."

"I wasn't about to," said Frisco. "All I was going to say is, we can take these horses over to the old north wagon trail and maybe sell them to one of the relay stations. They always have an eye out for fresh horses."

Dave thought about it for a second. "Is that on the way to catching up to Cherokee Earl?"

"Well, yes," said Frisco, sounding put out. "Why the hell else would I bring it up?" He shook his head as if in disgust. "You're going to have to start trusting me, Waddell."

"Yeah, I'll do that," snapped Waddell. "Now let's get going." He dropped his horse a step back behind Frisco and gestured with his pistol barrel.

Frisco heeled his horse forward, leading the string. He grinned to himself, staring straight ahead.

They rode hard the rest of the day, barely stopping long enough to rest the winded horses. It was late dusk before they stepped down and made a dark camp beside a thin trickle of water running down the middle of an otherwise dry creek bed. Frisco Bonham slept flat on the ground, snoring loud and deep, wrapped in a blanket from behind Stick's saddle. Dave Waddell also wrapped himself in a blanket, but he slept light. He spent the night with his back propped against the dirt bank, his big Colt still in his hand, resting across his lap.

At daylight, Frisco stood up and coughed loudly just to see how soundly Waddell was sleeping. When Waddell didn't stir, Frisco said in an urgent tone, "Waddell! Wake up! Time to get moving!"

But Waddell showed no startled response. Instead, he tipped his hat up calmly and looked at Frisco standing fifteen feet away in the gray morning light. "I'm not asleep, Frisco," he said. "I've just been waiting on you."

He flipped his blanket open, revealing the big Colt. After letting Frisco get an eyeful of the pistol and the way it had been lying there ready for him, Dave Waddell stood up, shook out the blanket, and walked to the horses.

Frisco grinned. "I always admired a man who looks out for himself."

They prepared the horses for travel, filled a canteen from the trickle of creek water, and, once on the trail, didn't stop until the sun stood high overhead.

They had stepped down from their saddles and led the horses for almost a mile when Dave Waddell asked, "How much farther to a relay station?" He felt light-headed from not having eaten since early the day before. His empty stomach growled.

"It's still ten miles or so," said Frisco. Looking all around the barren sand, cactus, and creosote, he added, "Hell, I ain't waiting any longer. I'm going to eat something even if I have to put down one of these horses." He looked Dave Waddell up and down and asked, "Have you ever et a horse?"

"No," said Dave, "and I'm not going to start today. Ten miles is not that far. We can hold off that long."

"Maybe you can," said Frisco, "but I'm a man who must fill his needs as quick as they arise." He stepped around beside the horse and reached for the rifle in the saddle boot.

But before he could draw it, he heard Dave say, "Hold it. Look at this!"

Turning, Frisco gazed out through the glittering sunlight. Three hundred yards away, a streaming rise of dust boiled up behind a rollicking stagecoach pulled by six galloping horses.

"Well, don't this just beat all? Ask and ye shall receive!" Frisco shouted laughingly, outstretching his arms as if embracing salvation.

"Thank God," Dave Waddell whispered. He let out a tired sigh of relief. Stepping forward, for the first time allowing Frisco behind him unwatched, Waddell raised both arms and waved them back and forth slowly. "He sees us," he said over his shoulder, still waving as the driver slowed the rig.

"Look at him," said Frisco as the stagecoach drew closer. "Not a care in the world . . . nobody even riding shotgun for him. That's dangerous as hell in this country."

At thirty yards, Dave Waddell saw the white beard of the lone driver as the man began slowing the coach horses down to a walk. At thirty feet, Dave called out gratefully with a hand raised toward the coach, "Much obliged, mister. We were just wondering if we were ever going to—"

The sound of the rifle blast so close behind him almost knocked Dave Waddell off his feet. "Jesus!" he bellowed, throwing a hand to his assaulted left ear. At the sudden explosion, Waddell had squinted and ducked his head to the side. Now, looking at the coach driver, he saw the red splotch on the man's chest, saw he'd slammed backward and fallen sidelong, the coach reins dropping from his hands, giving the coach horses free run.

"You son of a bitch!" Waddell yelled, turning toward Frisco and reaching for the big Colt in his belt.

But Frisco had already jumped into his saddle. The horse came streaking past Waddell, Frisco beating its sides with the rifle barrel as he nailed his spurs to it.

Sidling his horse up to the coach, Frisco dropped the rifle into its boot and leaped from his saddle. Catching the climbing rung, he swung up onto the driver's seat. He shoved the driver's body aside, snatched up the fallen reins, and reared back on them, bringing the spooked horses under control before they had time to get into a run.

"Whoa!" said Frisco, letting the horses circle out off the trail and back, settling them.

Dave Waddell watched the circling coach with fire in his eyes, his hand tight around the raised Colt, the rifle blast still ringing in his ears. "Get down from there, Frisco! You rotten, murdering—"

Again his words went unfinished. The coach came around onto the trail facing him, and from Frisco's right hand a cocked sawed-off shotgun pointed down at him. "If you keep calling me names, Davey Boy, you're going to hurt my feelings." He grinned.

Dave Waddell took on a sickly look. The pistol lowered to his side. "Don't shoot me, Frisco, please," he said. "All I want is my wife back. . . . I never asked for none of this."

"Shoot you, hell!" said Frisco. "Quit talking crazy. Put that pistol away and give me a hand here." He set the brake handle on the coach, rocking it to a halt as the horses stopped. "There's most always a dollar or two in these strongboxes."

"My God, we're robbing a stage?" said Dave as if he couldn't believe what was happening or how suddenly he'd become a party to it.

"I don't know how you can say we're robbing it," said Frisco. "This old buzzard's dead. He can't object."

"But—but he's dead because you killed him!" Dave exclaimed as if he had to point out to the man the terrible thing he'd just done.

"Davey Boy, you just keep going on about the same thing, don't you? Of course I killed him! How else was I supposed to get what he's got without him putting up a fight for it?" Somehow, the way Frisco said it, it all made sense in that twisted, vile way of thinking.

Dave shook his head as if to clear it. But he let the hammer down on the Colt and shoved it down into his belt. The shotgun in Frisco's hand made all the difference in the world. Now they were back on equal ground. He didn't want to get on Frisco's bad side, not after seeing how easily this man could take a life. He noted how, now that Frisco had the shotgun and had taken the edge from him, he'd gone right back to calling him Davey Boy. That meant something, Waddell was sure.

"Go back there and check under the luggage flap," said Frisco. "See if he didn't bring along some grub of some sort. I swear I could eat the hind end out of a running bobcat." He raised the heavy strongbox and pitched it out to the ground. "Here, shoot this lock off first."

Frisco watched closely and kept his hand ready on the shotgun until Dave reached down with the Colt and took careful aim. The Colt jumped in his hand, and Frisco laughed to see the lock disappear from the strongbox.

"Good shot, Davey Boy! Damn, I'll make a highwayman of you before it's over!"

He leaped down from the driver's seat and landed beside Waddell. Then he dropped to his knees, opened the lid to the strongbox, and rifled through the contents, keeping the shotgun in his right hand, the butt propped on his thigh.

As if having just become aware of Dave Waddell's presence, he looked back over his shoulder and said, "Are you going to check back there like I told you, see if there's any grub?"

Without a word, Dave Waddell turned and walked to the rear of the stagecoach.

"You're going to have to quit being so bashful, Davey Boy," Frisco called out as he began tearing open letters and checking for any cash in them. "We've got a long trail before us getting to Cherokee Earl and your pretty little wife. I'm counting on you to pull your own weight."

Dave Waddell stopped midstep at Frisco's words. He stood for a second, letting them sink in. Sickness almost overwhelmed him, but he fought it down, his fists clenched at his sides. His first thought was to make a break for the horses, jump into the saddle, and ride. Ride as far and as fast as he could. But then he pictured his wife with Cherokee Earl. His knees went weak for a second; then he forced the picture from his mind, swallowed the bitter taste in his mouth, and walked to the rear of the dusty stagecoach. God help him, he'd become one of them. He was no different in the eyes of the law from the man who had actually pulled the trigger and killed the stage driver. No court would listen to his flimsy excuse. He was an outlaw, plain and simple, whether he'd meant to be or not.

"How in the world did you end up here?" he asked himself, untying the dusty canvas flap and throwing it open. His eyes moved across the small wooden crates all neatly stacked and tied down, some of them stating their contents in black letters, others leaving it to his imagination.

"Anything to eat back there?" Frisco called out.

"Don't see anything," Dave replied. "But I'll search around some."

He reached in, untied the rope from the wooden crates, and pulled them down around his feet. Eagerly, he picked up the first one and began loosening its top. Since he was here, he might as well see what this life had to offer.

CHAPTER 11

By the time Danielle had reached the flatlands, she sat bowed in her saddle. The pain in her side had grown worse. The bleeding had slowed almost to a stop, but the flesh surrounding the wound had turned puffy and flaming red. The intense heat made matters worse, draining what strength the bullet in her side had not already taken away. It had been up to Sundown to lead them the last few miles to the beginning of the dirt street into town. Danielle sat slumped, suspended on a narrow edge of semiconsciousness and losing ground.

From an alleyway where he'd taken up a regular guard position ever since Cherokee Earl and his gang had raided the town, Leonard Whirley crouched with the ten-gauge shotgun—the same shotgun that had fallen from the dead sheriff's hand. Leonard could tell that this wasn't one of those who had sacked the town, but he remained cautious and slipped back through the alley and down behind the buildings until he reached the rear door of the doctor's office.

He knocked sharply and whispered to the wooden door, "Doc, it's Whirley! Open up! A woman's riding in. Looks like she's shot!"

"Shot?" Dr. Callaway slipped the bolt back on the door and stepped out into the alley, hooking his wire-rimmed spectacles behind his ears. "Another woman? This one's shot? What the hell's gotten into women around here?"

"I don't know, Doc," said Whirley. "I just thought you'd better know about it."

"Good thinking, Whirley," the doctor replied, buttoning his vest as the two hurried along the back alley.

On their way, they spotted a buckboard wagon loaded high with furniture and household items headed out of town along a back road.

"There go Orville Jones and his family," the old doctor said, shaking his head. "They're all leaving here like rats from a sinking ship. This town will be a dusty spot on the trail in another week."

"I know," said Whirley. "I'm already thinking of boarding up the New Royal and heading for New Mexico Territory. I'm giving up on Braden Flats."

"I hate saying it, but me, too," the doctor replied.

They rushed along until they reached the spot where Whirley had stood a moment ago. They saw the chestnut mare standing in the middle of the street. On the ground Danielle lay where she had fallen. The mare nudged her gently but got no response. Danielle appeared lifeless in the dirt. Dr. Callaway studied the situation for a moment, rubbing his chin.

"Come on, Leonard, this one looks like she's done in," said the doctor at length.

"Wait, Doc. This might be a trick," Whirley replied, his right hand going nervously to his toupee.

"Dang it, Leonard! Why would it be a trick?" He flagged Whirley forward with his hand. "Come on, help me get this poor woman off the street. Worry about your hair later."

After they rushed to the middle of the street, it took a few tries for Dr. Callaway to shoo the chestnut mare away from Danielle long enough for him and Whirley to scoop her up off the street and carry her back to his office. Sundown loped along behind them, her reins dragging in the dirt. As the men stepped up onto the boardwalk, the mare paced back and forth, shaking her mane and blowing out a restless breath.

"Don't you worry, ole gal," Doc Callaway said over his shoulder to Sundown from the open doorway. "We'll take good care of her."

When they laid Danielle on a gurney in the room next to the doctor's office, Doc Callaway said to the bar owner, "I'm going to have to undress her, Whirley. You go hitch the mare to the rail and see she gets some water and grain. I'll put her up at my barn tonight, since we've got no town livery barn left." Thinking about what had happened to the barn, Callaway grumbled under his breath as he unbuckled Danielle's trousers. "The dirty sonsabitches."

Whirley turned and slipped out the door. The old doctor eased Danielle's trousers down as carefully as he could. But still she moaned in unconscious pain.

"Whoo-ie," said the doctor, seeing the inflamed swollen flesh surrounding the small bullet hole. "Nothing worse than shooting a body with a dirty little derringer, I always say."

Danielle's eyes opened for a moment. "Who—who are you? Where am I?" she asked, reaching to grasp the doctor's wrist as he pressed his fingertip gently against the tortured flesh.

"Nobody you need fear," the doctor replied. He pushed her weak hand aside. "I'm Dr. Callaway. This is Braden Flats . . . what's left of it anyway. That's as much as you need to know for now. You got a nasty little bullet lodged in ya." He probed gently with his fingers. "We need to get it out of there before it festers up any worse. I'll have to do some cutting."

Danielle looked around the room with bleary eyes. "Is my mare all right?" she asked.

"Yeah, I'd say she's right enough. She gave us a hard time when we went to move you here."

Danielle gave a weak smile. "That's my mare for sure," she whispered. Then she lowered her head back to the pillow on the gurney and said with resolve, "Cut away, Doctor. I'm all yours."

Seeing she had slipped back into unconsciousness, Dr. Callaway rubbed her hair back off her damp forehead. "I'll make it as painless as I can, young lady," he whispered to her. "You look like you've been through plenty enough already."

For the next half hour, Whirley waited in the doctor's office, pacing to the window every few minutes and keeping an eye on the road leading out of town. While he stood at the window, he shook his head as he saw another heavily loaded wagon amble into the distance across the rolling flatlands.

"She's all stitched up now," said the doctor's voice from the door to the next room.

"Did she ever wake up, Doc?" Whirley asked, straightening his crooked toupee.

"Yep," said Dr. Callaway, "she woke up before I started, then again when I was closing the incision."

"Well, what did she tell you?" Whirley asked. "Had she run into the same bunch that raided us? Did they do that to her?"

"She said it was different men, but from the same bunch," said the doctor. "She's on their trail for doing the same in Haley Springs that they did here. They killed an old drover who rode with her. . . . They kidnapped that woman who was with Cherokee Earl." Considering the situation, he added, "I thought right off that there was something wrong there. I hate thinking that man took advantage of that woman right here in Braden Flats, and we never lifted a finger to stop him."

"Hell, Doc, we didn't know," said Whirley. "Besides, what good would we have done anyway? Our sheriff is dead from trying to stop them. What chance would we have had?"

"I don't know," said the doctor. "None, I suppose. I ain't got it in me to kill. Some men are born with a killing trait, but some of us ain't. Sometimes I wish it was otherwise, but I can't deny how I am."

"Then we did all we could," said Whirley. "So put it out of your mind and think no more about it."

"I reckon you're right," said the doctor. He looked off across the barren land to the slight rise of dust still stirred up from the wagon, which was long gone from sight. "This is a hateful, cussed place, Whirley. I wish to God I'd never laid eyes on it."

A silence passed. Then Whirley straightened his toupee and smoothed it down again with both palms of his hands. "Me, too, Doc," he said as if in defeat.

For the next week, Danielle, following the doctor's orders, was forced to rest and keep the wound treated in order to arrest any further infection. She did so grudgingly. She took her meals and lodging in the same small room where Dr. Callaway had treated her. She began moving around slowly with the help of a cane on the third day. Leonard Whirley managed to be close by her side every waking hour. Danielle could see the saloon owner was taken with her, and she tried to treat him as a casual friend, hoping that was as far as it would go. But Whirley grew more smitten as each day passed.

On the fourth day, having loosened the stiffness in her side, Danielle moved about the room and the doctor's office without the cane, limping slightly. The swelling had begun to dissipate from her wound. On the fifth day, when Whirley went to the doctor's barn to feed and water Sundown, Danielle was in her boots and went with him. She wore her gun belt to get used to the weight of it again, her Colt tied down to her right thigh.

"You sure heal quick," said Whirley, noting that she no longer limped as they crossed the empty street and walked toward the doctor's house on the outskirts of town.

"I have to heal quick," Danielle replied. "The longer I wait here, the colder the trail." She had filled in both Whirley and Doc Callaway on everything that had happened. "I owe it to the Waddell woman to find her and free her from Cherokee Earl. It makes no difference what her husband has done. I've got to help her. I'll deal with him when the time comes."

Whirley nodded as they walked along. Lifting a hand to his toupee out of habit, he said, "Miss Danielle, if I might be so bold, I think you are about the prettiest woman I ever laid eyes on."

"Well, thank you, Mr. Whirley," said Danielle, seeing where this might be headed and wishing she could stop it before it got there. But it was no use.

"The thing is," he continued, "I'll soon be leaving this shi—I mean, mudhole . . . and I'm going somewhere clean and sophisticated. Maybe

Santa Fe. Maybe Tombstone. I ain't sure." He stopped and turned to her, touching her arm gently and stopping her also. "But wherever I go . . . I'd be honored to have you by my side." He swallowed and ventured, "That is to say, as my lawful wife, Miss Danielle. . . . Everything would be on the up-and-up, of course."

"That certainly is a gentleman's proposal, Mr. Whirley," said Danielle, "and I appreciate it. But I'm afraid I must turn you down. I'm on the trail of these murderers, and I don't plan on stopping until I've finished what I started." She gestured toward the doctor's barn, and together they continued walking.

Whirley looked let down but at the same time relieved. "Well, at least I got a chance to ask," he said in all earnestness. "Some fellows never get this close to a respectable woman."

"I'm flattered you feel that way, Mr. Whirley."

They walked on.

"Can I ask you, Miss Danielle, is it me, or are you just not interested in marrying at this time?" Whirley's eyes turned soft, almost pleading for the right answer.

"It's nothing against you, Mr. Whirley, although you have to admit we hardly know each other. It's just that I'm not interested in marrying anybody right now. Someday maybe but not now. If I was, there's a man in Colorado. . . ."

"Well, I'm glad to hear that," said Whirley good-naturedly. "For a minute I wondered if maybe there was something wrong with you."

"You mean, if I'm not interested in marriage, there must be something wrong with me?" Danielle felt the tightness in her voice and tried to shake it off.

"I didn't mean that the way it sounded," said Whirley. "Of course there's nothing wrong with you."

Danielle offered a smile of reconciliation. "That's good to hear," she said.

Whirley shrugged. "But if you don't mind me saying so, Miss Danielle, I believe it's awful foolish of you . . . going out there after Cherokee Earl and his bunch."

"Oh, really? Foolish, you say?" Danielle cocked an eye.

"Well, yes, foolish," Whirley said with finality. "Doggone it, Miss Danielle, it don't make sense, a little woman like yourself trying to do a man's job. Heck, most men wouldn't attempt to go after Cherokee Earl even with a posse backing them up! You're talking about going after him alone."

"And because I am, it's foolish of me," Danielle said flatly, staring straight ahead.

"Please don't take offense," said Whirley, "but let's face it. That Colt is almost bigger than you are. If you ever had to draw and shoot at somebody, how do you expect to ever get it—"

The Colt streaked upward too fast for Leonard Whirley to see it clearly. All his eyes caught was a flash of sunlight on polished steel. Then four shots exploded as quickly as she could cock and fire. With each shot, a short length of chain holding a long wooden sign above the New Royal Saloon disappeared from one corner after the other until the sign collapsed to the street in a large puff of dust. Leonard watched, hunkering farther down with each shot, his arms rising and wrapping across his head as if to protect his toupee, his mouth agape.

"One thing's for sure—you know what to say to turn a girl's head." Danielle opened her Colt, dropped out the spent cartridges, and replaced them while smoke still curled from the barrel.

"Wait, Miss Danielle!" Leonard called out, staring at his downed wooden sign for a moment in disbelief as he hurried to catch up to her. "I didn't mean nothing by it, honest! I wouldn't say something to offend you for nothing in this world."

"I believe you, Mr. Whirley. I really, truly do," said Danielle. "It's just the way things are in this world. The only time I feel foolish is when I start making myself believe things might have changed." She walked on, still without facing him.

For the next two days she avoided Leonard Whirley, but on the morning she left Braden Flats, Danielle made it a point to stop by the New Royal Saloon and thank him for having looked after Sundown for her.

"I wish you would stay another few days," said Dr. Callaway

when she stepped into her stirrups out front of his office. "You've been the first paying customer I've had for the longest time. I hate to loose you."

Danielle smiled down at him. "I wish you and Mr. Whirley weren't leaving here," said Danielle. "I expect there will be no town here in a few weeks."

The old doctor scratched his head as if considering it. Then he said, "Well, I suppose we'll just have to wait and see."

With dried food in her saddlebags and grain for Sundown, Danielle turned the chestnut mare in the street and rode away at an easy pace, eyeing the burned remains of the telegraph office on her way. There was no way she would give up on hunting Cherokee Earl and his gang. The more she saw of their handiwork, the more she was convinced that she had to put a stop to them. She thought it a bit peculiar that neither the doctor nor Leonard Whirley had been able to tell from Ellen Waddell's actions that she was being held against her will. But she realized that in a life-or-death situation a woman might very well go along with her captors until she saw a chance to break away. At least Danielle hoped that was the case, having lost so much precious time here.

At the edge of town, Danielle brought the mare up into a trot, testing the tenderness of her healed wound, feeling no pain there. She studied the hoofprints in the dirt, knowing that the trail had grown cold. Cherokee Earl and his gang could be any number of places by now. Once again she was on her own, the same as when she'd hunted her father's killers. She was used to being alone, yet she missed having Stick beside her. From now on she had to watch her own back, not always an easy task for a woman unescorted in a man's world.

Danielle knew her best bet was to stay on the north trail, follow it toward the highlands, and see what, if anything, had happened along the string of towns that lay ahead of her. She was certain that a man like Cherokee Earl couldn't go along without causing more trouble. His gang had tasted blood at the past two towns in a row. She was betting they would be wanting more.

CHAPTER 12

Following a narrow stream running down from a stretch of rocky hills, for two nights in a row Danielle made her camp alongside the water's edge. The first night had been uneventful, sheltered as she was beneath a deep cliff overhang. But on the second night, in the hours before dawn, Danielle was awakened by Sundown nickering low and warily from where Danielle had grazed her in sweet grass less than twenty yards away. Hearing the mare, Danielle rolled quietly from her blanket, her rifle in hand. She crouched back out of the circling glow of firelight, listening for any sound out of the ordinary. For the rest of the night, she stayed back away from the fire, blanket wrapped around her, barely seeing the silhouette of the mare in the moon's glow.

At first light, Danielle picked up Sundown's bridle and walked down to where the big mare stood waiting. Sundown turned her head to face Danielle, and Danielle reached out a hand and rubbed the velvety muzzle.

"Easy, girl," Danielle whispered.

As she stroked the mare, her eyes searched along the stream, up along the rock ledges and into the darkened shadows and crevices.

"What was up there?" Danielle asked quietly as if at any moment the mare might answer. "Don't you worry," she added. "Whatever it is, if it's still there, we'll find it soon enough."

She lifted the bridle onto the mare's muzzle, adjusted it, and led the animal back to the campsite only a few yards away. Yes, there was someone watching her; she felt it plain as day. Unseen eyes followed her until she passed out of sight back into the rocks bordering the stream. Instinctively, she checked her Colt, then placed it back loosely into her holster.

"Yep," she repeated quietly to herself and the mare, "we'll soon find out."

Without preparing coffee or food, Danielle saddled the mare. Then she cleared the camp and rode off along the north trail alongside the stream before sunlight had crested the eastern skyline. Just past sunup she reached a place where the land flattened for the next few hundred yards before swooping upward again. Still following the stream, Danielle purposefully skylined herself to the hill trail below. She didn't let herself be seen for long, just enough for whoever might be watching to know that she was not using good caution. *Something a foolish woman would do,* she reminded herself with a wry smile.

Had someone well skilled with a rifle wanted her dead, right then would have been a good time to make their play. But they would have had to strike quickly and even then risk everything they had on one shot. With a fast break for cover, she could easily duck into the rocks before they set their sights on her again.

As she rode, she watched both right and left, barely turning her head in either direction but rather shifting only her eyes beneath her lowered hat brim. Along the way she caught a glimpse of a wisp of trail dust stirring from the rocks and scrub juniper running parallel below. Whoever was down there was hurrying now, wanting to get past her and climb up onto the trail inside the rocks. That made sense, she thought. They weren't out to ambush her. They wanted her to come upon them all at once in surprise, face-to-face. All right, she would give them that. At a point where the trail climbed back up into the rocky hills, she prepared herself, letting her right hand rest on her thigh only inches from the butt of her Colt.

With the craggy hillside rising on her left and the winding stream on her right, she eased the mare along at a slow walk until suddenly, as if out of nowhere, two men appeared on the trail before her. One man held a cocked rifle pointed at her from less than thirty feet away. The other stood confidently, with a pistol hanging loosely in his hand.

"Well, well, look here, brother Daryl," said the one with the pistol. "What a pleasant surprise."

"I was just thinking that very same thing myself, brother Lon!" said the one with the rifle. "You never know who you're going to come upon up here in these rocks. Could be a snake or a scorpion," he said, widening his eyes in mock fright.

"So true," said the other. "But then again it just might be some tender young dove."

Danielle stopped the chestnut mare with the slightest tap of her knees. The mare turned slightly, quarter-wise to the men, then stood as still as stone. "Your best hope is for the snakes and scorpions," Danielle said. "This dove ain't as tender as you'd like."

Both men had spread wolfish smiles, but the smiles melted away at her words. The one with the pistol said to the other without taking his eyes off Danielle, "Well, brother Daryl, there's our answer. It's her, all right. Cherokee Earl said she was a rash, rude, wished-she-was-a-man kind of woman."

Danielle felt her senses perk. Immediately, she picked up on the man's words and replied, "Didn't you wonder why Cherokee Earl didn't come looking for me himself? Why's he so busy he can't handle his own gun work?"

"He's busy sparking his new bride up in Drake," the man replied.

"Shut up, Lon," said the rifleman, stepping forward. "Can't you see she's just trying to milk you for information?"

"She can milk all day. It suits me," the other replied. His face turned stonelike, his eyes dark and caged. His voice went flat and ironhard. "She ain't going nowhere after today."

Danielle felt a cold, calm resolve wash over her. "I take it you two are brothers."

"That's right," said the one with the pistol. "Daryl and Lon Trabough, at your service." His death-mask expression remained the same. "I'm Lon," he added, "the handsomer one."

"What's it to you?" said the one with the rifle.

Danielle allowed a slight shrug. "Well, Daryl, I'm always curious about those I'm fixin' to kill."

"By God, let's go on and kill her and be done with it, Lon," said Daryl, working his fingers restlessly on the rifle stock. "I've no tolerance for a sharp-tongued woman!"

"Easy, brother Daryl," said Lon, still keeping his eyes on Danielle. "How often is a man blessed with this kind of situation? Earl wants us to kill her. He never said we couldn't have a little fun first."

"I don't like it," said Daryl.

"Oh, but you will, brother Daryl, by the time it gets around to you," said Lon.

Danielle sat silently, waiting, watching, knowing. Beneath her, the mare hadn't much more than breathed. Together, horse and rider could have been a statue except for the flutter of a hot breeze as it licked at Danielle's hat brim.

"Now lift that pistol, pitch it away, and climb down here," said Lon. "We're going to start by getting a good look at you without all them clothes hiding your better nature."

Danielle raised her knee and lifted her leg over the saddle slowly. She paused, suspended for a second, looking both men up and down. "You're about my size, aren't you, Lon?" She let herself slide down from the saddle and stood with her feet shoulder width apart.

Lon Trabough had a hard time containing himself. His lips quivered a bit at her words. "Oh, don't you worry, you sweet little morsel. I'm just exactly your size!"

"That's what I thought," Danielle said coolly.

"Now lift that pistol, and let's get started!" Lon demanded eagerly.

"Whatever you say, Lon."

Her first shot hit Lon in the dead center of his sweaty forehead, the impact of it flipping his hat backward off his head. The shot came so fast, her pistol only a streak of shiny metal coming up from her holster, that Lon stood staring blankly for a second, a stunned grimace on his face as blood spewed from the back of his head. Then he sank to his knees as if ready for prayer and collapsed forward onto his face.

"Lon, Jesus!"

Daryl Trabough saw the gout of blood and brain matter spray past him. It rattled him long enough for Danielle to almost take her time putting two bullets through his heart. He dropped limply in the dirt. Only then did Sundown seem to ease down and shake out her mane.

Danielle walked forward, reloading her Colt. When she reached out a boot toe and rolled Lon Trabough's head to the side, she saw only a minimal amount of blood on the back of his shirt collar and none down the back of the shirt itself.

"Yep, you're just about my size," she said quietly to herself. She holstered her pistol, stooped down, and began undressing him.

Stripping Lon Trabough down to his long johns, Danielle carried his clothes out into the shallow stream and scrubbed them with a small bar of lye soap she carried in her saddlebags. She rinsed them, soaped them again, rinsed them again, and hung them to dry over the rounded tops of scrub juniper and mesquite bushes. While she waited on the wet clothes to dry, she took down the lariat from Sundown's saddle, looped it around the corpses' feet, and dragged them both downstream amid jumbled piles of rocks and spilled boulders that years of wind and rain had washed down from the hillside.

She loosened the rope, looked down at the two bodies, and dusted her hands together. She stood silent for a moment and took off her hat in reflection. The mare stood close by her side.

"Lord," Danielle said, bowing her head slightly, "I know it's not right taking another person's life, and I wish I hadn't had to do it. But you saw how it played out. They couldn't have made their intentions any plainer and it still be fit for Christian ears." She paused for a moment with her hat in her hand. "I doubt these two snakes ever did anybody any good in this life. So whatever you do with them is fine by me and better than they deserve. Amen."

Danielle placed her hat back down on her head, tightened it, and turned and walked away, leading the mare back across the rocky ground to the trail. Having missed a lot of sleep the night before and breakfast early that morning, Danielle ate some jerked beef and dried biscuits, then napped for the next couple of hours. When she awakened she gathered the clothes, feeling where the trousers were still a bit damp, and walked off into the cover of rocks and brush. While Sundown waited, Danielle unwound the binder she'd carried for the past year in her saddlebags. She took off her women's clothes and wrapped the binder firmly around herself, flattening the curve of her breasts.

Once she had changed into the men's clothing, she took her time folding her doeskin skirt, her bell-sleeved blouse, and her long, soft leather riding vest. Back at Sundown's side, Danielle placed her women's clothing carefully down into her saddlebags, strapped the saddlebags shut, and patted them with her hands.

"I hope this is not for long," she said absently to the chestnut mare. "Looks like the only way to get respect in a man's world is to be a man."

Danielle unstrapped the rolled-up riding duster from behind her saddle, shook it out, and put it on. Then she stuffed her hair up under her hat, stepped up into her saddle, and patted the mare on the neck.

"Let's go, Sundown," she said. "We've been down this trail before."

DRAKE, NEW MEXICO TERRITORY

Cherokee Earl sat atop his horse and spoke down to Buck Hite, an outlaw gang leader he'd met upon arriving in town. Earl had decided that Buck Hite and his gang would fit nicely into his plans. Buck stood holding the reins to Ellen Waddell's horse. Ellen sat stone-faced, staring straight ahead.

"Don't wait around too long for Daryl and Lon Trabough, Buck," Earl said. "I need you and your gang in Cimarron as soon as you can get there."

"What day do you need us there, Earl? We'll make sure we get there on time."

Cherokee Earl gave him a blank stare. "If you knew what day the main silver load comes in, you wouldn't need me at all, now, would you, Buck?"

"I meant nothing by it, Earl," said Buck.

He tried to hand Earl the reins to Ellen's horse, but Earl refused to take them. Instead, Earl flagged Avery McRoy forward and gestured for him to take them. McRoy looked put out by the task.

"Just make sure you get there soon," Earl said gruffly to Buck Hite. "I only need men I can count on."

As Earl spoke to Buck Hite, Dirty Joe slipped his horse forward ahead of McRoy, saying to him in a guarded voice, "I've got her reins, Avery."

"Much obliged," McRoy whispered in reply. "Leading her has made my arm sore as a boil."

Earl leaned slightly down to Buck Hite and said, "Buck, I'll tell you this much. . . . Your boys Daryl and Lon killing that woman and old man for me has gotten you a top spot in my operation. Once we pull this bank job, you'll wonder why we didn't get together years before now." He gave a quick thin smile, then straightened in his saddle and leveled his hat. Looking back and forth along the street, he shook his head. "This whole damned town is made of mud. I'm glad you talked us out of burning it."

Buck Hite only nodded, tipping his hat as Earl, McRoy, and Dirty Joe backed their horses and rode away, Joe leading Ellen's horse, which stayed right up beside his.

"There goes trouble in the making," Buck Hite murmured to himself, seeing the flushed and aroused look on Dirty Joe's face and the guarded smile the woman passed to him. Buck shook his head and walked back to the Ace High Saloon, where his men awaited him.

At the edge of town, Ellen Waddell slowed her horse back a step, deliberately making Dirty Joe fall behind with her while McRoy and Cherokee Earl rode on ahead.

"Come on, Miss Ellen!" Joe whispered warily. "He's going to suspect something." He jerked her horse forward.

"All right," Ellen replied in a hushed tone, "but can't you see he's already tiring of me? He'll soon pass me off to McRoy or one of those men back there or anyone he feels like—"

"Shhh, don't say that, Ellen! I'm not going to let that happen to you. . . . I swear I won't."

"Then you'd better do something quick," Ellen said, letting her horse ride sidled against his, "or it's going to be too late, and you and I will never be together." She gazed deep into his eyes and said, "I can't stand the thought of us never being together, can you?"

"God, no!" he said, a slight tremor in his voice. "But what can I do about it right now?"

She moved her eyes from Dirty Joe's slowly, making sure that his eyes followed hers to McRoy and Cherokee Earl's backs. "You know what to do, Joe," she whispered with finality.

Dirty Joe stared at the two men for a moment, the tendons in his neck drawn tight at the thought running through his mind. "Soon, Ellen. . . . Soon, I promise."

Back in Drake at the Ace High Saloon, Eddie Ray Moon, Clifford Reed, and Fat Cyrus Kerr stood huddled at the bar and listened to Buck Hite talk about their newly formed alliance with Cherokee Earl and the plans for meeting him and his men for the upcoming bank robbery up in Cimarron.

"I'd feel better about everything if Daryl and Lon was already back here with us," said Fat Cyrus. As he spoke, he hiked his baggy trousers up under his belly, the weight of his gun belt constantly working them downward.

"Me, too," Clifford Reed agreed. "I'm a little spooked about it, to tell the truth."

"Spooked?" said Buck Hite, showing an amount of contempt for Reed's words.

Reed wasn't a bit embarrassed. "Damn right, spooked," he said with conviction. "It ain't natural, what Earl told us about this woman, and it was a mistake sending two of our men back to ambush her. How long should it take two men like the Trabough brothers to gun down her and one old man?"

"When you start running things, Clifford, you can ask them kind of questions," Buck Hite said, jutting his chin, not liking the way Reed questioned his judgment in front of the other men. "But right now I'm still the top bull of this herd." He tapped a thumb on his broad chest. "I sent them because I told Cherokee Earl I would. You don't throw in with a man like Cherokee Earl Muir unless you've got something to offer."

Fat Cyrus tossed back a shot of whiskey and wiped his thick hand across his mouth. "Earl was down to only two men and himself," he said, "not counting the fact that he's riding around with a woman draped across his lap. Looks to me like we're holding the most cards in this game."

"Yeah," said Buck Hite, "we might be holding the most . . . but the most ain't always the best. I don't care if he's got a woman and her house cat on his lap. We've thrown in with him." He looked at each of the three men's faces in turn. "Boys, Cherokee Earl is an old hand at this business. He knows the upper country and every hiding place up there. He knows ranchers who'll hide him out and crooked sheriffs who'll tip him off when the law's gotten too close." He leaned in closer and said almost in a whisper, "He's even got inside information on the bank in Cimarron . . . knows when there's a big shipment of money coming in to pay for silver from the silver mines all across the Territory."

"When is it?" Fat Cyrus asked.

Buck looked at him in disbelief. "Well, now, Cyrus," he said wryly, "if I knew when it was coming, I reckon I wouldn't need Cherokee Earl at all, would I?"

"Oh," said Cyrus, nodding. "I see what you mean."

Buck Hite shook his head, then said to everybody, "Don't ever think I enjoy giving my gang over to somebody else. But for now, if we ever plan on getting ahead, Cherokee Earl is the best way to do it. Sure, he's short of men right now . . . got somebody dogging his trail. But why else would he be taking us in?" He looked at each of them again, his eyes asking if they were with him.

Clifford Reed nodded. "I had complaints, Buck. I just needed some filling in."

"All right." Buck stared at him, his hand resting on his pistol butt. "Are you properly filled in?"

"Sure." Clifford shrugged, reaching for the whiskey bottle that stood on the bar. "I'm good."

"What about you, Cyrus?" Buck asked. "Anything else I need to fill you in on? I had eggs and potatoes for breakfast . . . went to the jake about an hour ago . . . been going pretty regularly the past few weeks."

Fat Cyrus looked away from Buck's cold stare.

"What about you, Eddie Ray?" Buck asked the thin, hollow-eyed gunfighter with a pointed chin.

Eddie Ray Moon had been rolling himself a smoke while Buck spoke to the other two men. Now he ran the cigarette in and out of his mouth, wetting it, and let it hang from his lips as he spoke, taking a long match from his shirt pocket. "Do I look like I give a rattling bag full of dry horse shit?"

Fat Cyrus and Clifford Reed chuckled as Eddie Ray struck the match and lit the cigarette. Turning his eyes to Buck Hite, he let go of a long stream of smoke and shook out the match. "Makes no difference to me who we ride with, long as the money's right." He shot Clifford Reed a look of contempt. "I'll try not to get too spooked by this woman and her grandfather or whoever the hell the old man is." He made a show of flipping the burned match away, then leaned back against the bar as if getting comfortable. "You figure out what you want done. Then just let me know. I'll kill them so quick, they'll forget they was ever born."

CHAPTER 13

Cherokee Earl and his party had been gone from Drake for three days when Danielle rode in on the chestnut mare. Dressed in the clothes she'd taken off of Lon Trabough, she looked exactly as she'd intended, a young gunman on the move: lean, wily, and sizing up everyone who passed before him. To Buck Hite and the others, the young gunman looked no different from any other saddle tramp coming in off the high range. Yet, watching the mare pass by the Ace High Saloon, seeing the young gunman with his duster open in front, revealing the big tied-down Colt perched on his hip, something strikingly familiar caught Fat Cyrus's attention. He just couldn't put his finger on it.

"What have we got here?" Cyrus said to Clifford Reed, the two of them standing on the boardwalk of the Ace High.

"Beats me," said Clifford. "But he sure carries himself like he's cock of the walk."

Both men watched in silence for a moment as the young gunman rode by.

"Nice mare, though," Clifford offered under his breath.

"Think I ought to go get Buck?" Fat Cyrus asked, hiking up his trousers.

"Why?" said Clifford Reed. "Alls he'll do is what we're doing—stare and ask questions."

From behind the batwing doors of the Ace High, Eddie Ray

said, "Don't you suppose it would be a good idea if somebody went and asked this newcomer what he's doing here in Drake? Don't know about you boys, but I always like to have an idea who might or might not be carrying a badge."

"That's no lawman," said Cyrus. "I'll wager you on it."

"No, I don't think so either," said Clifford. "There's something about a lawman you can always spot . . . too well fed or something. This boy is a straight-up gunman, an outlaw just like us, far as I'm concerned."

Eddie Ray stepped out onto the boardwalk and let the doors flap behind him. "One thing's for sure: Neither one of yas would ever know what he is if it meant walking your lazy behinds over and asking him."

"I'll go if Buck asks me to," said Fat Cyrus.

Both he and Clifford Reed watched the rider ease the mare up to a hitch rail out front of a low adobe-and-stone hotel.

Clifford Reed said, "You're right, Eddie Ray. We ain't going over and asking him a damn thing. . . . But you know what? I figure that's something you'd be wanting to do by yourself, tough guy that you are and all."

Eddie Ray took a deep draw on his cigarette and said through a stream of smoke, "Tough guy that I am . . . I think I'll do just that." He flipped the stub of the cigarette away and stepped down off the boardwalk. "Get us a beer, Fat Cyrus," he said over his shoulder. "This shouldn't take over a minute or two."

The two men watched Eddie Ray Moon saunter across the street and run his hand along the chestnut mare's damp side as he walked past the hitch rail to the door of the hotel.

"That damned fool," said Clifford Reed, staring alongside Fat Cyrus. "Whoever that gunman is, I almost wish he'd send Eddie Ray back out with a tin can tied to his tail."

"Yeah, me, too," said Fat Cyrus, easing forward down off the boardwalk. "Come on, let's get over there close to the window. I want to listen to this."

In the small lobby of La Rosa Negra Hotel, Danielle stood

signing the leather-bound guest register, her saddlebags over her shoulder, her rifle under her arm. She used the name she'd used in the past when she'd traveled as a man, Danny Duggin. Finishing, she slid the register across the ornate countertop into the waiting hands of the Mexican woman across the counter.

The woman started to close the register, but the voice of Eddie Ray Moon said firmly from the front door, "Not so fast, Falina."

He slipped over quickly beside Danielle and placed his hand down flat on the register. Danielle only stared at him from within the dark shadow of her lowered hat brim.

"I'd like to see who we have visiting us."

Falina drew her hands away from the register, shooting a worried look back and forth between the two faces at the counter. "*Por favor!* I do not want the trouble," she said in stiff English.

"And you won't have any trouble, at least not from me," said Eddie Ray, spreading a harsh grin at the stranger with the lowered hat brim. "What about you, Mr. . . . ?" He consulted the register, then finished his words. "Mr. Danny Duggin. Any trouble coming from your direction?"

Danielle lowered her tone of voice a bit and added some gravel to it. "If there was, you'd be past knowing about it by now," she said.

The words stung Eddie Ray. His grin disappeared. He took a step back from the counter, letting his right hand poise near his pistol butt. "Did I just hear a threat in there?"

Danielle stared at him from the darkness beneath the broad hat brim. "You figure it out," she said, swiping her free hand across the countertop and picking up the key to her room.

Seeing her gun hand busy holding the key, Eddie Ray grew bolder. As Danielle turned to walk away toward the stairs, Eddie Ray stepped around in front of her, blocking her way.

"I already have figured it out," he said, his fingers opening and closing near the pistol butt. "I say you and me are going have to do some settling up before you go a step farth—"

Danielle cut his words with her rifle butt, jerking it forward from under her arm to nail Eddie Ray's nose flat to his face.

Falina gasped and threw both hands to her face. Eddie Ray staggered backward, blood flying from his crushed nose, his arms flailing out at his sides. His bootheel caught the edge of a brass spittoon and caused him to lose balance for a split second. But that split second was all Danielle needed. She stepped forward quickly, sidled close to Eddie Ray, stuck the rifle barrel between his legs, and tangled his legs with a hard twist of the rifle. Eddie Ray went to the floor face-first, a muffled scream resounding as his smashed nose met the hard clay tiles. With the toe of her boot, Danielle reached out and kicked his pistol from its holster, then kicked it across the tile floor under a long divan.

Outside the open window of the hotel lobby, Fat Cyrus and Clifford Reed both winced at the sound of the rifle butt slamming into Eddie Ray's nose. They winced even more when they'd slipped a peep over the window ledge in time to see his face smack the hard floor. Seeing the young gunman walk away from where Eddie Ray lay writhing on the clay tiles, Clifford and Cyrus ducked away from the window and stared at each other.

"Suppose we best go help him," said Clifford.

"Why? Looks like it's over now," said Fat Cyrus. "Besides, that peckerwood has had that coming for the longest time. I'd have busted his head myself long before this except I know it would come down to gunplay. . . . Ain't no way I'm as fast as he is."

"Me neither," said Clifford. "Come on, we can at least drag him up off the floor."

"Yeah," said Cyrus, grinning, "I want to hear him explain how this all went wrong for him."

In her small hotel room, Danielle heard men's muffled voices as Clifford Reed and Fat Cyrus helped Eddie Ray Moon to his feet and half carried him out the door.

Falina, feeling bolder now that she'd seen one of the gunmen brought down a notch, ran over to the divan and pulled Eddie

Ray's pistol from beneath it. She quickly unloaded the pistol and dropped the bullets into her dress pocket. Then she ran to the door, holding the empty gun with two fingers.

"Here . . . take your stinking pistol with you!" she shouted, heaving the gun out into the dirt. "And don't come back to this place with your rudeness!"

The pistol hit the ground with a thud. Clifford and Fat Cyrus managed to keep from laughing aloud at the hapless Eddie Ray hanging between them, his boot toes still dragging in the dirt a bit as they walked. They looked down at Eddie Ray's gun.

"Damn, Eddie Ray," said Fat Cyrus with a grin as he stooped to pick up the pistol, "That fellow caused you to get your pistol all dirty." He shoved it down in Eddie Ray's holster. "Now you'll have to clean it."

"I'll kill him," Eddie Ray gasped, his swollen broken nose giving his voice a deep nasal twang.

"Kill him?" Clifford chimed in. "My God, man! You ought to thank him for not eating you alive. The shape you're in, he could have set your boots on fire and you couldn't have stopped him!"

"The hell did you say to him anyway?" Fat Cyrus asked, tormenting Eddie Ray.

"I forget," Eddie Ray mumbled as they dragged him on toward the saloon.

"If I was you, I'd sure try to remember," said Cyrus, "so you never make the mistake of saying it again!"

Danielle watched the men through a drawn window curtain she held slightly parted. When they went inside the Ace High Saloon, she took her hat off, poured tepid water from a pitcher into a wash pan, and washed her face. Then she placed her hat on her head, carefully stuffed her hair up under it, and picked up her rifle from where she'd laid it across the bed. A soft knock at the door drew her attention.

When she eased it open a crack, Falina held out her hand and said, "Here—I take the bullets from his gun so he cannot shoot anyone." She dropped the six bullets into Danielle's outstretched hand and smiled. "*Por favor*, do with them as you will."

"*Gracias,*" said Danielle. She returned the woman's smile and closed the door softly.

Pocketing the bullets, Danielle left her saddlebags in the room, walked outside to the hitch rail, and led Sundown around behind the hotel to a long row of stalls. There she grained the chestnut mare, watered her, and wiped her down with a handful of clean straw. Almost an hour had passed by the time Danielle left the row of stalls and walked back along the alley alongside the hotel.

Nearing the end of the alley, she saw two men step in slowly, blocking her way to the street. One held a pair of saddlebags in his hand. *Mine... ?* she wondered. Glancing behind her, she saw two more blocking her way back toward the stalls. One of these she recognized as the man from the lobby of the hotel. *Good,* she thought. They were coming to her no sooner than she'd arrived in town. She smiled to herself and slowed her pace, still walking forward.

"Hold it right there," said one of the men in front of her, seeing that she seemed to have no hesitancy about walking right through them. He held up a hand toward her. "Danny Duggin," the man said, "we don't like saddle tramps soiling up our town." He gestured a hand, and the other man stepped forward. "Clifford, give him his bags."

Clifford Reed pitched the saddlebags to Danielle's feet.

She glanced down at them, then slowly looked back at Clifford and Buck Hite. Behind her, Danielle heard footsteps hurrying, trying to sneak up on her. She spun, her Colt snapping up from her holster, cocked and ready, stopping Fat Cyrus and Eddie Ray Moon in their tracks.

"You're back for more?" Danielle said in her best man's voice, low and gravelly. Her pistol pointed straight at Eddie Ray's broken nose. A thin trickle of blood still ran down his upper lip.

Seeing how quickly Danny Duggin had gotten the drop on two of his men, Buck Hite said under his breath, "Jesus, boys, he could have killed you both." He stared at Eddie Ray Moon. "I thought you said he hit you while you weren't looking."

"That's the truth, Buck," said Eddie Ray. "We was just talking, then all of sudden, *bam*! He hit me with his rifle butt."

Danielle watched in silence, her pistol still cocked, still pointed. Fat Cyrus and Clifford Reed passed one another a knowing glance.

Buck Hite saw it and said, "Is there something you boys ain't told me? If there is, you'd best say so now before somebody gets killed here."

"We might have seen the whole thing through the hotel window," Fat Cyrus said hesitantly.

"You might have?" Buck Hite shouted. "By God, either you saw something or you didn't!"

"All right," said Clifford Reed, coming clean, "we saw this man bust Eddie Ray in the nose. . . . But he didn't do it on the sly. Eddie Ray had his bark on and was fixin' to draw on him." His finger pointed at Danielle. "This Duggin was just faster. He smacked the cold yellow piss out of him."

"That's a damn lie, Buck," said Eddie Ray. "This man ain't nothing!" He also pointed at Danielle. "I'm faster than he'll ever hope to be with a gun! I wasn't prepared, is all."

Danielle listened. If this was a chance for her to work her way into the confidence of some of Cherokee Earl's men, she needed to defuse the situation. She lowered her Colt and looked at Buck Hite. "Maybe you and your pals had better go somewhere and work all this out . . . figure who did what." She reached down and scooped up her saddlebags. "Meanwhile, I'll be at the saloon. . . . It's been a long ride up here."

"Not so fast, Duggin," said Buck. "You came up from the south range?"

"Yep," said Danielle.

As she spoke, she noted Buck Hite looking her up and down. Did he recognize the shirt she was wearing as once having belonged to Lon Trabough?

"I sent a couple of good men down along the trail—the Trabough brothers. They should have been back before now. Maybe you saw them."

"Yep, I saw them," said Danielle, draping the dusty saddlebags over her shoulder and raising her rifle up under her arm, the way she'd carried it earlier. Seeing the rifle butt up under her arm, Eddie Ray took a cautious step back from her. "They said they'd just finished up some messy business with somebody along the trail. Said they were on their way back to Drake."

"Oh . . ." Buck Hite eyed Danielle's shirt again. "Then I expect I should be seeing them here most anytime?"

"I wouldn't count on it," Danielle said flatly.

"Why not?" Buck asked.

"Because I killed them both deader than hell," Danielle said.

The men seemed to snap to attention.

"You what?" Buck stared in disbelief.

"They got belligerent and out of hand." Her eyes beneath the hat brim went to Eddie Ray. "They started asking too many questions, just like this one did before I rifle-butted him."

"You'll play hell ever getting the drop on me again, Danny Duggin!" Eddie Ray raged. "I can damn sure promise you that!"

Danielle looked down at the pistol in his holster, saw the dust still on the handle and the hammer, and took a chance on him not having checked or dusted it off since their earlier encounter. "Mister, I've got the drop on you right now. . . . You're just not smart enough to know it."

Shaking with anger, Eddie Ray touched a wadded-up bandanna to the trickle of blood on his upper lip. "Buck," he said. "Let me shoot this smart-mouthed turd, please! Right here, right now! I've got to kill him. . . . I've got to!"

Danielle spread a tight smile beneath her hat brim. "Give him the go-ahead, Buck," she said. "It ain't like he's apt to hurt anybody."

"That does it, Buck! Everybody, stand back!" Eddie Ray screamed, his face red, his purple nose appearing to almost throb with boiling rage. "I'm going to kill him!"

"All right, Mr. Danny Duggin," said Buck Hite, stepping back and making room. "Looks like you've gone and dug your own grave. Eddie Ray is not a man to fool with when it comes to a gunfight."

Danielle turned to face Eddie Ray. "Let's get to it, then, Eddie Ray," she said in a hissing voice.

"Damn right, let's get to it," said Eddie Ray. Then he said to the others, "Cyrus, Clifford, stay out of this. . . . He's all mine!"

Eddie Ray's hand streaked down to his pistol butt, but before he could lift the pistol, Danielle's Colt was out, cocked, and pointed at his swollen nose. Eddie Ray's face turned sickly green; his hand was frozen on the holstered pistol.

Danielle had him, and she knew it. But instead of firing, she let down the hammer on the Colt and spun it on her finger. Eddie Ray had another chance. He almost snatched his pistol up, but then stopped again when Danielle's Colt pointed at him, again cocked and ready. She moved closer to him.

"You just can't seem to get that gun out of the holster, can you, Eddie Ray?" she said, taunting him in a quiet voice.

She spun the pistol again, saw the thought cross Eddie Ray's mind again, then stopped the Colt and pointed it again just as he was on the verge of drawing. Again he froze. Again she came closer.

"Damn it to hell!" Eddie Ray shrieked, almost sobbing in his frustration and fear. "Either shoot me or back off! I can't stand this!"

"Then you've had enough?" Danielle asked, her Colt still menacing him.

Before he could speak, she spun the Colt again and stopped it, cocking it in his face only a few inches from his broken nose.

"I've had enough! Yes, I've had enough," said Eddie Ray in defeat, wincing, holding his free hand up as if to protect his swollen nose.

Danielle pulled the trigger on the Colt but caught it with her thumb just before it struck the bullet. Eddie Ray, Clifford Reed, and Fat Cyrus gasped. Buck Hite just watched, liking the way this young gunman handled himself.

"You wasn't going to shoot nobody anyway, Eddie Ray," Danielle said in a low gravelly voice. She lowered her Colt, reached into her pocket with her free hand, took out the six bullets, and pitched them to the ground at Eddie Ray's feet. "Your gun ain't even loaded. Think I'd trust you with a loaded gun . . . the way you was acting earlier?"

"You've got to be kidding!" said Buck Hite. He stepped over, yanked Eddie Ray's pistol up from his holster, slung it open, and checked it. His eyes widened, then narrowed as he turned them to Eddie Ray. "You stupid peckerwood! This man unloaded your pistol? You didn't even check it before coming back here looking for a gunfight? I ought to bend this barrel across your chin!" He drew the pistol back, then stopped himself, with Eddie Ray standing dumbfounded.

Danielle holstered her pistol and stepped away through an opening Buck Hite had left for her.

"Are you looking for work?" Buck asked before she had gone two steps.

"No, thank you," Danielle said over her shoulder. "Work is the last thing I'm looking for."

"Well, what the hell are you looking for?" Buck asked.

"Easy money," Danielle said, a flat smile coming to her lips.

There was silence for a second as her words sank in. Then Buck Hite chuckled, Clifford and Fat Cyrus slowly joining in.

"I figured it went without saying that you're looking for easy money," said Buck. "We wouldn't know how to spend any other kind."

"Now you're making more sense," said Danielle.

"Wait a damn minute," Eddie Ray demanded. He tuned to Buck Hite. "What about him killing two of our men?"

Buck Hite cocked his head at Danielle. "Yeah, what about that, Danny Duggin? Bad as I need men, you went and killed two of them."

"Yeah," said Danielle, "but I figure it's an even trade. I didn't kill Eddie Ray. That's one. . . . And I'm throwing in with you. That's two."

The men laughed, except for Eddie Ray.

"He's got a point there, Eddie Ray," said Buck. Buck looked at

Danielle. "Do you have any qualms about what you have to do to make this easy money?"

"Not in the least," said Danielle.

"Come on, then," said Buck, "I want to buy you a drink." He looked back at the others. "Boys, get your drinking done—we leave first thing in the morning."

"Where are we headed, Buck?" Danielle asked.

"We're headed north to meet up with a pal of mine named Cherokee Earl Muir." He beamed proudly. "Ever heard of him?"

"Sure have," said Danielle.

"Then I reckon you know that riding with him is about as big as you get in the business of outlawry."

"That's my thought exactly," Danielle said as they walked on.

Buck Hite hooked a thumb in his belt. "Stick with me, Danny Duggin. . . . You'll be glad you did."

"I'm glad already, Buck," Danielle replied.

CHAPTER 14

CIMARRON, NEW MEXICO TERRITORY

Sheriff Clarence Wright walked from the St. James Hotel back to his office two blocks away. He had a lot on his mind, most of it involving an already large amount of money lying in the Cimarron bank at that very moment and more money coming any day. Those unusually large amounts of money were sent to Cimarron to pay for the shipments of silver coming in from mining operations all across the Territory. Why the large mining company's home offices back East had chosen his town for this transaction was beyond him. But there was no use in him fretting over it. The money was there; the silver was arriving. All he could do was keep a tight rein on things. In his hand Sheriff Wright held a federal court summons he had just received. On top of everything else, he had now been called to appear in court. That would put his town in a dangerous position for at least a week. He sighed, folded the summons, and stuffed it inside his coat pocket.

Out front of his office, he stopped for a moment and watched the scruffy young man on the boardwalk sweep road dust off into the street. Sheriff Wright needed help bad. This man had shown up in town two weeks earlier, down and out and looking like the only thing that could save him would be the next drink of whiskey he poured between his lips. He'd drifted into Cimarron looking for work, and Wright had taken a chance on him. So far the man had stayed sober enough to sweep up and do some minor roof repairs on the jail building. But that was a long way from being trusted as a deputy, Sheriff Wright reminded himself, watching the broom swish back and forth.

"What the hell?" Wright murmured to himself. "I'm desperate." He called out as he walked up onto the boardwalk and opened his office door, "Carlyle, come in here for a minute. . . . We need to talk."

Tuck Carlyle followed the sheriff through the open door, a gnawing feeling already welling up in his stomach. His first thought was that he'd done something wrong. Why else would the sheriff want to talk to him?

Inside the office, before the sheriff got a chance to speak, Carlyle said, "Sheriff, I would have had the sweeping done a lot sooner, except the hitch rail out front had gotten wobbly. . . . I tightened it up some."

"Close the door, Carlyle," said the sheriff. "This ain't got nothing to do with the sweeping. You've done a fine job ever since you been here."

"Then—then what's wrong?" Tuck asked.

"Wrong?" The sheriff frowned beneath his bushy eyebrows. "Hell, there's nothing wrong. In fact, I want to see how you feel about taking on a better job here, maybe becoming a temporary deputy. If it works out, maybe even doing it full-time. You interested?"

"You know I was a drunk for a long time, Sheriff. Do you think it might be too soon yet to go trusting me with that kind of responsibility?"

"If I thought it was too soon, I wouldn't have asked you," said the sheriff, a patient smile forming behind his drooping gray mustache. "Now, back to my question. . . . Are you interested?"

"Well, yes," Tuck said hesitantly. "I suppose I am. "

"You suppose you are," said the sheriff, repeating his words. "You'll have to do better than that, Carlyle."

Tuck raised his head, squared his shoulders, and looked the sheriff in the eyes. "I *know* I'm interested, Sheriff. Thanks for having this kind of faith in me. I realize you don't know me, Sheriff, so you don't know how far I've sunk since my wife's death. But the fact is, I wasn't always a down-and-out drunkard. At one time I had my own spread. Before that, I was a trail boss, drove cattle for some of the biggest ranches in the country."

"No man was born a drunk, Carlyle, so I figured you must've been something else along the way. I might not know you real well, but I've watched you enough to see that you've just gotten pretty far down, and now you're trying to get back up. When a man does that," the sheriff said, stepping around behind his battered oak desk, opening a drawer, and taking out a tin badge, "I believe it's only right that the rest of us give him a chance. Someday you might again own your own spread. Who knows? I might come to you looking for work. Meanwhile, welcome to being my deputy."

"I don't know what to say, Sheriff," said Tuck, taking the badge and looking at it for a second before pinning it on his shirt.

"Just say, 'I do.'" The sheriff grinned. He held up his thick right hand and said, "Do you solemnly swear to uphold the laws of this town to the best of your ability so help you God?"

"I do," said Tuck Carlyle, quickly raising his right hand as Sheriff Wright spoke.

"There, it's done," said Wright. "You are now officially an officer of the law. Conduct yourself accordingly."

"I do. . . . I mean—I will," said Tuck. He lowered his right hand.

Sheriff Wright reached down and opened a larger, deeper desk drawer. "I don't suppose you own a gun, do you?"

"No, Sheriff," said Tuck. "My firearms got away from me soon as I started living on rye whiskey." He looked ashamed.

"That's what I figured." Sheriff Wright pulled a rolled-up gun belt from the drawer. The bone handle of a .45-caliber Colt stood above the well-worn holster. "It ain't loaded, but there's bullets in the drawer. I reckon you can still handle one of these without shooting your toes off, can't you?" He handed the shooting rig over to Tuck.

"I'm sure I can," said Tuck.

He slipped the pistol from the holster, held it sideways, checked it, then hefted it in his hand. He spun it once and caught it in place, his thumb cocking then uncocking the hammer sleekly.

Watching him, the sheriff nodded with satisfaction. "Yeah, I can see you're familiar with the workings of a pistol. Are you any good, drawing and firing if you had to?"

"Yes, I'm a fair hand with a gun, Sheriff," said Tuck. "But to be honest, I'm going to go practice somewhere before I try to show you anything." He offered a smile. "As rusty as I am from all the drinking, I don't want to make you change your mind and take the gun back."

"There's little chance of that," said the sheriff. "I need a deputy real bad, Carlyle. Take the rest of the day off, go somewhere, and practice as much as you need to."

"What about all the dust out there on the boardwalk?" said Tuck. "Shouldn't I finish sweeping first?"

"The dust was there when I come to this town. . . . It'll be there when I leave," said Wright. "Tell the liveryman to fix you up with a horse and go do some practice shooting. You might be needing it before long."

"Much obliged, Sheriff." Tuck reached down and picked up a wooden box full of bullets. Instead of putting the gun belt on right then, he stuffed the rig up under his arm and headed for the livery barn. "I appreciate all you've done for me. . . . I won't let you down."

Sheriff Wright nodded in silence until Tuck Carlyle closed the door. Then the sheriff let out a long breath and said to himself, "I hope you won't, young man. . . . Things might get awfully dangerous around here."

At the livery barn, Tuck Carlyle told the liveryman Old John what the sheriff had said. Old John eyed the badge on Tuck's chest, then walked out to the corral behind the barn. When he returned, he handed Tuck the reins to a big rawboned roan.

"He's uglier than mud," said Old John. "But he's the best on the place far as I'm concerned."

Tuck looked the big dapple roan up and down. The horse looked strong and full of energy.

"Take that saddle," said the old man, pointing to a battered saddle lying atop a pile of firewood.

"Much obliged, John," Tuck Carlyle said.

"Don't mention it." Old John watched him pitch a saddle blanket atop the dapple roan, then toss the saddle gently on the horse's back and shake it into place. Grinning across empty gums, the old liveryman said, "A deputy, huh?"

"Like I said, it's only temporary," said Tuck. "But I'm hoping it'll turn full-time for me. I need the work." As he spoke, he adjusted the worn gun belt on his waist, getting used to it.

Old John nodded, noting the tied-down Colt. "Ain't been long since you came here wanting to muck stalls for a place to sleep. . . . Now look at you, wearing a badge and a bone-handled pistol." He stepped forward and rubbed the roan's muzzle while Tuck drew the cinch and dropped the stirrups. "I'm pleased things have worked out well for you."

Tuck nodded. "Thanks, John. You letting me sleep here meant a lot to me. I won't forget you for it."

"Aw, go on." Old John waved Tuck's words away. "Get on your horse and get out of here. If you like that big roan, I'll give you a good deal on buying him. I picked him up from a trail crew on their way back from Montana a month back. He knows his way around, I reckon."

"Montana and back? I'd say he does," Tuck said, rubbing the horse's jaw as he led it outside. "I just might be talking to you about buying him, then, if my credit's good."

"As good as any," said Old John, stopping at the door rather than stepping out into the sunlight. "Ride him out first. Then let me know. We'll talk price later." He watched Tuck step up into the saddle, collect the horse, heel the animal toward the street, and ride away. "Good luck, Deputy," Old John said under his breath.

Tuck rode the roan three miles out across a stretch of land dotted with piñon pine, juniper, and spruce. He wouldn't have had to go this far to practice his shooting. But it had been a long time since he'd been clearheaded sober, and it felt good to just be in a saddle again and have some time to think about things. Losing his wife had been like suffering through a long illness. Grief had stricken him like some dark, terrible fever that had only recently broken, allowing some of his strength to slowly return. All the whiskey he'd drunk hadn't helped cure him. It had served only as a painkiller. The longer he stayed sober, the more he realized he had to give up the whiskey and simply learn to live with his pain.

He stepped down and hitched the roan to a piñon. He stepped off thirty-odd yards to a sun-bleached oak log and set a row of fist-sized rocks up along its surface. Back at his starting point, he held his right hand up flat in front of himself and eyed it closely. The shakes he'd been going through ever since he'd quit drinking had ceased almost entirely. Good. He raised the pistol stiffly from the holster, looked it over again, then held it out at arm's length, cocked it, and took careful aim. His first shot missed his rock target by three inches. Not good, yet not as bad as he had expected.

He holstered the pistol, shook out his right arm, and took a few deep breaths. Then he raised the pistol again, drawing it slowly, this time cocking it on the upswing. He had to relax . . . let his knowledge of shooting come back to him. *You've got all day if that's what it takes,* he told himself with resolve. The next shot left a skinned streak across the dried log less than an inch from his target. *Better,* he thought, cocking the pistol again and taking aim, *but still* . . .

Three hundred yards away, topping a low rise, Cherokee Earl Muir rode up to where Avery McRoy sat staring out at the lone gunman taking target practice.

"Is that who's doing all the shooting?" asked Earl.

"Yeah," said McRoy. "Best I can make out, he's shooting at a log."

"At a log," Earl said flatly. "Wonder what that log ever did to him. Must be a kid stole his pa's pistol out here hankering to learn how to kill somebody." He stared off with McRoy for a moment, then said, "I did the same thing when I was a youngster."

McRoy nodded. "Me, too, sort of."

"Hell, that's no kid," said Earl, staring harder.

"I never said it was," said McRoy. "He's right alongside the trail. What do you want to do, ride out wide around him?"

"Hell, no . . . we got nothing to hide." Earl jerked his horse around to face Dirty Joe as he rode up leading Ellen's horse beside him.

"Take that lead rope off her horse, Dirty," Earl demanded. He looked at Ellen. "I'm counting on you behaving yourself," he said coldly to her. "Make a run for it, the last thing you'll see is a bullet pop out of your belly. Do you understand me real clearly?"

"She won't try nothing stupid," Dirty Joe butted in.

"Oh? You do all her speaking for her now, Dirty?" Earl asked with sarcasm.

"No, boss," Joe said quickly. "I just meant that I'll keep a close eye on her, is all."

"You've been doing that well enough, Dirty," said Earl. He dismissed Dirty Joe and looked Ellen up and down. "Fix your hair up some. Keep that horse close to Dirty till we get on down the trail to town."

"Uh, boss?" said Dirty Joe, stepping his horse forward and untying the lead rope from the bridle of Ellen's horse.

"Yeah, what is it, Dirty?" Earl replied.

"I gave it some thought, and I just as soon you not call me Dirty anymore. My name's Joe. . . . I figure that'll be good enough from now on." He offered a faint half smile. "If it's all the same to you, that is." He coiled the loose lead rope and hooked it over his saddle horn.

Avery McRoy winced and looked away for a second, shaking his head slowly.

Cherokee Earl sat staring in silence for a moment, then looked back and forth between Joe and the woman and said with a slight shrug, "What the hell do I care, Dir—I mean, Joe." He said to McRoy, "Do you have any objections to just calling him Joe?"

Avery McRoy looked down as he spoke. "I don't care. . . . Whatever suits him, I reckon."

When he raised his eyes, he gave Joe a cautioning look. But Joe ignored it.

"There you are now, Joseph," said Earl with a sharp snap of emphasis. "Everything the way you like it?"

"I appreciate it, boss," Joe said quietly, appearing a bit embarrassed. He shot McRoy a defusing glance and rode forward, Ellen Waddell keeping her horse close by his side.

When Joe and Ellen were a few feet ahead of them, Earl and Avery McRoy rode forward side by side. In a lowered voice, Earl asked McRoy, "How long has this been going on?"

"What's that, boss?" McRoy asked in response, trying to sound unknowing of anything out of the ordinary.

"Don't play dumb with me," Earl hissed.

"Boss, I can't say one way or the other," said McRoy, begging off of the conversation. "I just came to do my job. You know that's how I am."

"Yeah, I know," said Earl, staring ahead at Joe Turley and Ellen Waddell. There was silence as they wound down toward the main trail into Cimarron. Finally Earl said in a secretive tone, "How close are you and Dirty Joe?"

"We just ride together," said McRoy. "I never knew him before I came to ride with you. Far as I'm concerned, he's just one more gun in a world full of them."

"Good," said Earl. "Once this bank is robbed and we're in the clear, I might ask you to do me a special favor, McRoy. Think you'll be up to it?"

Avery McRoy nodded. "I can't see why not."

Tuck Carlyle was so engrossed in his shooting that he didn't notice the approaching riders less than twenty yards behind him. Only when he heard a gruff voice call out, "Hello the camp," did he turn and face them, his pistol still in hand but lowered to his side.

At the sight of the tin badge on Tuck Carlyle's chest, Ellen's heart leaped at the prospect of freedom. She shot a quick look at the others, then almost bolted her horse forward, ready to cry out for help from this man.

"I've no camp here," said Tuck, "but ride on in all the same."

He gestured his free hand along the trail. "As you can see, this is a public road."

"I saw there was no camp," said Earl, drawing closer, having taken the lead farther back along the trail. Earl was now being followed by Joe and Ellen, who in turn were followed by Avery McRoy. "But we've been hearing your shooting a long ways off. Didn't know how close we ought to come before announcing ourselves."

Tuck raised the pistol slightly and turned it back and forth in his hand. "Just doing some practicing," he said.

He felt the woman's eyes burning into him. Her expression was puzzling. What was it he read there: fear, hope . . . a warning of some sort?

Nodding at the badge on Tuck's chest, Earl said, "I expect that's a prudent pastime for a lawman." He smiled flatly, his hand seeming to rest idly on the pistol at his hip.

Behind Ellen and Joe, McRoy had drawn his rifle from its boot as he came down the trail. It lay across his lap, his gloved hand near the trigger.

"In my case it is," said Tuck. "I just turned deputy today. I figure I need all the practice I can get."

Catching a quick glimpse of the woman's eyes again, Tuck saw a change in her expression. He tried to take a good look at the faces of the men, but their broad hat brims along with the bright sunlight served to obstruct his vision.

"Oh, I see," said Earl, his hand relaxing on his pistol butt, even sliding down an inch. "Then we'll not take up your time." He nodded along the trail. "I take it this is the best way to Cimarron."

"It is that," said Tuck. "Cimarron is only about three miles farther."

As he spoke, he looked the woman up and down, wondering what had happened . . . what had caused her to change so suddenly. But now her expression offered no clue. Her eyes turned downward as if afraid to face him.

"Have you traveled far?" Tuck asked Earl, taking his eyes from the woman, lest he appear to be staring.

"Does Texas sound far?" said Earl. "I'm Fred Bartlett. I own a cattle operation outside Haley Springs. Ever heard of the place?"

"So happens I have," said Tuck. "I'm a Texan myself. My name is Tuck Carlyle." He touched his hat brim. "I've passed through Haley Springs buying cattle, making up a herd, although it has been a long while."

Earl smiled. "Well, like as not nothing's changed there." He tipped his hat slightly, then said, "We'll be taking our leave now. I'm afraid we're all in sore need of a hot bath and some food that ain't still running from us. I suppose there is a decent hotel in Cimarron."

"Yes, there is," said Tuck. "There's the St. James. It's the finest hotel between here and Kansas City."

"Much obliged then," said Earl, touching his hat brim. "That's where we'll stay."

Tuck touched his fingertips to his hat brim again as the four riders filed past him, the woman not raising her eyes or acknowledging him again in any way. *A strange group,* he thought. He stood watching them until they rode down out of sight beneath the roll of the land. Then he turned back to his shooting, unable to get the woman's expression out of his mind as he raised the pistol and cocked it. He'd have to mention it to the sheriff tonight, he reminded himself. That was the sort of thing a deputy was supposed to do. This time his shot was perfect, shattering the rock like glass.

Just over the rise, Ellen Waddell looked back at the sound of Tuck's shot.

"You done real well back there," Earl said to her, cutting his horse to the side and stopping as she and Joe Turley rode past him.

Joe took the lead rope up from around his saddle horn and uncoiled it, ready to tie it to Ellen's horse's bridle again.

"Never mind, Joe," Earl said to him. "Long as she behaves, let her handle the horse herself."

"But, boss, I've been leading her all this way." Joe looked disappointed.

"You heard him, Joe," Ellen whispered in a sharp hiss, just

between the two of them. She jerked her reins away from Joe's hand before he even had time to reach out with the lead rope.

"Yeah," said Earl, with no idea what Ellen had just said to Joe Turley, "and now I'm telling you to leave her be. . . . We'll see how far we can trust her." He cut Ellen a dark stare. "Don't forget, little darling, I can still drop a bullet in you long before you get out of sight."

"I know that," said Ellen. "I'm no fool. I'll do as I'm told."

"There, Joe, you hear that?" said Earl. "This woman's not a fool. She wasn't about to say something back there to cause that poor deputy to get his eyeballs shot out. . . . The odds weren't right, were they, Mrs. Waddell?" he said with a sneer.

Ellen didn't answer. She rode on, looking down at the ground.

Avery McRoy took this time to say something he'd been wondering about for a while now. "How in the world are we going to keep her from shooting her mouth off once we get inside Cimarron?" he asked.

"We're not taking her into town with us," said Earl.

Joe Turley looked surprised. "But you just told that deputy we'd be staying at the hotel—"

"Damn it, Joe," said Earl, cutting him off. "I hope I ain't got myself in trouble, lying to a deputy of all things!" He feigned a look of fright.

"Joe, Joe, my goodness." McRoy stifled a laugh and shook his head at Turley's ignorance.

"There's a cabin I know about, four miles east of town," Earl said. "We'll hole up there until we get ready to do our raid."

"Buck and his men will be looking for us in town," said McRoy. "Want me to cut off from you and ride on in, keep my eyes open for Buck?"

"Tomorrow," said Earl. "We'll get a night's sleep, give that deputy time to forget our faces. Then we'll take turns going to town till we hook up with Buck."

"Sounds good to me," said McRoy, heeling his horse forward.

"I sure hope there is a washtub and a stove to heat some water at that cabin."

"Don't worry," said Cherokee Earl. "I think of everything." He tapped his horse up and rode beside McRoy, hearing another pistol shot resound behind them over the rise. "That's it, Deputy," Earl said to McRoy with a chuckle. "Better get good at it. You never know when it'll come in handy."

CHAPTER 15

THE UNSLED MINES, NEW MEXICO TERRITORY

Dave Waddell flinched at the sound of gunfire coming from inside the mining office shack, but he stuck to his job, holding the reins to Frisco Bonham's horse while Frisco performed the robbery. Since he and Frisco had joined up, it seemed that all they'd done was ride from one robbery to the next. After the stagecoach, they'd robbed a relay station north of Santa Fe, then a band of settlers headed for California. But according to Frisco, every step they took was leading Dave that much closer to finding his wife. He had to go along with things. What else could he do? he asked himself. Another shot resounded from the shack.

Dave sat watching tensely for any sign of trouble. "Damn it, hurry up, Frisco," he said to himself under his breath, seeing two miners step out of a toolshed a few yards away and look toward the office shack. Dave raised the rifle from across his lap and let the barrel loom menacingly toward them. "Get back inside, you peckerwoods! This doesn't concern you!" he shouted through the bandanna he wore as a mask.

The two miners ducked back inside the toolshed, but only for a moment. By the time Frisco came running out of the office with a canvas money bag in one hand and a smoking Colt in the other, the miners came out again. This time there were four of them. This time they each carried shovels or picks. One hurled a large rock that bounced off the door of the office shack just as Frisco ran for his horse. The rock came too close for comfort, and Frisco turned before stepping up into his stirrups.

"You sumbitch!" Frisco shouted. "Throw a rock at me?" He fired a shot.

The bullet nailed the miner in his chest, causing him to stagger backward, dropping the shovel he wielded above his head. The other miners caught their wounded comrade as he fell.

"Let's go!" Frisco shouted at Dave Waddell as he hurled himself up into the saddle.

"Jesus! You killed him!" Dave Waddell shouted as they batted their heels to their horses' sides and sped away from the shouting, cursing miners.

Frisco's only reply was a long, rowdy yell, followed by two pistol shots in the air. When they'd topped a ridge a hundred yards away, a rifle shot rang out from the direction of the mine's office. But by then it was too late. The pair of thieves rode down out of sight, onto the main trail. Then they rode at a steady clip for the next three miles.

Finally, Frisco slowed his horse a bit and laughed, pushing his hat up with a finger and jerking the bandanna down from across his face. "Now, that's the way to pull a payroll robbery!" he gloated, shaking the bag of money at Dave Waddell. They both slowed their horses even more.

"It went pretty smooth," said Dave. "That's for certain."

"Smooth? Hell, yes, smooth," said Frisco. "I'm talking about right in, right out." His chest swelled with pride. "There wasn't no fooling around like some robbers do." He shook the bag again. "Davey Boy, I believe you and me could make a good team on our own! We wouldn't even need Cherokee Earl and his boys!"

"You—you really think so?" Dave Waddell shot a nervous glance back over his shoulder, then yanked his bandanna down and ran a shaky hand across his forehead. "I don't mind telling you, I still feel pretty scared doing this."

"Like I told you, everybody gets a little spooked the first few times," said Frisco, dismissing it. "But how scared will you be running your fingers through this much money, eh?" Again he held the bag up for Dave Waddell to see. "This is the best we've done yet."

Dave Waddell studied the bulging canvas bag as their horses loped along easily. "How much you figure is in there?" Dave asked, settling down some.

"Oh, four, five thousand, easy enough," said Frisco. "Maybe even more. However much there is, it's all ours!" He shook the bag again, laughing loudly.

"So maybe we'd better stop somewhere and split it up?" Dave asked, his greed starting to get the better of him.

"Sure, we can do that," said Frisco. He nodded along the trail ahead of them. "Or I can hang on to it till we get to Cimarron. It's only another twenty or thirty miles."

"Cimarron," said Waddell. "What's in Cimarron? A bank? Another mining payroll?"

Frisco gave him a bemused look. "Both," he said. "But that ain't all that's in Cimarron."

"What else?" Waddell asked.

"It just might be that she's there," said Frisco.

"She who?" Dave asked. But then he caught himself and said, "Oh, you mean, Ellen, my wife?"

"Well, damn, Dave." Frisco chuckled. "Yeah, that's who I mean all right. Have you forgotten all about her?"

"Of course not," Dave responded, his face reddening. "It's just that we was talking about something else. It took me a second to catch up."

But Frisco wouldn't let him off that easy. He taunted Dave, saying, "You do remember your wife, Ellen, don't you?" As he spoke, he reached down into the canvas bag and pulled up a handful of dollars and gold coins and let them spill back down into the bag.

"Go to hell," Waddell said.

Frisco grinned. "I'm trying to just as fast as I can." He closed the bag and carried it on his lap. "Don't be so hard on yourself for not remembering your wife, Davey Boy. It could happen to anybody. A man gets out here, gets a taste of freedom, money, anything else he takes a hankering for . . . knows all he's got to do is reach out and take whatever he wants. . . . Nobody can stop him. That's a powerful pull on a man's better nature!"

Dave Waddell ignored Frisco's taunting and heeled his horse forward ahead of him. "You say Ellen might be in Cimarron."

"Yep, she sure might be," said Frisco. "I know Cherokee has been planning a raid on the bank there. He just needed something to get him moving in that direction." He caught up to Dave Waddell and stopped his horse in front of him, turning crosswise in the trail. "What exactly have you got planned for when you catch up to Cherokee Earl, if you don't mind me asking? Are you going to shoot him down where he stands? Maybe call him out into the street, face him down gun to gun?"

Again Dave Waddell ignored him. He tried reining his horse around him, but Frisco maneuvered along with him, blocking his horse's path, forcing him to confront the situation that he'd put himself into.

"Speaking of facing up to somebody, when are you going to face up to yourself? You've got no use for that woman, Dave! She's just something else you acquired along the way—something to prove to yourself how good you were doing, some pretty trinket that you could afford at the time. You knew she was something other men would see and be envious of. Now that other men have had her, is she still going to be worth as much to you?"

"You son of a bitch! She's my wife, damn you!" Dave Waddell raged.

He started to snatch the pistol from his belt. But he found himself looking down the barrel of Frisco's Colt.

"Yeah." Frisco grinned cruelly. "I'm that all right, a son of a bitch and worse. But I ain't the one having trouble choosing between my wife and stealing other people's money."

"Neither am I," said Dave Waddell. "I'm going after Ellen. If you say she's in Cimarron, that's where I'm headed. You can go or stay. I don't give a damn!" He started to spur his horse away, but then he stopped, looked at the canvas bag in Frisco's hand, and said, "I'll take my cut of the money now. I'll need it to live on in case Earl and Ellen aren't in Cimarron, and I have to go hunting them farther away."

"Hell, why not?" Frisco lowered his pistol, uncocked it, and let it hang loose in his hand. He pitched the bag to Dave Waddell. "Here, count out half of it for yourself. Leave my share in the bag."

"We both ought to count it," said Dave, wary of a trick, keeping a close eye on the Colt in Frisco's hand.

Frisco saw the apprehension in Waddell's eyes. He shoved the pistol down into his belt. "Count it yourself. I'm not worried about it. Money like that comes to me any day of the week I want to go out and get it."

Frisco watched Dave count the money onto his lap, then divvy it up and poke half of it back into the canvas bag.

"There," Dave said. "It came to eighteen hundred forty-seven dollars each." He folded the bills into a thick roll and shoved the roll into his coat pocket. The loose gold coins he shoved down into his trouser pockets. "Now I'm going to Cimarron. I can't say it ain't been fun, what you and I did. But I'm no outlaw, Frisco. You was reading me wrong in that regard." He backed his horse a step away and pitched the canvas bag to Frisco. "I'd never been out here if it weren't to save my wife. I might have dealt some stolen cattle, maybe done some other little things . . . but that's the limit. I'm stopping here before I end up on a rope or dead in the street some-where."

Frisco sat staring, his wrists crossed on his saddle horn. He nodded slightly, looking a bit bored. When Dave Waddell finished talking, Frisco said, "Well, all right, then. . . . Best of luck to you. Don't tell Cherokee you've seen me. I think it's time I go out on my own. make more, keep more. Okay?"

"Sure, I won't mention you one way or the other," said Dave. He watched Frisco lift his reins and start to turn his horse. "Where are you going, though?"

"That's not a good thing to ask," said Frisco.

Dave nodded. "All right." He started to turn his horse, but then he stopped and said, "You suppose when Earl gets tired of Ellen, he'll just turn her loose? I mean, I hate thinking he'd hurt her real bad or maybe even kill her."

"I doubt he would do that," said Frisco. "Hell, he just saw something pretty that he wanted, so he took it. Like I said about you a while ago." Frisco shrugged. "He'll turn her loose sooner or later." He watched as Dave Waddell looked all around, then stepped down from his horse and led it off the trail.

"Thought you was in a hurry to get to Cimarron," Frisco called out, a faint smile coming to his lips.

"I am," said Dave, "but it might be better to wait till tomorrow. Let the horse rest . . . give myself time to think what I ought to do once I get there."

"That's a good idea," said Frisco, stepping down himself and leading his horse off the trail. "I might rest mine awhile, too." Looking down at the trail, noting the deep wheel ruts in the soft earth, Frisco said, "I didn't mention it before, but I bet there's still a stagecoach runs through here . . . all the way up from Taos."

"Yeah?" said Dave. "Does it carry any money?"

"Oh, yes," said Frisco. "Last time me and Billy Harper robbed it we came away flush for the whole winter." He grinned and led his horse over beside Dave Waddell's, nodding down at the deep wagon ruts. "There's nothing I hate worse than passing up a nice fat stagecoach."

No sooner had Tuck Carlyle returned to Cimarron than he went straight to the St. James Hotel and rang the bell on the counter. A young man wearing sleeve garters came out from an office behind the counter. His hair was parted sharply in the middle and slicked down with hair oil. He ran a clean hand along one side of his head as if to make sure each hair was in its proper place.

"Yes, may I help you?" His eyes widened a bit when he recognized Tuck and saw the deputy badge on his chest. "Oh, you're a deputy now? The last time I recall seeing you . . . well, let's just say you were doing less meaningful work." He smiled. "Congratulations, I'm sure." There was a slight haughtiness to the young man that Tuck decided to overlook.

"Thanks, Eli," said Tuck. He got right to the point. "Three men and a woman rode into town earlier, said they would be staying here. The leader was a big fellow named Bartlett . . . Fred Bartlett. Did you wait on them?"

"No, sorry," said Eli. He gave Tuck a blank stare. "Anything else I can do for you, Deputy?"

"Do you suppose Henri Lambert waited on them?" Tuck asked, referring to the hotel's owner.

"No, sorry again," Eli said crisply. "Mr. Lambert is out of town for the week. If I didn't wait on them, they simply haven't been here."

"Are you sure, Eli?" Tuck asked. His eyes went to the guest register.

"Are you really going to ask me to check and make certain?" the young clerk asked, sounding a bit annoyed.

"No, I'm not," said Tuck, relenting. "It just seems strange they would tell me they were going to stay here, then it turns out they didn't."

"Be that as it may, they haven't been here. In fact, I haven't seen any party of four ride in off the trail all day."

"All right, then, much obliged," said Tuck. Turning to leave, he saw Sheriff Wright walking along the street toward the office and carrying a pot of coffee from the restaurant, a hot pad wrapped around the metal handle. "Sheriff, wait up," Tuck called out, hurrying to catch up to him.

"Good afternoon there, Deputy," Sheriff Wright said, stopping and waiting for Tuck. "I've never seen it fail. . . . I get a fresh pot of coffee, and folks call out my name from all across town. How did the shooting practice go?" he asked as the two of them headed on to the office together.

"It started out pretty bad," said Tuck, "but I got back into the hang of it by the time I ran out of bullets." He shook his head as they walked across the street and stepped up onto the boardwalk. "I feel bad about shooting up so much ammunition."

"Don't feel bad about it, Deputy," said the sheriff. "I call it an investment in both our futures. If we should get in a tight spot, I'd like to think you capable of shooting the eyes out of a blue fly if need be."

"I can't say I'll ever get that good, Sheriff," said Tuck, "but I promise you I'll always do my best or go down trying."

"I reckon that's really all I'm looking for," said Sheriff Wright, "just a deputy I know I can count on."

He swung open the door to the sheriff's office and walked inside, with Tuck right behind him. Setting the pot of coffee atop a small potbellied stove, he said, "I don't mind telling you, all this money arriving in town to pay for the silver is likely to draw some of the bad element. I expect to see some strange faces turning up most anytime."

"That reminds me, Sheriff," Tuck said, picking up two clean cups from a shelf beside the stove. "I saw my share of strange faces today." He filled a cup for the sheriff, handed it to him, and filled one for himself. "Or I should say I tried to see them. I only got a good look at two of them. The sun blocked the others' faces."

As they sipped the hot coffee, Tuck told him about the four riders he'd seen on the trail. Sheriff Wright listened intently, but then seemed to dismiss the matter no sooner than Tuck finished telling him. Seeing his waning interest, Tuck said, "Anyway, I thought it was peculiar, them saying they'd be staying at the St. James, then not doing it."

"I see," said the sheriff. He seemed to consider it for a moment, then said, "Do you suppose they might have just changed their mind, pushed on past town, maybe decided to make a camp?"

"Sure, they might have," said Tuck. "There was just something peculiar about them. . . . I can't really put my finger on it. Maybe I shouldn't have mentioned it."

"You did good mentioning it to me, Deputy," said the sheriff.

"I'd rather hear all day about things that mean nothing than miss hearing the one thing that could get somebody killed." He offered a tired smile. "We'll both keep a lookout for them. You might even want to ride out tomorrow along the old road and see if you spot where they might have made a camp overnight. With all this silver transaction going on, it won't hurt to keep an eye on the trails in and out of town for a while."

"Sure thing, Sheriff," said Tuck, sipping his coffee, feeling like he was once again a part of the world. He noticed his hand was steadier than it had been in a long, long time.

CHAPTER 16

For the next four days, Tuck Carlyle rode out, searching the countryside surrounding the town in all directions, looking for any sign of the men and the woman. He found no trace of them. On the second day, he found a recent campsite with its ashes still warm. But upon following the tracks leading away from the clearing, he soon caught up with four independent silver miners who were headed southwest toward their holdings along the winding Rio Grande.

"We ain't seen a soul since leaving Cimarron," one of the miners told him, speaking for all four. "Of course, we left there so drunk, they could have walked over the top of us and we'd never have known it."

Tuck tipped his hat and bade them a good journey.

Realizing the improbability of ever finding those four riders in the endless stretches of piñon forests and jagged bluffs, Tuck reminded himself that they weren't his only reason for being out there day after day. He made it a point to spend at least an hour a day practicing with his pistol until his hand was as steady, his draw as quick, and his aim as deadly as they had ever been. Luckily, the whiskey hadn't completely destroyed him, he thought, his hand streaking up from his holster and the pistol exploding three times just as fast as he could fire it.

Three rocks vanished in a shattered spray of dust. Tuck spun the pistol, holstered it, then drew it again and fired two more shots. Two more rocks vanished. As he walked to the log to set up more rock targets, he dropped the five spent cartridges and replaced them, having cautiously left one live round in the cylinder. When the Colt was reloaded, he spun the cylinder out of habit and twirled the pistol back into his holster. Reaching down to set up more rocks along the log, he stopped and listened to the sound of hooves moving steadily closer through a pine thicket twenty yards away.

Inside the thicket, Buck Hite raised a hand and brought Danielle and the others to a halt. They sat in silence for a moment; then Buck said, "Duggin, Eddie Ray, you two go check out that shooting, then catch back up to us."

"I'd sooner go by myself," said Danielle in her lowered voice, not wanting to risk Eddie Ray Moon trying to harm some innocent person and her having to shoot him before finding out where they would meet up with Cherokee Earl and his gang.

"I said both of yas. . . . I meant both of yas," Buck said, his voice growing a bit testy.

"Yeah, so come on, Duggin," Eddie Ray said to Danielle, heeling his horse forward.

Danielle nudged Sundown and caught up to him as Buck Hite, Fat Cyrus, and Clifford Reed rode on.

At the edge of the clearing, Eddie Ray stopped and looked back at Danielle right behind him. "You want to see some shooting, watch me," he said, barely above a whisper.

"Buck never said shoot anybody, Eddie Ray," said Danielle. "He just said check it out."

"I know what he said. I don't need you telling me." Eddie Ray looked her up and down scornfully. "But if the opportunity presents itself, I'll show you some shooting that'll cross your eyes."

"Hello the woods," Tuck called out, seeing the two riders just inside the tree line.

"Hello the clearing," Eddie Ray replied, his voice only vaguely concealing some sort of challenge.

Tuck! Danielle gasped, instantly recognizing Tuck Carlyle's voice. She leaned sideways to look around Eddie Ray Moon at the lone shooter standing across the clearing with the pistol hanging down at his side. *My God, it is Tuck!* Her mind raced. For a second she was caught completely off guard.

Having noted the tone of voice coming from the thicket, Tuck called out in a civil but not overfriendly voice, "Come forward and show yourselves."

"Stay behind me," Eddie Ray whispered over his shoulder.

"Like hell," Danielle hissed, coming to her senses quickly and heeling Sundown forward, forcing herself and the mare ahead of Eddie Ray and into the clearing. She made sure to tug her hat brim down. She held her reins with her left hand and made sure to keep her right hand away from her Colt. "Tuck? Tuck Carlyle?" she asked, wanting to let Eddie Ray Moon hear right away that she knew this person. "My ole trail pal from Texas?"

Tuck took a step forward, cocking his head slightly, trying to believe his eyes. "Danny Duggin?" Then he was certain. "Well, I'll be. . . . It is you!" He raised his pistol and slid it down into his holster.

Noting the badge on Tuck's chest, Danielle wished he'd kept the pistol in his hand. But it was too late to tell him that. "Yep, it's me all right, Tuck." She touched her fingertips to her hat brim, then stepped the chestnut mare forward. "Never thought I'd run into you again." She pulled the mare to one side and gave Eddie Ray Moon a look, letting him know that he'd better not start any trouble.

"Same here, Danny," said Tuck. "I've got no coffee to offer the two of you, but step down all the same. We can talk some."

"Much obliged, but not today, Tuck," said Danielle, shooting Eddie Ray a harsh glance as he started to swing down from his saddle. "We're on our way to Cimarron on business. Just rode over from the trail to see what the shooting's about." She nodded at Eddie Ray and said, "This is Raymond Moon. I'm riding with him and some other fellows."

"Oh, I see," said Tuck, sounding a bit disappointed, looking closely at Eddie Ray. "Well, I'm deputy in Cimarron now, so I suppose we'll be running into each other. Maybe we can a have a drink at Lambert's Tavern."

Danielle nodded at the badge on his chest. "I was going to ask when you took up a tin star. I have to say I'm little surprised by it. I always figured you for a cattleman and nothing else."

Sadness seemed to come over Tuck's face. "A lot has happened since we last met, Danny. I look forward to seeing you in town and telling you all about it."

Danielle backed her mare a step. Thinking about what had happened to Tuck's old friend Stick, she said, "I have some things to tell you, too, Tuck. Why don't we make it a point to meet tonight for that drink?"

"Sounds right to me," said Tuck, noting the faintest urgency in Danny Duggin's expression, which he didn't think the other man noticed.

Eddie Ray Moon cut in. "Duggin, the boss ain't going to want you wandering off tonight to talk about old times with your saddle pals."

Danielle gave him a cold stare. "Go on ahead of me, Eddie. Tell the boss I ran into an old friend of mine. Tell him I'm on my way."

Eddie Ray started to protest, but seeing Danielle slip a gloved hand down near the handle of the big Colt, he made only a gruff sound under his breath and jerked his horse around toward the thicket.

As Eddie Ray rode off into the dense piñon forest, Tuck said to Danielle, "Don't let me get you into trouble with your boss, Danny. We can meet tonight."

"Tuck, have you ever seen me worry about getting in trouble with a boss?" She didn't give Tuck time to answer. Instead, she said, lowering the range of her voice, "But listen to me. It's a stroke of luck, me running into you. I'm on the trail of some killers. These men I'm riding with are leading me to them. They're outlaws. . . . They think I'm riding with them to rob a bank."

"I figured something was up," said Tuck. "I couldn't see you riding with the likes of that one. I hope your knowing me, a deputy, ain't going to hurt you any."

"It won't, Tuck," said Danielle, cutting a glance into the piñon thicket. "Meet me tonight and I'll fill you in on everything."

"You got it, Danny," said Tuck. "I'll be there for sure."

He watched the big mare turn a short circle, rearing slightly on its hind legs, then come down and race away into the piñon. After a moment of reflection, Tuck turned and walked back to his horse. He had a feeling that he was about to get real busy. This was all the target practice he'd be doing for a while.

In a remote cabin tucked deep inside the woodlands alongside a wide, shallow creek, Ellen looked down at the butcher knife one of the men had left lying on a window ledge beside the woodstove. She gave a quick look at Dirty Joe Turley, who sat at the wooden kitchen table, his back turned to her. Her first impulse upon seeing the knife was to grab it and plunge it into his spine as deep as she could force it to go. But then she glanced out the window and saw that Cherokee Earl and Avery McRoy hadn't even made it out of sight yet. Their horses were still climbing the far side of the creek bank toward the trail leading to Cimarron.

Bide your time, Ellen's inner voice told her.

On the other side of the creek, Avery McRoy looked back once toward the cabin as their horses stepped up the bank and moved out of sight. "It's none of my business, boss," he said to Earl, "but knowing the shape Dirty Joe is in regarding that woman, is it a good idea leaving them alone like that?"

"Far as I'm concerned, Dirty Joe is a dead man soon as we get this bank robbed," said Cherokee Earl. "It's either leave him or you alone with her, and I need somebody I can trust beside me. That's why I brought you."

"Then I take it you're through with the woman?" McRoy asked.

"Yeah," Earl said sourly. "I've been through with her since Braden Flats. She ain't much. . . . She just looks full of promise, is all. Why?

You want her? If you do, she's all yours soon as we get back, provided Joe ain't killed her by then."

"No, boss, I think I'll pass," said McRoy. "It's business first with me. We get that bank money, I can buy all the women I'll ever need and be able to run them off come morning so's I don't have to hear them bellyache about anything that doesn't suit them."

Cherokee Earl grinned. "That's smart thinking on your part, McRoy. Soon as we take this bank, you kill that moon-eyed Dirty Joe—the woman, too, for that matter. You and me will be equal partners from now on. How does that suit you?"

"That suits me fine, boss," McRoy said, heeling his horse up beside Cherokee Earl's.

Inside the cabin, Ellen took one more look and, not seeing the horses now, felt her hand start to reach for the butcher knife. But just as she did, Joe Turley scooted his chair back from the wooden table, got up, and walked over to her, craning his neck to take a good look out the window toward the trail.

"Good, they're gone," he said, keeping his voice lowered as if they might yet hear him. He reached hungrily for Ellen, his hands grasping her waist and pulling her to him.

"Joe, please, wait a minute!" Ellen said, stalling the inevitable.

"Wait?" Joe said, repeating her, his voice trembling. "You must be kidding! Waiting is all I've been doing. I've got to have you right now!"

He forced a deep, wet kiss onto her mouth. His beard stubble assaulted her lips, her chin.

"Please, Joe!" She managed to force him away if only for a second. "You've got to give me a moment . . . to get in the mood."

"Honey, I'm in the mood," Joe rasped. He forced her hand down the front of his trousers and pressed himself against her, clawing at the front of her dress until it came open and her breasts stood out pale and quivering. "God, I've never been more in the mood than at this minute," he whispered lustily.

"Okay, okay, then," Ellen said, giving in, letting his mouth find hers again, allowing his free hand to knead and fondle her breasts.

With her left hand down his trousers, she squeezed him firmly down there and heard a long moan come from his throat. Yet, as he pawed and squeezed her and held her pinned to him, Ellen's right hand went around him, reaching the window ledge, searching frantically for the knife handle until she grasped it firmly. She felt him lifting her dress above her hips, felt his belt buckle dig into her flesh. He fumbled with his gun belt buckle, loosened it, and let his Colt fall to the floor. Then he loosened his trouser belt and let his trousers fall also.

"Now give it to me," he moaned.

Squeezing her eyes shut, Ellen stabbed the point of the knife sidelong into his neck two inches below his ear with all of her strength. She felt the knife blade go deep, and having done such a thing sickened her.

Joe lost his grip. His hands melted away from her and shook violently for a second until realization sank in. He stood staring in disbelief, his eyes wide in terror. Then he raised his left hand, found the handle, and grasped it tight.

"I—I thought you wanted me," he managed to say in a strained voice.

"No! Forgive me, Joe!" Ellen said shakily. For a second, she stood transfixed by fear.

"Damn you!" Joe yanked the blade out of his throat, and a spout of blood pumped long and hard from his severed artery.

Ellen came unstuck. She screamed hysterically and scooted back away from him, raising her hands to her face as if to hide the grisly scene from her eyes. Dirty Joe staggered forward, his life-blood leaving him quickly, his face growing pale white. He stabbed down at her halfheartedly.

"Joe!" Ellen sobbed. "I didn't want to kill you! I had to! God forgive me!"

She jumped farther back as he stabbed at her again. This time the knife slipped free from his weak, blood-slick hand and clattered to the floor at her feet. She snatched it up as, falling forward, he lunged at her, his hand grabbing for her. With a long scream,

Ellen dropped down into a crouch, drew the knife back, and with all her strength stabbed him again, this time burying the blade up to its hilt in his chest where the left and right sides of his rib cage came together.

"Ayieee!" His breath left him in a rattling gust. He stared down at the knife handle again in disbelief. His eyes seemed to say, *My God, you've done it again! You've stabbed me twice!* The stream of blood from his neck splattered down onto the rough plank floor, making a strange sound. He sank to his knees, his mouth gaping, his tongue thick and lolling between his lips. He managed to grip the handle with both bloody hands before he fell face forward.

"God forgive me! God forgive me! God forgive me!" Ellen stood wild-eyed, her hands clasped to her ears. Around her, the small cabin appeared to have been painted with blood by the hand of a blind madman. She stood stone-still for a moment, then looked around as if to see who might be watching as she drew the open front of her dress closed, hiding her blood-splattered breasts. Another deathlike moment passed before she began to tremble uncontrollably. Then she sank weeping to her knees, curled up in a ball like a small child, and lay quietly amid the carnage.

Whether she'd slept or not, she didn't know. But when she stood up, it was growing dark outside and an evening chill had moved into the cabin. She took a good look at the body of Joe Turley lying in the same spot where she remembered it being. Then she looked once again around the bloody cabin, pushed her hair back out of her eyes, and busily set about preparing herself for the trail.

The first thing she did was step over to Joe Turley's gun belt, which was lying on the floor in a drying puddle of thick black blood. She lifted his pistol, checked it, picked up a cloth from the table, wiped blood from the gun handle, and carried the pistol with her as she lit a lantern and rummaged through the cabin for a coat and some better clothes for the trail.

When she'd gathered a pair of trousers, a wool shirt, and some long underwear, she stepped out of her dirty, bloodstained dress and, standing naked in the dim circle of light, dipped a bandanna into a water bucket and washed herself free of the many spots and smears of dried blood. Finishing, she dressed quickly, still holding the pistol as if it were her personal talisman. Stepping around Joe Turley's body, she picked up his hat, looked it over, saw that it had only a few small blood spots, and put it on her head. Her red hair flowed beneath the hat brim.

Where was she going? "Anywhere but here," she murmured aloud to herself, taking a last glance around the grisly scene in the cabin.

She wasn't sure where she was going, but she knew better than to go toward Cimarron and risk running into Earl and McRoy—that much she knew for certain. She was free now . . . and she intended to stay that way. Besides, she'd seen what Cherokee Earl and his men had done to the last towns they'd ridden through. She wasn't about to pin her faith on a small-town sheriff, a deputy or two, and a handful of townsmen. Once she got onto the trail, she was heading in the opposite direction from Cherokee Earl. She'd overheard Earl and the others talk about the trail they'd been on winding downward and southwest to Taos. That was good enough for her.

Beside the door stood Joe Turley's Winchester repeating rifle. On a peg hung a bullet belt full of ammunition for the Winchester. She knew very little about rifles, but she reminded herself that she would never find a better time to learn. For one last time she looked over at Joe Turley's body and whispered, "I really am sorry I had to kill you, Joe. But it was life or death for me." Then she picked up the rifle, swung the bullet over her shoulder, and walked out the door.

CHAPTER 17

No sooner had Danielle and Eddie Ray Moon caught up to Buck Hite and the others than Eddie Ray began spilling his guts about Danny Duggin being friends with a lawman. When he'd finished, the men had all come to a halt and drawn their horses into a half circle around Danielle and her mare.

"Just how good of friends were you and this deputy, Danny?" asked Buck.

"We were the best of friends, Buck," Danielle replied. "But Eddie Ray has left out two important facts. First of all, it was a long time ago. . . . And second of all, Tuck Carlyle was not a lawman then. He was a drover." Danielle's eyes went across each man's face in turn. "Now, if anybody has a problem with this, we can work it out a lot of different ways right here and now." Her hand poised close to the pistol butt, she made no effort to hide her meaning.

Buck Hite noted that while she'd addressed all four of them, everything about her—her voice, her shadowed face, her gun hand—appeared to be focused toward him. Buck turned his face slowly to Eddie Ray Moon. "You didn't mention all that, did you, Eddie Ray? Reckon it must've slipped your mind?" He spoke low and even, but there was a threat in his voice that caused Eddie Ray to shrink back a bit.

"All right, listen to me," Eddie Ray said, raising a hand, his voice sounding a little anxious. "I knew this fellow was new at being a lawman—he said so himself. I also figured it had been a while since they'd seen each other, the way they talked about it. But, Buck, Duggin here was talking about getting together with this man later on. . . . Catching up on old times, they was saying." Now Eddie Ray turned an accusing gaze on Danielle.

"Is that true, Duggin?" asked Buck Hite. "You plan on riding with us and at the same time being good friends with the law?"

"Yep, you're damn right I do," said Danielle. She paused for just a second to make sure her words sank in. "I'd make friends with every lawman in this country if I could. The more information I can learn from lawmen, the better it is for me and anybody I ride with, the way I look at it."

Staring at her intently, Buck Hite finally offered a slight smile. "Pretty damn smart, Duggin," he said.

He shot Eddie Ray Moon a glance. Clifford Reed and Fat Cyrus backed their horses a cautious step away from Eddie Ray's.

"Buck, I did what I thought was best for all of us!" Eddie Ray said quickly.

"You've been on a slow burn against this man ever since he beat the shit out'n you. Now whatever you think you got to settle with him, you do it now and get it done."

"Buck, I—"

Buck cut him off. "Because we've got serious business to take care of in Cimarron, I can't have this kind of schoolkid bickering going on between grown men!" His voice grew more angry as he spoke.

"Buck, if you'll just let me explain," said Eddie Ray, growing more worried, especially now that he saw the mare take a step closer to him. Danielle had let her hand relax for a moment, but now she poised it again. "I felt like everybody here ought to know that Duggin—"

"There ain't nothing to explain, Eddie Ray," Buck shouted. He turned his stare at Danielle. "Duggin, do you think you can get close enough to that lawman tonight to find out how much silver and cash is lying in that bank?"

Danielle shrugged. "If Eddie Ray didn't put him on guard about what he tells me, yeah, I can get that close. . . . He trusts me."

A tense silence passed as Buck looked from one man to the next, then said, "See? That's called using our heads. Cherokee Earl is the one who's supposed to know how much money there is in there. But, boys, what if he's wrong? Or what if he's dead by now and ain't even showed up?" Buck raised an eyebrow, a gesture of wisdom. "It never hurts to know what a lawman's got to say." He turned back to Danielle. "Any chance this lawman could be cut in with us?"

"That's a thought," said Danielle, knowing better. "The thing is, what if I bring it up and he turns it down?"

"Yeah, good thinking," said Buck. He nodded toward a clearing ahead alongside the trail. "Let's camp out up there. We'll ride into town tonight. While Clifford and Fat Cyrus and me look for Earl and his boys, you keep Eddie Ray with you, find out what you can from the deputy. Does that sound all right to you, Duggin?"

"That sounds fine to me, Buck," Danielle said.

From beneath the shelter of her broad hat brim, she saw a faint smile of satisfaction come to Eddie Ray Moon's face. Danielle understood why. Even though Danny Duggin had just gained some important respect from Buck Hite, it was still clear to her that Buck didn't trust Danny Duggin completely. He was leaving Duggin and Eddie Ray Moon together, knowing that Moon still had enough of a grudge to keep a close eye on every move Duggin made. *So be it*, Danielle said to herself. Once in Cimarron she'd just have to find a way to shake loose from Eddie Ray.

All of that had happened earlier in the day. Now, after thinking about it for a few moments, Danielle stood up from lying back against her saddle in the thin shade of a cottonwood tree and dusted the seat of her trousers. After spending the afternoon resting the horses and themselves, Buck Hite and his gang were ready to ride the rest of the way to town. Eddie Ray seemed to have forgotten the near altercation between himself and Danny Duggin as they stood side by side, saddling their mounts and making ready for the trail. When the gang gathered at the edge of the clearing, Buck

Hite sat chewing a mouthful of tobacco. He spat and ran a hand across his lips.

"Boys, when we get into Cimarron, remember why you're there. We want to find Cherokee Earl and his men, nothing else. If you need to wet your whistles a little, that's fine by me. But remember this well." He raised a gloved finger for emphasis. "You're not there to chase whores, play poker, or get blind, staggering drunk. If you do, just expect that I'm going to put a bullet in you once we're out of town. We're there on business." He spat another stream, then turned his horse to the trail, the others falling in behind him single file. "Don't nobody make me say it again."

The men all nodded silently among themselves.

The last few miles into Cimarron went quickly, but by the time their horses gathered on the edge of town, darkness had fallen across a starlit sky. The sound of a tinny piano danced along the street from the direction of Lambert's Tavern, a building attached to the right side of the St. James Hotel. The tavern's front doors were wide-open, lantern light spilling out onto a dozen or more horses standing at hitch rails and hitch posts out front. A woman's shrill laugh resounded playfully along the street.

"I'm glad you said it was all right to wet our whistles, Buck," said Fat Cyrus. He licked his lips. "But suppose if I went out back with a whore only wasn't gone for longer than, say . . . three or four minutes? Would that be okay?"

"Good God, Cyrus," said Clifford Reed, shaking his head. "You ought not admit something like that."

"Like what?" Fat Cyrus looked confused. "I'm quick at most everything. A man ought to be proud how fast he can—"

"Shut up, Cyrus!" Buck Hite barked, cutting him off. He turned his gaze to Clifford Reed. "Clifford, keep his mind on what he's here for, or so help me. . . ."

"I'll try, Buck," said Clifford. "That's all I can do."

"Duggin," said Buck, turning to Danielle, "since you're going to meet this deputy at the tavern, you and Eddie Ray get on over there. Clifford, you and Cyrus start making some rounds—restaurants, billiard halls, faro tables, wherever you might run into Earl and his boys. I'll be lying back out of sight, keeping an eye on things."

Danielle and Eddie Ray Moon broke off from the others and rode their horses to Lambert's Tavern. They stepped down from their saddles and tied their horses to one of the crowded hitch rails. At the open front doors of the tavern, they both stopped dead still when two pistol shots exploded from the long, crowded bar inside.

"Don't turn your back on me, Mr. Deputy, you cowardly polecat!" shouted a raging young man with his pistol smoking in his hand.

Danielle stood transfixed, seeing drinkers clear away from the bar, leaving only Tuck Carlyle facing the young gunman, who had three more gunmen standing behind him. The three spread out slowly, taking a fighting position.

"Oops!" Eddie Ray chuckled beside Danielle. "Well, Duggin, looks like your law dog friend is about to become your ex–law dog friend."

Without answering, Danielle took a step inside the open doors and spread her duster back behind her pistol butt. The piano had abruptly fallen silent; the tavern customers stood tense and expectant.

"Hope I'm not interrupting anything, Deputy Carlyle," Danielle said, using her strongest man's voice.

Behind her, Eddie Ray Moon whispered, "If you'll just excuse me, Duggin. He's your friend, not mine."

Danielle heard Moon's boots hurry away.

At the bar, Tuck Carlyle said, without taking his eyes off the gunmen facing him, "Not at all, Danny. In fact, I was just wishing you'd pop by here, spread a little laughter my way." His voice was dead serious in spite of his dark irony.

"That's what I do best," said Danielle.

She stepped farther into the tavern, then stopped fifteen feet from the gunmen and planted her boots shoulder width apart, her hat low across her forehead, hiding her face.

"This ain't your concern," said the young gunman, his hand

seeming to get a little nervous now that someone had tipped the odds a little.

The three men behind him looked at Danielle. They, too, seemed suddenly put off by having the deputy in front of them and now a lone gunman taking off his right glove slowly, one finger at a time, behind them. They noted how the big tied-down Colt on the lone gunman's hip glinted in the light of the many lanterns flickering around the tavern.

"Now that makes me feel unwelcome," said Danielle.

"You ain't welcome!" the young gunman raged. "Now get out, or die here!" He half turned to face Danielle, something that even his friends behind him knew was a bad mistake: standing that close to a man he'd just challenged and then turning to face another gun halfway across the floor.

"I won't be doing either tonight," said Danielle, her voice strong as if tempered by iron.

She saw the slightest move among the three gunmen. Two of them reached for their guns at once. At the same time, she saw the gunman in front of Tuck start to cock his smoking pistol. But she paid him no mind. Instead, when her pistol streaked up from her holster, she threw her shots at the other two. Her shots fired almost as one, the first snapping the gun from one man's hand in a spray of blood and broken metal. Her second shot nailed the other man in his right shoulder and slammed him back against the bar.

"Jesus!" The third man bolted across the floor and burst through the rear door, his boots pounding loudly until they faded into the night.

On the floor at Tuck Carlyle's feet, the first gunman lay in a crumpled heap, his hat gone from the top of his head, replaced by a bloody knot the size of a duck egg. Tuck stood over the man with his pistol in his hand, having knocked the young man cold with the barrel.

Danielle walked to the bar with her pistol still cocked and ready. She looked at the other two gunmen as she spoke to Tuck Carlyle. "What about these two? Do you want them in jail or out of town?"

"Out of town will have to do," said Tuck. "The sheriff's gone for a few days. I haven't jailed anybody yet, and I'm not sure what to do." He gave Danielle a bemused look. "Sounds foolish, don't it?"

"Yep, a little," said Danielle. "But I suppose everybody has a first time for everything."

She and Tuck looked at the two men.

"Get Rance up from here and get him out of town," said Tuck. "If I see any of you again tonight, you'll all go to jail."

"What about my shot hand?" The gunman held up his wounded hand, blood running down between his thumb and finger, dripping onto the floor.

"What about it?" Danielle said coldly.

His eyes were wide with fear, anger, and pain. "I need a doctor or something! Damn! You can't just shoot a man and run him out of town with no medical attention! I could bleed to death!"

As he spoke, Danielle reached out, untied his bandanna, and yanked it from around his neck, stirring up dust. She flicked it once to get the rest of the dust off, then laid it across his wounded hand. "Wrap it tight until the bleeding stops."

"That ain't no way to treat a wound!" the young man bellowed.

"Keep running your mouth, and I'll see to it that you do bleed to death," Danielle said.

She turned to the other gunman, who stood with his back against the bar for support, a hand pressed to his bleeding shoulder. His face was stark white.

"What about you?" Danielle asked. "Are you able to ride, or are you going to need a doctor, too?"

"I'm able to ride," he said defiantly. "Just let me out of here. I don't want your help."

"Good," said Danielle. "You can help get this one out of here."

She and Tuck lifted the knocked-out gunman, who was now reviving, from the floor and stood him between his two wounded friends. He wobbled back and forth on spindly legs, looking unsure of himself, of who he was or where he'd been.

"If you come back here threatening me, boy," said Tuck, "I'm going to forget how stupid you are and go ahead and put a bullet in you." He looked closely at the young man, then gave up, realizing it was useless talking to him right then. "Get him out of here," Tuck said to the other two.

As the wounded, crestfallen gunman was dragged out through the front doors, Tuck turned to Danielle and said, "Much obliged, Danny. If you hadn't showed up when you did, I'd sure have had my hands full."

"Glad I could help, Tuck," said Danielle. Looking around to make sure neither Eddie Ray nor any of the others were present, Danielle added in a lowered voice, "Let me tell you while I can: These men I'm riding with are here to rob the bank." Seeing Tuck's expression turn concerned, Danielle went on. "Just listen for now while they're not around. The men I'm hunting are Cherokee Earl Muir and his gang. They have a hostage, a woman they took from her home near Haley Springs. Her name is Ellen Waddell—"

"Does she have red hair?" Tuck asked.

"Yes, she does," said Danielle. "Have you seen her?"

"I believe so," said Tuck. "She's traveling with a man who calls himself Fred Bartlett. There's two men riding with them, but I didn't get a good look at their faces."

"Fred Bartlett, my eye," said Danielle. "I bet that's Cherokee Earl. Do you know where they went?"

"No," said Tuck. "I even went searching for them, but I never came up with a trace of them. It seems like they've dropped off the face of the earth."

"They'll be back, Tuck—you can count on it. They've been leaving towns in ruins from here to Haley Springs . . . and they mean to rob the bank here. They know there's a big silver exchange going on."

"Then we've got to stop them," said Tuck.

"Yes, but we've also got to save Ellen Waddell," said Danielle. "If we jump too soon and tip our hands to the men I'm riding with, that poor woman will likely end up dead."

"All right, Danny, I'm backing you," said Tuck. "You call the play."

"We wait until the day they come in here all together. Then we take them all down at once. Meanwhile, I'll keep an eye on things, find out where the woman is so we can free her once they're all taken care of."

"Then that's how we'll do it, Danny," said Tuck. "I'll wait for your call."

"Thanks, Tuck. I knew I could count on you." Danielle hesitated, then said in a gentler tone, "And, Tuck . . . I hate telling you this, but two of these men killed our old friend Stick."

"Oh, no, Danny, not Stick," Tuck said, his grief showing instantly. "That man was like a daddy to me, Danny."

"I know he was, Tuck." Danielle hung her head for a moment. "Stick was on the trail with me, searching for these men after they stole the Waddell woman. But he and I started off looking for you. He told me what happened to your wife—I'm sorry, Tuck—and he told me you were somewhere drinking your brains out. We were coming to get you, see to it you straightened out. I'm glad to see that you've apparently already taken care of that."

Tuck looked pained and ashamed. "Yes, I've gotten over drinking my brains out. . . . But the other part, losing my wife, is something I doubt I'll ever get over. It hurts just as bad today as it did the day I lost her." He struggled silently for a second to keep from breaking down. "Something's missing inside me, Danny. I'm managing to get by without the whiskey, but that's just pure stubborn pride that keeps me going. I couldn't stand thinking that whiskey was going to kill me. So I'm fighting hard." He took on a determined expression and let out a tight breath. "But listen to me going on about my misfortune . . . while some poor woman is being held by outlaws."

"Don't worry, Tuck. We'll get her freed," said Danielle. "And once all this is over, you and I are going to have a long talk."

"About what, Danny?" Tuck asked.

"About me," said Danielle, aching to throw off her hat, shake out her hair, and tell him everything. "There's something I've needed to tell you for the longest time . . . Just seems like there's always something else going on to prevent it."

"Danny, are you all right?" Tuck asked.

"Yeah, Tuck, I'm all right. Now that I'm here, I'm fine. The rest will have to wait till later." Danielle had caught herself and settled her mind to the task at hand. "We'll be talking about it real soon, I promise."

CHAPTER 18

O ut of consideration for Tuck Carlyle and his battle with the bottle, Danielle did not drink any whiskey or beer. Instead, she drank the same thing Tuck drank: a cup of coffee from a fresh pot the bartender kept behind the bar. No sooner had the tinny piano started again and the smoke from Danielle's Colt drifted away than Eddie Ray Moon came through the front door of the tavern, a sheepish look on his face.

"I heard the shooting," he said, sidling up to her. "Thought I'd better come see how things turned out."

"As you can see," said Danielle, "we managed to get by without you." Tuck Carlyle had stepped out the rear door to relieve himself. Offering a wry smile and to show there were no hard feelings, Danielle asked, "Can I buy you a drink, Eddie Ray?"

Eddie Ray rubbed his lips, looking at the long row of bottles standing against the wall behind the bar. "I could sure enough stand one."

Danielle gestured for the bartender to pour Eddie Ray a shot of whiskey. As they stood watching the glass being filled, Eddie Ray looked at Danielle's coffee cup.

"I see you ain't drinking nothing yourself."

"That's right," said Danielle, not wanting to even try to explain why to the likes of Eddie Ray Moon. "While you were gone, did you see Cherokee Earl or any of his men?"

"Not a hair," said Eddie Ray. He raised the shot glass to his lips and drained it in a single gulp. He released a deep whiskey hiss. "But they'll show if they ain't been killed or caught."

The bartender had left the bottle of rye standing in front of them. Danielle picked it up and poured Eddie Ray another drink.

Eddie Ray grinned. "I think I might have been wrong about you, Duggin."

"Really?" Danielle looked surprised to hear him admit such a thing.

He looked repentant and shrugged. "Yeah . . . we just got off to a bad start. I never should have come to the hotel acting so pushy that day. I reckon I'm trying to apologize for it. See if we can't go ahead and become friends."

"You saw the whole shooting through the window a while ago, didn't you?" Danielle asked matter-of-factly.

Eddie Ray's face reddened. "Yeah, I might have," said Eddie Ray. "But still, I'm offering my hand in friendship. We're riding together, so we ought to try to get along, don't you think?" He extended his rough right hand timidly.

"Yep, why not?" said Danielle, shaking his hand, then turning it loose as soon as she could, lest she bring to his mind how small her hand was in his. "From now on we'll try to get along," she said, repeating his words.

Tuck Carlyle came back to the bar and, seeing that one of the outlaws they'd been discussing had joined them, remained friendly enough to his ole pal Danny Duggin yet a little standoffish toward Eddie Ray Moon. Raising his cup to this lips, finishing the coffee off, and setting the empty cup back on the bar top, Tuck took on an aura of authority.

"Well, it's time I got back to making my rounds. It's been good to see you again, Duggin. And I appreciate your help a while ago. But remember what I told you. It makes no difference what you and I done together in the past. Now that I'm wearing a badge, upholding the law comes first." His eyes drifted from Danielle to Eddie Ray. "I hope you and your friends understand that."

"Yeah, I understand that, Carlyle," said Danielle, sounding less than enthusiastic. "Good to see you, too." She touched her fingers to her broad hat brim.

"Evenin', then," said Tuck, tipping his hat and stepping away from the bar.

Danielle and Eddie Ray both turned and leaned back against the bar, watching the deputy leave.

"Well, there you have it," said Danielle, a sound of regret in her best man's voice. "Never stay friends with a lawman. That little piece of tin must have a way of changing a man through and through."

"I've always said that very same thing," said Eddie Ray. He chuckled and tossed back his rye whiskey. "And I'll drink to it every time."

Turning around to face the bar again, Danielle pushed the coffee cup away from her and, feigning anger, said, "To think I stood here drinking coffee like some sort of dandy." She gestured the bartender to her and said, "Clear these cups away and give me a shot glass. I've got some catching-up drinking to do."

"Now you're talking my language," said Eddie Ray.

As the two stood at the bar, Eddie Ray not seeming to notice that he was the one doing all the drinking, Avery McRoy, who had been watching them from a far corner, slipped in beside them. "Mind if I join you fellows?" he asked.

Danielle, who had noticed him watching them for the past few minutes, looked him up and down, then said, "That all depends, mister. What's on your mind?"

McRoy looked back and forth between them, then said, "I was hoping you could help me out some. See, I'm supposed to meet a fellow here on business. . . . His name is Hite. Either of you ever hear of him?" He gestured to the bartender for a glass, then filled it from the bottle on the bar.

"Yeah," said Eddie Ray, his voice starting to take on a whiskey slur, "we're riding with—"

"That all depends, too," said Danielle, keeping Eddie Ray from blurting anything out.

"A lot of things depend with you, don't they, mister?" said Avery McRoy in a testy tone of voice.

Danielle turned to face him, a hand on her tied-down Colt. "You came to us, mister, not the other way around. If you've got something to say, spit it out. If not, swallow it." She stared at him coldly until he was forced to look away.

"All right," said Avery McRoy, raising his hands chest high in a show of submission. "Maybe I shouldn't have approached you two this way. No harm done, I hope." His voice lowered almost to a whisper. "I'm looking for Buck Hite and his boys. Cherokee Earl sent me."

Danielle offered a half-friendly smile. "See, that wasn't so hard, was it?" She nodded. "Yeah, that would be us all right. Where's Earl?"

"Easy now," said McRoy. "I've never seen either one of you before. Earl sent me to find you boys and make sure everything is on the up-and-up the way we've planned it. I need to see Buck Hite so I'll know everybody here is who they say they are."

"Makes sense to me," said Danielle. "I'm Danny Duggin. This is Eddie Ray. Come on, we'll take you to see Buck Hite right now."

"Real good," said McRoy, raising the drink to his lips. He downed his whiskey, then looked closer at the shadowed face beneath the broad hat brim. "Duggin, you look familiar. Have you and I run across each other before somewhere?"

"Maybe." Danielle shrugged. "Who knows?" She stepped back from the bar and thumbed toward the door while the music from the piano filled the tavern. "Want to stand here all night talking about it or go find Buck and see what we've got to do to make some money in this wide spot in the road?"

"Mister, are you always this unobliging?" said McRoy, turning away from the bar.

"My pal Duggin here has no play in him at all," Eddie Ray chuckled. "I found that out the hard way."

Leaving Lambert's Tavern, the three walked along the darkened street until they spotted Buck Hite's horse hitched out front of a run-down saloon where a scraggly row of chickens sat perched along a wooden bench out front. As the three approached, the chickens protested in raised cackling and a flurry of batting wings.

"What the hell kind of place is this?" Eddie Ray Moon asked no one in particular, fanning small feathers from the air.

A fat black man stepped out of the dark shadows and said in a deep, flat voice, "This is Chicken Mama Loo's place, like the sign done said." He pointed a large, long finger up at a sun-bleached wooden sign hanging by one corner chain.

Eddie Ray Moon stopped fanning his hand and looked up in the darkness. "Jesus," he said in disgust. "That sign ain't said nothing since Napoleon wore Josephine's bloomers."

Upon hearing Eddie Ray's words, all cordiality left the big black man's face. "What you men want here? You come for some of the hot pipe?"

"I never use it," said Eddie Ray. "What about you, Duggin? Care for some tar opium?"

"I pass," said Danielle, stepping closer to the door.

Avery McRoy and Eddie Ray followed.

"Where you think you're going?" the black man asked.

"We're here to see the man who's riding that horse," said Danielle.

"He a friend of yours?" the man asked.

"If he wasn't a friend, we wouldn't be standing here asking— we'd already have shot him and you both."

The black man nodded, then looked at Buck Hite's horse and said, "Yeah, okay, he's in there." He stepped to one side, turned down a thick metal door handle, and shoved the door open. "I 'posed to ask for your guns, but I don't expect you'd give them to me, would you?"

"It ain't very likely," said Danielle, stepping inside the dark opium-clouded saloon.

The big black man laughed under his breath. "That's the same thing your friend told me. Yes, sir, he did."

A thick cloud of gray-brown smoke loomed heavily inside the small dirty saloon. Many of the drinkers stood slumped on the bar top. Others lay sprawled on tabletops, where candles stood in tin holders for the purpose of lighting the bowls of smudged opium pipes.

Danielle spotted Buck Hite lounging at one of the tables in the back corner, and she walked straight to him. "Wake up, Buck," she said, kicking the leg of his chair. "We've met up with one of Cherokee Earl's men."

"Hunh?" Startled, Buck Hite fumbled with his chair, trying to scoot it back from the table. "I ain't asleep," he said as if denying an accusation. "I was just watching these boys, seeing what all the fuss is about." He looked back and forth among the three figures standing over him in the swirling drift of smoke. "I never smoke this stuff myself." His eyes were shiny and red streaked. His voice sounded thick.

"Good," said Danielle. "Then you won't mind us pulling you away long enough to talk business."

She grabbed his chair and tipped him out of it. He staggered to his feet.

"Come on," she said firmly. "Let's go outside and get some air."

Buck looked at Avery McRoy and asked in an almost belligerent tone, "Where the hell is Cherokee Earl? We're supposed to meet with him, not one of his flunkies."

McRoy bristled at Buck Hite's words, but he managed to keep himself in check. "Earl sent me because I can be trusted. There's only three of us, and the third man is busy taking care of something."

They'd started for the door, but Buck Hite halted and looked at him pointedly. "There's only three of you? I thought this was going to be a big operation! Why am I throwing in with a three-man gang? I can get better than that on my own."

Avery McRoy walked on to the door as he spoke, causing Buck Hite to follow reluctantly. "We've got a couple of men still coming to join us. They stayed back along the trail to take care of some business." He stopped out front of the run-down saloon amid fleeing chickens and batting wings.

Buck Hite closed the saloon door behind them. "Still, this gang of Earl's ain't sounding as strong to me now as it did back when we talked about joining forces."

Avery McRoy started to speak, but from the darkness came Cherokee Earl's voice as he walked forward, kicking a chicken out of his path. "I'm going to pretend like what I'm hearing is just your dope talking, Buck. Otherwise you and me would be shooting holes in each other right here and now. I hate belligerence of any sort."

The sight of Cherokee Earl with his thumb hooked into his belt near his tied-down Colt had a sobering effect on Buck Hite. "Hell, Earl, you can't blame a man for asking questions . . . looking out for his own interest, can you?"

Cherokee Earl didn't bother answering him. Instead, he looked across the shadowed faces standing before him. "Like McRoy said, we're waiting for Harper and Frisco to join us. Unless something bad has befallen them, they'll be along most anytime." Nodding at Danielle, he said, "You picked up a new man?"

"Yeah," said Buck, trying hard to clear the opium stupor from his head. "This is Danny Duggin—a good gunman. He's riding with us now."

"Duggin," said Cherokee Earl, touching his fingers to his hat brim. Then he said to Buck Hite, "What about the two men you sent back to check for those troublemakers?"

"They're dead," Buck said bluntly.

"Who killed them?" asked Earl.

"Duggin killed them," said Buck. "They jumped him on the trail, and he took them both down. That's why I hired him. If he can handle Daryl and Lon Trabough, that's good enough for me."

Cherokee Earl took a step closer, suspiciously eyeing her up and down. "Duggin, huh?"

"Yep, Duggin," she repeated, standing her ground.

"So, Duggin, just what was you doing on the trail at that time?" Earl asked.

There stood the man responsible for Stick's death and all the other trouble she'd gone through. Danielle felt herself bristle slightly at his question. But she kept her anger in check and said coolly, "I felt a powerful urge drawing me in this direction . . . must've been so's I could get up here and answer a bunch of damn fool questions—why else?"

A tense dead silence fell over the group for a moment. Then Cherokee Earl let out a short laugh, saying, "I guess that's about as straight an answer as I'll ever get out of you."

"Just about," said Danielle flatly. "Anything else I say would just be me looking for the kind of answer I think you want to hear." She shrugged one shoulder. "Either you pards need me working for you or you don't." She looked back and forth between Buck and Cherokee Earl. "It's your call."

Cherokee Earl nodded, understanding that if this Danny Duggin had anything to hide, he sure wasn't worried about it. "Down to business, then," said Earl. "They've been moving lots of silver through this bank, but mostly in small lots from the independent mining companies. What we're waiting for is a large shipment that'll be here in two days. As soon as I get the word, you'll hear about it from me or McRoy here. Meanwhile, we sit tight, keep a man in town at all times so we'll know when to draw our men together."

Thinking about the Waddell woman and how to get to her to save her, Danielle asked, "Shouldn't we be camped together now? It looks like that would make it easier for everybody concerned."

"You're right, Duggin. It would," said Earl, again eyeing him as if wondering what his interest might be. "But I make it a practice to keep a large body of men spread out a little before a raid. It's a practice that has served the James-Younger Gang and others well over the years. I'm sticking with it." He grinned, looking from one to the other of the men. "Besides, I'm what you might call honeymooning right now. I need a little privacy, if you understand what I mean." He winked.

"Sure, no problem," said Buck Hite, still sounding a bit groggy from the opium. "So long as you drop her ankles and pull your pants on quick once you hear about that silver load."

The men chuckled, Earl included.

"Don't worry, Buck," he said. "I've been with this woman long enough that I'm losing interest. Far as I'm concerned, you can have her once we take care of business here."

"Much obliged but none for me," said Buck. "I know better than to take a woman offered to me for free. There's a catch to it somewhere."

"You might be right," said Earl. "If she was all that much, I wouldn't be getting rid of her. You saw right through that, Buck. Looks like you and me might be riding together for a nice long time."

His grin widened as a ripple of laughter stirred across the men. Danielle just listened, wondering how she would go about getting Ellen Waddell out of this alive.

CHAPTER 19

Ellen Waddell made good time starting out, riding down the steep, winding trail toward Taos. Yet once darkness had completely enveloped the land and she began to realize she had put some distance between herself and her captors, she slowed the horse to a walk and let the animal lead the way. Coming down out of a stretch of low hills onto some grasslands, Ellen caught sight of a campfire glowing in the distance. Using caution, she approached the fire as quietly as possible, the rifle lying across her lap.

When she reached what she judged to be a distance of a hundred yards, Ellen stepped down from the horse and led it through low brush and over loose rocky ground. She almost held her breath with each slight sound of the horse's hooves. Reaching a stand of scrub cedars, she stopped the horse and knelt in the darkness, listening until she heard the sound of two men's voices drift across the night. After a moment she stood up silently and whispered in the horse's ear as if it understood her words.

"You'll have to wait here," she said, tying the reins to a low scrub cedar.

She moved quietly, measuring and testing every step before setting her foot down firmly on the ground. She had no idea how long it took her to move the few remaining yards, but when she stopped again and sank down in the cover of wild grass, she could make out the fire clearly and see the two men huddled near it, their faces obscured by their wide hat brims. The smell of hot coffee and beans made her empty stomach moan softly. She knew she had to make a decision pretty soon whether or not to announce herself or move on. Looking down at the rifle in her hands as she smelled the food and coffee, she made up her mind.

Taking a deep breath, she stood up and called out, "Hello the camp," hearing the shallow sound of her voice in the broad, empty land.

"What the hell?" Frisco Bonham's coffee cup fell from his hand at the suddenness of a shrill voice reaching out of the darkness. His right hand clasped his pistol butt, but then stopped before drawing the gun from his holster. "That's a woman's voice!" he said, lowering his voice to Dave Waddell.

"Yes, it is," Dave replied, already recognizing his wife's voice but not yet daring to believe his ears. He stood up in the firelight, looking toward the voice. "Ellen? Ellen Waddell? Is that you? It's me, Dave!"

Frisco gave Dave Waddell a bemused look, thinking he'd just lost his mind. "Hey there, partner, you'd better try to get a grip on yourself—"

"Shhh," Dave said quickly, hushing him up. "That's my wife! I know it is!"

When she heard her name called out, Ellen's first instinct was to turn and run, fearing that these men were a part of Cherokee Earl's gang and that somehow Earl had informed them that she was missing. But seeing the man stand up in the glow of the fire, hearing his voice, and watching as he looked back and forth trying to locate her, Ellen gasped, "Oh, my God, Dave?" Then, realizing that it really was him, she called out loudly as she began to run toward him, "Dave! Dave! Yes, it's me!"

Dave jerked his hat from his head as if to better identify himself. "Ellen! My God, Ellen!" He ran to her as she came into the firelight.

Frisco Bonham stood watching, stunned, as the two met and sank to their knees sobbing, embracing. His eyes searched the surrounding darkness. If this woman was here, it was pretty good odds that Cherokee Earl and the boys were, too. He eyed the rifle that Ellen Waddell had dropped to the ground.

Dirty Joe's rifle, Frisco said to himself.

When Ellen could speak, she said to her husband, "I—I thought you were dead, Dave. I had no idea . . ."

"That I would be searching for you?" Dave said, finishing her words for her as he wiped his eyes. "Ellen, I've nearly gone crazy looking for you!" He nodded quickly toward Frisco, then said, "This is Frisco Bonham, one of Cherokee Earl's men. He's been leading me to Earl . . . so I could come get you."

Ellen tensed in her husband's arms, having heard Frisco's name spoken by Dirty Joe and others of Earl's men. She looked up at Frisco just as he bent down and picked up the rifle she'd dropped.

"Evening, ma'am," Frisco said, nodding with a slight grin. He held the rifle up, looking it over. "This belongs to Dirty Joe Turley. . . . Ain't no way he would have given it up. So I figure you got it some way and snuck off with it."

Ellen gave her husband a terrified look. The two rose from the ground. Dave drew the pistol from his waist on their way up. He held it pointed at Frisco as he drew Ellen tight against his side.

"It makes no difference how she got the rifle. She's here now, and that's all that—"

"Hey, hey, take it easy," said Frisco, grinning, raising his hands chest high and waving them back and froth. "I'm with you, pard, remember? I'm the one brought you two happy young lovebirds back together!"

Dave Waddell eased his grip on the pistol and on his wife. "He's right, Ellen," Dave said. "If it hadn't been for Frisco, I wouldn't have been here tonight."

"Ma'am," said Frisco, "I might be an outlaw . . . but your husband will have to admit I've been a man of my word. I told him to stick with me, that I'd bring him to you. And so I did." In a grand gesture, Frisco swept off his hat and took a short bow.

"The most important thing is we're back together now," said Dave to Ellen.

"Yes, we're together," Ellen said, still standing against her husband's side, "but we might not be for long if we don't clear out of here before Earl finds out I'm missing."

"If you don't mind me asking," said Frisco, "how did you manage to get away?" He studied Dirty Joe's rifle in his hands as he asked.

Ellen looked into her husband's eyes for support, then turned to Frisco and said bluntly, "Earl left Dirty Joe to watch me. I killed Dirty, took his rifle, and made my getaway."

"Killed him how?" asked Frisco with a wry smile. "Dirty Joe Turley was no easy piece of work as I recall."

"All right," she said, tilting her head up as if telling herself and the world that she was not ashamed of what she'd done. "I gained Joe's confidence. . . . Then, while he wasn't expecting it, I stabbed him to death with a butcher knife."

"Ouch!" said Frisco, still grinning. "I bet ole Dirty didn't care for that one bit."

Ellen turned her gaze back to her husband. "But like you said, the important thing is that we're together. Now we need to get out of here quick."

There was a questioning expression on Dave Waddell's face as he asked her pointedly, "Gained his confidence how?"

Ellen just stared at him for a second. Then, before she could respond, Frisco cut in, saying, "I don't mean to throw cold water on whatever high opinion you might have of yourself, ma'am, but if Cherokee Earl's in Cimarron, you won't have to worry about him looking for you. He's got plans for a big robbery there . . . big enough that he won't let losing a woman interfere with it."

In spite of Frisco's reassurance, Ellen looked skeptical. "I think we'd better get moving, Dave."

"Sure thing," said Dave, holding her close with his arm wrapped around her shoulders, his free hand stroking her hair. "God, I've missed you so much!" Then he snapped a glance back to Frisco and asked, "Just how big is this robbery you're talking about?"

Frisco shook his head back and forth slowly as if in awe at the thought of such an amount of wealth. "It's big enough that even once it's split a bunch of ways, nobody involved will ever have to pick up another branding iron for as long as he lives . . . unless he does it to light his cigar, that is."

"Dave?" said Ellen Waddell. "What does that matter? We're leaving right now . . . aren't we?"

Dave seemed not to hear her until she shook his coat sleeve. "Aren't we?" she repeated.

"Uh, yeah," Dave said finally, snapping out of a deep train of thought. "We're both heading out of here. We're not taking a chance on Earl showing up, robbery or no robbery."

"All right, pard," Frisco said reluctantly. "But I've got to say, it's a damn shame, you missing out on this big job after coming all this way."

"What is he talking about, Dave?" Ellen asked. "Why does he keep calling you pard?"

"It's a long story, Ellen," said Dave Waddell. Dismissing her question, he turned to Frisco. "My wife's right, Frisco. She's the reason I came this far. Now that I've got her, all I want to do is return home and live in peace." He drew Ellen even closer. "For my wife and me, this nightmare is over."

"In that case," said Frisco, pitching Dirty Joe's rifle to Dave Waddell, "I'll take my leave and go on to Cimarron."

"You're not going to tell Cherokee Earl where we are, are you?"

"Of course he will," Ellen cut in.

"No, ma'am, you're wrong there," said Frisco. "I won't mention you two if you don't want me to. But believe me, it ain't as important as you think it is. Sure, Earl did a wrong, stealing you the way he did. But if he wasn't through with you, he wouldn't have left you in Dirty Joe's care in the first place. The fact is, if Dave showed up with me, Earl would cut him right in on this robbery and let bygones be bygones." He shrugged. "That's just how he is . . . all us outlaws, for that matter."

"Don't take me for a fool, Frisco," said Dave. "You mean, he would still let me ride on this big job after all that's happened?"

"I'm saying he would," said Frisco. "He'd forget the past if you would. And sure he'd let you ride with us after all the thievery you and me's done together. . . . You're an old hand at it now."

Ellen looked on in disbelief. "Dave, what is he talking about, all the thievery you've done together?"

"Like I told you, Ellen, it's a long story," said Dave.

"I have time to listen," said Ellen, pulling away from his encircling arm.

Over the next few minutes, while Ellen Waddell sipped coffee from Dave's battered tin cup, she listened to her husband tell her about everything that had happened since she'd last seen him lying in the dirt out front of their home. Dave told her how their neighbor Danielle Strange and the old man Stick had ridden by searching for Cherokee Earl. He told her how the two had found him there and brought him along to search for her. Then he went on to tell Ellen about Billy Boy Harper shooting Danielle Strange and about Frisco shooting Stick. Ellen sat amazed, a tear falling from her eye as Dave told her about the robberies he'd committed with Frisco in order to raise money and supplies to keep on her trail. When he'd finished telling her the whole story, he let out a long breath and sat slumped for a moment.

"Ellen," he said at length, "I'm ashamed of these things I've done . . . but I had no choice." Now a tear ran down his cheek as well. "I had to find you. I couldn't give up the hunt until I knew you were all right."

"But, Dave, those people . . . they were innocent, hardworking folks for all you know. How can you justify robbing them? You have to do something to make all of this right."

"Uh, well, it's something I'll sure do some serious thinking about," he said to Ellen, shooting Frisco a knowing glance as he spoke.

In telling Ellen his story, Dave had failed to mention that there had been murder committed and that, although he hadn't been the one to do the killing, he was still in it up to his neck. Legally, he would hang alongside Frisco if the law ever found them.

"You'll *think* about it?" said Ellen, surprised by her husband's attitude. "You'll simply have to go to the law and tell them what happened. You'll explain why you did what you did and that you'll pay back every dollar you took."

Dave Waddell wiped his eye, gave Frisco another glance, then said, "Ellen, believe me, sometimes it's better to just let things lie. In the long run everybody will be better off."

Listening closely, Frisco shook his head and cut in long enough to say, "If you two will excuse me, I'll just get my stuff, get saddled up, and move right along."

"In the middle of the night?" Dave asked.

"Yeah, I think so," said Frisco. "I know when I'm the third wheel."

"But you can wait till morning," said Dave, half rising from the ground beside the fire.

Ellen stared at him curiously.

"Thanks but no, thanks," said Frisco. As he walked away toward the horses, he paused for a second, looked around at Dave Waddell, and said, "Not saying that you will of course, Dave . . . but if you should change your mind for any reason and want to join me, I'll be riding the Cimarron trail all the way to town."

Dave glanced at Frisco only long enough to see the knowing smile on his face. Then Dave hung his head and said, "No, Frisco, I reckon I'll be riding on back home now . . . my wife and I."

Ellen still only stared at him, not sure how she should take his words. Was there a sound of defeat in her husband's voice? The two sat in silence until Frisco stepped up into his stirrups and rode off into the darkness.

"Well, that's that," said Dave Waddell, standing up beside the fire, shoving his hands down into his trouser pockets. "It would probably be best if we moved our camp away from here."

"Yes, I believe it would be wise," said Ellen. She stood up beside her husband, studied his face in the fire glow, and said quietly, "You want to ride into Cimarron with him, don't you?"

"What? No . . . Hell, no," said Dave Waddell. But the look in his eyes told her he was lying, and he knew it. He relented a bit and said in a softer tone of voice, "Well, let's face it. He's talking about a lot of money. It would sure make up for what all we've lost these past days.

"So you do want to ride with Cherokee Earl?" Ellen asked.

"Well . . ." Dave let his words trail. Then he said, "But even if I did, what about you? We need to get you home, let you put all of this behind you."

Ellen caught herself again staring at her husband, wondering how she could have lived with a man so long and never realized until now just how little she knew him. "You would ride with the men who kidnapped your wife," she said flatly.

"No," said Dave, "because as you can see, I'm still right here, ain't I?" He spread his hands to take in the campsite. "Right here where I should be. By your side."

Ellen detected a faint sourness in his voice, but she let it pass without commenting on it. After a lengthy, awkward silence, she said, "A lot has happened to us, Dave. We'll need to take some time to let things heal."

"I know," he said. "And we'll take all the time we need." After another pause, he said, "I—I don't dare ask how you were treated or what he and the others did to you."

"Thanks, Dave, for understanding," Ellen said softly. "It's something I can't talk about . . . not now, perhaps never."

Facing away from her and staring down into the fire, Dave said, "I'm sure you did whatever you had to to stay alive, so I'll never question your judgment . . . or blame you for any of it."

Blame me . . . ? She stared at him. "Dave, no matter what I did or didn't do, I was kidnapped . . . taken against my will, forced against my will to do whatever that dog—" She stopped, then said aloud to herself, "What am I doing? Defending *my* actions?"

"No, don't, please," said Dave. "We don't need to go over the details."

"Good," Ellen said sharply, "because for a moment there I was afraid you might not approve of the way I allowed myself to be pawed and violated by that sweaty, greasy pig."

"Please, don't!" said Dave. "I know it wasn't your fault, none of it. I just have to find a way from now on to accept the fact that another man has—" He stopped himself, then said, "Well . . . you know."

"Oh, well, thanks," said Ellen sarcastically. "I feel much better now."

"I didn't mean it like that, Ellen," he said, reaching with both arms to hold her.

"I'm sure you didn't," she replied, backing away.

"I'm sorry," said Dave. "That's all I can say. Think of me here, of what I've been through . . . knowing what was happening, being powerless to stop it. I've been through hell!"

"Yes," she said, "what time you weren't robbing people with your pard, Frisco Bonham!" She looked him up and down. "Frankly, Dave, you don't look all that hurt to me."

"Yeah? Well, neither do you if I might say so," Dave hissed, his temper rising.

"What is that supposed to mean?" Ellen asked heatedly.

"You're a woman of the world now," said Dave. "You figure it out."

"A woman of the world?" Ellen repeated his words, feeling rage begin to boil inside her. "Because I'm not standing here with my face beaten in, my bones broken! Because of that, I have somehow let you down? I turned loose of my virtue too quickly, too easily? Is that what you mean?"

"Did you even put up a fight?" Dave asked, holding nothing back now.

"No!" Ellen shouted. "I did not put up a fight! I let him do whatever he wanted to do to me. I made no effort to stop him! I lay there like a sack of feed while he grunted and slobbered and bored himself inside me!"

"Stop. That's enough!" Dave shouted, unable to abide the terrible scene her words evoked in his mind. "I don't want to hear any more!"

"You're a liar, Dave." Her voice dropped low like the harsh purr of a mountain cat. "You want to hear more. . . . You want to hear every sick detail. But you want to hear it on your terms. You want me to clean it up, tell it to you in a way that will allow you to forgive me for it." Her voice rose suddenly. "You son of a bitch! You want to know if I enjoyed it! You stupid bastard! No, I hated it! If I hadn't managed to play Joe Turley along, make him promises of giving myself to him, let me tell you what I would have done."

"No, stop!" said Dave.

But she ignored him and continued. "I would have given myself to Earl on the ground, buck naked, while the whole gang watched!"

"I mean it, Ellen—stop it!" Dave threatened.

She didn't seem to hear him. "If I would have had to, I would have groaned and moaned and screamed in delight! And while I did so, I would have been slipping my hand along his thigh until I could close it around his pistol!"

"Damn you! Shut up!" Dave slapped her.

She reeled but refused to stop. "Then I would have blown my brains out!" Her hands covered her face. She wept violently.

Dave stood helplessly by, unable to approach her, unable to console her. When her crying subsided and she wiped her eyes and stared into the fire, she said in a calm voice, "Dave, there is something about me you should know." She hesitated, then went on. "Before I met you? Remember I told you I was away in a ladies' business college? Well, that wasn't true. I lived on my own, Dave, in Washington, D.C., less than three miles from the White House. I made a living entertaining men in private."

"What? My God!" said Dave. "I had no idea!"

"I know," said Ellen. "I kept it a secret from you." She sniffled and wiped her nose on her coat sleeve. "When I met you in Colorado, I knew I could make you a good wife. After all, I know how to please. . . . I should. I've done it often enough."

"I'm not going to listen to any of this," said Dave. "I think you're making it up. I think you're talking out of your head. We shouldn't have ever let this conversation get started. Let's stop it right now."

Her face still stung from where he'd slapped her. "There's no stopping now, Dave. It's all coming out into the open. I don't want to hide who I am or what I've done. It's all that's kept me alive throughout this ordeal." She paused and considered things, then said, "Funny, isn't it? I left that life because I felt like public property to any man who would pay me. Now, all these years later, I used the skills I learned in that life in order to keep myself alive—protect your personal property, so to speak. Now it appears that my having done such a good job of staying alive is being called into question." She sighed long and deep, then murmured, "Men . . . what the hell do you fellows want?"

"I don't know," said Dave, his whole demeanor suddenly rigid and unyielding, "but after this conversation, I don't think it's you." He refused to face her as he spoke. "I think when we get somewhere where there's a stagecoach, it would be best to put you on it. I often thought there were things I didn't know about you. You've deceived me all along. I will never be able to get over that."

"I understand," said Ellen. "I suppose I wouldn't expect you to."

As Dave stared into the fire, Ellen walked away for a moment.

"I know I ain't perfect," said Dave. "Maybe I've dealt a little dirt in business deals. I've put my hands on stolen cattle. But up until this thing happened, I've never robbed anybody, brought harm to anybody. I've done only what a man does. All I ever wanted was a good, decent, honest wife," Dave said down to the licking flames. "I thought that was what I had. Now it turns out I was wrong."

"I've let you down something terrible, haven't I?" said Ellen.

"Let me down? Ha! To say the least, you've let me down." He turned his eyes to hers as she returned to the campfire. "I wish to God we'd never met," he said bitterly.

"So do I," said Ellen.

Dirty Joe's rifle bucked once in her hand, the explosion causing something above them in the scrub cedars to take flight, letting out a short screech and a windy sound of powerful beating wings. Dave Waddell hit the ground stone-dead, one arm flinging over into the licking flames of the campfire.

Ellen reached out with the toe of her scuffed and ragged shoe and flipped his arm from the flames just as the skin on his hand began to sizzle and blacken, peeling back in layer after layer. She looked around the small campsite, then back down at the body of her husband lying dead on the ground.

"Earl, you son of a bitch," she hissed as if Cherokee Earl was standing there. "I've got one more stop to make. . . . Then I'm going home."

CHAPTER 20

Frisco Bonham had heard the gunshot as he rode toward Cimarron. While the echo of the explosion still rolled across the land, he'd smiled to himself and said to his horse and the surrounding darkness, "Looks like they just settled their differences the hard way." Laughing aloud at his little joke, he batted his boots against his horse's sides and rode on toward Cimarron. Less than a mile from town, as his horse rounded a turn in the road, Frisco came upon Cherokee Earl and Avery McRoy as they made their way back to the shack hideout.

"Damn, Frisco," said McRoy, settling his startled gelding, "don't spook the horses!"

"I didn't come looking for you just to spook the horses," Frisco replied, his horse turning a complete circle before coming to a nervous halt. He studied their shadowed faces in the thin moonlight. "What's the odds of me running into you two?"

Both Cherokee Earl and Avery McRoy looked equally surprised to come upon Frisco so suddenly in the dark of night.

"Pretty damn good, I'd say," Earl chuckled. He leaned slightly and looked along the trail behind Frisco. "Where's Billy Boy?"

"Billy Boy's dead, I reckon," said Frisco, his voice taking on a sad edge.

"You *reckon* he's dead?" said Cherokee Earl, sounding a bit testy about Frisco's answer. "You mean, you don't know for sure?"

"Boss, Billy Boy shot that woman you sent us back to ambush. He shot her with that hideaway gun he carried. But then she nailed him with a Colt Forty-five. So yep, I'd say for sure poor Billy Boy's dead."

"All right," said Earl. "At least he managed to kill the woman for me." He eyed Frisco. "What about the old man riding with her? Is he dead?"

"He is," said Frisco. "I shot him myself, left him dead on the trail."

"Good enough," said Earl. "Things are starting to come together for us. We didn't need those two dogging us."

"Hold on to your boots, boss," said Frisco. "I got some strange news for you."

"Yeah? What's that?" asked Earl.

"I fell in with Dave Waddell on the way up here. He was with the old man and the woman when we ambushed them."

"I thought I left him in the dirt," said Earl.

"I know," said Frisco. "That's what he told me. Evidently, the woman and old man showed up and saved him."

"Then why didn't you kill him when you had a chance?" Earl demanded.

"Kill him, hell," said Frisco. "He saved me from those two. Besides, he helped me rob a stagecoach and some settlers on the way here."

"That figures," said Earl. "I always knew he was an outlaw at heart."

"Yeah, well, he said you stole that pretty redheaded wife of his." Frisco spat, wiped his mouth, and chuckled. "The damned fool said he aimed to take her back from you."

"He's welcome to try," said Cherokee Earl. "The fact is, I wore out on her awfully quick . . . but I promised her off once I was through with her. I'll just have to explain all that to Dave if he shows up." He grinned. "I hope he understands."

"I don't think that matters now, boss," said Frisco. "It's a fifty-fifty possibility he's dead by now. Him or that redheaded woman."

Earl and McRoy stared at him in the darkness. "What are you getting at, Frisco?" asked Earl.

"Boss, me and Dave ran into his wife on the trail. She told us you left Dirty Joe watching her, and she stabbed him to death with a butcher knife."

"Damn it to hell!" Earl cursed. "Here I am needing men to rob a bank and that damned Dirty Joe goes and gets himself killed!"

"I know, boss. It's a shame," said Frisco. "I hate being the bearer of bad news, but I thought you'd want to know before you ride on to the hideout and find Dirty Joe bled out all over the floor."

"This leaves me stuck with Buck Hite, who's a dope smoker, and his three men, a bunch of idiots, all of them together too damn dumb to prime a dry pump." Earl shook his head slowly in disgust and dismay. "It's getting harder every day to hold a good gang together. Sometimes I wonder why I even try."

"For the money, that's why," said Avery McRoy, hoping to cheer Earl up. He looked at Frisco. "Why do you figure it's a fifty-fifty chance one of the Waddells is dead?"

"I left because I saw a big fight coming," said Frisco. "They were all lovey-dovey when they first got back together. But it didn't take over five minutes until she was on the verge of riding him out about helping me rob the stage."

"That's a woman for you," said McRoy.

"Yeah," said Frisco, "but I could also see that it wouldn't be long before Dave was going to start asking her some questions himself." Frisco nodded solemnly. "You could tell Dave is a greedy, jealous man. I left before the sparks started to fly. Then I heard a rifle shot before I'd gone a mile."

"That don't mean one of them killed the other," said McRoy as if looking for a brighter outcome to the story.

"Let's put it this way," said Frisco. "They was both armed and ready for some serious marital discussion." He gave each of them a look of dread. "And it was too dark out to be shooting at rattle-snakes."

"Then I suppose you're right," Earl said to Frisco. "One of them's dead and the other is long gone would be my guess."

"Say the word, boss," said Avery McRoy. "Me and Frisco will find out what's gone on."

"No," said Earl. "It's no big concern to me. We've got business to take care of. Besides, I'm sorry I ever wasted my time on that woman. Far as I care, they can kill each other." He let out a sigh. "They always struck me as one of those couples who just weren't meant to stay together."

He heeled his horse forward at an easy walk. McRoy and Frisco rode along, flanking him on either side.

"Is losing Dirty Joe going to leave us shorthanded?" asked Frisco.

"It would have," said Earl. "But lucky for us, Buck Hite took on a new man . . . a young gunman called Danny Duggin. Ever heard of him?"

"No," said Frisco, "can't say that I have."

"Me neither," said Avery McRoy. "And believe me, I know every foulmouthed, low-down, back-shooting, murdering, crazy sumbitch in this territory."

"So do I," said Cherokee Earl. "That's what worries me about him."

"You seemed to trust him all right back in town, Earl, from all outer appearances," said McRoy.

"Get this straight, McRoy," said Earl, turning in his saddle to face him. "From all outer appearances you would think I trust my own mother . . . but you'd be awfully wrong thinking it. I'm going to stay one step ahead of Mr. Danny Duggin. You can count on that."

"Stay one step ahead of him how?" McRoy asked.

Cherokee Earl gave them both a smug, crafty smile. "For starters, did either of you know there's a shortcut runs from behind our hideout all the way back to Cimarron?"

The two looked at each other. "No," said McRoy. "We had no idea."

"Well, there is," said Earl, "and we're fixin' to check it out. Don't get too comfortable tonight, boys. Things are going to be happening fast and furious."

McRoy and Frisco grinned at each other.

"We can hardly wait," said Frisco.

McRoy said, "You mean, there's something you know about when the money's arriving that you ain't told nobody yet?"

"You saw the shape Buck Hite and his boys are in," said Cherokee Earl. "Would you trust telling them fools anything?"

When neither man answered, Earl said, "Boys, I know when the money is coming. . . . I've got inside information on it. We're going to use Buck Hite and his boys in case things don't go the way we want them to. But I wasn't about to tell them anything until it's time to make our play. We'll round them up on our way to town."

"See?" McRoy said to Frisco. "I knew the boss had this all taken care of."

They rode farther along on the main trail until they came to a fork, where they turned toward the secluded hideout.

Had Earl, McRoy, and Frisco lingered a few moments longer at the fork in the trail, they would have heard the hooves of Ellen Waddell's horse and met her as she rode through the night, headed for Cimarron. For a cautious second, Ellen stopped the horse on the trail and stared upward along the dark path toward the shack. She was struck by the sudden urge to ride up there tonight, stick the rifle barrel through a crack in the wall, and blow Cherokee Earl to kingdom come. But she fought the urge, reminding herself how it would be for her should something go wrong and land her right back into captivity.

"I'll wait," she whispered to herself. "And I'll be there when the time is right."

In the gray hours of morning, Eddie Ray Moon, Clifford Reed, and Fat Cyrus Kerr lay snoring in their blankets. Buck Hite sat slumped beside the fire in a glaze-eyed opium stupor, a long wooden pipe lying across his lap. As she lay with her head on her saddle, her hat pulled low across her face, Danielle's eyes darted back and forth beneath her lowered hat brim. Satisfied that no one would be awake for at least another couple of hours, she stood up and walked quietly to the horses, carrying her saddle with her. Checking again over her shoulder, she took Sundown's saddle blanket from the bough of a tree, smoothed it onto the mare's back, then pitched the saddle upon the mare and cinched it.

When she'd finished preparing the mare for the trail, she walked the animal away from the campsite to a place alongside the road where the night before she'd arranged for Deputy Tuck Carlyle to meet her. As soon as she stepped out upon the trail, she saw him riding out from Cimarron. A half mile behind him, the town's rooflines loomed in a silvery mist.

As Tuck rode up, he glanced off the trail toward the high curl of smoke from the spot where Buck Hite and his gang lay drunk and unconscious around the low fire. "Think things will be okay here, Danny?" Tuck asked.

Danielle stepped up into her saddle, making sure to turn up her coat collar and lower her hat brim. "Yes, these boys will keep until we're finished with Cherokee Earl. The main thing is, we've got to get Ellen Waddell safely away from Earl before all hell breaks loose. We'll take care of the Buck Hite Gang on our way back to town." She looked off toward the snoring campsite with a wry smile. "Provided they're sober enough to stand up by then."

"Are you the one who's supposed to be in town keeping an eye out for the big silver load?" asked Tuck.

"Yes," said Danielle, "I'm the man in town today. That gives me a reason for not being here when they wake up."

"Good thinking," said Tuck.

They turned their horses and rode off along the main trail. But before they'd gone three miles, they sighted a riderless horse grazing along the edge of the trail, its reins dangling freely in the dirt.

"Whoa, Sundown," said Danielle, reining the chestnut mare down far enough back not to spook the grazing horse.

Tuck reined down beside her.

"What do you think, Danny?" asked Tuck, slipping his pistol from his holster. "Think it might be a trick of some kind?"

"I don't know," Danielle said in a soft tone. "Cover me from back here. I'll go check it out."

She stepped down from the mare and handed Tuck her reins. Then she walked the few yards separating her and the riderless horse with her hands out to her sides in a show of peace.

"Easy there," she whispered, getting closer.

The animal nickered low but didn't spook and bolt away. When she got close enough, she took ahold of the dangling reins and ran a gloved hand down the horse's muzzle, calming it. She looked all around and started to lead the horse back to where Tuck sat keeping her covered.

But Danielle stopped abruptly when she heard a moan coming from a patch of waist-high wild grass. Upon looking closer toward the sound, she saw a woman's red hair glisten through the tall, swaying grass.

"Tuck, over here," she said, gauging her tone of voice, keeping it loud enough for Tuck to hear but not loud enough to carry much farther. Leading the horse, she hurried to where the woman sprawled facedown. Recognizing Ellen Waddell, Danielle knelt quickly and turned her over, laying Ellen's head on her lap.

"Take it easy, Mrs. Waddell," Danielle said, feeling Ellen try to resist even in her weakened condition. "We're not going to hurt you. You're safe here."

Catching a glimpse of Danielle's face before Danielle lowered her hat brim between them, Ellen squinted her eyes and said, "Who are you? I've . . . seen you before somewhere."

"No, ma'am," said Danielle. "You don't know me, Mrs. Waddell. But I know you. I've been hunting you ever since you left your place near Haley Springs."

"You're not . . . one of them?" Ellen asked, her eyes beginning to well with tears.

"Them? You mean, one of Cherokee Earl's gunmen? No, ma'am. I'm Danny Duggin. I started out hunting them for what they did in

Haley Springs . . . but then I began hunting them to get you away from them."

Tuck stepped in, carrying a canteen of water. "And I'm Deputy Tuck Carlyle. You're under our protection now. Don't worry about a thing."

He twisted the cap of the canteen free and passed it to Danielle, who in turn helped Ellen raise it to her lips. She took a long sip, then closed her eyes for a moment as if trying to accept that this was real, that she was finally free. When she opened her eyes again, tears ran down her cheeks.

"I didn't know anybody was trying to save me," she said. "I thought I was all alone."

"No, ma'am," said Danielle, "I was there right behind you all along. Now you take it easy for a minute or two, make sure you've got your head clear."

Danielle gently touched the large bump on Ellen's head. Luckily, it was only going to leave a large bruise. The skin was not broken.

"I fell off the horse last night in the dark," Ellen said. "I must've hit my head pretty hard."

"Yes, ma'am, you did," said Danielle. "But you're going to be fine, I can tell."

"Thank you, Mr. Duggin," Ellen said in a weak voice.

She tried to reach a hand to the rifle lying nearby. Danielle reached over, picked it up, and laid it across Ellen's lap.

"There you are, ma'am, if holding it makes you feel better. As soon as you feel like getting up on the horse, we're going to take you to Cimarron and get you looked at by a doctor."

"Deputy," aid Ellen, trying hard to focus on Tuck Carlyle, "I think you need to know that Cherokee Earl and his men are intending to rob your town's bank." She paused, then said, "That's why I was headed to town: to warn you about it." She wasn't sure how to present what had happened between her and her husband.

"Much obliged for the information, ma'am," said Tuck. "But thanks to Danny here, I already know about it. I'm ready for them anytime they feel like taking me on."

"The fact is," Danielle said to Ellen, "we were on our way to try to find you this morning and see if we could sneak you away from Earl and his men. We weren't about to hit the gang nose to nose until we knew you were safely out of our line of fire." Danielle looked at Tuck and nodded, then looked back at Ellen. "Now that we know you're all right, ma'am, there's nothing to keep us from hitting them as hard and as fast as we can."

"Now you're talking, Danny," said Tuck.

Together they reached down and helped Ellen to her feet, holding her between them.

"I don't want to hold you up from getting to them," Ellen said. "Help me up onto the horse. I'll go with you."

"No, ma'am," said Danielle. "That's out of the question. Tuck and I both have more experience at this sort of thing. Let us handle it."

"Why, Mr. Duggin?" Ellen asked. "Because I'm a woman?"

"No, ma'am, that's not it at all," said Danielle, thinking how ironic it was that Ellen Waddell should think such a thing. *If you only knew,* Danielle thought. But all she could say was "Ma'am, it's not because you're a woman that we can't take you with us. Tuck and I just know about how each other works, is all."

"Mr. Duggin, I want you to realize what this animal has done to me," said Ellen. "To be honest with you, now that I know how to fire this rifle . . . I want to kill him. I know that doesn't sound very ladylike, but it's—"

"Ma'am," Danielle said, interrupting her, "you've taken a hard lick on the head. We can't afford to take you out there and find out you're hurt worse than we thought. I hope you understand that."

Ellen relented and said with a trace of regret, "All right, Mr. Duggin, you win. I'll go to town and see the doctor."

CHAPTER 21

CIMARRON, NEW MEXICO TERRITORY

Danielle and Tuck escorted Ellen Waddell immediately to the doctor's office and waited in an adjoining room while the young doctor examined her. While they waited, Tuck walked to the front window, pulled back a curtain, and looked out along the main street.

"There was a lot of townsfolk watching us ride in. They'll be having questions about who she is and what happened to her. Do you suppose I ought to let a few of them know what we're expecting here?"

Danielle walked over and looked out with him. "Now that the woman is safe and we know where to look for Earl and his men, go ahead and tell them before we leave town. It was important to keep this a secret before. But now it's better that these people be prepared in case Earl manages to get around us and hit the town while we're not here."

Tuck nodded in agreement, then said, "Before leaving town, we might just as well round up Buck Hite and his boys. Once we throw them in the slammer, we'll have that much less to deal with."

Staring out along the street to the north, Danielle saw the large green-and-red express wagon come lumbering into town, flanked on either side by a horseman riding guard, each carrying a rifle across his lap.

"Uh-oh," she said. "I think the silver exchange money is arriving right now!"

Now Tuck Carlyle saw the wagon. "That's it, all right. I wish Sheriff Wright was back. We're going to get spread awfully thin here if we ain't careful."

"This changes our plans," said Danielle. "We can't run the risk of going after Cherokee Earl and leaving the money or this town unguarded."

They watched the wagon stop out front of the bank. The two guards and the wagon driver stepped down and began opening a steel security box that stood bolted to the floor of the wagon.

"Right," said Tuck. "The first thing I'd better do now is let the townsmen know we've got trouble coming."

"You do that," said Danielle. "I'll go tell the wagon guards and driver the same thing."

As Danielle and Tuck turned from the window and headed for the door, she said, "There's three more guns on our side." They stepped out onto the boardwalk outside of the doctor's office, and Tuck closed the door behind them.

In the other room of the doctor's office, Ellen Waddell heard the front door close. She sat halfway up, seeming startled, and said, "Doctor, was that Mr. Duggin and the deputy leaving? Where are they going?" Her eyes went to the rifle she'd clung to throughout her ordeal. "Hand me that, please," she said, struggling to raise herself the rest of the way up from the cot. "I've got to get up from here and get busy."

Out front, Tuck said to Danielle, "I'll hurry, Danny. As soon as I tell them there's outlaws coming, I'll—"

"Save yourself the trouble, Tuck," Danielle said, nodding toward Avery McRoy, who stood in his long riding duster and leaned against the front of a building. "The outlaws are here already."

"How in the world . . . ?" Tuck's voice trailed as the two of them sidestepped along the boardwalk, then down into the shelter of a narrow alley.

"Cherokee Earl and his men must have doubled back along a side trail in the night," said Danielle, scanning the street now for any other familiar outlaw faces. "There's Eddie Ray Moon," she added, gesturing toward a stack of nail kegs out front of the town mercantile store across the street from where Avery McRoy stood with his head bowed, trying to go unnoticed. "Earl and his men must've gotten them up right after we left this morning."

"He's gotten ahead of us on knowing the money was arriving today," said Tuck. "But how?"

"I don't know," said Danielle. "But any minute now this street is going to turn into a battlefield." As she spoke, they both saw Fat Cyrus and Clifford Reed stepping down from their horses at the edge of an alley that ran between the mercantile store and the barbershop. "Why didn't they hit the wagon while it was on its way here?" Danielle asked.

"Because they're greedy," said Tuck. "This way they hit the bank and get the money plus the silver."

Danielle nodded. "Then it will be their greed that causes their downfall."

"Let's hope so," Tuck said. He looked back and forth quickly, taking in the street. Then he said, "You stay here. I'll circle around behind the buildings, get to the guards, and let them know what's about to happen."

"Go ahead," said Danielle. "I'll keep watch from here. As soon as I can get to my saddle without tipping our hand, I'll get my rifle and keep this end of town covered."

"Be careful here, Danny," Tuck said.

Danielle only nodded as he turned and hurried away along the alley.

"You, too, Tuck," Danielle whispered under her breath, scanning the street like a hawk. "I don't want to lose you again."

Running in a crouch, keeping close to the side of the building, Tuck hurried to the long alley running behind the town. As soon as he knew there was little chance of being stopped from the street, he came out of the crouch and ran faster, his Colt in his hand.

At the rear door of the bank, he pounded hard until he heard the voice of the bank manager say, "Who goes there?"

"Mr. Scally! It's me, Deputy Tuck Carlyle! Open the door quick!"

"Now see here, Deputy," said the manager's gruff voice. "I never open this door unless it is an extreme emergency!"

"This is an extreme emergency!" Tuck said, trying to keep from shouting. "There's a robbery about to take place!"

"A robbery?" The manager's voice sounded suddenly hushed and anxious. "One second, sir!" He shakily turned a key in the lock, then threw back a heavy steel door latch and swung the door open a few inches. "Now what are you talking about?" He stood blocking the door with his square, portly chest.

"I'm coming in, Mr. Scally." Tuck shoved the man back out of his way and stepped inside. On the other side of the room, the two guards stood holding their rifles at port arms. Upon seeing Tuck shove his way inside, they both leveled their rifles at him.

"Easy, fellows. I'm on your side," Tuck said, raising his hands chest high and at the same time nodding at the badge on his chest.

"What's going on, Deputy?" the bank manager asked.

"There's a gang in town, Mr. Scally," said Tuck. "Don't ask me how, but they knew the money was arriving today." He looked at the two guards. "They'll be coming any minute. I've got a man covering the other end of the street. He'll move this way once the shooting starts."

"The shooting? Oh, my!" said the bank manager as if the possibility of getting shot had just crossed his mind. "What on earth shall I do?"

"Get a gun," Tuck said flatly.

"I have no stomach for this sort of thing, Deputy," said the manager. He placed a hand to his sweat-beaded forehead in anguish and terror.

"Then take cover and stay out of our way," Tuck said. "These guards and me will have our hands full."

"That's right, mister," said one of the guards, a tall rawboned man with a sandy red mustache. "We won't have time to wet-nurse you."

As he spoke, he stepped over beside Tuck and looked out through the empty bank lobby to where the wagon driver stood staring out the front window. "Fred? How do things look out there?" the guard asked.

"So far, so good," said the wagon driver, a grizzled old teamster with a tobacco-stained beard.

"All right, then," said the guard. He gave Tuck a smile of confidence and nodded. "Everything is under control."

But as he turned to step back over beside the other guard, his free hand snatched Tuck's Colt from his holster. Before Tuck could react, the guard swung a hard blow with the pistol barrel and cracked Tuck across the side of his head, sending him to the floor.

"Damn, Roy!" the other guard shouted. "What the hell are you doing?" As he asked, he swung his rifle barrel and pointed it at Roy. His thumb went across the hammer, ready to cock it.

"Sorry, Smitty," said guard Roy Sadler to the man who had been his partner for the past year. "You just got put out of work."

The rifle bucked in his hand. Smitty slammed backward against the door of the big vault, then slid down to the floor.

"My God! Help!" the bank manager shrieked, throwing his hands up and cowering back against the vault door. His plea was directed at the wagon driver in the other room. "We're being robbed!"

"Is that the truth?" the old wagon driver called out, a slight chuckle to his voice.

"Yep. It's the truth, so help me," Sadler replied, smoke curling up from his rifle barrel.

The wagon driver called out, "What the hell happened back there? You wasn't supposed to do any shooting until everybody got in here."

"I know it," said Sadler, "but Smitty here had more guts than I thought. He was all set to cock and fire on me. I had to kill the idiot."

"Damn it, that rushes everything up too much," said the wagon driver. "You could have slugged him. Why did you have to pull that damn trigger?"

"It couldn't be helped," said Sadler. "I don't like slugging a person. It's bad on a gun barrel. Now wave Earl and the others in here,

Fred. . . . Let's get this damn thing done and clear out of town." He
turned to the terrified bank manager. "Old buddy, you'd better get
that safe open like your life depends on it because it *does*." He
jammed the tip of his rifle into Scally's big belly.

"Oh, dear, oh, dear!" said the frightened bank manager, his
trouser legs shaking along with his trembling knees. "My mind has
gone blank on me. I'm too scared to remember the combination!"

"Then you'd better take a few deep breaths, count to ten, and
start remembering. Otherwise, I can't think of any reason not to
kill you right now." Roy cocked the rifle. "I'll even count to ten
with you." He pointed the rifle into Scally's round belly. "One . . .
two . . . three . . ."

"Wait! Please! Just give me a moment!" Scally pleaded. "It's
coming to me. . . . Yes, I think I remember now."

He turned to the vault and began quickly turning the combination dial. His fingers shook violently. Then he stopped twisting the
dial, turned the steel door lever, and swung the big door open with
both hands.

Sadler grinned, looking inside the vault at stacks of silver bars
in the middle of the floor and stacks of cash on shelves reaching
almost to the ceiling. "I find that looking down a rifle barrel always jogs the memory." He shoved the manager inside the large
vault and into an empty corner. "Now, you sit your scared-to-death
ass down and don't open your mouth, *comprende*?"

"Yes, sir," the bank manager said shakily, covering his face with
his forearms.

At the far end of the street, when Danielle heard the rifle shot,
she immediately ran to her saddle and snatched her rifle from its
boot. Now, as she turned toward the bank, she saw Avery McRoy
and Frisco Bonham hurrying through the door.

"Tuck!" she said aloud to herself, the rifle shot having conjured
up all sorts of dark possibilities.

Down the street she saw Buck Hite, Cherokee Earl, Fat Cyrus,
and Clifford Reed, all four mounted and wearing long dusters, converging on the bank with their pistols blazing in every direction.

Townsfolk scattered and sought shelter where they could from the barrage of gunfire. At the wagon, Eddie Ray leaped forward and grabbed the reins to the team of horses to keep them from spooking and bolting away. Instead of dismounting, the men rode their horses right inside the bank building, leaving Eddie Ray Moon standing outside as a lookout. Danielle saw Eddie Ray pull a double-barreled shotgun from under his duster. In a flash it came to Danielle that the key to breaking up this raid and saving Tuck Carlyle—if he was still alive—was to take control of the wagon. Without the wagon, the silver ingots weren't going anywhere. Turning, Danielle swung up atop Sundown and heeled the mare straight toward Eddie Ray Moon.

"It's Danny Duggin!" said Eddie Ray, seeing the horse and rider pound toward him. He raised his hands and waved the shotgun back and forth above his head. "Hurry up, Danny! The raid's already commenced!" he shouted. "Get on in there—you're missing everything!"

Before he realized what was happening, Danielle swept past him on the big mare, jerked her boot from the stirrup, and kicked Eddie Ray solidly in the jaw, sending him sprawling. While Eddie Ray rolled on the ground, still grasping the shotgun, Danielle slid the mare down to a halt and leaped from the saddle into the wagon seat. She grabbed the discarded traces and slapped the horses' backs.

"Yieee!" she shouted, sending the horses lunging forward into a run down the middle of the street.

Feeling the wagon slide a bit sideways turning the corner around the livery barn, Danielle caught sight of several townsmen encircling the bank with their rifles and shotguns in hand. When she'd hitched the wagon and jumped down with her own rifle, she heard Cherokee Earl's gruff voice shout from the boardwalk out front of the bank, "Where the hell is the wagon?" Then rifles, shotguns, and pistols began to explode all at once.

Danielle made it to the front corner of the livery barn in time to look across the street and see Eddie Ray Moon hurrying to the door of the bank on all fours, his shotgun still in hand. Rifle shots from a rooftop across the street followed him in a jagged row, ripping up splinters from the boardwalk.

"Boys, that damn Danny Duggin stole our wagon!" Eddie Ray shouted loudly.

"What?" said Cherokee Earl, who'd just stepped out the door and been met by whistling bullets slicing past his head.

He had been carrying two bags, one full of silver bars and the other full of money. But he dropped the silver bars and backed inside to the shelter of the bank, his big Colt blazing in his hand, returning fire.

In the back room of the bank, Tuck Carlyle had regained consciousness enough to realize what was happening. He'd managed to inch his way closer to the rear door when the shooting began out front.

The guard Sadler saw Tuck reaching out for the partly opened door. "Where do you think you're going, law dog!" he growled, raising a boot and slamming the door shut. He pointed his cocked rifle down at Tuck's face.

"Don't shoot him," Cherokee Earl commanded. "He's our free ride out of here."

Sadler stared at Earl, along with the others, while bullets pounded the front of the building.

"They've got our wagon, damn it!" Earl shouted above the roar of gunfire. "We'll have to trade him for it if we're going to take everything here with us."

"Forget taking everything, Earl," said Buck Hite. "Let's grab whatever we can carry! They've got us pinned down here like ducks in a shooting gallery. Let's load these horses down and get the hell out of here!"

"Like hell," said Earl. "I planned this job to be big, and by God it's going to be big!" He glared at Buck Hite. "Show some guts here, Buck. We don't have to settle for less. Let's be bold as brass! Any objections?"

"No, sir," Buck Hite said, looking down at the smoking Colt in Earl's hand. "None at all."

"Good!" Earl said sarcastically. He looked back at Sadler and said, "Bring the deputy up here and stick him in the door where the town can see him."

Sadler dragged Tuck through the bank, then pulled him to his feet with Earl's help.

Earl held Tuck by his lapels and said close to his face, "Your friend Danny Duggin took our wagon, law dog. Now we're going to give you a chance to see just how good a friend he is."

"I'm not telling Danny to deal with you, Earl, if that's what you're thinking," Tuck said defiantly. Blood ran down his cheek from the short gash the pistol barrel had left on the side of his head.

Cherokee Earl grinned. "I knew you'd say that. You law dogs are all alike . . . always looking for a way to be some kind of half-assed hero!"

He looked at Eddie Ray Moon, held out his hand, and said, "Eddie Ray, give me your belt and shotgun."

"My gun belt? My shotgun?" Eddie asked, looking worried, afraid he'd be blamed for letting the wagon get away from him. "Why, Earl?"

"No, not your gun belt, idiot!" said Earl, snatching the shotgun from his hands. "Give me your trouser belt. Come on, hurry up!" He snapped his fingers impatiently.

"All right," said Eddie Ray, reluctantly unbuckling his belt and pulling it loose. He looked to Buck Hite for support but saw none. "But now my britches are going to fall down." He clasped his trousers at the waist to keep them up.

Bullets continued to whistle in from across the street and pound the front of the building. At the broken front window, Clifford Reed and Avery McRoy returned fire. Behind them their horses stamped back and forth in fright on the bank's polished floor.

"They've surrounded us now, Earl," shouted Fred from the back room.

Three bullets pounded the back door like someone knocking with an angry fist.

"Somebody get these horses in the back room," Earl demanded.

He turned Tuck around and drew Eddie Ray's belt snug around his neck. He wrapped the length of the belt back along the shotgun barrel until he held it gripped in place, his finger across the triggers. The tip of the barrel pressed securely against the back of Tuck's head at collar level.

"Now let's see what this town really thinks of you, Deputy! Get over here in the door!"

"Go to hell!" Tuck said, standing firm. But it did him no good to resist.

"Not without you, I won't!" said Cherokee Earl. He yanked hard on the belt around Tuck's neck and pulled him fully into the open doorway, in plain sight from all directions.

"Here's your deputy, folks!" Earl shouted, standing directly behind Tuck.

Firing stopped immediately.

Cherokee Earl gave his men an I-told-you-so look, then grinned and shouted out to the street, "That's it, gentlemen. Hold that fire! If I hear one more shot out there, I'll make a dead law dog out of this boy. I swear I will."

There was a tense silence for a second. Then Danielle said in her best man's voice, "All right, Earl, what is it you want?"

"Why, Danny Duggin!" said Cherokee Earl in feigned surprise. "Is that you out there?"

"You know it's me, Earl," Danielle said flatly. "Now what's your deal?"

Cherokee Earl wasn't ready to make a deal just yet. "What are you doing, siding with the townsfolk? I thought you were in with us on this raid."

"I changed my mind," said Danielle, her firm tone of voice unchanged. "Now what's your deal?"

"Imagine my sore disappointment," said Earl, still putting off any serious discussion about Tuck Carlyle, "looking out there and seeing you on the side of law and order. It nearly shook my faith to the foundation." He cackled aloud behind Tuck Carlyle.

Danielle shot a glance along the boardwalk, where townsmen

looked at her with uncertainty. "Don't worry," she said. Lowering her voice to the men huddled with their rifles and shotguns behind wooden shipping crates and rain barrels, she added, "He's looking for any opening he can find."

"Who are you, mister?" asked Angus O'Dell, the owner of the town's mercantile store.

"My name's Duggin, just like he said. I'm a friend of Tuck Carlyle." Danielle nodded toward Cherokee Earl standing hidden behind Tuck Carlyle. "If I was riding with these outlaws, would I have taken off with their getaway wagon?"

"He's got a point there, Angus," said John Dash, the town barber. Along the boardwalk heads nodded in agreement.

Angus O'Dell asked Danielle, "What about the wagon, then, Mr. Duggin? Are you going to give it back to them?"

Danielle didn't answer right away. Finally she said, "We'll see." Then she turned away from the townsmen and called out to Cherokee Earl, "The town knows whose side I'm on, Earl. Now what's your deal?"

"You know I need that wagon, don't you, Danny? That is why you took it, right?"

"Yep, that's why," said Danielle without mentioning the fact that her greater reason for taking the wagon had been to either trade it for Tuck Carlyle or at least to slow things down long enough to find a way to free him. Now that the time was at hand, she waited, saying no more about it. It was Cherokee Earl's move.

"The deal is this, Duggin," said Cherokee Earl. "I get the wagon and a free ride out of town with my money and silver. You folks get this deputy back with his head still sitting up on his shoulders. You can't ask for better than that, can you?"

As Earl spoke, he motioned Buck Hite forward. "Take over for me, Buck. I need somebody I can trust," he whispered.

Buck stepped in, taking the offered shotgun from Cherokee Earl's hand as Earl stepped back and let Buck take his place.

"Good man," Earl whispered, patting Buck Hite on his shoulder before stepping farther back. From her position across the street,

Danielle saw some movement behind Tuck Carlyle, but she didn't manage to see the exchange take place.

"No deal," Danielle called out to Earl, hoping her concern for Tuck's well-being didn't show in her voice. "I'll give up the wagon for the deputy, but from there we go back to where we started. You've got to get out of this town the best way you can."

Danielle had been checking her rifle while she spoke. She took out a cartridge, checked it for perfect roundness, checked the casing, then put the cartridge up into the chamber. She licked her thumb, rubbed the tip of the front sight, and did the same to the rear sight. Then she took a firm grip on the front corner edge of the building protecting her, making a shooting brace, and laid the rifle into the V of her thumb and index finger.

"God help me, Tuck, this had better work," she whispered to herself.

"Get out of here the best way we can?" Earl called out from a few feet behind Buck Hite. "Hell, Danny, that's no kind of deal at all!"

Earl and Frisco began busily tossing bags of money and silver back across the floor to McRoy and Clifford Reed, who had moved from the front window to the back room. They caught the bags and loosely piled them near the rear door, where the horses stood nervously, ready to bolt and run should the opportunity present itself.

"That's the best deal you're going to get from me today, Earl," Danielle said. "Take it or leave it."

"I'll leave it, Duggin," Earl called out from the back room of the bank while he and the others stuffed the bags of money and silver into their saddlebags and readied the horses.

Holding the shotgun to the back of Tuck's head, Buck Hite looked over his shoulder and saw what Earl and the men were doing. His face turned pale. "Hey, am I missing something here? You're not leaving me holding the bag, are you?"

"Hell, no, Buck," said Cherokee Earl. "Whatever gave you that idea?" As he spoke, Earl tied more bags of money to his saddle horn.

"What gave me that idea is that you're doing it!" Buck stared wide-eyed.

"Buck, listen to me," said Earl, slowing for a moment to explain things. "Somebody has to hold things down here while the rest of us get away. This time it's you. . . . Next time, who knows? It might be me. But it's always somebody's turn, ain't it?"

"So I'm staying here to face this whole town?" Buck couldn't seem to grasp what was happening to him.

"You heard Duggin," said Earl. "He ain't going to make a deal that suits us. And like you said yourself, it looks like this is all we're going to get."

"So you're just leaving me here alone?" Buck Hite had begun to sweat profusely.

"Why do you keep asking me that, Buck?" said Earl. "You're my right-hand man. If I don't leave you in charge, who'll keep this whole thing from falling apart?"

"By God, I don't know," said Buck, "but it for damn sure ain't going to be—"

"What about the rest of us—Eddie Ray, Fat Cyrus, and me?" asked Clifford Reed, cutting in. "Are we supposed to just stand here, too, get shot to pieces while you and your men ride away with the money?"

"Well, no," said Cherokee Earl, sounding put out with the man for asking. "When we throw this back door open, you do whatever you need to do to get away. Now, have you got any more stupid questions?"

Clifford Reed looked stunned. He turned to Buck Hite. "Damn it, this ain't right, Buck. I might not know much, but I know that this ain't right!"

While turning his attention to the back room, where Cherokee Earl and his men were preparing for their getaway, Buck Hite had not kept Tuck Carlyle directly in front of him in the open doorway. Tuck knew it, and he had inched as far to one side as he could. He looked toward the corner of the building where Danielle knelt, holding the big rifle poised for a precision shot. Unable to nod or give any kind of a signal, Tuck hoped his friend Danny Duggin could read the expression on his face and take action.

"Don't move on me, Tuck," Danielle whispered, her sights already fixed, her finger already beginning to squeeze the trigger. "Whatever you do, please don't move."

CHAPTER 22

Get ready to open the door when I tell you to," Cherokee Earl barked at Fat Cyrus and Eddie Ray Moon.

The two bewildered outlaws looked helplessly at their leader, Buck Hite, for some sort of guidance. But they turned their attention back to Earl when he swung up into his saddle, cocked his pistol in their direction, and said, "You'd better do like you're told, then grab yourself a horse and make tracks out of here."

"Damn it to hell, Earl!" Buck Hite shrieked. "I ain't going to forget this. I swear to God I ain't!" As he raved at Cherokee Earl, he let himself take a half step farther out from behind the shield of Tuck Carlyle. "No matter where you go, no matter how long it takes—" His words stopped abruptly as Danielle sent a bullet spinning through his brain.

"Lord God Almighty!" Clifford Reed shouted, seeing Buck Hite's wide-brimmed hat sail off his head in a long, spraying mist of blood.

The shot resounded from across the street. The impact flung Buck Hite's body forward like a bundle of loose rags. The shotgun flew from his hands, so did the belt around Tuck Carlyle's neck.

Tuck didn't hesitate. As soon as Danielle made the shot, he hurled himself forward, through the front doors, off the boardwalk, and into the street, coming up into a full run.

"See," said Cherokee Earl, gesturing down at Buck Hite's body.

"He's forgot it already." Earl swung his cocked pistol at Fat Cyrus. "Now open this damn door, or you'll be lying there with him!"

"Hell, I'll open the door," said Sadler, reaching down from atop his horse and grabbing the door handle. "Everybody ready?" He looked around at Fred, riding double behind him, then at Earl, McRoy, and Frisco.

"Hell, yes! Let her rip!" said Cherokee Earl.

Out front, taking Danielle's shot as a signal and seeing their deputy freed and rushing to safety, the townsmen opened fire once again. Bullets zipped through the bank building like hornets. As the men bolted their horses out into the back alley, where more gunfire awaited them, the bank manager, still cowering in the vault, eased forward across the floor, reached up with both hands, and began easing the vault door closed.

Seeing what the man was doing, Fat Cyrus flung himself inside the vault out of the hail of gunfire.

"Please, don't shoot me!" shouted the bank manager.

"Shut the hell up! Scoot over!" Fat Cyrus screamed above the deafening roar of gunfire, shoving the manager back into the corner. "I'm worried about getting shot myself!"

Clifford Reed and Eddie Ray Moon made their way out of the bank building and onto the dirt street before the townsmen's bullets began slicing through them. Clifford Reed fell first, managing to crawl a few feet before additional rifle fire tried to pound him into the ground.

"You dirty sumbitches!" Eddie Ray Moon screamed as bullets nipped at him, taking off chunks of flesh and leaving bloody rosettes in their wake. "I dare any one of yas to come face me one-on-one. You damn cowards! Guess you're too damn scared to do that, ain't you?"

The firing stopped short. Eddie Ray Moon looked around, stunned to think that his words could have had such a powerful effect on these people. "Well, now! That's more like it," he said, a slight smile of satisfaction coming to his bloody face. "Let's do this thing face-to-face. Give a man a fighting chance!"

He lowered his bloody pistol into his holster and spread his wobbly feet shoulder width apart, preparing himself for a show-down. "Now, send one of yas on out here," he said.

"Ready . . ." a voice said along the boardwalk.

Eddie Ray Moon's smile melted at the sound of the voice followed by the sound of many rifles and shotguns cocking at once. "Now wait a damn minute!" he screamed.

"Aim . . ." said the voice as if not having heard Eddie Ray's command.

"Well, shit," said Eddie Ray. "I mighta known. There ain't a real gunfighter in the bunch of yas."

"Fire . . . !" said the voice.

Danielle hadn't stuck around to see Eddie Ray Moon and Clifford Reed die in the street. As soon as Tuck Carlyle ran out of the bank building, the belt around his neck trailing in the air behind him, Danielle met him in the street, her rifle in one hand and her Colt in the other. Already figuring out that the rest of the men would be making a break out the rear of the building, Danielle pitched her Colt to Tuck Carlyle, saying, "Come on, Tuck, they're getting away!"

Together they ran toward the alley. Yet even as the two hurried to catch Cherokee Earl and his men behind the bank, Earl, leading the others, had to rein his horse down hard as a rifle shot hissed past his cheek.

"What the hell is this!" Earl shouted, the men and horses bunching up behind him in the narrow alley. At the far end of the alley stood Ellen Waddell, looking like some wild-eyed ghost straight out of a nightmare. Because she was bareheaded, her red hair stood out sidelong on a passing wind. Having shed her riding clothes and hat, she wore nothing except the thin cotton nightgown the doctor had provided her. The wind pressed the flimsy cotton against her body, revealing her every curve and feature as if she were nude.

"You weren't leaving without me, were you, Earl?" she called out in a strange, maniacal voice. "Me? The woman you had to have? The woman you couldn't seem to live without?" A shot blossomed and exploded from her rifle, slicing through the air close to Cherokee Earl's thigh. "Come take me with you, Earl! I'm free now. My husband is dead. Come take me, Earl."

"You crazy bitch!" Earl fired his pistol twice, but was too far out of range.

The shots kicked up dirt four feet in front of Ellen Waddell. Oblivious to the danger, she stalked forward slowly, levering another round into the rifle, her tender bare feet not noticing the sharp, stony ground.

Earl slapped a hand to his rifle boot but found it empty. "Damn it! Somebody shoot her!" he shouted over his shoulder, where both horses and riders were waiting impatiently. The horses stomped back and forth, crowding and butting one another.

"I've got her, boss!" said Avery McRoy, raising a rifle and taking aim, his restless horse keeping him from getting a good bead on her.

Ellen fired again. This shot grazed Cherokee Earl's horse and sent it rearing upward in a frenzy, twisting and turning in the air. Earl lost his reins and fell backward, coming out of his saddle but getting one boot stuck in a stirrup.

"Help me! Damn it!" he yelled after hitting the ground.

But with his big horse turning on the other riders who were jammed together in the tight alleyway, it was all the men could do to keep from falling themselves.

"That's all of you!" Avery McRoy shouted at Ellen Waddell.

He fired, and he didn't miss. His shot hit Ellen squarely in her left shoulder, sending her spinning backward until she crumpled to the ground, the rifle still grasped tightly in her hand.

Coming around the corner of the alley, Danielle and Tuck Carlyle saw what had happened. Danielle's rifle came up to her shoulder and she fired into the tangle of men and horses. Avery McRoy flew from his saddle with a bullet through his heart. The others tried to turn their horses and make a run for it in the other direction, but Tuck and Danielle gave them no opportunity. They fired on Sadler and Fred, sending both men from the horse they were sharing. Fred hit the ground dead, but Sadler came up onto his knees with a rifle and began screaming as he fired.

Frisco Bonham, seeing Sadler make a dying stand, turned his horse and heeled it hard in the other direction. He turned the corner of the alley toward the street just as Cherokee Earl's boot came loose from his foot and left him sliding to a halt in a cloud of dust.

"Hot damn! What a ride," said Earl, reaching up for Frisco as Frisco slowed his horse enough to reach down and grab his stranded leader. "I hope one of you killed that crazy redheaded woman!" he shouted, swinging up behind Frisco.

"McRoy shot her," said Frisco. "I don't know if he killed her or not."

"I hope to hell he killed her," said Earl. "She's been nothing but troublesome ever since I laid eyes on her." He drew a pistol from his waist and checked it quickly as Frisco heeled the horse toward the street. "Get us past these townsmen. Then stop at the first horse you see unattended."

He looked around Frisco at the bags of money tied to his saddle horn, then stared back and forth along the street as Frisco turned the horse onto it and spurred the animal hard. Shots fired in their direction. Frisco leaned low on the horse, spurring it harder and harder, sending it out of town.

Cherokee Earl fired back at the townsmen until his pistol was empty. Then he snatched Frisco Bonham's pistol from its holster and continued firing. "Give me that rifle, quick!" he demanded of Frisco.

"It's not loaded," said Frisco, still spurring the horse for greater speed.

"Stop up there!" said Cherokee Earl, pointing at a barn fifty yards ahead, where he saw a corral fence. Shots whistled past them from the direction of the boardwalk across from the bank. "Maybe we'll find a horse there!"

"Good thinking!" said Frisco Bonham. He spurred the horse to the barn, then slid it to a halt. Looking all around the corral, he said, "Damn, you're out of luck, Earl. There ain't a horse in sight."

"Hellfire!" Earl cursed, and looked back toward the street through the center of town. "They'll be coming any minute! Are you sure that rifle ain't loaded?"

"Yes, I'm sure," said Frisco. "I fired it out back in the bank. I've got bullets in my saddlebags, but I ain't had time to reload it."

"I see," said Cherokee Earl. He poked the pistol barrel against Frisco's head. "Get down. I'm taking the horse!"

"Do what?" said Frisco, not believing what he heard.

"I said, get the hell down from this saddle, or I'll blow your stupid head off! I'm taking the horse. You'll have to find you another one."

"But where? How?" Frisco looked all around, then said, "What about my money? You're not taking it, are you?"

"You tell me," said Cherokee Earl. He poked the pistol barrel harder.

Frisco slid down from the saddle and looked up at him. "If it hadn't been for me, you'd be lying back there in the alley, waiting for the town to come string you up."

"I know," said Earl, "and don't think I ain't grateful for it. It's just time we split up and go our separate ways. . . . You need to stand on your own."

"Like hell," said Frisco. "I know when I've been double-crossed. I'll find me a horse all right, and when I do, I'll—"

"Then you'd better get to looking quick," said Earl, cutting him off. He gestured his pistol barrel back toward town. "They'll be getting here any minute." He swung the horse around and spurred it out back onto the open trail. *"Adios!"* he called out over his shoulder in a grandiose manner, raising a hand in the air.

Frisco Bonham just stared in bewilderment as his horse and money rode farther and farther away.

E llen, are you all right?" Danielle asked, once again holding Ellen Waddell's head in her lap.

Ellen looked up at her, struggling to remain conscious, the impact of the bullet through her shoulder having nearly knocked her cold.

"Did . . . I get him?" Ellen asked.

Danielle looked at Tuck, then back down at Ellen. "Yes, ma'am, you got him. You got him good. Now I'm going to go find him and finish him off for you, all right?"

The sound of gunfire from the street told Danielle there were still outlaws there making their getaway.

Ellen smiled weakly but with much satisfaction. "That son of a bitch . . . he'll never do another woman . . . that way."

"He sure won't, ma'am," said Danielle, handing Ellen over to Tuck. "Take her back to the doctor's, Tuck," she told him. "I'll see what's left to do out there."

"Wait. I'll go with you, Danny," said Tuck.

"No," said Danielle. "This is your town—stay and take care of it. I'll be back soon."

"You'd better be, Danny," said Tuck. "You told me we needed to have a long talk. I'm curious to find out what about."

"And we will have that talk, I promise you," said Danielle, turning to leave as scattered gunfire from the street continued.

"Be careful, Danny," said Tuck, standing with Ellen Waddell in his arms. "We've both been lucky so far. . . . Let's keep it that way."

Danielle nodded in agreement. She ran to where Sundown stood at the hitch rail out front of the doctor's office. In a moment, Danielle was racing the big chestnut mare down the middle of the street in the direction the townsmen stood pointing. Now that someone was on the outlaws' trail, the townsmen all lowered their rifles and began shaking hands and slapping one another on the back for a job well done. A few of them ran to their own horses, mounted up, and heeled out in the same direction Danielle had taken, although knowing it would be difficult to catch up with the big mare.

Tuck Carlyle carried Ellen Waddell to the doctor's office and laid her back on the cot where she'd been lying earlier. The doctor hurriedly rolled up his sleeves and leaned down, examining her shoulder wound.

"I'm sorry I've been such . . . a bother, Doctor," she murmured.

"Nonsense, no bother at all," said the doctor, "although you will owe me extra for a new cotton gown, having gotten a hole shot in this one."

Tuck Carlyle smiled and watched the doctor cut the bloody gown with a pair of scissors in order to get to the wound. Outside, the street had grown quieter, but as Tuck began to relax a bit, a shot resounded from the direction of the bank building. Even before Tuck could get through the door to the street, a small boy came running in out of breath, crying, "Deputy! Deputy! Come quick! There are still outlaws robbing the bank!"

Tuck ran quickly ahead of the boy, drawing the pistol Danielle had given him from his belt. "Stay back, young man," he said. "This might be dangerous."

The boy lagged back a little, but wasn't about to stay too far away and miss all the action.

"The shot came from the bank, Deputy!" shouted a townsman as Tuck ran past the crowd in the street and on toward the bank building. "Mr. Scally is still inside. We heard him holler like somebody was killing him!"

"All right, stay back behind me," said Tuck, the gun in his hand cocked and ready.

Tuck slipped inside the open front doors to the bank with his pistol ready to fire. Gathered behind him, the townsmen stood with their rifles ready. But once inside the building, Tuck froze at the sight of the bank manager being held from behind with a gun barrel to the side of his head.

"Easy, fellow," Tuck said to the frightened face looking at him over the bank manager's plump shoulder. "Nobody has to die here."

"The hell they don't," said Fat Cyrus Kerr, his voice trembling in fear. "Either way it goes, I'm done for. I'll either hang or get shot down in the street. I've already reconciled myself to it, unless I can get me a fast horse and a clear run out of town!"

Tuck kept his pistol steadily poised, but he tried to appear at ease. "If that's all it takes, we'll get you a horse. We'll even back away and give you a clear run out of here, provided you do Mr. Scally no harm."

"Then quit talking and get moving!" said Cyrus. "I want out of this place bad!"

"All right, take it easy," said Tuck. Without taking his eyes off Fat Cyrus, he called out to the townsmen gathered outside the doors, "Somebody get this man a horse. . . . No tricks either. We don't want to get Mr. Scally hurt, do we?"

The townsmen grumbled quietly among themselves. Then one of them said, "All right, Deputy, we'll get him a horse. He can ride out of here. But he gets no promise that some of us won't be on his trail by dark."

"Is that fair enough, mister?" Tuck asked. "You can't expect them to let you get away without trying to catch you, can you?"

Cyrus considered it for a second, then said, "I'm taking this man with me!"

Tuck shook his head slowly and called out to be the townsmen. "Never mind getting him that horse. . . . He's not going anywhere after all."

"Wait!" said Cyrus. "I ain't taking him with me. Go on. Get me a horse. The bank manager stays here."

"You heard him," Tuck said to the townsmen. "Get him a horse after all." He looked squarely at Fat Cyrus Kerr and said, "Now, how are you going to turn him loose?"

Fat Cyrus looked perplexed, having not thought things through that far.

"Mister," said Tuck, "I've been a deputy only a short time, so I don't know how this kind of thing usually goes. But I give you my word nobody here is going to try to stop you. Is that good enough for you?"

"Your word?" said Cyrus in disbelief. "Hell, no, that's not good enough! What good is your word to me? I'm the one who'll have every gun in this town pointed at him! There ain't a sumbitch out there who wouldn't love to put a bullet in me!"

"That might be true," said Tuck. "But if I give you my word nobody is going to try to harm you, that's a fact."

"Words, facts—this is all moving too damn fast to suit me!" Cyrus raged.

Tuck could see the man was getting confused and anxious. He tried to calm him. "All right, then . . . you tell me what you want to do. I'll go along with—"

"Shut the hell up!" Cyrus screamed.

He panicked, shoved Scally forward, and began backing quickly to the vault room, where the open back door beckoned to him. Screaming, firing the pistol as he went, Cyrus left Tuck no choice but to return fire. As the fourth shot exploded from Cyrus's pistol, Tuck put two shots into the big outlaw's chest, slamming him against the back wall. Once again Earnest Scally found himself huddled on the floor with his arms wrapped around his head. Behind Tuck, the townsmen rushed in through the front doors.

"Get that bastard!" one of them yelled.

They hurried past Tuck and into the next room. There they stopped, seeing the dead outlaw on the floor slumped against the wall, a smear of blood down the wall from the exit holes in his back.

"Whoo-ee!" said one of the townsmen. "Good shooting, Deputy! Damn good shooting!"

When Tuck didn't answer, the men turned as one and saw him standing slumped against the edge of a desk, leaning on one hand, his other hand pressed against the bloody bullet hole in his lower-left side. The pistol had fallen from his hand and lay on the floor at his feet amid widening drops of blood.

"Oh, Lord, no, Deputy," said the same townsman. "You've been gutshot something awful."

"I know," said Tuck in a strained, breathless voice, his face pale and bloodless. "Tell Danny I did the best I could. . . ." Then he fell to the polished floor.

CHAPTER 23

At the barn outside of Cimarron, dust from the outlaws' horse still hung in the air when Danielle slid the chestnut mare to a halt and slipped quickly down from the saddle. Hearing a commotion from inside the barn, she slapped Sundown on the rump and shooed her out of harm's way. When she saw dust hovering above the trail leading off to the lone rider in the distance, it only took a second for Danielle to put together what had taken place between the two outlaws. With her Colt drawn, Danielle hurried quietly to the front of the barn and stood with her back pressed to the weathered boards, listening intently to Frisco Bonham cursing a donkey and the donkey braying as if in reply.

Inside the barn, Frisco grumbled, "I don't like this a damn bit more than you do, you stiff-tailed little peckerwood! Now stand still!"

He tried to toss a saddle upon the animal's thin, knobby back, but the donkey would have none of it. The animal brayed loudly, spinning and kicking at Frisco.

"Damn you!" Frisco raged. "If I didn't need a ride, I'd put a bullet in you . . . if I *had* a bullet!" There was a brief pause; then Frisco said despondently, "What the hell am I talking about, a bullet? I don't even have a damn gun."

Danielle heard him clearly, yet she wasn't taking any chances on him being unarmed. She looked back toward Cimarron at the fresh dust rising up behind the townsmen who had grabbed their horses and followed her. She wasn't going to waste time here and let Cherokee Earl get away. Just as she was about to grab the barn door and swing it open, she saw the door come swinging open from the inside.

"All right, you stubborn, good-for-nothing dog bait!" Frisco shouted, dragging the donkey forward an inch at a time by a six-foot length of lead rope.

The donkey brayed and resisted strongly.

Danielle stood back with her Colt drawn, watching. Frisco was so engrossed in his struggle with the stubborn animal that he didn't notice her standing only a few feet away.

"I swear to God!" Frisco said to the donkey. "If I get away from here, I'll roast you over a fire and eat you quicker than a wolf will eat a jackrabbit!"

He tried twice to swing a leg over the donkey's back, but each time the nimble little animal stepped out of the way. His second try landed him facedown in the dirt. As he tried to stand up, Danielle planted a boot on the back of his neck and pinned him down.

"It's the end of the line for you, Frisco," she said, making sure he heard her cock the Colt only inches from his head.

"Damn it!" said Frisco in a release of breath. "I have never been so put upon in my life! Cherokee Earl abandoned me. I guess you know!"

"Yep, that's what I figured when I got here and saw somebody out there making tracks for the high country," said Danielle. "How is he armed?"

"Oh, he's armed fine, the rotten turd!" said Frisco. "He's got my pistol and my rifle!"

"Your rifle, too, huh?" said Danielle, gaining information that might come in handy real soon.

"Yes . . . and I hope you kill the sucker! If you kill him, tell him I said good riddance! Will you do that?"

Danielle didn't answer. Instead, she stared down, watching him prepare for his next move. Even as he spoke, she saw his right hand reaching down toward his boot. As he bent his leg to bring his boot up into reach, Danielle saw the top of the knife handle sticking up.

"For two cents I'd let you go ahead and pull that pigsticker, Frisco," she said. "After what you did to my friend Stick, there's nothing I'd like more than to empty this Colt into you."

"Oh," said Frisco.

His hand stopped reaching; his leg straightened. He turned his head enough to look up at the face above him, squinting in the afternoon sun's glare. With Danielle's face hidden by the darkness beneath her wide hat brim, Frisco saw nothing.

"Do I know you?" he asked, turning his gaze up the open bore of the cocked pistol.

"Not if you thought you could pull that knife on me," Danielle said flatly.

"You said your friend Stick," Frisco said. "Do you mean the old man I shot and killed a while back?"

"Yes, that's who I mean," said Danielle. Thinking about it caused her hand to tighten on the pistol butt.

"You're not . . . ? You're not that blasted woman, are you? The one what gave me and Billy Boy Harper such a hard time?"

"What do you think?" Danielle asked.

Frisco considered it for a moment, then slumped onto the dirt. "Naw . . . hell, no. She was a tough little filly. But no woman could have stuck with it, stayed on our trail all the way up to this Cimarron country. That's too crazy to imagine!"

"Yeah, I suppose you're right, Frisco," said Danielle, not wanting him to know who she really was since she would be sending him back to Tuck with the townsmen. Telling Tuck who she was would be something for her and her alone to do. "A woman tracking you, Cherokee Earl, and that bunch? That would be too crazy to imagine."

Danielle reached down and pulled the knife from Frisco's boot. She cut the lead rope from the donkey and tied Frisco's hands behind his back. Then she helped him to his feet, walked him to the corral fence, and, with the remaining length of the rope, tied him to a post. The donkey followed her like a pup and watched with great interest.

"This ought to hold you until those fellows get here," she said, nodding in the direction of the approaching horsemen from town.

"They're just going to hang me," said Frisco with certainty, bowing his head at the thought. "You'd do me a favor if you'd just put a bullet in my head and go on."

"I don't owe you no favors," said Danielle.

She walked to the mare, stepped into the saddle, and began riding away. Before she'd gone thirty feet, she heard the donkey braying loudly again. She looked back and saw Frisco spitting and cursing.

"Get out of here, you sumbitch!" Frisco screamed. "Now you want to be pals! Get the hell away from here!"

But the donkey stepped forward and stuck its wet muzzle to his face as Frisco screamed and spat at it.

"Stick," Danielle said under her breath, "that's the best I can do for you right now."

She heeled the mare up into a run and rode toward the lone rider in the distance.

A mile ahead, Cherokee Earl looked back as he pushed the tired horse up off of a stretch of flatland into some low hills. The horse faltered, slowed, and finally came to a staggering halt, having started out at a full run carrying two men and the bags of silver and cash. Now, although one man was gone, the poor horse had spent itself. Going from the flatland onto an uphill trail was more than the animal could take.

"This can't be happening to me!" Earl ranted, jumping down from the saddle and trying to pull the horse up the steep trail by its reins. "You ain't giving out on me now, you ornery bastard!"

But the horse not only couldn't take another step; it dropped down onto its knees and lay there, its breath pounding like a broken bellows. White froth swung from its mouth and streaked its sides.

Earl dropped the reins and looked back at the lone rider gaining ground. Beyond that rider came other riders, but it looked as if they would never catch up.

"All right," Cherokee Earl said to the front rider as if he could actually be heard, "you've got a good, fast horse. . . . I can see that." He grinned. "Real proud of that horse, are you? I bet you are."

Stooping down, still watching the approaching rider, Earl took some rifle cartridges from the saddlebags and slipped the rifle from its boot. The winded horse started to struggle upward onto all fours, but Earl pressed a hand on its neck.

"Naw, you lie still, you lazy hunk of hide. . . . You're fixing to be replaced by a big, fast ground stormer."

He loaded the rifle and leaned it against his side. While he waited for the rider to draw closer, he loosened the bags of money and silver bars from the saddle horn and stacked them neatly at his feet.

Looking back again in anticipation, he said, "Bring that horse on up here. I ain't got all day." Then he cackled aloud to himself. "Damn it, Earl boy," he said to himself, "you never cease to amaze me!"

Drawing nearer, Danielle caught a glimpse of Cherokee Earl ducking behind a rock a few yards farther up the trail from the downed horse. Knowing he had a rifle, Danielle stopped the mare a long way out, taking as much advantage of the sun glare as she could get. To the left of the flat trail, a mazelike string of rocky ground reached upward for the hills. She pulled the mare over into cover and studied the hillside carefully, keeping herself out of sight.

Seeing how the rider had stopped far back on the flatlands, Cherokee Earl slumped and shook his head. "Thank you all to hell, Frisco, you bigmouthed sumbitch!" said Earl as if talking to Frisco Bonham in person. "I shoulda known you'd spill your guts the first chance you got . . . tell him I've got a rifle! I hope you're lying back there right now with crows plucking your lousy eyeballs out!"

After a silent pause, Earl stood up halfway behind his rock cover and looked down in the direction where he'd seen the rider lead the horse off the trail. A watery veil covered everything Earl looked at out in the harsh sunlight.

"Danny Duggin? Is that you?" He waited, squinting beneath the shelter of his hat brim.

Danielle could hear his voice only with the assistance of its echo off the rocky hills. She didn't answer.

"If you can hear me, Duggin," Earl screamed out, "I've got a proposition for you."

Danielle still didn't answer.

"Damn it, man," Earl bellowed, looking back along the trail, searching for the other riders but not finding them. "Talk to me here. We can work something out! I've got money—silver! By God, don't tell me you can't use some silver!"

Danielle ignored the outlaw's rolling, jumbled echo and sat with her back against the rock. While Earl went on shouting his enticements, she raised the long-range sight on the rifle, rubbed it clean with her fingertips, raised it to the five-hundred-yard mark, and tightened it into place. Satisfied, she turned around, laying the rifle barrel up over the top of the rock.

"Duggin, listen to me," Earl called out. "This ain't no small amount of money! You can go anywhere in the world with this kind of money!"

Danielle half closed her eyes for a few seconds, looking down within the circling shadow of her hat brim on the rock, keeping her eyes relaxed, avoiding any strain from the sun glare. Even when she opened her eyes and adjusted the rifle into the pocket of her shoulder, she didn't look down the sights just yet.

Save it for the shot, she told herself.

"Duggin, are you listening to me?" Cherokee Earl shrieked. Then he said in a lowered tone to himself, "All right, by God, you want to play this way? I can play this way. You want a shoot-out, boy, you're going to get a shoot-out!" He snatched the rifle up and stared down through the harsh sun glare. "I wanted to do this different . . . get you off guard, kill you unexpected-like and take that horse. But no," he said, making a face, "you won't do it that way. All right, suit yourself. . . . I can do it this way. Makes me no difference!"

"Duggin!" Cherokee Earl bellowed even louder than before,

looking out and seeing the riders now. They were tiny black dots in the wavering heat, yet with every passing second, Earl knew they were drawing closer. "Duggin! Damn it to hell! Will you answer me?"

He rose up above the rock, exposing himself from the waist up. With one gloved hand cupped to his mouth, he screamed even louder, "We've got to get this settled! Before they get here!"

I've got you, Danielle thought to herself, looking down the long-range rifle sight at the third button on Cherokee Earl's dusty shirt. She had to make her move quick before the sun glare got to her or before Earl dropped back down out of sight. She took a breath, let it out, then cut it off. The rifle settled dead still in her hands. She began to squeeze the trigger, but at the last second moved the sight up his chest and a bit to the left. Through the recoil of the rifle, she could see the puff of dust as the bullet nailed through his shoulder. There was a spray of blood that seemed to hang in the air after Earl had already flown backward and down out of sight. His hat, too, seemed suspended in the air for a second. Then it fell zigzagging to the ground.

Danielle stood up and dusted her knees and her seat and leveled her hat down onto her forehead. She looked back toward the oncoming riders, then walked to the mare, took up the reins, mounted, and rode to where Cherokee Earl lay bleeding into the dirt. When she reached the spot where the downed horse lay breathing heavily in the thin trail, she stepped down and coaxed the winded animal up onto all fours. The horse stood wobbling for a moment while Danielle slipped off its saddle and bridle. A bit more rested now and carrying only its own weight, the horse shook itself out and walked away, down to the flatlands.

Danielle left Sundown on the trail and stepped up among the rocks where she'd seen Cherokee Earl fall. She knew she'd hit him good and hard, yet she used caution until she stood upon a rock, saw the smear of blood, and looked down to where he lay on the rocky ground. His rifle lay a few feet away, but looking up at her, he made no move for it. That told her something. She waited for a second, then leaped down easily and stood over him, her rifle in hand.

"That was . . . nothing but a lucky shot, Duggin," Earl rasped. "You'd never do it again. No man shoots that good."

"You might be right, Earl," said Danielle. "But then, I'm not a man."

"Hunh?" Earl stared in stunned silence as Danielle reached up, pulled off her hat, and shook out her long, flowing hair. "You're not a man? You're not Danny Duggin?" he asked, appearing completely dumbfounded.

"That's right, Earl. I'm not a man. I'm not Danny Duggin," Danielle said.

"Then who or what the hell are you?" Earl asked, his weakened voice growing stronger all of a sudden.

Danielle saw his right hand crawl beneath his back, but she glanced away as if not seeing his move. "I'm just a woman, Earl, a woman no different from Ellen Waddell or any other woman you've mistreated your whole worthless life. This is for Ellen," she said. She cocked the big Colt with her thumb.

"Hold on now! I never mistreated that woman—that's just a damn lie! All I've ever done to any woman is what she wanted done to her. I'm a man. . . . Don't blame me for doing what any man does. I never forced myself on Ellen Waddell. . . . Well, not that much anyway," he said. "There was no harm done! I never hit her! She's got nothing to complain about."

"You stupid bastard, you really believe that, don't you?"

"Damn right I do!" said Earl. "Anyway, look at me now. What chance have I got to defend myself? You women are all alike. You listen only to what you want to hear! What chance has a man got? I reckon I'm at your mercy. . . ."

His words trailed off hopelessly. But Danielle saw that his hand under his back had found something there. She saw his arm tighten as he grasped the hidden pistol butt.

But before drawing the pistol from behind his back, Earl saw the look in Danielle's eyes and stopped short. "Huh-uh," he said.

"I'm giving myself up. I see what you're waiting for—I see what you want."

"Do it, Earl," Danielle whispered, stepping in close and standing astraddle of him, her feet spread apart. She looked down at him, her hand holding the big Colt. "Pull it out, Earl," she whispered, her voice sounding almost seductive. "Pull it out and show me what you can do." Without her hat on, the wind swept her long hair across her face like a veil.

Staring up at her, Earl imagined her smiling at him behind that veil. Smiling? No, laughing! Laughing at him.

"Why, you man-teasing, no-account little bitch!" he shouted.

His gun hand came out quickly from under his back but not quickly enough. He saw her eyes, cold, haunting, and without mercy, like the reflection of his own eyes in the face of every woman he'd ever seen that close and under those circumstances. "No!" he said. "No, please! *Please!*"

Danielle didn't seem to hear him.

My God!" said Angus O'Dell. "What's going on up there?" As one, the townsmen reined their horses to a halt and stared at the hills lying ahead of them in the afternoon heat. They listened as the big Colt fired steadily, one shot after another until, after the sixth shot, it fell silent.

"Whoo-ee!" said another of the townsmen. "I'd hate to have been on the wrong end of that gun battle!"

"I hope Mr. Duggin is all right," said O'Dell, heeling his horse forward again now that the shooting had stopped.

He looked back at one of the townsmen leading the donkey. Over the donkey's back lay Frisco's body, flopping up and down with each bouncing step, his blue-veined hands still tied behind his back, a gaping black bullet hole glistening on his forehead.

"Hundley," said O'Dell, "you can't hurry that little donkey. We're going to ride on ahead in case Duggin needs our help. You catch up as you can."

"Yeah, why not?" said Hundley, the town auditor. "Go on ahead. I'm in no hurry to get shot at anyway."

He watched the others gallop ahead while behind him the little donkey took its time carrying Frisco Bonham's body. After a while, Hundley grew impatient and jerked hard on the lead rope.

"Come on, you little varmint! I'll see to it you get up some speed!"

But the donkey went wild, kicking and braying until it jerked the lead rope loose from its bridle and took off out across the open wilderness, the body of Frisco Bonham appearing to stare back at the bewildered auditor.

"Well, I'll be," said Hundley to himself. "Now what do I do?"

He stared after the donkey for a moment, then shrugged, heeled his horse forward, and rode hard to catch up with the other townsmen.

By the time O'Dell led the townsmen to the spot along the upper trail where the chestnut mare stood pulling at a mouthful of tall wild grass, Danielle had tucked her hair back up under her hat and stood replacing the six spent cartridges in her Colt.

"We heard a bunch of shooting up here, Duggin," said O'Dell. "Are you all right?"

Danielle only nodded. "I thought I heard a shot back there a while ago," she said. "Did you find that outlaw tied to a fence pole where I left him for you?"

The townsmen looked at one another, avoiding Danielle's eyes. Finally, Angus O'Dell said, "Aye, we found him. But the belligerent arse that he was, he tried to put up a fight. One of us had to shoot him."

"*One* of you had to shoot him?" asked Danielle. "You know who?"

"As long as we can't remember who," said O'Dell, "we won't have to worry about getting anyone in trouble, now, will we?"

"I don't know," said Danielle. "In this case, I don't expect the law will press too hard."

"Just dandy, then." O'Dell grinned. "And what about the one you chased here? I presume he is dead."

"Deader than he ever hoped to be," said Danielle.

"What happened with him—more of that same outlaw belligerence, I take it?" asked O'Dell.

"Yeah, you might say so," said Danielle. "He went for a gun. I wasn't in the mood for it." She nodded upward toward the rocks where she'd left him. "I was just getting ready to go drop a loop on his ankle and drag him down here."

"Nonsense, Mr. Duggin," said O'Dell. "You take yourself a breather. We'll take over from here."

"Much obliged, then," said Danielle. "I've got somebody I need to have a long talk with back in town."

She smiled, touching her fingertips to her hat brim, then walked to the chestnut mare, stepped up into the saddle, and rode back toward Cimarron. On the way, she passed Hundley on the trail. When he excitedly told her what had happened to Frisco's body, Danielle shook her head and looked all around the vast, empty land.

"I don't know what I should do," said Hundley. "I don't want to get out there and get lost. This can be dangerous country, especially at night."

The two looked around, noting how their shadows had grown long on the ground.

"Wait here for the others and don't worry about it," said Danielle. "That donkey has probably kicked itself free of the body by now. If not, it will soon enough."

"Goodness, I hope so," said Hundley. "There are settlers scattered out through there. What a terrible surprise that would be, finding something like that in their front yard."

Danielle thought about it for a moment, then shook her head to clear it of such a thought. "Let's hope for the best," she said. "I'm going back to town."

She nudged the mare forward and didn't look back.

EPILOGUE

D anielle was not prepared for what she met upon her return
to Cimarron. The first person she saw was Ellen Waddell,
who came running to her as soon as Danielle had guided Sundown
to a hitch rail.

"Mr. Duggin, something terrible has happened," Ellen said.

"What is it, ma'am?" Danielle asked, swinging down from the
saddle and spinning Sundown's reins around the rail. She didn't
like the tragic look in Ellen's eyes.

"It's your friend, the deputy. He's at the doctor's. I'm afraid he's
been badly shot!"

"Oh, no," said Danielle.

Without another word, she rushed to the doctor's office, barely
aware of Ellen Waddell beside her, still talking.

"Did you find Cherokee Earl?" Ellen asked, running out of breath
in keeping up with Danielle.

"Yes," said Danielle absently. "Earl's dead. He won't be bothering you anymore." Then, without missing a beat, Danielle asked,
"Who shot Tuck?"

"It was one of those outlaws. He stayed behind and hid in the
bank vault. The deputy killed him, but not before getting shot
himself. Are you sure Cherokee Earl is dead?"

"Without a doubt," said Danielle, still hurrying.

"Thank God," said Ellen, and with that, she stopped in the street and just stood there as Danielle continued on to the doctor's office.

Once inside the office, she walked right on into the back room, where Tuck lay unconscious.

"Mr. Duggin! Sir!" said the doctor. "You shouldn't be in here right now! I've given your friend the deputy something to make him sleep. He'll need plenty of rest."

"How bad is he, Doctor?" Danielle asked, going straight to Tuck's side and easing down into a chair close to the bed.

"Well, he's lucky," said the doctor. "The bullet went through him, so I haven't had to do any cutting. What bleeding he's done has been good and red, so it looks as if nothing vital has been damaged."

"Thank God!" said Danielle. "Then he's going to be all right?"

"Unless he takes some unforeseeable bad turn, yes, I believe he'll pull through just fine. He'll need rest and healing."

"I'll see to it he gets plenty of both," said Danielle. She reached a hand over and placed it gently on Tuck's forehead.

The doctor gave her a peculiar look. "Mr. Duggin, is there something about you and the deputy you'd like to tell me?" he asked carefully.

"No, Doctor," said Danielle. "It's just that I love him so much . . . and I was afraid I was going to lose him again."

"Oh, I see. . . ." The doctor stood dumbfounded, not knowing quite how to respond.

At the touch of Danielle's hand on his forehead, Tuck Carlyle stirred, opening his eyes slightly. "Is that you, Danny?" he asked, barely above a whisper.

"Yes, Tuck, it's me," said Danielle, moving from the chair over onto the edge of the small bed.

The doctor's eyes widened in astonishment as Danielle clasped Tuck's hand.

"Am I—am I going to be all right?" Tuck asked, his voice weak and groggy from medication.

"Yes, Tuck, you're going to be all right," Danielle said, feeling the tears spill down her cheeks. "You're going to be fine! Just fine! I'm going to take really good care of you from now on."

Even in his semiconscious state, Tuck seemed surprised at his friend's words and manner. "Danny?" he asked. "Are you . . . crying?"

"Yes, Tuck," Danielle said, offering a tight smile through her tears. "I am crying. So what?"

Tuck closed his eyes and shook his head back and forth slowly. "My, my. I never thought I'd see you crying, Danny. This certainly has been a day full of surprises. . . ."

"Surprises?"

Danielle sniffled and wiped her eyes. She could see that he had drifted back off to sleep, yet she continued speaking to him all the same. With her free hand, she reached up, pulled off her hat, and sailed it across the room. She shook out her long hair, hearing the doctor gasp then sigh in relief behind her.

"Just you wait, Tuck Carlyle," she said. "You haven't seen surprises yet."

Ralph Compton stood six foot eight without his boots. He worked as a musician, a radio announcer, a songwriter, and a newspaper columnist. His first novel, *The Goodnight Trail*, was a finalist for the Western Writers of America Medicine Pipe Bearer Award for best debut novel. He was the *USA Today* bestselling author of the Trail of the Gunfighter series, the Border Empire series, the Sundown Riders series, and the Trail Drive series, among others.

Ready to find
your next great read?

Let us help.

Visit prh.com/nextread

Penguin
Random
House